A Fox in Shadow

What Reviewers Say About Jane Fletcher's Work

Silver Ravens

"Fletcher serves up tasty, trope-filled political intrigue with a side of wholesome lesbian love. …Fletcher succeeds in crafting a gentle, fanciful lesbian love story about questioning cultural bias."—*Publishers Weekly*

"*Silver Ravens* flows nicely and Lori's adventures have kept me deeply engaged. Though my first try at Fletcher's works, I am now convinced I have to read more of her novels."—*Hsinju's Lit Log*

Isle of Broken Years

"Fun, fast, and deeply entertaining, *Isle of Broken Years* is one of the better uses of the Atlantis myth I've yet seen in fiction. I enjoyed it a lot, and I feel confident in recommending it."—*Tor.com*

"*Isle of Broken Years* is an amazingly inventive story that started off being the tale of a noblewoman being captured by pirates and veered off into something way more interesting and fantastic."—*Kitty Kat's Book Review Blog*

Exile and the Sorcerer

"Jane Fletcher once again has written an exciting fantasy story for everyone. Though she sets her stories in foreign worlds where the traditional role of women are reversed, her characters (are) all too familiar in their inner lives and thoughts. Unlike the Celaeno series (which I highly recommend) where there are no men, this series incorporates male characters that help round out the story nicely. …Fletcher has a way of balancing the fantasy with the human drama in a precise way. She never gets caught up in the minor details of the environment and forgets to tell the story, which happens too often in fantasy fiction. …With Fletcher writing such strong work, readers of fantasy will continue to grow."—*Lambda Book Report*

"*The Exile and the Sorcerer* is a mesmerizing read, a tour-de-force packed with adventure, ordeals, complex twists and turns, and the internal introspection of appealing characters. The author writes effortlessly, handling the size and scope of the book with ease. Not since the fantasy works of Elizabeth Moon and Lynn Flewelling have I been so thoroughly engrossed in a tale. This is knockout fiction, tantalizingly told, and beautifully packaged."—*Midwest Book Review*

"Tempura Mutantur" in *Women of the Dark Streets*

"This is certainly a haunting and love intensive story. A darkly and overpowering obsession morphs into a reunion that knocked my socks off. Splendiferous!"—*Rainbow Book Reviews*

Wolfsbane Winter—*Lambda Literary Award Finalist*

"Jane Fletcher is known for her fantasy stories that take place in a world that could almost be real, but not quite. Her books seem like an alternative version of history and contain rich atmospheres of magic, legends, sorcerers, and other worldly characters mixed in with ordinary people. The way she writes is so realistic that it is easy to believe that these places and people really exist. *Wolfsbane Winter* fits that mold perfectly. It draws the reader in and leads her through the story. Very enjoyable." —*Just About Write*

The Shewstone

"I was hooked on the plot and the characters are absolutely delightful." —*The Romantic Reader Blog*

The Walls of Westernfort

"Award-winning author Jane Fletcher explores serious themes in the Celaeno series and creates a world that loosely parallels the one we inhabit. In *The Walls of Westernfort*, Fletcher weaves a plausible action-packed plot, set on a credible world, and with appealing multi-dimensional characters.

The result is a fantasy by one of the best speculative fiction writers in the business."—*Just About Write*

"...captivating, well-written stories in the fantasy genre that are built around women's struggles against themselves, one another, society, and nature."—*WomanSpace Magazine*

"*The Walls of Westernfort* is not only a highly engaging and fast-paced adventure novel, it provides the reader with an interesting framework for examining the same questions of loyalty, faith, family and love." —*Midwest Book Review*

"*The Walls of Westernfort* is...a true delight. Bold, well-developed characters hold your interest from the beginning and keep you turning the pages. The main plot twists and turns until the very end. The subplot involves likeable women who seem destined not to be together."—*MegaScene*

"In *The Walls of the Westernfort*, Jane Fletcher spins a captivating story about youthful idealism, honor, and courage. The action is fast paced and the characters are compelling in this gripping sci-fi adventure." —*Sapphic Reader*

"Jane Fletcher has a great talent for spinning yarns, especially stories of lesbians with swords. *The Walls of Westernfort* is a well written and suspenseful tale. ...Fletcher effectively intertwines the intrigues of the assassination plot with a young woman's inward exploration...and yes, there is romance. ...This book is a page-turner; you will have a hard time finding a stopping place."—*Lesbian Connection Magazine*

Rangers at Roadsend

"In *Rangers at Roadsend* Fletcher not only gives us powerful characters, but she surprises us with an unexpected ending to the murder conspiracy plot, pushing the story in one direction only to have that direction reversed more than once. This is one thrill ride the reader will not want to get off." —*Independent Gay Writer*

"*Rangers at Roadsend*, a murder mystery reminiscent of Agatha Christie, has crossed many genres including speculative fiction, fantasy, romance, and adventure. The story is an incredible whodunit that has something for everyone. Jane Fletcher, winner of the Golden Crown Literary Award 2005 for Walls at Westernfort, has created an intelligent and compelling story where the reader easily gets drawn into the fascinating world of Celaeno, becomes totally absorbed in the well-designed plot, and finds herself completely enamored with the multi-faceted characters. Jane Fletcher, an amazing talent, gifted storyteller, and extraordinary plot developer, is one of the best authors of contemporary fiction today—in all genres. *Rangers at Roadsend* will convince you of that."—*Just About Write*

Dynasty of Rogues

"Jane Fletcher has another triumph with *Dynasty of Rogues*, the continuing story in the Celaeno series. This reviewer found the book clever and compelling and difficult to put down once I started reading and easily could be devoured in one sitting. Some of the characters in *Dynasty of Rogues* have visited us in other Celaeno novels, but this is a non-linear series, so it can be understood without having read the other stories. ...*Dynasty of Rogues* has it all. Mystery, intrigue, crime, and romance, with lots of angst thrown in too, make this fascinating novel thoroughly enjoyable and fun."—*Just About Write*

"When you pick up a novel by Jane Fletcher, you will always get a riveting plot, strong, interesting characters, and a beautifully written story complete with three-dimensional villains, believable conflicts, and the twin spices of adventure and romance. Ethical and moral dilemmas abound. Fletcher writes real characters, the type that William Faulkner once said 'stand up and cast a shadow.' The reader can't help but root for these characters, many of whom are classic underdogs. I give the highest recommendation for *Dynasty of Rogues* and to the entire Celaeno Series."—*Midwest Book Review*

Temple at Landfall—*Lambda Literary Award Finalist*

"*The Temple at Landfall* is absorbing and engrossing tale-telling of the highest order, and the really exciting thing is that although this novel is complete and 'finished,' the door is left open to explore more of this world, which the author has done in subsequent books. I can't wait to read the next Celaeno Series volumes, and this book is a keeper that I will re-read again and again. I highly recommend it."—*Just About Write*

"Jane Fletcher is the consummate storyteller and plot wizard. Getting caught up in the action happens as if by magic and the fantasy elements are long forgotten. The world Fletcher creates, the characters she brings to life, and the rich detail described in eloquent prose, all serve to keep the reader enchanted, satisfied, yet wanting more. A Lammy finalist, *The Temple at Landfall* is surely a winner in this reader's book. Don't miss it."—*Midwest Book Review*

By the Author

Celaeno Series

The Temple at Landfall

The Walls of Westernfort

Rangers at Roadsend

Dynasty of Rogues

Shadow of the Knife

Lyremouth Chronicles

The Exile and the Sorcerer

The Chalice and the Traitor

The Empress and the Acolyte

The High Priest and the Idol

Wolfsbane Winter

The Shewstone

Isle of Broken Years

Silver Ravens

A Fox in Shadow

A Fox in Shadow

by

Jane Fletcher

2022

A FOX IN SHADOW

ISBN 13: 978-1-63679-142-5

This Trade Paperback Original Is Published By
Bold Strokes Books, Inc.
P.O. Box 249
Valley Falls, NY 12185

First Edition: June 2022

Credits
Editor: Cindy Cresap
Production Design: Susan Ramundo
Cover Design By Jeanine Henning

Acknowledgments

Thanks go to everyone in Swallows—Gill, Anne, Sherry, Isa, and Joanie—for your support and feedback. Writing is a solitary process. Having you along made it a lot more fun.

Cassie

A gentle breeze through the window stirred the lace drapes, driving ripples of hazy shadow across the bed sheets. Wisps of hair tickled Cassie's forehead and the nape of her neck. The air drew cool fingers over beads of sweat on her back and thighs, in heady contrast to the firm body pressed against her and the hot hands grasping her hips.

Other senses, other contrasts. Lea's lavender perfume overlay the musky scent of her body. Her lips were honey-sweet, her neck salty. Cassie flicked her tongue against the beating pulse point and heard a groan. One more small victory to chalk up. She raised herself on an elbow to take in the view.

A band of sunlight slipped between the drapes. Dust motes sparkled in the air. Lea's breasts rose with each ragged breath, her legs spread in invitation, skin flushed against the white sheets, eyes closed, lips parted. She was beautiful and knew it. Her confidence in her ability to attract was unmistakable in her games of "look but don't touch," turning men and women into lovelorn puppets. But this time Lea was outplayed. Cassie had her helpless with desire.

Lea caught Cassie's wrist, trying to drag it downwards, her goal obvious. "Please."

Cassie slipped her hand free. After months of game-playing, it was Lea's turn to wait.

"Please, Cassie, I need—"

Cassie silenced her with a kiss.

The city of Kavilli was basking in midsummer. Familiar sounds were softened by the heat—market traders' cries, bells from a distant clock tower, the clatter of cartwheels on cobbles, the clop of a horse's hooves in the courtyard below. Then came the creak of a saddle, boots hitting the ground, and a man's growl, his words too low to make out. Someone mumbled a reply.

Did Lea understand what was said? The effect on her was dramatic. She shoved Cassie aside and scrambled away.

"I don't care." This time the man spoke loudly enough for Cassie to catch his words.

On the other side of the bed, Lea had her back pressed against the headboard, knees drawn up. Her fists were balled under her chin, clutching the corner of a previously discarded sheet. The white cotton partially hid her nakedness, but only succeeded in making her look more guilty.

Her expression was one of horror. Her lips quivered. "Oh, shit, no. My husband."

❖

"What did you think you were doing?" It was a silly question, even by Jadio's standards.

Cassie relaxed on the couch and watched him stomp back and forth. How did someone so prudish cope with army life? She loved her younger brother, she truly did, but it was hard to believe they were related. Maybe they shared the same wavy black hair and dark brown eyes, but when it came to personality they could not be more different.

"It's not a case of 'think.' I knew exactly what I was doing." As, by now, did the rest of Kavilli. "How much detail would you like?" Cassie plucked a grape from a bunch on the side table.

Jadio broke off mid-stride and glared at her as if she were a new recruit who had forgotten to salute.

"I was having fun." Cassie popped the grape into her mouth

"Fun!"

"Yes. You should try it sometime."

"This isn't a joke."

"Most people disagree. Haven't you heard the gossip making the rounds?"

"Everyone in Kavilli is laughing at our family and you don't care."

How could Jadio be so dense? "It's not us they're laughing at. The jokes are all about Senator Flavinus and his floppy sausage. The only ones acting prissy are jealous. You might be an exception, but there aren't many, male or female, who'd turn down the chance to hop into Lea's bed."

"It was Senator Flavinus Ennius pars Avitae dom Tribonae's bed."

As if his full name made a difference. "He wasn't there at the time."

"You don't care do you?"

"No."

"We have the family's position to think of."

"The family's position?" Cassie affected a thoughtful expression. "Is that the one where you put your legs over the—"

"Cassie!" Jadio turned to Mother. "Can't you make her see how she's sullied the family name?"

Mother remained standing at the window and gave no sign of hearing him, although of course she had. Nothing escaped her notice.

Cassie helped herself to another grape. "You're being overdramatic. Anyway, it's more likely to aid the family."

"And there's a flock of pigs swooping overhead as we speak."

Mother left her contemplation of the rose garden. "Import taxes on wine are due for review when the Senate reconvenes. It affects our southern estates. We could use a few more votes swung our way. This distraction from Cassie is actually just what we need, if we play things right."

"Why do you always side with her?"

"Oh, Jadio, don't be so childish. You're thirty, not three." Mother settled on a chair. "I only agree with Cassie when she's right. And stop marching around. You're not on the parade ground."

Jadio's expression would doubtless have his subordinates quaking in their hobnail boots. However, Cassie merely continued demolishing the grapes, while Mother poured herself a glass of lemon water. Finally, he flung himself onto a couch as though trying to see whether it would break. "All right. Explain how Cassie playing the harlot helps us."

"Harlot!" Jadio was not getting away with that.

"If the shoe fits."

"Just because you can't get—"

Mother raised her voice. "Stop it, the pair of you. Try to act like adults."

"No chance of that with Cassie," Jadio muttered, before adopting a firmer tone. "I don't see how sleeping with his wife will entice Senator Flavinus into voting with us."

"That's not how it works," Cassie said. "Flavinus and the rest of the Tribonae family wouldn't support us, even if I'd seduced him, rather than his wife." Which was not an image she wanted to play with. "It's the effect on everyone else."

Jadio turned to Mother, incredulous. "You agree with that?"

"Oh yes. Cassie's handed me a useful weapon. Nobody will bring it up on the Senate floor, but in private will be a different matter. I will, of course, express my deep disapproval at suitable moments, just to keep the gossip bubbling. Flavinus is the best orator the Tribonae have, and they'll be relying on him to make their case. But now, whenever he stands up in the Senate to challenge me, people at the back will be sniggering, and that's a hard audience to carry. I doubt anyone will pay attention to a word he says."

Jadio's scowl deepened. "I can't imagine you'd be so happy if I was the one caught shafting a rival senator's wife."

This was too tempting to ignore. "I can provide a list of candidates if you want to give it a try."

Mother sighed. "Cassie, don't tease your brother. And, Jadio, of course it would all play out quite differently."

"For starters, if I'd dishonoured another man like that, he'd challenge me to a duel."

"Exactly so. In fact, that's the main reason I wanted to talk to you both. You've hit on our most pressing issue."

"I couldn't ju—" Jadio stopped, clearly caught by surprise. "I have?"

Cassie was equally confused. What rabbit was Mother chasing?

Mother put down her glass. "Senator Flavinus has never been one for duelling. Hired assassins are more his style. But if gossip gets out of hand, he may feel he has no option other than to challenge Cassie's closest available male relative in her place. Which currently is you."

Of course. That was the rabbit. A rather tricky rabbit that completely eluded Jadio. He gave a bark of laughter. "What's the problem? I'd beat him easily."

Cassie groaned and put a hand over her eyes. By all accounts, Jadio was a skilled military commander. He must be able to look beyond the obvious, though he showed no sign of it in everyday life. "Think it through."

"Think what through? I'd win, even with one hand tied behind my back."

"You're missing the point," Cassie said. "Everyone's laughing at Flavinus. If he dies in a hopeless duel, defending his honour, it won't be funny anymore. The rush of sympathy won't do him any good when he's dead, but it'd swing votes against us."

Mother nodded. "At the moment Flavinus is a liability to the Tribonae. We need him to stay alive."

"If he challenges me, I can't refuse," Jadio said.

"Quite. So you need to make yourself unavailable before things reach that point."

"What?"

"You must leave Kavilli. Rejoin your legion."

"I've still got a month of my leave left. I've got plans."

"Plans can be rearranged."

Jadio launched himself to his feet. "I don't believe it. Cassie whores herself around the city and I get banished."

"I wasn't—"

"Cassie, be quiet." Mother raised her voice. "And, Jadio, you're not banished. You just need to be somewhere else for a while."

"It's not fair."

"Act your age."

"Flavinus could still challenge our family, even if I'm not around."

"Then it would be up to your uncle Ullesso to stand in Cassie's place," Mother said.

"But he's eighty and half-blind."

"Exactly. Challenging Ullesso would open Flavinus to yet more mockery. He won't risk that." Mother's tone softened. "Oh, go fortify somewhere. Win a battle or two. You know you enjoy it more than slouching around Kavilli."

This was undeniably true. However, Jadio was unwilling to give up. "What about Salicia? Doesn't she get a say?"

"Then take her and the children to visit her parents. She'd like that. And, now that I think of it, you're overdue a visit."

Jadio's face dropped and Cassie felt a twinge of sympathy. Jadio's mother-in-law was more terrifying than a horde of barbarian warriors.

The fight went out of him. He ran a hand through his hair. "I'll talk it over with Sal."

Mother nodded. "You don't need to go today. Just make sure you're out of town before the Senate reconvenes."

Jadio bent to give Mother a peck on the cheek. "I'll see you before I leave."

"Good. We need to discuss your next promotion."

Cassie stood to give him a hug. "Tell Sal I'll bring presents over for her parents."

A suitable gift would soothe the way with his in-laws. Teasing her little brother was fun, but they were on the same side, and always would be. Family was what counted. It was the foundation the Kavillian Empire was built on.

After he went, Cassie returned to her couch and the grapes. Then she noticed Mother's eyes fixed on her. "Is there something else?"

"Do you need to ask?"

There was always something else on Mother's mind, usually several somethings, but this probably related to the Lea debacle. "You need to make a public show of reprimanding me, so the Tribonae family can't accuse you of secretly approving?"

"I certainly don't approve. Keeping your brain between your legs is supposedly a male failing. But you could do with taking lessons from your brother."

Arguing was unwise, and apologising was pointless. Mother would not be deflected by either. Cassie swivelled to sit up straight and waited for her to continue.

"You were 'having fun.' I think that was your phrase. Now it's time to be serious. We must make plans for you."

What sort of plans? Marriage was unlikely. Cassie would get married again, of course, whenever it was to the family's advantage. For the aristocracy, marriage was always a political matter. Love and lust were reserved for outside the marital bed, tolerated as long as one was discreet. But, given her recent display of indiscretion, a prospective husband might expect concessions. Negotiations would proceed more smoothly once the fuss died down.

Cassie was in no hurry. In truth, neither of her marriages had been dreadful, but being unmarried was more fun. Both divorces had been due purely to shifting power dynamics in the Senate. Just as well she had not loved either man, and Mother had secured good divorce settlements. All three of Cassie's sons had stayed in the family, although they came with a bittersweet cost.

As with every male born into the aristocracy, all were destined for the army. The oldest, fifteen-year-old Rufio, had just received his first deployment. It would be twelve years before he could honourably take up civilian life. Even then, he might become a career soldier, like Jadio. Her youngest son, Derry, had gone to the military academy on his seventh birthday a few months before. The house was so quiet without him. How much was the pursuit of Lea an attempt to fill the gap he left? Cassie pushed the thought aside. Mother did not tolerate lapses in attention.

"There's something I need to do?"

Mother's expression sharpened. "Think. I don't expect it of your brother, but you have no excuse. What trouble do you foresee? I've already mentioned it."

She had? "Senator Flavinus might…" Cassie racked her memory.

"Yes. Senator Flavinus. As I said, he's quick to use assassins."

"You think he'll try to have me killed? Risk a blood-feud over Lea?"

"I'd be surprised if he isn't already checking his contacts."

"He's got no real interest in her. He's keener on the houseboys."

"I agree Leasilla is irrelevant in herself. But you've publicly humiliated him. That's one thing Flavinus cannot bear. We must keep you safe until he's calm enough to act sensibly."

"How long will that take?"

"Too long for you to remain in the city. You won't be able to avoid his agents." Mother pointed to a leather dispatch wallet on a table in the corner. "An issue has cropped up in a remote location, so I'm sending an envoy to handle things at the source. Xeranius was my first pick for the role, but it will be good experience for you and will get you safely away from Kavilli."

Jadio would be pleased when he learned she was also leaving the city. Not that Cassie minded. Much as she enjoyed Kavilli's social whirl, a change of scenery offered new opportunities.

"Where am I going?"

"The far northwest. Into the Shadowlands."

Or maybe not so many opportunities.

Cassie had assumed her mission would be to an outlying province, exotic but civilised. The Shadowlands were ill-defined regions, lying beyond the empire's border, but engulfed by its shadow. They were home to barbarian tribes, who were allowed their autonomy mainly because the land held nothing worth fighting over.

Mother continued. "The region is known as the Western Uplands. From which you might deduce it's mainly mountains. Take the dispatch wallet with you to read later. It has maps and information."

"What sort of problem will I be dealing with?"

"The only resource of any value in the area is mining, and even with that, the quantities were too small to bother about, until a rich vein of iron and tin was discovered two years ago. Since then, provincial representatives have tried to secure access to the ore, but the local king has rebuffed them. You'll be representing the Senate, adding its authority to renewed negotiations."

"Why negotiate? Can't we simply send in the legions?"

Mother nodded. "We could. In fact, the army is under orders to annex the region. But that's where we get to the heart of the problem. The legate is the person asking for my help."

"An army commander wants diplomatic support? Why?"

"Rather than me tell you, see if you can work it out for yourself."

All right. "Talking has got nowhere, so now the army's involved." Cassie voiced her thoughts aloud. "Barbarians and mountains are a tricky combination, but nothing that can't be overcome with enough troops. If the legate has doubts about conquering the region, the first thing he'd ask for is reinforcements rather than a trade envoy. So…" Suddenly, it became clear. "His request has been denied. Someone's pulling strings to block him. Either they want him to fail, or they're using the threat of defeat to put pressure on the commander's family. Since he made an appeal to you, we must be the family at risk."

"Good." Mother smiled. "The commander is your second cousin, Legate Quelinus Regulus con Cavionae dom Passurae. The Sabrinae family are the ones pulling strings, trying to force our hand over the upcoming governorship in the Tarrallo province. I'd rather one of our people was governor, but we can't risk having a military disaster dumped on us. Unless you find a way to resolve things, we'll have to concede the nomination."

"I'm to negotiate a mining deal?"

"If you can get one the Senate finds satisfactory."

"Is it likely?"

"Frankly, no."

"So what am I really doing there?"

"If nothing else, buying time while I look for a counter weapon to use against the Sabrinae and force a compromise. I've got the Senate to agree that military action can hold off while this final attempt at negotiation goes ahead."

"Can we stall until after the Tarrallo governorship is settled?"

"Unlikely. The vote is still months away."

"Is there more I could be doing in the Shadowlands?"

"Of course, though it'll depend on what you find when you get there. See what Legate Quelinus can suggest. Ideally, we like him to sidestep the Sabrinae and annex the region without needing reinforcements." Mother pursed her lips. "Divide and conquer. That'll be your best option. It's just as effective with barbarians as it is in the Senate. Look for tribesfolk who can be brought over to our side—maybe a rival claimant to the throne who'll be happy to trade ore in exchange for a few cohorts to boost his own supporters. Failing that, you'll be working as a spy. Accurate enemy numbers and resources might reveal a weakness Legate Quelinus can exploit. Never forget the importance of good recognisance."

"I'll do my best."

"You'll have to do that, and more. Make no mistake, it won't be easy." Mother stood and returned to the window with its view over the rose garden. "The chances are, one day, you'll lead the family. Jadio doesn't have the ability. But do you have the self-control? Consider this a test. Indulging in childish pursuits will not remain fun for long. You'll be on your own, in an unpredictable situation. If things go wrong, you'll have to handle the consequences."

"I understand."

"Do you? Time will tell. However, I have more advice, if you want it."

"Of course."

"The various tribes in the Western Uplands are forever fighting among themselves and taking slaves. Some end up in the empire. The tribe you'll be dealing with call themselves the Lycanthi. Check the slave market for any on sale. Returning them to their homeland would start negotiations with a friendly gesture. More importantly, it'll give you a chance to learn as much as you can about them. You'll be on the road for two months. See what you can find out."

Arian

Arian's face ached from holding her false smile. She had totally lost track of the stream of gossip. The pretence of listening to meaningless chatter had got harder as the afternoon wore on. What her cousins were not saying was far more important.

Her son, Feran, was asleep on her lap, his head nestled against her shoulder. He stirred and murmured. Was her tension getting to him? Arian stroked the blond hair from his forehead and he settled back. She envied his carefree slumber. Last night she had lain awake for ages while the moon rose over Breninbury.

Pointless to tell herself she need not worry. What did it matter if none of the Lycanthi had witnessed Yehan's birth? They had Merial's word on it. That ought to be enough. But the knot in Arian's guts would not go away. She just wanted the ceremony over.

The taste of dust and dry grass hung in the air, along with sweet smoke from the cooking fire. The sun was dropping as midsummer's day drew to a close. The shadow of the Great Hall lay over half the meeting ground.

Folk were gathered, ready for the coming celebration. Women wore their finest shawls and jewellery. Men had their beards freshly braided. The children were in high spirits, running and whooping. Dogs scattered before them. If anyone shared her anxiety, they were hiding it behind a mask of restraint. Flasks of mead had not yet made an appearance. Might the drink blunt someone's better sense? Arian bit her lip. Was she reading too much into the occasional shrug or wry pout?

A liquid chord rippled over the babble. The bard had finished tuning his harp. Arian slid along the bench to get closer, careful not to jolt Feran. Voices hushed in anticipation, broken by shouts from a group of children.

Sharp words sent them off to continue their game out of earshot. Thankfully, Eilwen was not among them, though this did not mean she was not making mischief elsewhere.

Listening to music was better than worrying. As a child, Arian had believed the sagas to be true. Now she saw their value lay not in a bald recounting of facts. Even if the heroes had never performed the feats claimed, there was truth in lessons they taught.

Dark the hall, and cold the hearth.
Grim the foe, and hard the path.

Familiar words, and normally Arian's favourite, the tale of Rigana, the Sword Maiden. Although she was a woman, Rigana had taken up arms to avenge her brother. It was a heroic tale of courage rewarded, and order restored. But maybe it was not the best choice for the occasion, starting as it did with the death of Cadryn, first king of the Lycanthi. Some might see it as a poor omen.

Why had the bard not picked Cadryn's own saga, and sung of the semi-divine hero's quest to rid the land of monsters? In reward, his mother, the goddess Alwyni, gifted the land to Cadryn and his descendants until the world's ending—descendants who included Arian and the rest of the royal family.

The saga was barely begun when Feran stirred. Arian had hoped he would sleep a while longer, so as to stay awake for the coming ceremony. With his third birthday just a few days off, Feran would be too young to remember anything, but the day was important for their kin. Eilwen might even stop chatting with her friends long enough to notice.

Feran squirmed to be set down, then grasped her hand. "Hungry, Mama."

"The food won't be ready yet."

Feran was undeterred and leaned with his whole body weight, trying to pull her to her feet. "Hungry. Come."

Arian let herself be towed to the hog, roasting over the flames. Nobody would eat from it until Tregaran had led his fellow priests in making an offering to the gods. However, Daegal, who was overseeing the work, gave Feran a slice of goose breast that had been roasted earlier.

"Thank you," Arian said, since Feran had stuffed the meat in his mouth and was unable to speak on his own behalf.

"That's the summer-born for you. I swear they come into this world twice as hungry as anyone else."

"And with worse manners."

Feran chewed away, happily and noisily.

"I like to see a boy with a good appetite." Daegal ruffled Feran's hair. "He's a proper summer-born princeling, right enough."

"Shame he's the only one in Breninbury." The muttered words from behind were so low it was likely Arian was not intended to hear.

She did not bother looking around. Did it matter who had spoken? A renewed rush of anxiety made a fist in Arian's throat. Was holding Yehan's rite of passage on midsummer's day wise? The day was normally seen as auspicious. But did it merely invite comparison with Feran's birth?

Five years had passed since Merial returned to Breninbury, bringing her empire-born son with her. Simmering disquiet had grown ever more vocal as this day approached—the day when Yehan became a man and was acknowledged as Gethryn's eldest nephew and heir.

Arian glanced across the meeting ground, to where her brother, Gethryn, was surrounded by a group of his friends. Beside him stood Nelda, his bedfellow. Even though the birth was months away, her bulging belly was unmissable. Just as evident were her fantasies, taken from the empire. So what if Gethryn had played a part in creating the baby. The Lycanthi were not conquered serfs and would never forsake their traditions. Boy or girl, the baby was not of Cadryn's blood, and could not be Gethryn's heir.

But would anyone dare challenge Yehan's right to one day take the throne?

"Bring forth the boy." Tregaran's voice resounded over the meeting ground.

The urge to check the surrounding ring of faces was overwhelming, but Arian's position by the fire was too conspicuous to permit nervous fidgeting. She looked up at the sky. Red flames snapped at the night. Sparks were carried up to dance among the stars. The priests would have studied the constellations. What fate had they foreseen for Yehan?

The door of the Great Hall opened. For a few seconds there was nothing, then Merial appeared followed by Yehan. They joined the small group in the firelight, Yehan beside Tregaran, and Merial with Arian and their aunts.

Tregaran spoke again. "I call on the witnesses."

Aunt Ireni, as eldest, went first, by necessity, modifying her oath. "I swear Yehan is the true born son of Merial, sister to King Gethryn. This I know to be true."

Arian was next. "I swear Yehan is the true born son of Merial, sister to King Gethryn. This I know to be true." And it was true. She did know Yehan was her sister's son. Merial would not lie about something so important. But Arian had not witnessed the birth. Nobody in Breninbury had.

Other witnesses repeated the oath.

"The gods hear your words." Tregaran raised his hands to the night sky. "As do we. If any here dispute Yehan's birth, now is your time to speak."

A rustle of murmurs and shifting feet rolled in a wave around the meeting ground, and then faded. The only sounds were Arian's heartbeat thudding in her ears, the crackle of flames, and a breeze whispering over the rooftops.

"So is it avowed. Cadryn's blood flows in Yehan." Tregaran slipped into the rhythmic chant. "The seasons turn. The boy becomes a man. The man becomes a warrior. The seasons turn…"

Ritual words, heard so many times before. Tension dissolved in Arian's gut, flowing through her in a surge of relief, threatening to buckle her knees. Nobody had spoken out. Yehan was Gethryn's heir, and all the stupid gossip could stop.

"The land is in our blood. Our blood is in the land. This is our bond." Tregaran ended his chant and held up the knife.

Now came Yehan's turn. "By my blood, I swear to keep faith with my ancestors. The land is in my blood. I give my blood to the land."

The glass blade was as black as the night. Yehan did not flinch as Tregaran drew it across his palm. Even in the firelight, it was too dark to see Yehan's blood drip onto the ground, but the land would know. The oaths were given. The bond was made.

Tregaran continued. "Yehan Cadrynson. In the sight of the gods, and the name of the ancestors, you are bound to the land, as its defender. Uphold this sacred bond, it is time to leave childhood behind."

Yehan faced the burning logs, stacked waist high. He took one deep breath and set off. Three strides running and then he jumped, clearing the top by a hand's breath. For an instant, he hung in space as the flames parted around him. Then he landed on the other side, chased by a flurry of sparks, a child no more. Gethryn and two warriors stood ready to welcome him into manhood. They pulled Yehan into a huddle, arms around shoulders, brows touching.

And there it was for all to see. Three blond heads and one black.

Yehan was so dark. How much easier if he had taken Merial's colouring. Easier to fit in, easier to ignore the lies. Instead, he stood out, the only head of black hair in Breninbury.

Gethryn broke from the huddle. "This is Yehan, my sister's son, and my heir. He will be king after me, guardian of the land. May he walk in the footsteps of Cadryn, our forefather."

The men crossed the meeting ground to the Warriors' House. It was the first time Yehan had been allowed to enter, and he would not leave again for six days. Arian did not know what happened in there—no woman did—but when he emerged, his face would carry the blue tribal tattoos, the stylised wolves. He would be a warrior of the Lycanthi.

Once Yehan earned his place in the warband, there would be an end to it. That was the way a true prince answered those who doubted him.

Feran was asleep even before the blanket was tucked around him. The moon was high in the sky. Enough light slipped past the door hanging to show his outline. Arian sat on the ground next to him, hands clasped around her ankles. Nearby, Eilwen was snoring softly. She had taken herself to bed in a sulk after falling out with a friend. Doubtless it would be forgotten by morning.

Although Arian's home was on the opposite side of the Great Hall from the meeting ground, the sounds of revelry split the night. She should go back, but first she wanted a few moments to gather herself.

The day had gone to plan. Yehan had been named Gethryn's heir and nobody had tried to start a pointless quarrel over Feran. Arian remembered the years of overheard gossip, folk stirring up discontent. Not that anything had ever been said to her face. Maybe this should have been a pointer. The troublemakers had lacked the courage to poke their heads over the palisade beforehand. It was unlikely they would suddenly discover a backbone during the rite of passage.

Arian pushed herself to her feet. Time to have fun.

Familiar faces greeted her return. Everyone had eaten their fill. Some had already drunk more than was wise. Arian drifted between the groups, intercepting a flagon of mead, clapping in time to a song, laughing at the punch-line of a joke. Kinsman hailed her. Friends beckoned to join them.

After a circuit of the meeting ground, Arian paused to take in the scene.

"Your son's asleep?" The elderly woman was from an outlying steading and had come to Breninbury with her thane for the ceremony. Arian did not know her name.

"Yes."

"He's a fine looking lad. A shame he's not older."

"True. I'd have liked him to remember this night."

"That wasn't what I meant."

"What did you mean?" Though Arian already had a good idea.

"Him being true Lycanthian, and summer-born."

"Yehan is true Lycanthian."

"Weeeeell." The woman drew the word out. "So they say. But a lot of folk think it would've been better if your sister had stayed away. Then your lad—"

"Yehan is the rightful heir. Feran will be a loyal companion to his king."

"Oh, I don't m—" The woman's expression changed to a bland smile, as her eyes fixed over Arian's shoulder.

"There you are. I wondered where you'd gone. I was looking for you." Merial arrived.

Arian gave the elderly woman a last frown—age was no justification for her words—then turned away. "I was putting Feran to bed."

Merial looped arms with her. "Let's go somewhere quieter."

They steered a path between the houses to the relative peace of the palisade. Cloud was rolling in from the south, cloaking the stars. The valley below was a patchwork of moonlight and shadow. No lights showed. The farming folk and their herds were asleep.

Arian slipped her arm free and leaned against the palisade. "Was there something you wanted to talk about?"

"Not really. Just to share my relief that today is over."

"I know. But you needn't have worried. Yehan is Gethryn's rightful heir, and nobody was going to deny it. We won't forsake our traditions. Not now, not ever."

"Nothing lasts forever. The world will change no matter what we want." Merial was facing east, towards the empire. "One day we'll be just a memory."

"No. This land is ours, from now till the end of time."

"The land is ours because the empire doesn't want it."

"We've paid for it over and again with the blood of our warriors. As the empire will discover if they dare attack us."

"Oh, Arian." Merial sighed and took her hand. "You've no idea about the size of the empire. They can overwhelm us any time they choose. We'd be washed away like ants in a thunderstorm."

Arian hunted for something safe and ordinary—a joke, gossip, plans for tomorrow, but then surprised herself by blurting out, "Why did you go away?"

Merial laughed softly. "Do you know you're the only one who's ever asked me that? All I get from anyone else is, why did I come back?"

"You came back because this is where you belong—you and Yehan and your daughters."

"Do we?"

"You can't be serious. This is the land of your ancestors. It's in your blood. It will always call you back."

"Do you never hear the call of the empire?"

"No. Of course not." The idea was ridiculous. "What does the empire have to offer anyone? Forget about it."

"We can't. The empire's a seductive monster. We'll end up inside it, either all at once, or little by little. If it doesn't swallow us, we'll crawl up its arse."

"That'll never happen. We'll win in the end."

"We've already lost."

"No. We still…" Arian shook her head. "Why do you say that?"

"Because you're the only one who's never asked why I came back."

"Have you been drinking?"

Merial laughed. "Some, but not nearly enough. Come on. Let's see if we can fix that."

Arian poked her head into Merial's room. "Can you listen out for Feran and Eilwen, if they wake?"

Merial nodded, and then groaned, clearly regretting the motion. Her face twisted in a grimace. Not surprising. She had drunk considerably more than Arian the previous night, and Arian's head and stomach were delicate enough.

She was not the only one who had overindulged, judging by the pained expressions Arian saw as she made her way across Breninbury. The main gate was already open. She paused just outside and drew a deep breath. The morning breeze over the hillside was cool on her face. Briefly, the thumping at her temples increased, and then faded.

Had Merial's grimace been due to something other than a straightforward hangover? She rarely mentioned the time she had spent away from Breninbury, and what she did say was usually cryptic and lacking detail. But even by this standard, Merial had excelled herself. Leaving had been a mistake and that was all there was to say. It was not worth dwelling on the why of it.

The sun peeked over the hilltops to the east, lighting the familiar scene that had greeted Arian every day of her twenty-five years. Each tree, each rock, each bend in the river, was precious. It was her people's birthright and was not going to change. She would not let it. Merial was wrong.

Arian set off downhill, weaving through the series of defensive earthworks. After the last embankment she turned onto the well-worn track to the sacred spring.

An ancient oak grove surrounded the spring and pool, nestling in a hollow near the foot of the hill. Rocky ground and thin soil meant the trees grew barely twice Arian's height. Roots clawed around fallen clumps of boulders. Trunks were twisted and knotted. Far taller trees grew farther down the valley, yet none carried the weight of this grove. Years hung on the oaks, heavier than the moss draped over their intertwined branches. The air was thick, like water in Arian's lungs.

The rustle of the breeze through the leaves was hushed. Even the birds seemed wary at breaking the solemn silence, leaving only the trickling of clear, fresh water, bubbling from the ground. It washed over smooth pebbles, before spilling into the sacred pool. Even with the brightening sky, the water was dark. Surrounding trees cast shadow, but no reflection.

Arian slipped the copper bracelet from her arm. The pool accepted her offering with hardly a splash. The circle of ripples spread and faded. Arian knelt and dipped her fingers. The water was chill on her forehead, her throat, and finally her lips. She closed her eyes and let her thoughts still. The ancestors' spirits were here. She could sense them enfolding her, their strength and their love. A stirring of breeze was a mother's kiss where the water had touched her skin.

A prayer for Yehan's future. That was why she had come. Arian opened her mouth but was caught by unexpected doubts. Merial was wrong. Utterly wrong. The Lycanthi would never submit to the empire dogs. The ancestors would not allow it, and this sacred spring was the last place on Earth to waste a moment over the nonsense.

Arian tried to regather her sense of peace, but then came the sounds of someone approaching. Tregaran emerged from between a knot of trees. The high priest was also making a dawn visit to the sacred pool.

He smiled at her. "Well met, Arian. It's good to see you here."

"I wanted to make an offering for Yehan." Not that any reason was required. "He needs the ancestors to intercede for him"

"As do we all."

"Yehan needs more help than most."

"Does he?" Tregaran lowered himself onto a boulder. Age was creeping up on him. His hair was more white than blond, and deep lines were etched on his face, but his eyes were as sharp as ever. "Yehan may embody the menace we face, and will have his own trials to face, but I do not think he stands in any greater danger than the rest of us. Dark clouds are on the horizon, drawing close. I fear the coming storm."

"You're worried about the empire?"

"Aren't you?" Tregaran stared at the water. "It's my sacred responsibility to guide our people on the path the gods have decreed for us. I pray I will be up to the task. If I fail, we lose everything. This is the land our ancestors fought and died for. We must stay true to them. We must stay strong."

"If the empire dares invade, they'll discover just how strong our warriors are."

"The threat we face can not be defeated by swords and axes."

"You think the empire would win?" Arian shook her head. "We'll fight until the last drop of blood has been spent. We'll never surrender."

"If it were as simple as a battle, it would not be so important whether we won or lost." Tregaran sighed. "Even if every last man, woman, and child were killed, we wouldn't be shamed in the sight of our ancestors. We would have kept faith with the gods. Yet some are already tempted to stray. What I fear most is the slow creep into the trap. Some of our folk are falling for the lie that as long as you leave most of the palisade in place, it doesn't matter if you give a few timbers away. But that's how the empire will defeat us. One log at a time."

The words had an uncomfortable ring. “Merial said something like that last night.”

“Did she? It’s not surprising. Your sister knows the empire well. And the temptations to be found there.” Disapproval was clear in Tregaran’s voice.

“But she came back. She rejected the empire in the end.”

“It might have been better had she stayed away. Now every time anyone looks at her, or her son, it raises questions.”

“They belong here. And Merial doesn’t talk about the empire.”

“That only makes it worse. It leaves every fool free to imagine the answers they want. And there has never been a shortage of fools.”

Gethryn. Arian was happy to supply a name. A question pushed into her head. “I…”

“Yes?”

“I asked Merial why she left Breninbury. She wouldn’t answer. She never does. But I wondered if it might be because she hoped, without her, Gethryn would learn to stand on his own feet.”

“I cannot speak for your sister.”

No. Of course he could not. And it would not be fitting for a priest to voice criticism of the king. Arian bit her lip. If Merial had hoped Gethryn would become more independent, it had not worked. He just clung onto someone else as a prop. There was no iron in Gethryn’s soul.

Tregaran patted Arian’s shoulder and pushed up to his feet. “I’ll leave you to your prayers.”

Arian watched him disappear between the oak trees. Alone once more, she turned back to the sacred spring. Tregaran and Merial shared a fear of their people abandoning their traditions and willingly adopting the decadent empire ways. Why? What did they see as the lure? Why would any of the Lycanthi want to become a slave to foreign overlords?

Again, Arian dipped her fingers in the water and dotted it on head, throat, and lips. She closed her eyes, the request of the ancestors coming quickly and easily this time. “Please, let the world Feran and Yehan inherit be the one you left for them.”

Cassie

"I've jotted down a few notes for you. Vague ideas you might want to think about." Mother held out a folded sheet.

"Thank you." Anyone with sense would pick Mother's vague ideas over other people's meticulously worked out plans.

"You're all set?"

Cassie slipped the paper into the pouch on her belt. "I believe so. They should have finished loading the wagon by now."

"Good. If you leave soon, you'll reach the hostel at Piola before dusk."

A definite hint to get moving.

Mother followed Cassie from the room, still talking. "Have you spoken to the slaves Amillia found for us?"

The three men and two women were all tall and blond, with ages ranging from late teens to mid-forties. Even though the summer sun had tanned their skin, they were still much paler than Cassie. Two men had blue tattoos on their faces but were otherwise unnoteworthy.

"Briefly, last night. I explained they were now free and I was taking them home."

"What did you make of their reaction?" An edge to Mother's voice implied she had picked up on something.

"I don't think they got beyond surprise."

"Well, after a night to sleep on the news, one strikes me as quite interesting."

Which one? Cassie went with a hunch. "The man without tattoos?"

"Why him?" Yet Mother's tone made it clear the hunch was right.

"He kept looking sideways at the others. Everyone else just stared at me."

Mother nodded. "I'd say he isn't overjoyed about returning, which suggests he left enemies behind. He might be an exiled criminal. Whatever his reason, keep an eye on him. I don't know if he'll cause trouble, but he's your most likely source of information for things the Lycanthi would rather you didn't find out."

They reached the stable yard where grooms were harnessing horses to the open wagon that would carry the freedmen. Cassie had her own private carriage, decorated with the Passurae family crest, a silver fox on dark blue background.

The sun had cleared the horizon, although the yard was still in shade. The air was pleasantly cool on Cassie's face. It would not stay that way. Clear sky promised a long, hot summer day. Thankfully, the carriage roof would provide shade, and windows allowed a through draft.

The vehicles and their crew would only go as far as Verina, the empire's last outpost. Thereafter, Cassie and her entourage—a lady's maid, two bodyguards, and the freedmen—would make do with whatever transport the Shadowlands could offer and take their chance with the weather.

The freedmen were already in the wagon, talking among themselves, except for the man without tattoos. He sat apart from the others, staring at the boards between his feet. Mother was right, as ever. He looked decidedly ill at ease.

The bodyguards stood to one side, clad in thick leather armour and iron helmets, with an assortment of weaponry strapped to them. They would ride in the wagon, taking turns to sit beside the driver, on the lookout for trouble. Their presence was reassuring. Both Massillo and Palonius were trusted, long-term family retainers.

The same could not be said of Tullia, who had entered the Passurae household only a few months before. Currently she was showing far more interest in a good-looking footman than attending to her duties. Admittedly, there was nothing Cassie needed help with, but a lady's maid should be more diligent.

"Who selected Tullia for me?" She would not have been Cassie's first choice.

"She's youngest and easily replaced. And apparently, she volunteered. Though the word 'volunteer' should be taken with caution." Mother gave a snort of amusement. "None of the senior maids had any urge to see the Shadowlands."

Cassie yawned. Being awake this early was not unusual for her, but only because she had not yet made it home to her own bed. With luck she could catch up on sleep in the carriage.

The lead driver shouted, "We're all set, my lady."

Cassie turned to Mother. "I'll send word when I get to Verina."

"Do that." Unexpectedly, Mother wrapped her in a hug. Displays of affection were rare. "Take care, and come home safe."

"I will. I promise."

A footman held the carriage door and offered an arm to help Cassie in. Tullia joined her a few moments later. "Is there anything you need, my lady?"

No point asking now. Cassie bit back the rebuke. "No." Better to start on friendly terms. They would be together for months.

To the creak of harness, the carriage followed the wagon through the archway and onto the street. Wooden wheels rumbled over the cobblestones.

The Passurae mansion lay at the heart of town, close to the main plaza and imperial senate buildings. The white marble pillars were interspersed with sentries, resplendent in red and gold uniforms. Banners fluttered in the breeze, displaying insignia of the senatorial families, including the Passurae silver fox.

From Kavilli's administrative centre, the route continued along a tree-lined boulevard, passing temples, markets, theatres, and government buildings. Already people were out and about, the porters, traders, and craftsmen of the city. Merchants threw open storefront shutters. The carriage crossed a small square, where a gaggle of slaves clustered around the fountain, collecting water for the day. The familiar sounds of the city surrounded Cassie. How long before she heard them again?

More sentries manned the city gates, but rather than standing to attention, they were actively monitoring the flow of traffic. At the sight of the Passurae crest they pushed the crowd back, clearing the way.

The buildings did not stop at the gates. Kavilli had long outgrown its walls. However, there was a sharp change in architecture. Far less pleasing to the eye, the tenements of common labourers were interspaced with workshops, before degenerating into a shantytown of hovels and rubbish dumps.

Cassie turned to Tullia. "Have you been in the Shadowlands before?"

"No, my lady."

"Me neither. What's the farthest you've been from Kavilli?"

"Nowhere, my lady."

"So it'll be an adventure for us both."

"Yes, my lady."

"Are you looking forward to it?"

Tullia's lower lip quivered. "If you say so, my lady."

Volunteered? My arse she did. But could Tullia not manage a little more spark? It was, unfortunately, too late to request a change of maid.

Hot water has its own special magic. Cassie bent her knees and ducked down until she was neck deep. Steam-dampened hair stuck to her cheeks and forehead. The warmth seeped into her muscles, easing the stiffness and aches. How could sitting in a carriage make her so sore? Was it the hours spent tensing in anticipation of the next pothole?

Thankfully, the hostel had first-rate facilities, with both communal and private baths. Dinner had also been excellent, reflecting Piola's location, a day's travel from the capital. Doubtless the accommodation would become more basic and the food worse, the farther she went. What chance they had hot baths in the Shadowlands?

The temptation was to make the most of civilised comforts while they were still available. Cassie could happily have stayed in the water until her skin was wrinkled like a prune, but there were things to do.

After a few more minutes to soak away the dust and sweat of travel, she levered herself from the water. A hotel servant brought a towel and robe. This should have been Tullia's job, and, to be fair, the maid had offered to assist with Cassie's bath, but after a day stuck in the carriage together, Cassie needed a break. Tullia's expression had fluctuated between a tense smile and a bored pout. Her conversation had not gone beyond agreeing with everything said to her.

Cassie's entourage was still in the common room when she returned. Dinner had been cleared away and a game of dice started among the coachmen and bodyguards. The freedmen hung to the side, clearly unsure whether they were allowed to join in, although one tattooed man looked as though he was summoning the courage to ask.

Tullia was also at the gaming table, although she did not appear to be taking an active part. No coins lay before her. She sat next to Massillo, the more handsome of the two bodyguards. Given the size of the bench, she was far closer to him than necessary, and for the first time that day, her air of listless unease had vanished. She nudged Massillo and said something. He grinned broadly and drained his tankard, before taking his turn with the dice.

Tullia finally noticed Cassie's return. She slid from the bench and scurried over. "Do you need anything, my lady?"

"I'm going to my room."

"Yes, my lady. Do you wish me to come with you?" Tullia's face made it clear she hoped for a no.

"Stay here. But send him"—Cassie pointed at the freedman without tattoos—"to see me."

Many owners would not hesitate to bed slaves of either sex. Tullia's flicker of surprise changed to a knowing smirk. "Yes, my lady."

One more down-mark against her. House servants ran the best-informed rumour mill in Kavilli. Either Tullia had not been paying attention to gossip, or she did not believe what she had heard. Regardless, Cassie was not about to explain she purely wanted to speak with the man.

She had just poured a glass of wine and settled on a couch when the knock came. "Come in."

"You wish to see me, Mistress?" He stood awkwardly in the entrance. Judging by his expression, the freedman was also uncertain of her intentions. His eyes flitted anxiously around the room.

"Yes. Shut the door and take a seat." Cassie waited until he was perched on a stool. "What's your name?"

"My last owner called me Branius."

"What did your parents call you?"

"Bran, normally. Short for Branan." Despite a strong accent, his Kavillian was easy on the ear. He sat with his knees pressed together, hands clenched in fists on his lap.

"There's no need to worry. I only want to talk to you."

Bran glanced up. "Yes, Mistress."

"And you're a free man. I'm not your mistress. You may call me my lady, or Lady Cassilania. Whichever you prefer."

"Yes, m…my lady."

"Are you looking forward to returning to your homeland?" How would he answer?

Bran hesitated. "I'm very grateful to you."

"But you have misgivings."

"I...I mean...of course. I..." He swallowed.

"Do you have enemies there? Are you a wanted criminal?"

"No, my lady. Nothing like that."

"Then what?"

"I've got nothing to go back for."

"Nothing?"

Bran's shoulder twitched in a shrug. "No, my lady."

What was he not saying, and was it relevant? Cassie took a sip of wine. "Have you heard anything about why I'm making this journey?"

"No, my lady."

"I'm an imperial envoy. I want to negotiate a trade deal with your people, the Lycanthi." Best to start with the story she wanted spread. "Unfortunately, information about your homeland is very sparse. That's why I'm talking to you. I'll do the same with the others. I want to know as much as I can about what to expect."

"I don't know what I can tell you."

"Anything. Everything. From my viewpoint, there's no such thing as being too well informed."

"What you want to know?"

"Start at the beginning. Tell me about your life before you were captured."

"I was a farmer."

"You had your own farm?"

"It was my lord's. My family worked on it."

"Who was in your family?"

"My mother, my aunt, my grandmother..." His voice died away.

"Anyone else?"

Bran's eyes fixed on his knees. "My brother. My aunt's bedfellow. Two cousins and their children. We shared a home."

"How long ago was this?"

"Fourteen years."

"You must've been..." Bran was, at most, a year or two older than herself. "Twenty or so. Did you have a wife? Children?"

"We don't have wives, like in the empire. But there was a woman in the village. I was her bedfellow, on and off. She had a baby, a little boy. You might call him my son."

"Don't you want to see him? He'll have grown. He'll be a young man by now. Don't you want to know what became of him?"

"Nothing became of him. He's dead. I might find his grave, but that's all."

"Your wife—bedfellow? The rest of your family?"

"Those who weren't worth taking as slaves were killed. My grandma and the baby, they..." Muscles bunched in Bran's jaw. "The Endridi warband did it. They took everything of value, sheep, cattle, people, and destroyed the rest." He dashed a hand across his eyes. "As I said, I've got nothing to go back for."

So only bad memories were waiting for him. Yet something about his manner nagged at Cassie. There was more to Bran's unwillingness to return.

"You'd be with your people and a free man."

"Freedom is..." Bran gave another shrug. "I'd rather live in the empire."

Now that was surprising, and interesting. "You aren't forced to stay. You're free to go where you want."

"The lordly folk wouldn't agree with that. They like their common folk to stay put. Otherwise there'd be no one to do all the work." His voice and expression sharpened.

"You resent them."

"Why shouldn't I? The lordly folk live in their hillforts, with walls to keep them safe, eating the food we grow. They say we need them to protect us, as if we ought to be grateful. They took their tithe of our food but didn't protect my family. The only reason they care whether we live or die is because they'd starve without us."

More and more interesting. "Don't you feel any loyalty to your leaders?"

"The king and his warband?" Bran's tone verged on contempt. "They make out they're better than us. They sing songs about the old heroes. Fighting and raiding. It's a game to them—like dice. And we're the stakes they play with. Warrior is just a nice name they use, because it sounds better than murderer. But that's all it amounts to. They kill people for fun and call it honour."

"My brother is an officer in the legions. Tribune Jadioleus Camillus con Nerinae dom Passurae. Would you call him a warrior?"

"I didn't mean any criticism, my lady." Bran shrunk back on his chair. "And it's different. Soldiers in the empire, it's a job for them, not a game. They make sure ordinary folk can go about their lives in peace. If someone invaded the empire, the legions would rush to face them, not hide in their forts until the enemy had gone. After my village was ransacked, my king would've gone on a revenge raid against the Endridi. His warband would have overrun a village, taken some other poor sods as slaves, murdered their weak and destroyed their homes, just because they lived on the other side of the river. What good does that do?"

Cassie sipped her wine thoughtfully. Bran's worldview was undoubtedly coloured by his experience, and might be neither fair nor accurate, but there was obviously potential for conflict between farmers and nobility. This was all the more useful since nobles needed farmers far more than the other way round. How widespread was Bran's attitude? And could she make use of it? *Divide and conquer.*

Bran glanced up. "Anything else, my lady?"

"Oh, yes. Lots, but this will be all for tonight. You've been very helpful. You can go, but send one of the other freedmen to talk with me."

Bran looked surprised, as if for the first time truly believing Cassie wanted nothing other than conversation. "Yes, my lady. Thank you, for listening."

"Thank you, for talking." Cassie gave her warmest smile. "We'll speak again."

A blanket of cloud had rolled in overnight. Presumably, the sun had risen, though it was yet to have much impact. The sky was leaden, heavy with the promise of rain. A moist breeze picked at the hem of Cassie's robe and wriggled its way under her collar. The coachmen had erected a canvas over the wagon. Inside would be protected from a downpour, but hot, cramped, and airless. The damp would get its clammy fingers into everything.

In a corner of the yard, Tullia had latched onto Massillo like moss around a tree trunk. It was obvious she was flirting shamelessly and Massillo was a willing target. Cassie shook her head. He was welcome to her. Tullia was pretty, in a vacuous sort of way, but utterly lacking vitality.

Nor had she shown any hint of possessing a sense of humour. Two essential traits in a woman, as far as Cassie was concerned,

Tullia remained oblivious to Cassie's arrival until alerted by a coachman's discreet cough. She trotted over. "Is there anything you require, my lady?"

The negligent attitude made up Cassie's mind. The weather was dull enough. She needed better company than Tullia. "I want to talk with Bran, the freedman. He'll ride in the carriage with me. You'll be in the wagon."

"Yes, my lady."

Tullia's smug smile was most likely in anticipation of a day spent crushed against Massillo, though it was possible she once again misinterpreted Cassie's wish be alone with Bran.

He was by far the most interesting of the freedmen. The oldest was a woman, enthusiastic and grateful to be reunited with her family, but with nothing to say beyond how she expected her children and grandchildren to now look. The other woman had been sold as a child and scarcely remembered her homeland. She had no clue about politics and power struggles.

The tattooed men had been captured in battle and were eager for revenge. They clearly considered themselves superior to the others—certainly so, now that they were about to resume their former lives. Their insight into upper-class Lycanthian culture would be invaluable, as well as providing a counterbalance to any bias from Bran. However, care was needed in teasing out information. Their loyalty to their king was absolute.

Bran appeared at the carriage door. "Lady Cassilania? Your maid said you wanted me to ride with you."

"Yes. Get in."

He settled on the seat opposite, looking slightly less nervous than the previous evening.

At the driver's command, the horses began the day's journey, passing from the stable yard onto the road outside. The hostel was the only structure of note in Piola. The rest was a jumble of stone huts with fields of grain beyond. Sheep grazed in the distance. A peaceful landscape, looking suitably rural as the rain started to fall.

Cassie waited until they had left the village. "I have a proposition for you."

"Yes, my lady?"

"You're worried a noble in your homeland might enslave you."

"It wouldn't be so blatant, but that's what it'd amount to."

"Supposing you're my employee? My guide. Translator. I'd grant you full citizenship and pay a fair wage. When the mission's over, you can return to Kavilli with me. Would you be happy with that?"

"Yes. Yes, I would."

"Would the Lycanthian nobles be willing to accept that you're a free Kavillian citizen?"

"Probably. If I was working for you, I wouldn't be up for grabs."

"Then this is your task. I want you to teach me as much as you can about your people. Everything. Your history, your culture, your laws. Tell me about your king and the other nobles."

"I don't know much. We didn't mix with the lordly folk on the hill. You'd learn more from the other two. They're warriors."

"Is that the significance of their tattoos?"

"Yes. They get them after their rite of passage."

"Do common folk have their own rite of passage?"

Bran laughed. "No. Of course not."

"Is there any other meaning to the tattoos?"

"They're wolves. That's the totem animal of our tribe. Like the otter is for the Endridi."

"Are wolves important to your people?"

"Only in myths. The different tattoos let them know who's who in battle."

"Like a family crest?"

"Sort of."

Cassie nodded. "Right. So start at the top. What can you tell me about your king? And I don't want to know what his supporters would say. I want the gossip you shared after a few beers at the end of the day."

"Maddock was king when I was captured. But his nephew might have taken over by now."

"His nephew? Didn't he have children of his own? What's the story there? Was he married?"

"We don't have husbands and wives like in the empire."

"All right, they're not the same ceremonies, but you still…"

Bran was shaking his head. "No. It's different. Totally different."

"Then tell me how your families work."

"Blood is what counts. It's the only thing that counts. Of course, we know a man plays a part when a woman gets pregnant. You can see how some children take after their mother's bedfellow, but there's none of the man's blood in the child."

"Yes, there is." What was she missing?

Bran shifted awkwardly. "I don't mean to be crude, but when a man….you know, with a lover. It's just clear liquid."

"You mean there's no blood in semen?"

Bran nodded. "A baby is born covered in its mother's blood. And every drop of blood in its body has come from her, and just her."

"All right. What does that mean for your families?"

"It means the children a man's bedfellow gives birth to aren't his blood-kin."

"So who is?"

"His sisters' children. A man and his sister—they came from the same woman, covered in the same blood. If he really wants to be sure who his blood-kin are, he can watch his sisters give birth, though most take the midwives' word on it. When it comes to the king's sisters, all his female relatives witness a birth. Like I said, blood is the only thing that counts."

"That's why it's the king's nephew who takes the throne after him?"

"Yes."

"Doesn't it matter at all who the father was?"

"No. Even the mother mightn't know for sure."

Cassie yelped with laughter. "The king's sister can put herself about, and nobody cares?"

"If she wants. It wouldn't matter. In the empire, men try to control who women sleep with because it's the only way they can claim children as their own. Our way is simpler. And we all know the children an empire woman gives birth to aren't always her husband's."

That's one thing I can't be blamed for. "Still, don't men get jealous if their lovers sleep with someone else?"

"Oh yes. But that's a personal thing. It doesn't affect which family a child belongs to, or who gets to inherit what."

"So women can sleep with whoever they want? No problems?" Maybe this would be fun, after all.

"Pretty much. Though it can get a bit unruly if one woman takes another woman's bedfellow." Bran grinned.

"And if she wants the woman herself as a bedfellow?"

The grin froze on Bran's face before dissolving in embarrassment. "That's different. We don't do that sort of thing."

"You don't take same-sex lovers?"

"No. Never. It's forbidden. I mean, we'd all heard stories about folk in the empire. We made jokes about it. Even so, I never really believed it was true until I was taken to Kavilli and then…" He swallowed.

"It must have been a surprise."

"Yes. My first master, he…" Bran stared out the window, clearly working at controlling his expression. "I got used to it. Then I was sold to an older woman who liked pretty young boys." He tried to smile. "I didn't qualify."

"Don't worry. I don't take unwilling lovers, slave or free." *And certainly not male ones.* Where was the challenge? A criticism that applied equally to slaves and men. "Maybe your people ban same-sex lovers. But people break rules. Are you telling me nobody ever does it?"

"Some do, I suppose. But it's against the law. If they're caught they'd be exiled, maybe executed."

"Executed!"

"If one man had forced himself on the other."

"Would the same apply to women?"

"It should, according to the law. But people might not take it so seriously." Bran glanced at her. "I've heard the stories going around, about you and the senator's wife. I mean, it's gossip. I don't know if it's—"

"It's true."

"Right, well. When you're with my people, it would be better if you…umm, don't."

"Right."

"I mean, our laws won't apply to whatever has happened here. But it'd be best not to say anything. And you won't find any women who'll…" He shrugged. "You know. They won't. They just won't."

Making laws was not going to stop people being people. Whatever Bran might think, Cassie had no doubts about finding some women who would. Though it did sound as if more discretion than normal was advisable.

Cassie looked out the window. The road had left the farmland behind and entered a forest. The sky had brightened, although the ground under the trees was shrouded in gloom. She already had much to think about. It was time to move on.

"I want to learn what I can of your language. But don't let anyone know you're teaching me." Unguarded comments could be so useful.

"All right."

"So, let's start." She pointed. "What's your word for tree?"

"Please let the commander know Lady Cassilania Marciana pars Vessiolae dom Passurae is here to see him."

"Yes, my lady." The officer on the gate signalled to a subordinate.

While waiting, Cassie looked back at the town. Verina gave the impression of being an afterthought, tacked onto the side of the legionary fort. From the gateway, unpaved roads fanned out like the work of a drunken spider. It was clear the town existed mainly to provide entertainment for off-duty soldiers. Cassie mentally ticked off the establishments lining the main street. *Tavern, brothel, bathhouse, brothel, tavern, tavern, gaming den, bathhouse, brothel, not sure but possibly illegal, tavern, brothel.*

The hostel was one of the few reputable businesses in town, and thankfully only a stone's throw away. Even with her bodyguards, Cassie would not feel safe walking around after dark. If Verina was in any way typical of army postings, how by all the gods did Jadio remain so prudish?

"Lady Cassilania?"

Legate Quelinus Regulus con Cavionae dom Passurae was identifiable by his commander's uniform, though Cassie fancied she could catch a hint of Jadio in the shape of his nose and chin. They were related via her grandfather's sister. The only time Cassie remembered meeting him, she had been six, and he a little older. Her main recollection was him shouting at her, *Shove off, snot-face.* What had their argument been about? She had no idea.

"Please, call me Cassie."

He gave a warm smile. "And you must call me Quelin."

After entrusting Massillo and Palonius to the care of the gate officer, Quelin led the way through the fort. The contrast to the scene outside could not have been more marked. Soldiers in their pristine uniforms marched with straight backs. The buildings were laid out with military precision, walls freshly whitewashed. The ground was free of rubbish and weeds.

From the outside, the commander's house matched the surrounding buildings, but the interior revealed a comfortable family home. In winter, underfloor heating would keep the rooms toasty warm, no matter what the weather. Wall hangings softened the sounds, giving an intimate feel. Mosaic scenes covered the floor in vivid colours. The furniture in the dining room they entered was polished wood with inlaid patterns in mother-of-pearl.

A slightly overweight woman rose to greet them.

"My wife, Emilia." Quelin made the introduction.

"How lovely to meet you. I'm dying the hear all the latest gossip. You've no idea how tedious it is out here in the backwaters." Emilia was bubbling with excitement. "We're always the last to hear anything. I keep hoping Quelin will get a posting closer to Kavilli." Emilia settled back on the dining couch and gestured for the attendants to begin serving dinner. "So tell me, what's the hottest scandal in town?"

"That doesn't involve me?"

Emilia giggled, no doubt assuming Cassie was joking. Maybe Lea was better left until after a few glasses of wine. Fortunately, talk of scandal in Kavilli could easily fill a week of dinners and still leave the juiciest bits over for the bathhouse.

"I take it you haven't heard about Senator Albanus and his wife's birthday surprise?" The story was as good a place to start as any.

"No, no, please. Do tell." Emilia took a bite of spiced sausage.

Cassie selected a stuffed vine leaf and dipped it in sweet sauce. The meal was more limited in range than would be normal in Kavilli, but well prepared. Quelin clearly had the services of a skilled chef. Cassie launched into an account of the ill-fated birthday.

Quelin and his wife were easy hosts, who laughed in the right spots. Time passed quickly, but eventually, Emilia put down her empty glass. "It's been wonderful meeting you, but I must see to the children, and I know you two have much to discuss."

After she had gone, Quelin dismissed the attendants and refilled Cassie's wineglass. Alcohol and business were a poor combination, but she was in safe surroundings. Who knew when she would taste good wine again?

Quelin returned to his couch. "I appreciate you coming here. I've been able to stall while you were on the way, though it's purely a delaying tactic. Unless things change, I'll have no option other than to invade, and that won't turn out well."

"I'll do what I can. If nothing else, I'll drag the negotiations out for a couple of months,"

"Do you think you can manage that? Once winter sets in, I won't be able to lead the legion out until spring and the snow melts. Maybe someone will have seen sense by then."

"What's the current situation?"

"I've secured a promise of safe passage for you to visit their main settlement. You'll be a guest of their leader. He styles himself as King Gethryn, though he's more of a petty tribal chieftain. He's been fed the story you hope to strike a deal for iron and tin."

"You say that as though it's not true."

Quelin's expression hardened. "It's all a charade. The Lycanthi aren't going to agree to a deal. We both know that."

"Not a complete charade. Regardless of how the negotiations go, the Senate is determined to get access to the mines."

"Then the Senate ought to give me enough troops to see it through. I've got the army hierarchy on my back, pressing me to annex the region, but every request for reinforcements gets turned down. Some bastards are playing silly games."

"It's the Sabrinae family. They're the bastards in question. They've packed Western Regional Command with their own appointees and are making the most of it."

"What do they have against me?"

"It's not you, personally. They want their candidate put in place as governor of Tarrallo province. If there's a military disaster here that can be blamed on our family then—"

"So my men's lives are just stakes in the game. Damned politicians." A sentiment shared by many.

"Don't worry. It won't come to that." Cassie helped herself to honeyed dates. "Worst-case, if we haven't resolved things by the start of spring, Mother will concede the nomination for governor." It would be less damaging politically in the long run. "You'll get your reinforcements then."

"If she's willing to do that, invent an illness to stay here. That'll work as a delaying tactic. Emilia would enjoy the company."

"We don't want to give up on Tarrallo that easily."

"You'll be safer here."

"You think I might be in danger in the Shadowlands?"

"They're barbarians. Anything could happen. The safe passage won't count for much if things go bad. To be honest, when I heard you were being sent here as envoy, part of me wondered whether someone was hoping you'd be assassinated, so I'd have no option but to take immediate retaliation."

"I'll try not to get myself killed."

"Thanks. It'll make my job easier. Just watch your back."

"Has there been much trouble with the tribes?"

"There was a flare-up twenty years ago, but they learned their lesson. In the two years I've been here?" Quelin shook his head. "Mostly quiet. A few skirmishes with raiding parties. They fancy themselves as noble warriors, but they're just cattle thieves. They have more fun fighting among themselves, anyway."

"Would it be difficult to conquer the Uplands?"

"All of it? It'd take the entire imperial army. Even Western Command aren't being that unreasonable. It's just the region controlled by the Lycanthi they're pushing me on. But as for that..." Quelin sighed. "It'd be straightforward if I had the troops. The barbarians lack discipline. Their idea of warfare is to strip semi-naked and hurl themselves at the enemy. We'd cut them to ribbons in a pitched battle, but after the first few defeats they'd retreat to their hillforts. We'd have to lay siege to each one in turn, while trying to stop the others from regrouping. With my current resources I'd give myself an even chance of conquering the region, and be lucky if I lost less than a third of my men doing it."

Cassie finished off a berry-and-cream-filled pastry. Her wineglass was also ready for refilling. "I picked up a few Lycanthian slaves in Kavilli. The plan is to return them to their families as a friendly gesture. Except one has no wish to be returned, so I'm employing him as a translator. He used to be a farmer before he was captured. Talking to him has been very enlightening. He holds a lot of resentment for his former lords."

"Doesn't surprise me. It's the same in most places." Quelin pursed his lips. "I get the feeling Gethryn isn't popular. And the traders certainly like the weight of empire gold in their pockets. Trouble is, the power is with the warrior class, and they hate the empire and everything in it. They want nothing to do with us."

"If that's the case, how did you get an agreement for me to talk to the king?"

Quelin smiled. "They hate us because, deep inside, they're in awe, and it hurts them to admit it. I sold Gethryn on the idea that the mighty empire was desperate to talk with him. It was too flattering for him to ignore. It makes him look important. He'll want you to beg for the ore, so he can gloat over saying no."

Cassie swirled the wine in her glass. "What we need are a couple of nobles who're willing to fight on our side."

"I don't rate your chances. The warriors don't want increased trade, because that'll give more clout to the traders and miners. The last thing they want is lowborn serfs getting ideas. They're happy with things the way they are and won't support us, no matter how much gold we dangle before them."

"I wouldn't dream of offering money. I have a pair of Lycanthian warriors who I picked up with the farmer. Honour is everything to them. So maybe they could be spurred into fighting because someone badmouthed someone else's mother. It'd be more workable, and a lot cheaper."

Quelin shook his head, clearly amused. "If you can manage that, I'll be forever in your debt."

"I'll see what I can do."

"You're serious?"

"Totally. Though it might take more than badmouthing a mother. Throw in a couple of insulted grandmas as well."

He did not look convinced. "Anything else you want to know?"

There was bound to be more, although nothing sprung to mind. She would sleep on it and speak with him again before leaving. Cassie drained her wineglass. "Can you remember meeting me at my grandfather's house when we were children?"

"Vaguely."

"What made you call me snot-face?"

Quelin threw back his head and laughed. "That I don't forget. You dropped a worm down my neck."

ARIAN

Arian wound the new yarn on the shaft, then made a loop around the hook at the top. A flick of her fingers set the spindle twirling again. Carefully, she teased out more fleece, watching the spindle's slow descent. The action was rhythmical, calming. Her fingertips were softened by oils in the wool. Fibres slid between them smoothly. Another flick. Another few inches of yarn.

Breninbury's Royal Quarter basked in afternoon sunlight. The weather was warm, but not so hot as to make her hands sweat, perfect for sitting and spinning wool outside the home she shared with Merial. A light breeze carried whiffs of smoke from the bread oven and bleats from sheep grazing on the hillside beyond the palisade.

Other familiar sounds came from closer at hand—the clash of sword and shield, laughter, and shouts of encouragement. Warriors were honing their skills on the meeting ground, at the other side of the Great Hall. Even nearer, soft and calming, was Merial, singing Perri to sleep inside the house. Arian paused her spinning to listen, leaning back against the wall. The sun-baked stone was warm through the material of her dress.

Nearby, a huddle of three aunts stood outside their house, picking over the gossip.

"She never did!"

"Oh yes. Twice."

"What can you say to that?"

Who were they talking about, and what had she done? Arian had not paid attention to the start of the story. Then Wenda, Feran's favourite playmate, burst from between two houses. In either hand she held a crow feather, which she was flapping up and down, as if hoping to fly.

Feran toddled after. "My turn. My turn."

Smiling, Arian went back to her spinning.

A shadow fell across her lap. She looked up. Yehan had a bundle of clothes under his arm. A scrape marred the tattoo on his check, and his knuckles were bloody, presumably from an accident at sword practice. His expression was probably intended to appear aloof, although it reminded Arian more of someone trying not to fart. The aunts stopped gossiping to watch.

"Do you know where my mother is?"

Who did he think was singing? "She's inside."

Yehan hesitated. His training must not yet have covered the proper way for a warrior to get his mother's attention. Had Arian been feeling generous, she might have offered to fetch Merial, but it was more entertaining to watch Yehan puzzle it out for himself.

Eventually, he braced a hand on the wall and stuck his head through the entrance, while keeping the rest of his body outside the house. Setting foot inside his childhood home would obviously be an affront to his status as a warrior and a man.

"Mother." Yehan's shout was far louder than necessary, upsetting his infant brother. He stumbled back as high-pitched screams erupted.

A mighty warrior running from a crying baby. Arian bit her lip to hide her smile. The aunts were not so successful.

"Look what you've done." Merial emerged from the house with Perri wailing in her arms.

"Men do not concern themselves with crying babies." Yehan's show of disdain was unconvincing. He dropped the bundle of clothes on the ground. "These need to be washed. I'll pick them up tomorrow."

Merial sighed. "They'll have to wait until the day after."

"You should have a bondservant do it."

"They're all busy."

"I need the clothes clean for tomorrow."

"Then wash them yourself."

"I'm not a—" Yehan broke off at the sound of choked laughter from the aunts. His face darkened in a flush, either anger or embarrassment.

Did warriors get into arguments with their mothers over laundry? And what should they do if they were losing in front of an audience? Yehan was clearly in over his head and finally realised his best option was to cut his losses and leave. He stalked away. The aunts began eagerly dissecting this new source of gossip.

Arian waited until Yehan was out of earshot. "Don't worry. He'll eventually work out the difference between a warrior and a spoilt brat."

"Are you sure there is one?"

"I hope so. It's only a dozen years until Feran gets there." The future warrior had claimed the crow's feathers and was making his own attempts to fly, jumping up and down.

"He won't have as much to prove. Yehan finds it difficult because…" Merial shook her head sadly. "Listen to me. What mother doesn't make excuses for her children?"

Yehan certainly needed excusing more than most. Merial turned her attention to her younger son, and walked to and fro, rocking Perri back to sleep while Arian resumed spinning. The baby stopped crying.

Merial had just gone to put Perri to bed when a shadow again fell across Arian's lap. She looked up, expecting Yehan back, either to apologise or to restart the argument. Instead, Gethryn had arrived, along with Nelda, who was heavily pregnant. The child must be due any day. Two bondservants carrying bags stood behind her.

Gethryn puffed out his chest—always a bad sign. "Nelda will be sharing your home for a while."

"What?" Had she heard him right?

"Why?" Merial appeared at the doorway, looking as surprised as Arian felt.

"Someone else will be using her house."

"Nelda isn't our sister."

Arian might as well have not spoken. Gethryn's attention stayed with Merial. "Nelda needs a place to stay."

"Why our house?"

"You've got room. Especially since Odella has left. All five of King Maddock's sisters used to live here."

Arian rose from the bench. "That's not the point. This house is for the king's sisters, and nobody else. It always has been."

Still Gethryn ignored her. "Nelda won't be with you for long."

"Why can't she stay where she is?" Merial asked.

"I told you. We need her house for someone else."

"Who?"

"The Kavillians are sending an envoy to speak with me."

"What!" Was Gethryn insane? "You're going to let one of their rats inside Breninbury? Why not have a couple of legions tag along as well?"

This time, Gethryn turned on Arian. "It's not for you to question my decisions."

"Somebody needs to."

"I am the king."

"That's no excuse for acting like a—"

Merial stepped forward, putting herself between them, before things became more heated. "Arian's overreacting, but not totally wrong. The envoy is most likely a spy. The Kavillians are up to something." Her tone was composed and level but had limited effect on calming Gethryn.

"You think I haven't worked that out? That's why she's staying where I can keep an eye on her. I want to know where she is every second of the day."

"She? The empire is sending a woman?" Merial asked.

"Yes."

Nelda had remained in the background, looking sullen. She now gave a soft gasp and put a hand on her stomach. Gethryn glanced her way, then leaned closer to Merial. His voice dropped. "Please. As a favour to me. Nelda will give birth soon. She doesn't have any kin in Breninbury and she'll need help. I don't want anything happening to the baby."

Merial's expression flitted through a range of emotions, ending with resignation. She sighed and held out a hand to Nelda. "Come on, I'll find space for you." She ushered her into the house. The bondservants tagged along after them.

Arian slumped back on the bench. Gethryn was going too far. It had been bad enough when he gave Nelda the house. She was not of their bloodline and had no business being in the Royal Quarter. But this?

Down the generations, the house had belonged to the king's sisters, and to them alone. It was the birthplace of every king of the Lycanthi. Was that why Gethryn wanted Nelda to move in? Not that it would achieve anything. Cadryn's blood did not flow in the child Nelda carried. Boy or girl, it could never be Gethryn's heir.

The news about the envoy was equally unwelcome and, if Arian were to be honest, more serious. Why was Gethryn willing to welcome a Kavillian spy into the heart of his kingdom? Nothing good could come of it. But there was no point saying anything to him. He would not listen to her. He never had. Merial's opinion carried more weight, but even her influence was waning.

Gethryn dithered outside the house, as if uncertain whether to leave or to follow Nelda.

"Is it all sorted?" Leirmond swaggered up.

Immediately, Gethryn changed his posture in an attempt to match his friend. His shoulders went back, his chin up. His feet moved into a wider stance. Who did he think he was fooling? Gethryn was a sheep, and everyone in Breninbury knew it. Arian restrained the urge to shake her head. Of all the people her brother might have latched on to, Leirmond would not have been her choice.

"Merial's sorting out which room she'll be in." Gethryn gestured to the entrance.

From the lift of Leirmond's eyebrows he found something droll about the house. His gaze passed over Arian as if she were not there. He tapped Gethryn's shoulder. "Fine. Leave the women to it."

"I want to check Nelda is settled."

"Why? It'll be a while before you'll get to test her bed out again." He started to shepherd Gethryn away.

Saying anything was pointless, but Arian had to try. "Leirmond."

He stamped to a halt, then slowly turned back. His expression was midway between a scowl and a sneer. "What?"

"You can't agree with letting this Kavillian bitch come here. Can't you make Gethryn see sense?" The empire was one of the rare subjects she and Leirmond agreed on.

"Your brother is king. It's not your place, or mine, to challenge his decisions." Which was nonsense. Leirmond was quite happy to do Gethryn's thinking for him.

"The king should take advice—"

"From his chiefs and elders, not from women. Not even you."

"The envoy's a woman. Will you listen to her?"

Leirmond laughed. "Only if she's pretty."

"The empire isn't a joke."

"Oh yes, it is. Their fighters have got balls the size of a gnat. They call themselves men, and then they let women boss them around." He took a half step back towards Arian. "It isn't happening here." He turned away, putting his hand on Gethryn's shoulder. "Come on. We've got better things to do."

Merial returned. She took a seat beside Arian. "I've put Nelda in Odella's old bed. I thought you'd prefer her on my side of the house." She was not wrong.

Arian watched Leirmond and Gethryn disappear from view. "Why did you give in so easily?"

"Being overly concerned for his bedfellow isn't Gethryn's greatest fault. As for Nelda? It's hard, giving birth so far from your family."

"She should have gone back to them, when she was still in a fit state to travel."

"That bird has flown." Merial being right did not make it any less annoying.

"And letting a spy into Breninbury. What is Gethryn thinking?"

"Thinking isn't our brother's greatest talent."

"I tried to get Leirmond to back me up. But…" Arian teased seeds from the fleece on her lap. "Maybe I should have said I thought having the Kavillian here was a great idea."

Merial laughed. "Then he'd have taken the opposite view?"

"It's what he usually does." Arian looked up. The aunts had gone in search of a wider audience. This latest gossip was too good to keep to themselves. Feran, Wenda, and the crow feathers were also out of sight. "How long do you think it will be before Leirmond gets over me refusing him as a bedfellow?"

"A few more years, at least."

"Why? It's not as if there's any shortage of women keen to have him in their bed."

"Leirmond doesn't take well to being told no."

Arian hesitated, before asking, "Have you ever…"

"No. But then, he's never asked me. Unless it was during the Night of the Ancestors."

"Never?"

Merial shook her head. "I'm too old."

"You aren't that much older than him."

"I'm old enough to remember him learning to walk. He's always had a thin skin."

"Leirmond?"

"Don't be fooled by the swagger. It's an act. Small boys have trouble accepting they aren't always the best at everything. Leirmond has never grown out of it."

Nelda shuffled out to join them and carefully lowered herself onto the end of bench.

"Welcome to our hearth and home." Arian made a belated attempt at good manners.

"Thank you." It was no consolation that Nelda appeared just as unhappy.

"What do you think about this envoy?" Maybe Gethryn would listen to his bedfellow.

"It's awful. Gethryn wanted me to share my house with her." Nelda shuddered "I wasn't standing for that. You know what they do? I'd have to keep a knife under my pillow. Gethryn was going on about how I needn't worry because our warriors will protect us. Who was going to defend me if this slut tried crawling into my bed one night?"

Merial shook her head, a despairing smile on her face. "Is that all you're worried about?"

"You lived with them. Maybe you got used to the way they are. But I'll gut her if she tries laying her filthy paws on me."

"Believe it or not, in all my years in Verina, I never once had to resort to violence to keep another woman out of my bed."

"You share a house with her then. I'm not having her anywhere near me. Filthy perverts."

Arian sighed. Much as she sympathised with Nelda, it was not an argument likely to sway Gethryn.

In summer, the fire was no more than a token hearth-warming. The sweet scent of burning herbs filled the Great Hall. Fresh reeds lay on the floor. The walls were hung with swords, axes, shields, and trophies captured in a hundred battles, cleaned, sharpened, and polished. The trestle tables used for the nightly feast had been taken down and the benches pushed back against the wall to allow more people to be present.

Arian retreated to the darkest corner of the hall, wishing she could think of an excuse to leave. However, Gethryn insisted the entire royal family attend in their finest clothes, along with the clan elders and a guard of warriors. He was preparing to receive the envoy with all the honour due a visiting chieftain. Had Arian been given a say, the Kavillian bitch would have been dumped in a pigsty, except it would not be fair to the pigs.

"You don't look happy." Tregaran joined her. He wore a circlet of sacred oak leaves and the Totem of the Ancestors around his neck. The bones were brown with age and rattled as he moved.

"Is that surprising? It's bad enough Gethryn is welcoming this spy inside our walls, without insisting I have to take part."

"I admit I'd much rather this Kavillian envoy was not here."

"So why is she? What's the reason? Do you know?"

"Supposedly, she wishes to negotiate for trade in iron and tin from our mines in Yanto's Leap."

"Supposedly? You don't believe it?" The empire could keep its thieving hands off.

"It doesn't matter whether it's true or not." Tregaran's lips made a thin line. "I cannot claim to care about the ore. But I don't want the empire to gain more influence in our land. This envoy will only spread doubt and discontent."

"As well as spying on us. That'll be what she's after. To learn our strengths and weaknesses. Doesn't Gethryn see that?"

"You're not the first to express the same concern." Tregaran sounded weary. "It has been said many times in the Council of Elders. The planning has being going on for over a month."

"I'm not surprised Gethryn kept quiet about it. The first I heard was yesterday, when Nelda moved into our house. Gethryn promises it won't be for long, but one day is too much." Frustration made it hard to stand still. Arian wanted to kick something. "Can't you persuade Gethryn to send her straight back to where she came from?"

"I've counselled the king, as is my duty. But there are other competing voices."

"Then talk to Leirmond. Gethryn listens to him."

"Unfortunately, Leirmond has spoken in favour of the envoy's visit."

"He has? Why? Leirmond hates the empire."

"He hates the empire in the same way heroes in sagas hate monsters. Leirmond hopes to win glory by defeating its legions. I fear he wants the envoy here so he can provoke her into starting a war."

"He's said that?"

"Not in so many words, but his intent is clear—to my mind, at least. Though I doubt your brother realises it." Tregaran's voice dropped to an undertone. "In looking at the empire, Leirmond sees only a dragon he can slay. We must pray he doesn't bring us all down in flames"

A disturbance started by the entrance. The Kavillians had arrived. Tregaran patted Arian's arm before joining the elders around Gethryn's throne. Arian sidled over to where Merial and the other women of the royal household gathered to one side. A guard of warriors strode into the hall. Arian could not stop herself from craning her neck for a first sight of the envoy. Everyone around her was doing the same.

And what was she expecting? Legionnaires in gold armour? A woman bedecked like a shameless vixen, with painted face and provocative clothing? A carnival of depravity?

Instead, the five Kavillians turned out to be a disappointment. Their appearance differed from that of the Lycanthi, but in a mundane, unremarkable way. Two looked like fighters, strongly built men, encased in reinforced leather jerkins. The most noteworthy thing was their iron helmets with nose and cheek guards, as befitting cowards. True warriors did not hide their faces. Dying foes should know who had defeated them.

A third man was dressed in a thigh length robe over leggings. His hair was cut short and his face was smooth shaved like a Kavillian, but this could not hide the fact he was blond—the only one in the party. Beyond this, something about the way he held himself said he was from one of the tribes.

A young woman scuttled along, cowering between the two fighters in obvious disquiet. Pleasing though it would have been, if this were the Kavillian envoy, quivering in fear, there was no mistaking the true leader.

The woman serenely paced the length of the Great Hall, a step ahead of her companions. She was dressed in a loose white tunic reaching to her ankles. The material flowed around her, as though it were weightless. It glistened with a sheen in the firelight when she passed the hearth. A geometric purple design lined the hem. The colour matched the cloak draped across her shoulders which was held in place by an ornate pin. Open leather sandals were on her feet.

Her face had finely chiselled cheekbones, a long, thin nose, and narrow lips. Black braids framed her face. The rest of her hair was pinned at the back of her head in an elaborate bun. Her expression was impassive, unreadable. Her gaze swept the hall with a cool confidence, like a lazy fox scouting out a henhouse. Arian's fists clenched instinctively. The urge to knock the arrogant disdain off the envoy's face was overwhelming.

The fighters and young woman stopped by the hearth, while the envoy and blond man continued until they stood before the throne.

Gethryn spoke first. "Welcome. I am Gethryn, King of the Lycanthi and protector of the land. I greet you with the hand of friendship and offer you the hospitality of my hearth and hall. Relax after your journey and be at ease. We have made lodgings ready for you. Food and drink will also be provided. While you are in Breninbury you will be my honoured guest."

The blond man bowed low, then translated Gethryn's greeting into Kavillian, while the envoy listened solemnly. Many folk in Breninbury understood bits of the language, picked up from travelling bards and traders. Some even thought it clever to sprinkle the odd word into everyday conversation. It was not a fad Arian ever indulged, even though she spoke Kavillian far better than most.

The envoy replied. "Thank you for your gracious welcome. I am Lady Cassilania Marciana pars Vessiolae dom Passurae. I'm honoured to be here on behalf of the imperial Senate. I trust we will work together, in friendship, for the benefit of all."

The blond man repeated her words in Lycanthian. His accent left Arian in no doubt. He was a traitor who had gone over to the empire. A lowborn cur.

The envoy continued, gesturing to the man. "This is Branius, my translator and secretary. He is an empire citizen, as are my maid, Tullia; and my guards, Massillo and Palonius."

Gethryn responded in kind, introducing the elders, followed by yet more bland assurances of friendship and vague hopes for working together. He finished with, "My sisters will show you to your lodgings."

Why did it have to be her and Merial? An aunt could have handled the envoy and her lackeys. However, Arian had no option other than to follow Merial to where the vixen stood.

By all accounts, Kavillians were a short, stunted people. However, this envoy almost matched Arian in height. Seen up close, her skin was free of blemish, although darker than any of the Lycanthi. The blush on her cheek might have been natural, although the blue shadow above her eyes was not. Apart from the ornate cloak pin, in the form of a fox, her only jewellery was a fine gold chain around her long neck. Her eyes and hair were both dark. Her expression remained fixed in a mask of haughty appraisal, except for a hitch to one eyebrow when she looked at Arian, as if she had seen something amusing. Once again, Arian's hand itched to slap her.

Merial spoke in Kavillian. "Welcome to our home. I am Merial, and this is my sister, Arian. If there is any way we can be of assistance, please just ask. I look forward to getting to know you better."

The envoy gave a blatantly insincere smile. "Thank you. I hope, in time, to call you both friends."

Arian did not wait for a translation. She raised her voice but kept her tone and expression neutral. "I doubt it. I have higher standards. You might call me a friend, but I'll have a different name for you." Let the traitor deal with that!

The translator hesitated for a moment. "The king's sister regrets that your differing loyalties might stand in the way of friendship."

Did a hint of a smile touch the envoy's lips? "That's sad. But maybe, in time, I'll put her fears to rest."

Merial spoke before Arian had a chance to say more. "Please, come with me. A house has been set aside for you in the Royal Quarter. I'm sure you wish to rest after your journey."

She led the way through the small rear doorway. Arian tacked on at the back. Merial was more than welcome to the role of kindly hostess.

As they filed out, noise in the hall rose behind them. A burst of laughter made Arian glance back. Leirmond was surrounded by a group of warriors. His eyes fixed on the envoy, then he said something which provoked laughter, even more raucous than before.

What was so funny? Or maybe the joke was on them all.

Cassie

"I trust this is acceptable to you."

Was there a trace of doubt in Merial's voice? Even so, Cassie could hardly say no. "Yes. Of course."

"Over by the granary is a kitchen and bakery where you may collect meals if you do not wish to prepare food for yourselves."

"I think we'll take that option." Unless Tullia demonstrated an unexpected talent for cooking.

"I know you won't object to men and women eating together."

"No. Of course not." Did anyone?

"I'll have your possessions sent here."

"Thank you." All Cassie's self-control was needed to maintain her polite smile until both sisters had left.

The journey from Verina had taken five days, over the course of which they had passed several villages. Cassie had seen what constituted housing among the Lycanthi but had clung to a naive expectation the king's capital would offer something substantially better.

She was wrong.

She might even have wondered if she had been put in an animal pen as an insult. It certainly smelt like one. But although the building was smaller than most houses in Breninbury, it appeared otherwise identical.

The thick outer wall stood slightly over head height and formed an oval, forty feet or so by twenty. It was constructed from irregular rocks, that had clearly been found lying on the ground rather than quarried. An opening in the middle on the long side gave access to a central area, open to the sky.

On opposite ends of this courtyard were rooms, with grass growing on the turf roofs. The doorways had no doors, only hanging blankets to keep out the cold and offer privacy. The structure was obviously intended to provide housing for all of them. Fortunately, the freedmen, other than Bran, had already left to rejoin their families.

Just inside the courtyard entrance, a hurdle of interwoven branches leaned against the wall. Presumably, it was placed over the entrance at night, although it was hard to imagine the barrier keeping out a determined rabbit, let alone a wolf or a thief.

Cassie pinched the bridge of her nose. With hindsight, she should have set up her travelling pavilion at the foot of the hill before setting foot inside Breninbury. Doing so now would mean throwing the king's hospitality back in his face and would be decidedly undiplomatic. She would have to make the best of it.

Cassie pulled aside the blanket over one of the inner doorways and stuck her head inside the room. The animal stench went from strong to eye-watering.

She jerked back. "It smells like shit." There was no other word for it.

"It would be." Bran was at her shoulder.

"Would be what?"

"What you said, shit."

"This used to be a latrine?"

"No. It's the daub in the walls. It's made from straw, clay, and horse dung."

"Why?"

"To keep the drafts out."

"I mean why do they use dung?"

"There's plenty of it about, and it does the job. It's not so bad, once you get used to it."

Cassie managed a weak smile. "I now understand why you want to live in the empire."

"You should see what common folks' homes are like."

After hitching the blanket over the edge of the roof, in the hope of letting in fresh air, Cassie ducked through the doorway. Bran joined her a moment later.

The egg-shaped room had a dirt floor. The fireplace was a ring of stones in the middle. Obviously, carpets or underfloor heating were not to be expected, but flagstones would have been nice. A circle of posts supported a roof that was blackened by generations of smoke.

Opposite the doorway, a crescent shaped cubbyhole was set in the thickness of the outer wall. Was it for storage or a child's bedroom? It was too small for an adult to lie out flat.

"What this?"

"It's called a passage chamber."

More passage than chamber, except it did not go anywhere. "What's it for?"

"Whatever you want. Sometimes we'd nurse sick lambs in ours."

This passage chamber appeared to be mainly used to give spiders somewhere to practice. Back in the main room, a pair of three-legged stools were the only furniture, apart from a low wooden platform along the side. The top was piled with furs and blankets over a layer of straw.

"I take it that's the bed?" Cassie pointed to it.

"Yes."

The reek of stale smoke mingled with the stench of dung. "I know you said there wouldn't be a bathhouse, but I assumed there'd be somewhere to get clean."

"The river at the bottom of the hill."

"And a latrine?"

"Try the wicker shack we passed. There'll be a pit inside, with a couple of poles balanced on trestles to sit on."

Someone was going to pay for this.

Bran continued. "If it makes you feel any better, pity the poor sod who has to dig it out each night."

"I'm going to kill Mother when I get back to Kavilli."

"The baggage is here, my lady," Massillo called out.

Cassie returned to the courtyard which now contained the pack mules. "Tullia and I will share this room." She indicated over her shoulder. "The men will take the other."

She left Tullia and the bodyguards to do the best they could with unpacking and gestured for Bran to join her outside the main entrance, with a clear view of her surroundings. No potential eavesdroppers were in sight.

"I know you told me what life was like here, but I wasn't building the right mental picture."

"It's a shock for me too, coming back after all these years." Bran sounded bemused. "It's not quite how I remembered it."

"You say peasant housing is worse." Was it possible?

Bran grinned. "Thirty people would live in a house half this size. Sheep, pigs, and chickens would be running in the yard, so there isn't just shit on the walls. Goats graze on the roof and sometimes fall through. You'd sleep on the ground. The rooms aren't high enough to stand up in. And the roofs leak when it rains, especially where the goats have been."

Cassie glanced over her shoulder. Would their roof fare any better? "At least it'd let the smoke out. Has nobody thought about chimneys? I nearly choked in the hall." Thankfully, at that time of year they would not need a fire in the bedroom.

"A hearth fire is a traditional welcome. They were putting on a show to impress you. People were wearing their best clothes, and they'd put fresh rushes on the floor."

"Rushes? I don't impress that easily."

"How about the braided beards?"

"It made for a striking display." That much she could grant. "Especially the old man on the king's left."

"Tregaran, the high priest."

"I assumed that's who he was. Either that or the village idiot who'd been sticking leaves in his hair. His necklace looked like finger bones."

"It was. It's called the *Totem of the Ancestors*. It's a relic of our most important forefathers. He'd only wear it on special occasions. And you've been housed in the Royal Quarter. You're being honoured. Usually, only the king's blood-kin live here."

"I'll try to feel flattered. Though I suspect it's more to do with Gethryn wanting to keep an eye on us." Or not having far to walk if he wanted to murder them. "Did you pick up any sign of trouble?"

"No. Everyone was very formal and polite."

"Except the king's younger sister. I followed most of what she said, enough to know it wasn't a compliment."

"But it wasn't a threat. And she was the only one to insult you."

Cassie could not help laughing. "Isn't that always the way? She was easily the prettiest woman in the hall."

"Um...yes, maybe." Brad looked uncomfortable before moving on. "Did you notice Yehan, the king's heir?"

"Of course. He did stand out. Aren't the Lycanthi supposed to be blond?"

"Exactly."

"Oh, right. You mean his mother has been straying further than most?"

"Yes."

"I wonder what the story is there." It made for interesting speculation. "If he's the king's heir, he'll be the firstborn nephew, but it won't matter which sister was his mother. Have I got that right?"

"Yes. Though I'd have said it was the older sister. The other was too young."

"You're probably right. I just wondered if the straying wasn't voluntary. It would explain her hostility."

"If that was the case you'd be in line for a knife in the gut rather than mere insults."

"Then let's hope it was a love match."

"I'll see what I can find out."

"Do that. There's no saying what's going to be important."

Tullia appeared in the entrance. Her lower lip trembled. "I don't know how to unpack, my lady. There are no drawers or cupboards."

Cassie fought back a groan. Maybe she had inadvertently offended one of the gods. Overhead, the first stars pricked the sky, between wisps of orange clouds. Was it too late to make a suitable offering?

The act of swallowing made something scratch the underside of Cassie's jaw. She put her breakfast bowl down and carefully teased the hay stalk from her hair. Her neck was sore from dozens of scratches acquired overnight. *My own fault.* She had not wanted to examine the bedding too closely before going to sleep, fearing what she might find. In the future, she would take more care and ensure there was no loose straw on the blanket. The hay stalk joined others, littering the floor. Was it worth asking Tullia to sweep up?

Cassie took another spoonful of breakfast and grimaced. She had eaten worse things, but only as a dare. "Are you sure there was no honey?"

"Yes, my lady."

"What else did they have in the kitchen?"

"Bread."

"Why didn't you get some?"

"It was black."

"Burnt?"

"No. Black on the inside."

"Rye?"

"I don't know, my lady."

Could it be less appetising than the oatmeal porridge with stewed vegetables and shiny fat globules floating on the surface? "You saw the ingredients available if we want to prepare our own food?"

"Yes, my lady."

"How are you at cooking?"

Tullia's panic-struck face said it all. "Do you want me to try?"

"Probably not." Cassie forced down another mouthful. "Any idea what's giving the musty flavour? Did the cooks mention any local herbs?" Other options did not bear thinking about.

"You don't suppose it might be poison, do you?" Tullia's eyes were wide.

"No." Mother had taken care that both she and Jadio could recognise common poisons by scent or taste before getting a fatal dose. However, Cassie had eaten all she could bear. Some things were worse than death by starvation. She put the bowl down. "Tomorrow, I'll try the bread."

"Very good, my lady."

The sky was dull grey and the air heavy with moisture. A band of rain had swept through overnight. For now, it had blown away but threatened to return later. Surprisingly, the roof had not leaked, but the ground outside was covered in a slick layer of mud. It oozed over the sides of Cassie's sandals and between her toes. Boots such as the Lycanthi wore would be more practical, if she could bear putting her feet in anything so ugly.

Bran was off seeing what he could pick up from the servants. Without him to play the role of translator, Cassie was left to practice her eavesdropping. It was also worth letting her face become known around Breninbury. Once she was no longer a novelty, people would relax around her. Body language needed no interpreter and gave away so much.

Various people were out and about. Two men, bent under the weight of sacks, were heading to the granary. Young children were jumping in puddles, squealing loudly. Cassie smiled. Toddlers were the same everywhere. A huddle of older women stood gossiping, heads together. Could she get close enough to listen without it being obvious?

However, there was a better option. Merial sat on a bench nearby, nursing a baby. It presented an ideal opportunity for some mother-to-mother bonding. The king's sister was definitely a friendship worth cultivating. Her fluency in Kavillian was a reminder to take care when speaking. Others among the Lycanthi would understand what was said.

Cassie tiptoed between puddles, trying to keep the hem of her robe dry. She failed. Wet material slapped at her ankles, cold and gritty.

Merial looked up and smiled. "Good morning."

"Good morning." Cassie joined her on the bench.

"Did you sleep well?"

"Yes, thank you." Not strictly true, but far from being the biggest lie Cassie had ever told. "That's a good-looking baby."

"I think so too. His name's Perri."

Cassie tickled a tiny pink foot and was rewarded with a gurgle. "I remember mine being this little."

"You have children? I—" Merial broke off. "Sorry. Silly question. You just said you did. How many?"

"Three boys."

"You left them with their father?" Interesting the word *father* came so naturally to Merial.

"No. The youngest two are at the military academy. Rufio is my oldest. He's just taken his first posting, adjutant to a tribune in the sixth legion. I miss them, but we wouldn't be seeing anything of each other, even if I'd stayed in Kavilli."

"It must be hard, sending them away."

"I always knew they wouldn't be with me for long." Cassie forced a smile. As a child, she had cried for days after Jadio left for the academy. A bitter lesson that she had carried with her. Much as she cherished her sons, some part of her heart had always been sealed off, a defence against the inevitable separation. Was that why she had allowed herself to pour so much love into her daughters? And as it turned out, they had not stayed with her for long either.

"How old is he, the one who's in the army?" Merial asked.

"Fifteen."

Merial's expression was tinged with sadness. "You start them young, like we do. Before I know it, this one will be calling himself a warrior and running around waving a sword." She wiped a dribble of milk from the baby's chin before returning it to the nipple. "I'd once hoped for something different." The final words were a whisper, as if she was talking more to herself.

"Don't we all wish the best for our children? But no matter how hard we try, they'll end up making the same mistakes we did, and adding a few new ones of their own." A sentiment Mother would certainly agree with.

"I've given him plenty of mistakes to choose from."

And what were these mistakes? However, the question was one that could wait until they were better acquainted. "How many other children do you have?"

"Four. Three girls and another son."

"Your older son, was he the one standing beside King Gethryn yesterday, his heir?"

"Yes." She met Cassie's eyes. "The one with black hair, which I'm sure you noticed."

Was this one of the mistakes? "I did notice the colour. I've also noticed you're fluent in Kavillian. Is there…" Cassie paused. The question was potentially awkward, if the answer was no.

Fortunately, Merial smiled. "A link? Yes. I lived on the outskirts of Verina for ten years."

"Really? Why did you go there?" *And what on earth made you leave?*

"Partly I wanted to see the world. But mainly, because I fell in love. Clavius was a blacksmith. He came to Breninbury to see if there was a market here for him. He didn't have much luck selling swords, but I took one look at him and…" Merial sighed. "I was lost."

Good news for the outlook concerning knives in the gut. "What happened to him?"

"Nothing, as far as I know. After eight years, the magic had faded. Another two and I was ready to leave."

"You could have stayed in the empire. Don't you miss…" *Living somewhere better than a shit-covered collection of hovels?* Cassie settled for a vague wave of the hand.

"Baths, sweet red wine, honey-coated dates, and all the rest?"

"Well, yes."

"This is home. For now at least. I admit I wouldn't mind a few empire luxuries making their way here. And it would be nice not to—"

"Why are you talking to her?" The sharply spoken words were in Lycanthian.

Cassie looked up.

Seen in good light, Arian was even more attractive. Given a wash and a civilised haircut, she would be utterly stunning. Even without it, she was very easy on the eye. Her triangular face ended in a delicate chin. Her eyes glinted green. Her hair was the gold of ripe wheat. A pout accentuated her full, highly kissable lips.

Working against this, she was dressed in a shapeless, rough-spun smock with a cord tied around her waist as a belt. The green-and-blue chequered shawl draped over her shoulders was a simple square, secured with a copper pin. The edges were frayed. Her hideous leather boots looked as though she had stuck her feet into overcooked pies.

What would she look like dressed in elegant, fashionable clothes?

What would she look like naked?

Focus on the task in hand. So easy to say, so hard to do.

"The envoy is our guest. It is ????? that we act ?????" Merial had switched to Lycanthian, and presumably said something along the lines of *required that we act courteously*.

"She can ??????? back to the ???? empire, for all I care."

More unknown words, but easy enough to follow in general terms.

Merial reverted to Kavillian. "Please excuse my sister. She's a little agitated."

"Please tell your sister I'm sorry if my arrival has disconcerted her. I hope to put her mind at rest. I only wish the best for both our peoples."

"No reason why you can't tell her yourself. As children, we were looked after by a nursemaid, taken from the empire. Our uncle wanted us all to learn Kavillian. Gethryn struggles with it, but Arian understands your language almost as well as I do."

"I can also ????? like a sheep. Doesn't mean I'm going to ???? her ??????"

"Arian, you should be more ??????" Merial snapped back.

"You can ????? the ????? ????? yourself."

Cassie worked at maintaining the polite smile of someone who has no idea what is being said. When they had a chance, Bran ought to teach her a few obscenities, purely for interest's sake. Arian's intent was quite clear, without needing translation.

Merial turned to Cassie. "You asked about my time in Verina. Yes, life was easier in many ways, and there was a sense of being part of a larger world. That was good. But there were things I missed desperately. My family, obviously. But also the way people treat each other here. What they mean to each other. I had friends in Verina, but it was weak, temporary. I hadn't known them the month before, and in another month they could be gone. In Breninbury, I know everyone. Their families. Their history. We all mean the same things by the same words. We understand what's important and what's not. It's something Arian goes on and on about. But she's happy to throw away our heritage when it suits her."

"No, I don't." Arian continued to speak Lycanthian, although she clearly understood what Merial had just said.

"Then how about hospitality? The courtesy due a guest? The disgrace it brings if anyone is so ill-mannered as to show disrespect to a stranger who's been welcomed into hearth and home?"

A flush heightened the colour on Arian's cheeks, and for a moment she looked adorably flustered. *Stop it, Cassie. Stop it.*

Arian's expression hardened. "You want me to show ????? to someone who has no idea of ?? ?????? I know all about ??????? in the empire. Even animals know women don't ??????? other women and men don't ??????? other men. Why don't you ask her how many women she's ??????? in bed? She needs to ????? ????? herself, or she'll be sorry."

What an interesting direction for the conversation to shoot off in. Cassie had to work even harder on controlling her face. Bran really had to teach her a few phrases.

"There's more to the empire than that."

"It tells me all I need to know. All I want to know." Arian stalked away.

Merial sighed. "I apologise for my sister. She can be a little…"

"It's all right. I have a brother who is socially inept at times."

"Oh, when it comes to brothers, that horse is halfway to sunrise." Which was most likely Merial's literal translation of a local phrase, and one more thing to ask Bran.

The gaggle of elderly women had watched the entire interaction with unmistakable interest. Had it met their quota of gossip for the day, or were they hoping for more? Regardless, it was time to go, not least because the clouds were thickening. Rain was on the way. After a polite goodbye, Cassie puddle-dodged her way back to the pigsty passing for a home.

She ducked into the house as the first splats landed and sat on the three-legged stool, staring at the cold hearth. The sound of male voices and Tullia's giggling came from the other room. Cassie was more than happy to be left alone. She had quite a bit to think about. Some of those thoughts even related to her mission.

❖

Cassie leaned against the wooden palisade and peered over the top. Gaps had appeared in the heavy clouds as night approached, allowing through a last weak shaft of daylight. The distant mountains were lost in gloom. Trails of smoke seeped from the houses in the valley below, but the only activity came from the milling herds. Farming folk rose early and did not stay up after dusk.

"What does *guilrhul* mean?"

"Depends." Bran was standing beside her. "I don't suppose the person was speaking of carpentry?"

"Very unlikely."

"Then it was a crude way to talk about having sex."

"That's what I thought. And if a horse is halfway to sunrise?"

"It's so far gone there's no point chasing it."

"Makes sense."

A drawn-out howl echoed around the valley, making the hairs on Cassie's neck stand up. "How do farmers protect their animals against wolves?"

"Dogs."

"How are the farmers armed?"

"Farm tools."

"What happens if they're attacked by raiders?" Defences around the farming village were notable by their absence.

"This close to Breninbury?" Bran wrinkled his nose. "It'd be too much of a challenge for the warriors to ignore. They'd come charging down the hillside to show off their courage. Somewhere out of sight?" He shook his head. "The poor sods would end up like my village."

"Hmmm." Cassie turned to view the interior of the hillfort. "Strategy and logistics."

The area inside the palisade was about four hundred yards east to west, and half that north to south. Upwards of a hundred structures were scattered about. The largest by far was the hall where she had met Gethryn. It was also the only rectangular building, with a high pointed roof. The smallest was the latrine. There were granaries, but no well or other source of water.

A vast effort had gone into digging a monumental series of ditches and banks around the top of the hill, but the ramparts were merely for show. They looked impressive, but the hillfort was critically lacking, from a military viewpoint. Breninbury was designed to intimidate and to withstand a raid, but not a siege.

"Pardon, my lady?"

"The difference between winning a battle and winning a war. When it comes to managing an army, warriors need food and water more than a sword. Weapons can be improvised. Water can't."

Bran laughed. "Good luck getting this lot to admit that."

"They might change their mind if they were besieged."

"It'd take a while, if they started out with their granaries full of food."

"Do they take much of the farmers' produce?"

"Depends on the harvest. In a good year maybe only a tenth. In a bad year they'll grab over a third."

"That must leave the common folk on short rations."

"And then some."

"Do people resent it?"

"What do you think?"

I think it wouldn't be hard to whip up support for the empire. "Anyway, food is irrelevant. They'd run out of water first."

Other than putting the king's hall in the middle, and a horse paddock by the main gate, the hillfort lacked any sort of planning. But of all its failings, the absence of a well in Breninbury was easily the most critical. Was Quelin aware of this oversight?

"Talk me through things. Who lives where?"

Bran pointed to the west side. "That's where the bondservants are." The hovels were even more decrepit than the rest.

"How do bondservants differ from other sorts of servants?"

"They're even lower than serfs. They belong to the hillfort."

"They're slaves?"

"In everything bar name. Tribesmen aren't supposed to be sold for money. But they can still end up in the empire. Like me."

"How does someone become a bondservant?"

"Some are Lycanthian criminals who've lost their freedom as punishment. Some are captured from other tribes. I heard the last king bought a woman from the empire to look after his sister's children. She'd have been a slave, and she probably got treated better than the bondservants."

Which matched how Merial said she learned Kavillian.

Bran pointed to the building on the opposite side of the meeting ground from the Great Hall. "That's the Warriors' House."

It was easily the second largest building in Breninbury, although its construction had more in common with the oval dwelling houses. "What happens in there?"

"Rituals of some sort. I don't know for certain. They don't let folk like me in."

"The warriors live there?"

Bran shook his head. "No. If they aren't with a bedfellow, they sleep in the Great Hall. And that's where they eat every night. Gethryn caused a stir when he gave his bedfellow a house in the Royal Quarter. Only descendants of Cadryn are supposed to live there, although guests can stay for a while as a mark of honour. Like with us."

"Who's Cadryn?"

"The first king of the Lycanthi. His mother was a goddess."

"Aren't they always." The myth was hardly original.

"Gethryn didn't stop with giving her a house. If he hadn't upset folk enough, he's gone a step further and moved his bedfellow into his sisters' house."

"That must put a damper on the nights of passion."

Bran laughed. "Not many of those at the moment. Her name's Nelda, and she's about to give birth any day. As for why, it freed the house for us."

"It's where we're living?"

"Yes."

What a shame this Nelda had not refused to budge. "What counts as the Royal Quarter?"

"Those buildings behind the Great Hall. You see the shallow ditch? That marks it out."

"I'd assumed the ditch was for drainage." A silly idea, now that she thought about it. The hillfort did not have a cistern to channel rainwater into. Cassie turned and continued her stroll around the palisade.

Bran fell in beside her. They were developing a good working accord. He was amenable, observant, and quick on the uptake, as well as showing a talent for sifting information from gossip. Even before meeting her, Bran had taught himself to read and write. He was wasted as a slave, and Cassie planned to offer him a permanent place in the Passurae household, once they returned to Kavilli.

"Now that we've settled in, I'll speak to King Gethryn tomorrow and ask permission to visit the mining region," Cassie said.

"I doubt he'll let you go."

"I know, but he'll be expecting me to do it. I should be predictable. I want him to think he knows what's going on. Plus, the chance to say no to me will make him feel in control. It's much easier outmanoeuvring someone when they're not worrying."

Bran laughed. "A fox is the right animal for you."

"It's a pun on my family name. In the old northern dialect that nobody speaks anymore, surie means silver. Passa is a fox, and it also means sly. The name fits my mother very well, especially now that her hair has turned grey."

"Not just your mother, if you don't mind me saying so, my lady. Except for the hair bit."

"You haven't dealt with Mother—Doyenne Pellonia Valeria dom Konithae ado Passurae, to give her full name."

They reached Breninbury's main entrance where the hill's gradient was gentlest. The heavy timber gates were closed and barred for the night. A wooden tower stood at one side, manned by a lookout.

Cassie waited until they had moved out of earshot of the sentry before continuing. "Did you pick up any other useful gossip today?"

"I don't know how useful it is, but Merial is Yehan's mother."

"Yes. I spoke with her. What does the gossip say?"

"It agreed on the what, though not the why. Merial went off to the empire, either to spite her brother after an argument, or because a trader lured her away. Or she was always a wilful child, who wouldn't have anyone tell her what to do."

"Her account fits with the trader. Though there's nothing to stop all three versions being true, in varying degrees."

"Anyway, it was all right for her to do it. Lordly folk can come and go as they want. Common folk have to stay put. A farmer who ran off wouldn't dare come back. They'd be looking to spend the rest of their life digging out the latrine."

"But nobody minded Merial heading off to see the world?"

"I wouldn't go that far, but most criticism was over her leaving her brother and sister. Siblings are supposed to stick together, especially since their mother was dead."

"How old were they?"

"When Merial left, or when the mother died?"

"Both."

"Their mother died giving birth to Arian. Gethryn was five at the time. Merial was twelve. She looked after her younger siblings until Gethryn had his rite of passage."

"And then she went?"

"Yes."

"So Arian would have been ten or so?"

"About that."

"I wonder how she felt at being abandoned, once Gethryn no longer needed his nose wiped for him."

"If she was upset, she got over it. Gossip says the two sisters are close. Gethryn though…" Bran shook his head. "Him and Arian have never got on."

"He blamed her for taking his mother away?"

"Maybe."

"How about Gethryn and Merial?"

"She was his substitute ma. Since she's been back, they've butted heads a few times. But the folk I spoke to reckon Gethryn still looks up to his big sister more than he'd want to admit."

"How about other people in Breninbury? How do they see Merial's escapade?" And what might it reveal about the way the empire was viewed?

"The main upset is over her children by the man in Verina. Obviously not the baby, or the oldest girl. She was born here before Merial left."

"She'd be an adult by now?"

"Eighteen or so. Odella is her name. She didn't get on with Yehan and moved in with her cousins. You can imagine what the gossip made of that. I don't think she has a problem with her mother, but she hasn't moved back even though Yehan's no longer there."

"Enjoying her independence."

"Maybe. Or too many angry memories linked to the house. Yehan is good at upsetting people. And not just by his hair colour. Though it would sit easier if he took more after his mother. Both his sisters born in Verina have her colouring, but not him. People really aren't happy about the next king looking like a Kavillian."

"It must be a real dilemma for the die-hard traditionalists. Poor lambs. They'd like to disinherit Yehan because of a father they can't acknowledge as being anything to do with him."

"Exactly. The best hope was to question Yehan's birth, since nobody witnessed it. But they missed their chance. Arian's son as heir would go down much better. But they aren't getting any help from her, since, like I said, she's fond of her sister."

"They argued today."

"That's sisters for you. I bet it would have switched quickly enough if you'd got involved."

"No one can insult my sister but me." Just like nobody could insult Jadio in her hearing. "What do you know about Arian's children?"

"She has two. A boy aged three and a girl aged seven. Both summer-born."

"Does that mean something special?"

"The Night of the Ancestors comes midway between the autumn equinox and midwinter. It's one of the big festivals. A few men are chosen to put on masks with stag antlers and dance around the bonfire. The priest calls on the spirits of the ancestors to possess them. Then they go house to house and have sex with as many women as they can."

"Don't the women get a say?"

"And defy the ancestors?"

"So that's a no."

"To be honest, most people are too drunk to say anything."

"Presumably not the men wearing the masks."

"Probably not, judging by the number of children born nine months later." Bran shrugged. "Anyway, they're the summer-born. They're touched by the ancestors and seen as lucky."

"Both Arian's children are a result of this festival?"

"So I've heard."

"Any stories of other men? Lovers? Bedfellows?"

Bran shook his head

"Interesting. During the argument with her sister, Arian launched into a full-blown rant about same-sex lovers."

"Like I said, it's forbidden."

"But she's the only one to bring the subject up out of nowhere and lay it on so thick. Arian was going all-out to show how disgusted she was. The question is, who was she trying to convince?"

Bran frowned. "I don't follow you."

"It shows the subject is on her mind. Neither I nor Merial said anything to spark it. The rant came out of nowhere. She was overacting, in an attempt to hide the truth."

"You think she's got a woman lover somewhere?"

"Actually, I don't. I think it was all for her own benefit. She's trying to persuade herself she isn't attracted to women."

"You weren't raised here. You don't know how deep the taboo goes."

"I know people. And I know they wouldn't bother making laws if nobody ever wanted to do it."

Bran was clearly unconvinced, although he said nothing.

"Let me put it another way. Arian has to be blind drunk, and inspired by religion, before she'll have a man in her bed. What does that say?"

Now Bran looked alarmed. "You really think she wants…"

"Yes."

"What are you going to do?"

"Nothing. Don't worry. It's not worth the risk. She's attractive, but not that attractive."

The circuit of the palisade had taken them back to the Royal Quarter. Cassie and Bran parted in the courtyard of the house. Tullia was already asleep and snoring. Cassie sighed. The room was too dark now to hunt for hay stalks. Another night of scratched neck and ankles lay ahead. Tomorrow she would check her bedding and pray she did not find bugs.

Arian

"Thinks a lot of herself, doesn't she? Look at her, with her nose in the air." Nelda was watching the envoy tiptoe around puddles.

"Maybe it's so she won't see the mud on her feet."

"Ha. Stupid shoes. They're more hole than leather. What'll she wear in winter?"

"Who cares?" Arian certainly did not, except for a hope the vixen bitch would be long gone by then, taking her pet cur with her.

"Him. He's one of us." Nelda jerked her thumb at the blond man tagging along behind. "But he shaves his face. Doesn't he care if it makes him look like a girl?"

"He looks like the lowborn dog he is." The lack of tattoos was no surprise. "I wonder what dung heap she found him on?"

"I wish Gethryn would make them all leave. Send them back to the empire."

One issue on which she and Nelda were in total agreement. "Can't you say anything to him?"

"I tried. But Gethryn says Cassin…Calla…Cassia…oh, whatever her stupid name is."

Stupid was right. Did she think having a name it took all day to say made her sound important? And Merial was doing no better, calling her by the diminutive Cassie, as if they were friends.

Nelda continued. "Gethryn says she's no problem, and I needn't worry. He's just stringing her along, and he's not going to agree to anything the empire wants."

Which would be far more comforting if Arian had any faith in Gethryn's negotiating skills, even with Leirmond in support. Something about the imperial envoy was deeply unsettling. Her face was a mask, set in a fake, sickening smile. She was doing her own share of stringing people along. Arian was sure of it.

"She's asked to speak with him today," Nelda added.

"She's done what?"

"The king's council. That'll be where she's going now, to join the other plaintiffs."

Whatever the woman was up to, Arian wanted to know. She left Nelda and slipped in at the rear of the Great Hall. Gethryn sat on his throne with his trusted advisers gathered around, but most others had gone. By the look of it, the major petitions were over, leaving only a gaggle of lesser folk. The envoy joined the ragged peasants jostling at the far end of the hall, finally in her rightful place.

A farmer was speaking. "The young lordlings were only playing. I know that, but they killed two sheep, my Lord."

"Would you recognise these boys?" Gethryn asked.

"No, my Lord."

"Then what do you expect me to do?"

"Your pardon, my Lord, I wasn't thinking you could do anything. There's nothing can be done, now that the sheep are dead. And I'm not saying the young lordlings were acting unlawful, like. I just hoped the sheep could count towards my tithes."

"Did the boys take the sheep with them?"

"No, my Lord. They left them lying in the field."

"If you wanted the sheep to count towards your tithe, you should have brought them here when they were in a fit state to be eaten."

"Yes, my Lord. I have. The sheep were only killed yesterday, they're outside now." The farmer pointed in the direction of the main door.

Leirmond was standing beside the throne. He leaned over and whispered to Gethryn, who nodded. "I've been told we don't need mutton at the moment."

"I was fattening them up for winter, my Lord."

"They were lambs?"

"Half grown. Born in spring."

Gethryn glanced up at Leirmond, but there was a limit to how much advice a king should need over the fate of two sheep. The decision was his. "They were half grown, so they can count as a half share towards your tithe. I'll remind our young warriors that farm stock aren't for target practice."

"Thank you, my Lord." The farmer did not look overjoyed, but clearly recognised the judgment was the best he would get. He bowed and left the hall.

Although the other peasants had been there first, the steward, Emlyn, now called out, "Lady Cassilania, stand forth and make your case." How did Emlyn remember the absurd name?

The two-faced vixen advanced closer to the throne than she had any right, all the while smiling as if she found everything quaintly amusing.

She inclined her head in the faintest of bows. "Thank you, King Gethryn. With a view to the establishment of mutually beneficial trade, I request permission to visit the mines around Yanto's Leap. I'd like to appraise the situation and confer with the local lord. I'd also like to contact representatives of the miners."

Had Gethryn anticipated the request? He spoke as soon as the translation was complete, without needing advice. "Earl Kendric is lord of Yanto's Leap. I'm sure he'll be keen to speak with you, but as this matter concerns all the Lycanthi, I'll need to be present. I'll summon Earl Kendric to Breninbury."

"Your inclusion will be most advantageous. However, I'd still like to visit the mines in person."

"The road to Yanto's Leap is in poor condition and the journey would be an unacceptable hardship for a woman of your breeding." *Breeding!* How did Gethryn say it with a straight face? "You're under my protection, and I cannot allow you to take the risk. Earl Kendric is familiar with every aspect of the land he commands. He can be here in ten days and will be able to answer all your questions."

The envoy and her pet traitor spoke together quietly before she again addressed Gethryn. "I'll be pleased to take advantage of Earl Kendric's experience. Thank you for your help in this matter, and for exercising your knowledge on my behalf." After a last round of translations, she gave another regal nod and swept from the hall.

They would have to put up with seeing her smug face around Breninbury for a while longer. Arian would happily have sent her off to the back end of hell—the farther, the better. Yet a spy could not be allowed to roam unchecked. Had Gethryn worked that out for himself?

Emlyn summoned the next plaintiff. The peasant seemed to have an issue about boundary posts and ploughs. However, he mumbled into his unkempt beard, so it was hard to be sure. Whatever the issue, it was of no interest to Arian. She left through the rear door and collided with the envoy, who was hanging around on the other side.

"I'm sorry, Arian. I didn't mean to get in your way." She did not sound at all apologetic.

Arian matched the false smile and said in Lycanthian, "That's what happens when you stand in a stupid spot." She made to walk away, but the vixen took a small sidestep. This time there was no doubt that getting in the way was fully intended.

"Though, now that you're here, I wonder if I could ask a favour."

The traitor had gone. Either Arian replied in Kavillian or she ignored the request. Curiosity won out. "I don't know what you think I can do for you."

"Don't you?" The smile grew even more annoying, as if to a private joke. "I've heard so many interesting things about you."

"I can't help what people say."

"No. None of us can do that. But how would people pass the time of day without rumour and scandal for entertainment?"

"I don't concern myself with idle gossip."

"You should. You can learn so much from it."

"It's more lies than truth."

"Oh, yes. I agree. That doesn't stop its usefulness, once you learn to see through the facade. The truths people choose to ignore can be no less revealing than the lies they choose to tell."

"What lies are people telling about me?" Arian could not stop herself asking

"Actually, it's what they're not saying I find the most intriguing."

"I don't know what you mean."

"Are you sure? You can't think of anything about yourself that people either haven't noticed or don't like to mention?" The sly vixen was playing games, taunting her.

"You think you know something about me?"

"I could make a guess."

"I can assure you, Cassan…Cas…" Damn. She had fallen into the same trap as Nelda and ruined any attempt at sounding assured.

"Cassilania." The blatant amusement on the woman's face made it worse. "But please, call me Cassie."

I've got to call her something. Why waste more breath than necessary? "Whatever you think you know about me, Cassie, you're wrong."

"That's a bold statement. But time will tell."

"The less time I spend anywhere near you, the better."

Cassie sighed, like a mother exasperated with a wilful toddler. "You're saying there's no hope of us becoming friends?"

"None whatsoever. I want nothing to do with a pervert like you."

"Pervert?"

"You know what I'm talking about."

"Suppose I don't. Please, enlighten me."

"We've all heard the stories."

"About me?"

"You don't care who you have in your bed."

"That's not true." Cassie's face held no trace of awkwardness. "I have standards. Personal hygiene, intelligence, a sense of humour. Things like that."

"You don't care whether you're with a man or a woman."

"Again, not true. I have an overwhelming preference for women. Men are necessary for children, but when it comes to having fun, there's no comparison." Even with Cassie's light-hearted delivery, there was no doubt she was speaking the truth. No shame. No alarm. No denial.

She's done it. She's really done it. She's had female bedfellows. Had Arian truly believed it before? Her skin prickled as the blood drained from her face, then burned as it surged back in a red-hot blush. Her stomach turned to ice. The accusation had been intended as an insult rather than a statement of fact. Yet Cassie was happy to confirm it and did not look the least bit insulted.

The silence grew while Cassie's smile spread to her eyes. At last, she took a step back. "I won't keep you any longer. Good morning."

Arian forced herself to speak. "I thought you wanted to ask a favour of me."

"It was nothing. And besides, I'd never pressure an unwilling woman into doing anything she wasn't comfortable with."

Their eyes met. The lilt in Cassie's voice, the depth in her tone, the teasing smile. The scheming bitch was toying with her, implying far more than her words said. Then Cassie turned and strolled away.

❖

A scream ripped through the night.

Arian stood at the entrance of the house. Sleep was impossible, but she had the beauty of the stars to compensate. The crescent moon had set long ago, and nothing now competed with their brilliance. The familiar constellations moved through their majestic dance. What would the priests read in them? What did they foreshadow for the child about to enter the world?

She glanced back at the sound of footsteps in the courtyard. Merial had come to join her, carrying a small oil lamp. Arian put her arm around her sister's waist and pulled her close, partly for shared warmth, partly for support.

"How's it going?"

"The midwife says it won't be long."

"Good."

"You could show a little sympathy. We've both been there."

"The problem is she's here. I'd have more sympathy if she was in her own house, not ours."

Another whimper ended in an agonized groan. Arian bit her lip. If truth be told, it was far too easy to get caught up, reliving the birth of her own children—the two who had survived, and the one who had not. Except everything blurred in her mind. It had hurt, and gone on far longer than expected, but memory of the pain was overridden by the joy of holding her babies for the first time.

A figure appeared between two houses, a man, judging by the height. At first it looked as though he might slip back into the darkness, but then Gethryn stepped into the light. "Why are you out here? Why aren't you helping with the birth?"

"The midwives know what they're doing," Arian answered.

"Yes, but they're just…"

"What?"

The last trace of uncertainty vanished. Gethryn squared his shoulders. "I want you to witness the birth."

"Why?"

"Supposing it's a boy."

"What if it is?"

"He's not our kin." Merial joined in, her tone gentler but no less pointed.

"Nelda doesn't have any sisters here to speak for her and the baby."

"She'll have the midwives," Arian said.

"They're not of royal blood."

"Neither is the baby."

"That's not—"

A drawn-out screech rose in tone and volume, loud enough to be heard the length of Breninbury. The cry cut off abruptly. Silence held for a dozen heartbeats, until broken by the squall of a newborn infant. Gethryn pushed past Arian and Merial, who followed slowly.

A large lamp and the remains of a fire lit the room. The scent of burning herbs masked that of hard-worked bodies. Nelda lay exhausted, tended by two midwives. Sweat-soaked hair clung to her forehead. Dark stains marked the blankets. Blood. The blood linking Nelda to her baby, and to all who had gone before her.

Gethryn knelt by the bed, cradling the wailing infant in his arms, his face an image of entranced wonder. "It's a boy."

"Yes. A healthy child," one midwife agreed.

"I'll hold a feast for his naming."

"Gethryn!" Arian was outraged. Even the midwives looked surprised.

"Why shouldn't I?"

"Apart from anything else, it's a matter for Nelda's brothers, not you."

"They won't mind."

"That's not the point. You make it sound as if…"

"As if what?" Gethryn's tone was angry, defiant.

"As if you're claiming him. You can't. He's not of your blood."

"It's not a question of blood."

"Then what?"

"He's not my heir and never will be. But I helped make him. That should count for something."

"To the Kavillians. Not to us."

"Then maybe we need to rethink things."

Merial stepped in before Arian could say more. "This isn't the time. We're tired. Let's be happy for the birth of the child and leave everything else till tomorrow." She placed a hand on Arian's arm and steered her out and across the courtyard to the other side of the house.

"Gethryn can't do this." Arian kept her voice low.

"He's the king. He's allowed to call feasts."

"He thinks he can claim Nelda's child as his own. It's that fucking imperial envoy. It's her doing."

"I'm quite sure Cassie hasn't said a word to him on the subject."

"She doesn't have to. Just her being here makes people think. Makes them question things that don't need questioning."

"Asking questions is never a mistake."

"What if they reach the wrong answer?"

Merial sighed. "Go to sleep. There'll be time to argue and shout tomorrow."

Not that it would do any good.

The bed was vacant. All the children had been sent to stay with Odella once it was clear the birth was coming. Arian slipped off her outer clothes, crawled under the covers, and rolled over to make room. But sleep would not come to her.

Arian lay awake, staring into the darkness, listening to Merial's soft, even breaths. The words from months before echoed in her head. *"The empire's a seductive monster. We'll end up inside it, either all at once, or little by little. If it doesn't swallow us, we'll crawl up it's arse."*

Cassie. There was a seductive monster for you. How long before her influence poisoned everyone? Arian scrunched her eyes shut in a grimace as another memory washed over her. The memory that would not leave her head. The memory taunting her throughout the day and plaguing her dreams at night. The memory of Cassie, brazen and utterly without shame, smiling as she confessed to having taken women as bedfellows.

Seductive monster? Arian would rather die than let herself be seduced, in any meaning of the word. But it was so damned hard to stop thinking about the woman.

Gusts of wind ruffled the surface of the sacred pool. Arian stared at the water, trying to catch her reflection, but the distorted image revealed only dark clouds. Her face was a featureless outline, a shadow. Was it a message from the ancestors?

"You look troubled."

Arian jerked back, startled. How long had Tregaran been watching?

"I…Yes, I am."

"Can I provide guidance?"

"It's not for me." Her own difficulties did not require advice. The answers were both obvious and unworkable. She had to stop thinking about Cassie. But how?

"Have you spoken to whoever it is?"

"He doesn't think there's a problem. It's about Gethryn."

"Ah." Tregaran's expression was unreadable.

Arian waited until he had taken his usual seat on the rocks. "You've heard about Nelda's baby? Gethryn is holding a feast for its naming."

"Yes."

"He wants to claim the baby as his son."

"I cannot speak as to his motives."

"I can."

"In that case, I'd say you know more on the subject than your brother does himself."

Despite her tangled emotions, Arian could not help smiling. Gethryn always let others do his thinking for him. And it was easy to know where this idea came from. "It's that damned envoy. We need her gone from Breninbury."

"Removing one woman will not solve everything. The empire still casts its shadow over us. Although I agree her presence is a focus for discontent and foolish dreams."

"Dreams like calling yourself a *father*?" Arian was forced to use the Kavillian word, since there was not one in Lycanthian.

However, Tregaran did not seem confused by it. "We should not be surprised if men are jealous of their sisters and the blood bond between mother and child."

"Is this what you were talking about before? Giving away one log from the palisade?"

Tregaran nodded slowly. "Yes. And, as is the way with these things, it's a log set in soft ground. Borrowing the idea from the empire might seem a minor thing. After all, who can look at Yehan and doubt his mother's bedfellow played a part in his making? But it's a mistake to think you can take a piece from one pot and insert it in another. They will need to shatter the pot first, and it will never go back together again. If we step off the path the gods have decreed for us, then we lose our claim on the land." The calmness in Tregaran's voice did nothing to limit its force. "I will not stand by. I promise you, as long as I live, Nelda's son will never be king. We have the law as laid down by the gods. I will let no man or woman break it."

"You should speak to Gethryn."

"What makes you think I haven't spoken already?"

"Have you?"

"If I had, it would be a private matter between high priest and king."

And if you have, Gethryn is paying no attention. Arian stared into the water of the sacred pool, remembering the expression on Gethryn's face as he held Nelda's baby. He had done nothing more than the bare minimum to acknowledge Feran's birth.

"What are you thinking?" Tregaran asked.

"About Gethryn and me." Arian clasped her hands on her lap. "I know he blames me for killing our mother. And that's not guesswork. He said it often enough when we were children."

"You aren't children now."

"Merial did her best to hold us together, while we were growing up. She was like a mother to us. But then she…" Arian tried to keep her lips steady.

"She left you."

The scene blurred as tears filled her eyes. "The empire took her. The thrice damned, fucking empire."

"You blame the empire in the same way Gethryn blames you. Both lost a mother you loved."

"No. The empire's a monster. Our mother's death was…" Arian concentrated on breathing. "Women can die in childbirth. It's nobody's fault."

"But you find it easier to blame the empire than Merial for abandoning you?"

"No. It's not like that. When she came back, it was hard at first. But she's still my sister, and I love her. But Gethryn? That horse is halfway to sunrise." If not somewhere out in the stars.

"You have—"

Tregaran broke off at the sound of people approaching, low voices and the crack of a branch under foot. Everyone was free to pray at the sacred pool, at any time of day or night. However, the pair who emerged from the trees had no right to be there. Cassie and her pet traitor.

Arian jumped to her feet. "What are you doing here!"

"I'm sorry." Cassie gave one of her utterly insincere smiles. "I was told I could walk as far as the river. I thought here would be included." She looked around. "What is this place?"

"Somewhere you shouldn't be."

The man spoke. "It's the sacred spring. The water that wells up here is the lifeblood of the land. It symbolises the ancestors' bond with the people."

"What do you know of the ancestors?" How dare he speak of them. Did he still hope they would welcome him into the afterlife?

"My ancestors' blood has soaked this land, as truly as yours. I watched it happen. My grandmother—"

Cassie put a hand on his arm. "Peace, Bran."

So that was the traitor's name. Arian half-remembered him being introduced in the hall but had wiped it from her mind.

Cassie continued. "Angry words are not fitting for a holy place. Please translate for me." She turned to Tregaran. "I mean no disrespect to you or your beliefs. Indeed, I'd be eager to learn more of the ways the gods reveal themselves in your land."

"Learn more? I doubt you know the first thing about our gods," Tregaran responded scornfully to Bran's translation.

"I know how the gods reveal themselves in Kavilli and something of the many forms they take across the empire. I know that here, in your lands, they'll be both familiar and yet different."

"You think your gods hold power here?"

"Do you think there's a limit to their reach? They're everywhere."

"You'd impose your gods on us?"

Cassie laughed. "What sort of power-crazed fool do you take me for? I don't know what myths your people tell, but ours are full of mortals who thought they could defy the gods. It never worked out well. The gods have chosen how they wish to manifest themselves to you. I couldn't change the slightest detail, even if I wanted to. I'm here to learn, not to challenge."

And if you believe that, you'll believe anything.

Tregaran was equally unconvinced. "You think your Kavillian gods are the same as ours?"

"Not exactly. Everywhere, people worship different gods with different names, different rites, and different myths. Our priests teach that all these gods are aspects of a single divine spirit. But a spirit so vast the human mind cannot comprehend it. So the spirit manifests itself to us in varying aspects, embodied by the gods. These vary from place to place, as is divinely ordained. If the gods have chosen to reveal themselves in a certain way here, I'd be insane to defy their will."

"How would you know their will?"

"I'd listen to you, of course."

"You'd take instruction from us?" Incredulity was clear in Tregaran's voice after Bran's translation.

Arian did not believe her either.

Cassie's smile did not waver. "Who else? Your people have thrived here. Obviously, you're doing things right. Your farmers understand the climate and your priests understand the gods. To worship alien gods here would be as foolish as trying to grow olives in the snow."

Arian could keep quiet no longer. Everyone knew the empire would bend all into its own likeness, given the chance. "Just how gullible do you think we are?"

Cassie turned to her. "I'm serious. For example, the Freyans worship Ularice as the goddess of love, the Neraloni call her Kathair, to the Savestain she's Thalima. Depending on who you ask, her sacred animal is a cow, a bear, or a snake. Different names, different attributes. Yet, when you lie in your lover's arms, feel your skin pressed together, and stare into…" She paused. "…his eyes, the love you feel is nameless."

Having to rely on translation, Tregaran was oblivious to any innuendo. But he was still not taken in by the nonsense. "Would you try to pretend these are all the same?"

"No. But love's the same bittersweet gift, regardless of which god bestows its blessing, and the form its expression may take. Some gods allow as a pure joining of hearts what may be a reviled perversion elsewhere. Our challenge is to better understand the gods' will."

Arian could not stand it a moment longer "I must be going."

She headed back through the grove, her thoughts seething. Cassie was playing games, creating mazes from words. Tregaran might be able to see through her, but would others be taken in? How many would she seduce with her lies?

"I name this child Tolred." Nelda's oldest brother, Rhys, held the baby up for all to see. Firelight painted the scrunched little face even redder.

"He is my sister-son and will forever stand with me amid the ranks of our ancestors. Blood of my blood."

"Gethryn didn't think it through, did he?" Arian muttered under her breath.

"What?" Merial leaned closer since Arian could not move due to Feran clinging around her legs.

"Having a full naming ceremony. It means everyone gets to hear Rhys claim the baby. Gethryn wasn't thinking ahead."

"He never does."

The newly named Tolred had been quiet but now started to squall. Rhys looked ill at ease. He was clearly uncomfortable around babies and anxious to pass his nephew back to Nelda. Possibly, he was also unsettled by Gethryn, dithering in the background like a nervous cat.

Fortunately, the naming ceremony was nearly over. The midwives had attested to witnessing the birth, and Tregaran had recited the traditional prayers for the boy's ancestors to seek the gods' favour on his behalf. All that remained was for all of Nelda's brothers to kiss the baby's forehead and welcome him into their family. Soon, Tolred was back with his mother, and the feasting could begin.

"Mama, is Tolred my cousin now?" Eilwen appeared at Arian's side.

"No. Of course not. Why do you ask?"

"Linna said so. But I said she's wrong."

"Yes. She is. And you can tell her that from me."

Eilwen looked satisfied and skipped off to rejoin her friends.

The gathering was breaking into groups. Gethryn displaced Nelda's brothers at her side. Had he crawled far enough up the empire's arse to think of himself as Tolred's father?

Merial laughed. "Don't scowl like that, Arian. Supposing the wind changes and your face gets stuck that way."

"I don't need..." *I don't need anyone else to irritate me.*

Arian was not going to get her wish. Cassie was heading their way. Arian's stomach flipped, sending ripples down to her knees. She would have tried to make an escape, leaving Merial to deal with Cassie, but Feran had her trapped.

Cassie's face was fixed in her normal, patronising smile. "Do you always hold a feast when you name children?"

"It's usually a small, private affair," Merial answered.

"Your brother made an exception to please his bedfellow?"

No. It's purely for his own sake. Arian bit back the words. She tried to loosen Feran's grip.

"Partly." Merial was more diplomatic.

"The child won't count as part of his family?" Cassie asked.

"No."

"And the timing, seven days after the birth, is that traditional?"

"It takes place as soon as possible, so if the child dies, it'll still be known to its ancestors. But we had to wait for Nelda's brothers. Her family live in Drusbury. That's another hillfort."

Ten days. That was how long little Olin had lived. The memory of her first son was a raw wound in Arian's heart. She had to get away from the string of pointless questions. Merial could satisfy the imperial idiot's curiosity.

Finally, Arian detached Feran from her legs so she could pick him up and clasp him tightly, drawing strength from his warm, strong little body in her arms. He did not replace Olin, but he softened the pain. "I've got to take Feran home. He needs to sleep."

It was not merely an excuse. Feran had wrangled his way to a full stomach before the ceremony started and his eyelids were drooping. He had been clinging to her as much for support as anything and was asleep as soon as he got to bed.

Arian pulled the cover over him and stroked his head. A flurry of emotions churned inside her. She ought to return. Her absence would be noticed and commented on before long, but it was so tempting to stay where she was. She could hide under the blanket with Feran until the vixen had gone back to the empire.

Everywhere she looked, Cassie was there. And even when she was out of sight, thoughts of her filled Arian's head. Dreams were no more safe. *Damn the woman.* The woman, who so casually admitted being a lover of other women. Arian groaned. Why was the memory so hard to wipe from her mind? Was anyone else in Breninbury haunted in the same way? She could hardly ask around.

Arian shoved herself to her feet and strode from the house. This was her home. Her land. She would not hide away like a coward. Her footsteps faltered just as the meeting ground came into view. Was she facing down her inner demons or running to embrace them? How would it end?

True night had fallen while she was away. Light from the bonfire flowed over the gathered crowd. Warm brown shadows flooded the gaps between the houses.

There was no sign of Cassie. Arian tried to persuade herself she was not looking for her. Gethryn held Tolred, cradling the baby like a nursing mother. Nelda's brothers were busy getting drunk. It was an excellent idea. Arian looked for a flagon of mead to intercept.

"You go with me? Yes?" Words spoken in clumsy Kavillian came from behind a nearby house.

"Pardon? What did you say?" That was Cassie.

"You. With me. Good. Yes?"

"No. I don't think so."

Arian backtracked and sidled around the side of the house. The waxing full moon was rising in the sky, casting as much shadow as light, just enough to identify Leirmond. He had cornered Cassie in the angle where two walls joined. Neither showed any awareness of Arian.

"No. You no..." He switched to Lycanthian, searching for words. "Understand. Understand. Um..." Then back to Kavillian. "You. Me. We go bed. Yes?" Unsubtle as ever, Leirmond thrust his hips forward. But he had clearly been drinking, and the action made him stumble.

Cassie took the chance to dodge past. "No."

"I good at bed. You want it like—" Leirmond punched his fist into the palm of his other hand to illustrate.

"Thank you for your kind offer, but I must decline. However, I'm sure you'll find someone who'll be happy to take you up on it." Cassie backed away.

Leirmond would not have understood what she said, but it was unnecessary. Her mocking tone was unmistakable. His face twisted in anger. He stabbed a finger towards her and shouted in Lycanthian, "Miserable cow. I wouldn't want to hammer it home with you anyway. You wouldn't know what to do with a hard cock, and you'll never find out, because no real man would want you."

"What girl could resist a chat up line like that?" Cassie's ironic undertone could only be intended for her own benefit. She still seemed unaware of Arian's presence.

"Are you missing the women back home? Everyone knows empire men have cocks as soft as butter. That why the women have to hammer each other."

Cassie continued to back away. "Best get a craftsman who understands the equipment if you want a job done prop—" She was now within arm's reach of Arian, and finally spotted her in the darkness. For a split second, the amusement on Cassie's face wavered, before returning. "I'm not sure what he's saying, but I fear I've offended him."

The realisation hit Arian. *No. You do understand.* The sneaky, treacherous, lying, devious, underhand vixen. She could speak Lycanthian.

After another amused smile in Leirmond's direction, Cassie turned and strolled back to the meeting ground and the two Kavillian fighters. Despite her air of indifference, she obviously wanted support in case Leirmond tried his luck again.

Arian sagged against the wall, trying to remember everything she had ever said in Cassie's hearing. People should be warned.

Leirmond had vanished in the other direction. Not that Arian would have picked him as the first person to share the news with. No doubt, he had gone in search of a woman who would welcome his attention. On past form, this would not take long. Most women would be more than happy to take him as a bedfellow. Was it possible she and Cassie were the only women in Breninbury ever to turn him down? Arian closed her eyes. If so, it was the only point of similarity between them.

Voices erupted on the meeting ground. "Shut your fucking mouth, or I'll shut it for you."

"You wanna try?"

Heads turned. A fight was about to break out amid a knot of young men. Those on the outside stepped back, forming a ring around Yehan and another youth. The adversaries were unsteady on their feet, manifestly the worse for drink.

"I will if you don't watch yourself." Yehan's words were slurred.

"Come on then." The rival poked Yehan's shoulder in deliberate provocation. "If you think it's so great there, why don't you fuck off back to—"

Yehan swung at him wildly. The punch was clumsy and easily blocked, but the weight of his momentum carried Yehan stumbling into his opponent. Both were wearing heavy cloaks, which tangled around arms and legs, bringing them to the ground. They grappled in the dirt, untidy and awkward, each fighting with himself and his cloak as much as the other. Yehan managed to get astride his opponent's chest, raining down blows with his fists, but few punches, if any, made clean contact. The other youth bucked him off. Neither combatant was able to get to his feet unaided.

Fortunately, both were unarmed. By tradition, all weapons were forbidden at feasts. The bondservant cooks could carve anything needing a knife. Supposedly, it was a symbol of the sacred truce, although it surely owed more to limiting bloodshed in the drunken fights between warriors, which were far from rare.

Normally, men would be left to sort out things between themselves, but this was turning into an embarrassing spectacle. At some point, Leirmond had arrived on the meeting ground. With another warrior, he stepped in to drag the youths to their feet and then hold them apart. Yehan had a nosebleed, probably due to falling on the other's elbow, since neither had landed a straight punch.

"This place is a dung heap. When I'm king, things'll change. You'll see." Yehan was not ready to let the argument drop. "You're going to learn some lessons from the empire, whether you like it or not."

Leirmond turned Yehan around to face him. "I don't know what started this off, but the empire dogs will be the one learning the lessons."

"Ha! My father will show what a real battle is. You think you're warriors. He'll scatter you like the sheep you are." Yehan shook free and wiped his nose on the back of his hand. Blood smeared his cheek. "You'll be leading the warband only because you're running away the fastest."

Leirmond's fingers curled into fists. For a moment, it looked as though another fight would start, but he settled for giving Yehan a firm shove. "Go clean your face."

Yehan stumbled back. He glared at Leirmond, then turned and staggered away from the meeting ground, vanishing into the darkness.

The other youth opened his mouth, as if to send a challenge after Yehan. Instead, he threw up. Most of the vomit went down his front. Everyone else jumped back. The man holding him let go. "You need to clean up as well. Get someone to help."

The excitement was over. People returned to feasting and gossip.

"Young fools."

"Like you were so different at their age."

Foolish or not, Arian wanted a drink.

"What was that about?" Merial appeared.

"You didn't hear?"

"I wouldn't have asked if I had."

Arian shrugged. "Stupid stuff. They were drunk."

Merial looked in the direction Yehan had taken. "I wonder if I should..."

"You have to let him fight his own battles."

Merial sighed. "You're right."

"He'll be fine." Arian put a hand on Merial's arm. "But listen, I've discovered something."

"What?"

"Cassie. She can speak Lycanthian."

"She can do what? When?"

"Just now. Leirmond was trying to get into her bed. He was doing his best to speak Kavillian, though he could hardly string two words together. When she got the idea, she turned him down."

"I bet he wasn't happy."

"He wasn't. He started throwing insults in Lycanthian. The thing was, she understood what he was saying."

"How do you know?"

"By her comments."

"In Lycanthian?"

"No, Kavillian. She was speaking under her breath. She didn't know I was near enough to hear her. But it was obvious she was responding to what he was saying."

"Are you sure she wasn't simply picking up on his tone?"

"No. It was quite specific."

"What did she say?"

"It was..." *About having women bedfellows.* Arian could not force the words out. "I can't remember exactly."

Merial laughed. "Leirmond's line in seduction isn't strong on subtlety. A deaf woman would know what he was after. And maybe Cassie's picked up a few words while she's been here. I'll ask her, next time I see her."

"No. It's all right. Maybe she was..." In truth, Arian was no longer quite so sure. Had Cassie merely been making assumptions from Leirmond's tone?

Arian ran a hand through her hair and sighed. Where was the mead? She really needed a drink.

The top of Arian's skull was about to split. Her pulse hammered at her temples. Her tongue was coated with sawdust. She groaned and squirmed out of bed, trying not to wake Feran or Eilwen. Dressing was a battle, as if her clothes also wanted to spend the day lying on the ground. How much had she drunk last night?

Outside was painfully bright, even though dawn was some way off. Stars still pricked the midnight blue overhead. The eastern horizon was outlined in orange. Arian stood in the courtyard of the house taking deep breaths to calm her stomach, then staggered to the water bucket. She needed a drink and to splash her face.

Empty.

Typical—as was the memory of wobbling home and her foot catching the bucket, sending it flying. She could not even blame anyone else. Arian picked up the bucket. The bondservants would be busy with their morning tasks, and she was not willing to wait until one became available. She needed water now.

This early in the day, the main entrance would still be closed and barred. Arian was not strong enough to open it unaided, which meant detouring via the small side door. She was not the first that day to leave the hillfort by this route. The bar was out of its socket and the gate ajar when she got there, although no one was in sight.

Arian stepped outside and stood a moment, fighting to maintain the precarious hold on her stomach. Wind gusting over the hillside cooled her face and cleared her head. The light was strengthening, but just about bearable if she squinted. Another deep breath and the world steadied. However, it was still something of a surprise that she made it to the bottom of the hill, without either throwing up or falling.

Water rippled over the rocks lining the riverbed. Arian knelt and cupped her hands to take a deep draught. A wave of cold spread through her chest, clean and pure. Her stomach settled. More water washed the grit from her eyes and the fog from her mind.

The dawn chorus was in full spate. Sheep bleated in the fields and a dog barked as the sun broke the horizon. Arian let her head roll back and closed her eyes, taking in the sounds and scents. She concentrated on breathing until the pain in her head eased. It was a new day. A gift from the gods, and finally she felt halfway ready to face it. Arian took another deep breath and dipped the bucket in the water. With luck, she would still feel this good by the time she climbed back to the top of the hill.

Out of habit, Arian had gone to the upstream end of the shingle beach to drink, even though nobody was washing that early. As she stood, she caught sight of a heap of clothes at the downstream end. They lay, more in than out of the water. Had someone left their laundry behind? She shielded her eyes for another, better look. Not a pile of laundry. Someone still wore the clothes. Someone who was not moving.

Arian dropped the bucket and scrambled along the beach. A man lay face down in the river with his cloak wrapped around his chest and head. The weight of the waterlogged wool had him anchored against a rock in the shallows.

"Here. I need help. Someone's in the river." Arian screamed the plea.

Few people were in sight. A huntsman carried a deer over his shoulders. Two bondservants strolled down the path. A young shepherd sat by his sheep. Without waiting to see who would come, Arian splashed into the river and grabbed a fistful of cloak. The wet cloth tore at her hands.

The huntsman joined her in the water. Together they freed the body from the anchoring rock and hauled it onto the beach. But already Arian knew the person was beyond help. The body was rigid with the stiffness of death. The only question was the identity. The cloak was tightly wrapped around the body, resisting Arian's efforts to loosen it. Then suddenly, an end came free, revealing locks of black hair. The huntsman peeled away the rest of the cloak.

There was no need to search for a pulse. Yehan's face was bloodless, too pale for any hope of life. His eyes showed only the whites. His arms, that had been trapped inside the cloak, lay on his chest, crossed at the wrists, as if already laid out for his funeral. Yet still the huntsman pressed his ear to Yehan, listening for a heartbeat.

Arian stepped away. *How am I going to tell Merial? How?*

She was half aware of more folk arriving. The group around the body grew—warriors, farmers, bondservants. Leirmond arrived, taking charge, and shouting orders. Gasps and muttered remarks jumped from person to person.

"He was so drunk last night. Someone should have kept an eye on him."

"He must have slipped. Hit his head."

"Your cloak gets a mind of its own when it's wet. You can't do anything."

"Nearly happened to me once."

Arian had to find Merial and break the news. But her legs were lead. Her knees buckled.

And then Merial was there. She threw herself on her son's body. Arian knelt and hugged her sister as best she could. "Oh, Merial, Merial. I'm so sorry."

An elderly woman helped Arian gently ease Merial away. Under Leirmond's command, a group of warriors carried Yehan up the hill on his last journey. Arian wrapped her arms around Merial and held her as she sobbed. Together they followed the sad cortege.

The blankness lifted from Arian's mind, replaced by a whirlwind of thoughts and questions. How had Yehan died? When? Where had he gone after the fight?

When I'm king, things'll change. Yehan's defiant words of the night before. A promise that would never be fulfilled. Feran now was Gethryn's heir.

CASSIE

Honey cakes, stuffed vine leaves, spicy dipping sauces, pickled quail eggs. Everything looked so good. Where to start? Except the quails wanted their eggs back and were strutting under her couch, muttering. Who knew quails could mutter? In the corner, Tullia was milling grain on a grindstone. Then the quails turned into a gaggle of Lycanthian women, with Arian at the front. They hung around the door, shouting about a blocked drain.

Cassie opened her eyes. What the…

The tendrils of her dream evaporated. *Damn.* The food had looked wonderful, and she had not tasted a bite. Maybe tomorrow night. However, the shouting outside continued, supplemented by snores from Tullia. Was that the reason for her inclusion in the dream?

A weak band of daylight squeezed beneath the blanket over the doorway. At a guess, it was morning, not long after sunrise. What was the fuss about? After ten days in Breninbury, Cassie knew the daily routine, and this was unusual. She sat up. Surely the party was long over. It had been tailing off when she left, and the voices did not sound happy.

The crown of Tullia's head was visible at the far end of the bed. The platform was long enough for them to sleep top to toe, with little overlap. Even so, Cassie would be woken more often than not, when Tullia slipped into bed after her nighttime meetings with Massillo. The lady's maid and bodyguard were unquestionably lovers.

Tullia half roused herself with a rasping snore. She mumbled, then rolled onto her side. Her breathing dropped to soft grunts. Tempting though it was to kick her awake, there was no point sending her to find out what was happening. Tullia could not speak Lycanthian, and would not be a reliable news source, even if she could. She was incapable of looking beyond the obvious or picking up on innuendo.

A few slaps on the wall by the door were a substitute for knocking. "My lady? Are you awake?" Bran's voice was soft but urgent.

"Yes. What is it?" Cassie sat up, pulling a fur around her shoulders.

Bran stuck his head in. "The king's nephew, Yehan. He's been found dead."

"What?"

"Just now. Down by the river."

"Has..." Dozens of questions leapt into Cassie's head. "I'll be out in a moment. See if there's anything more you can pick up."

"Yes, my lady." Bran let the blanket fall back.

Cassie slipped from the bed, leaving Tullia to sleep. It was a maid's job to assist with hair and clothes, but her fussing would only slow things down. Cassie's robe from the previous night was hanging from a nail. The fine satin smelt of smoke and looked exactly as might be expected after ten days in a shit-covered hovel, but was no worse than her other clothes. Maybe she should try to dream about a bathhouse and laundry.

Cassie wound her hair in a bun and pinned it in place. That should keep it out of the way for now. Her long blue cloak would ward off the dawn chill, and as a bonus, the hood covered her hair. She slipped her feet into sandals and left the room. Tullia had not stirred.

Bran was outside the house, talking to a bondservant who was pointing towards the main gate. Leaving him to finish gathering information, Cassie walked to a quiet spot by the palisade, with a clear view across Breninbury.

The hillfort was in upheaval. Cassie could feel the ripples of excitement flowing between the buildings. Clusters formed and separated as people went from group to group, exchanging whatever news and speculation was to be had. Bran joined her at the palisade, just as Gethryn appeared from the Great Hall, backed by three attendants. They strode across the meeting ground and ducked into the Warriors' House.

"I take it that's where Yehan's body is." Cassie indicated the building.

"Yes."

"What have you discovered?"

"He was in the river. Drowned. People are saying it was an accident."

"Are they really?"

"You have doubts?"

"I can think of a dozen people who might want him dead. I'll keep an open mind until I know more. Is nobody else voicing suspicion?"

Bran shook his head. "All I'm hearing is how drunk he was, and that he could barely stand up. Once he fell in the river and his clothes got waterlogged, the weight would've held him under."

"As would someone kneeling on him."

"You really think he might have been murdered?"

"When it comes to people in power, unexpected deaths should never be taken at face value, unless you don't mind being the next victim."

"Yehan didn't have any power."

"Not at the moment. But he was in line for it." Cassie paused. "Arian's son is Gethryn's heir now."

"Yes. And she was the one who found the body."

"Hmmm." Was that just a coincidence?

Cassie turned and stared into the valley. The river threw a silver loop around the base of the hill. Given Yehan's state the previous night, him falling in and drowning by accident was not impossible. But then again, the graveyard in Kavilli was full of senators who had been too quick to accept similar stories. If Yehan had been murdered, then somebody was playing for high stakes.

She needed to know what the game was. "I'd like to check the body."

"They won't let you."

"Can I do it unofficially?"

"You're serious, my lady?"

"Deadly."

"Women aren't allowed in the Warriors' House. Common folk like me aren't either. If anyone sees you there…" There was no need to finish the sentence.

"Can I get in when nobody is watching?"

"Well." Bran ran a hand through his hair. "There shouldn't be anyone around at night."

"We'll do it then."

"Very good, my lady." He did not sound happy.

"I won't need long. I know what to look for." Cassie patted his shoulder and started back towards their house. Breakfast was not going to match her dream, although maybe there would be meat left over from the feast. The one bright spot in the barbarians' cuisine was their roast pork.

Bran fell into step beside her. "Oh, and I found out something else. Unrelated to Yehan's death."

"What?"

"Arian had another son, but he died when he was just a few days old."

So Arian knew that pain too. Cassie nodded but said nothing.

"He was summer-born, just like the others."

Cassie managed a sad smile. "Now there's a surprise."

Dawn was several hours away. Breninbury lay peaceful in the moonlight, coloured in blues and greys. The stars glittered with icy purity. The constellations of the hunter and the hare were rising in the east, while Draconis, the imperial dragon, hung high overhead—surely a good omen. However, banks of heavy cloud were building to the west, threatening rain. Soon they would cover the moon.

Cassie stood with Bran in the shadow of the Great Hall, watching and listening. The only living things in sight were two cats engaged in a staring contest, and the silhouette of the sentry, on guard duty above the gate. Noise carried on the night air, the hoot of an owl, one forlorn bleat from a sheep, and somewhere, a baby cried. From inside the Great Hall came the snores of men sleeping, but no sound of movement.

The first tendril of cloud swallowed the moon. The darkness thickened. As quietly as possible, Cassie scuttled across the meeting ground and through the outer entrance of the Warriors' House. Unlike the homes, the open forecourt had only one room leading off. Light glinted behind the door hanging. Cassie's oil lamp and tinderbox would not be needed, but was someone inside?

Bran thought the body would be unguarded. But he was relying on hearsay when it came to warrior rites. An honour guard or priest might keep vigil through the cold, lonely hours of the night. Yehan had been heir to the throne.

Cassie cautiously inched back the hanging blanket, first on one side then the other, but saw no one. Taking her chance, she slipped through the doorway. Bran joined her a moment later.

The circular room was many times larger than Cassie's bed chamber but of similar construction, with daub covered walls and a ring of posts supporting the roof. A stone structure stood opposite the entrance. Was it a shrine? In the middle of the upper shelf was a human skull, decorated with stag antlers and black seashells for eyes. More sets of antlers hung from the rafters, along with shields and weapons.

Yehan lay on a low altar before the shrine. The corners were marked by oil lamps. Old, dried blood coated the stone. Was it from sacrificed animals, or the warriors' own blood used as part of a ritual? Not that it mattered. Cassie reached down to touch him but paused. Wisps of fuzz coated Yehan's cheeks, black against the deathly pallor. The blue tattoos were equally stark. He was young, maybe even younger than Rufio.

Where was her eldest son at that moment? A junior adjutant would not normally be on the front line in battle, and the borders had been peaceful for years, but it would not last. Peace never did. Suppose Rufio was marching towards danger. Supposing he was already lying dead on a distant battlefield? Cassie closed her eyes and took a breath. She did not have time to waste with pointless fears.

Cassie knelt beside the altar, then moved an oil lamp closer and took hold of Yehan's hand. His knuckles were scraped, and his fingernails chipped, which might be from his fight with the other boy. The rigor mortis was showing the first signs of easing, no more than a hint of flexibility in his little finger. It was enough for her to see a ragged cut on the underside, no doubt got during his struggle to push up from the stony riverbed. But was it an attacker or the weight of his own clothes pinning him down?

"Help me turn him over," Cassie whispered.

She was able to lift Yehan's shirt high enough to examine the middle of his back. However, the dark purple mottling made picking out bruises impossible. Not that it was necessary. The discolouration held her answer.

"He was found lying face down in the river, you said?" Cassie asked.

"Yes, my lady. With his cloak wrapped around his arms and head."

"It was staged. Someone positioned him in the water after he'd been dead a while. They wanted to make it look like an accident"

"How can you tell?"

"See how the blood has pooled. He initially lay on his back long enough for it to settle. In fact, I should have spotted it immediately, from how pale his face was."

"If he didn't drown, how did he die?"

"I don't know."

Cassie moved to Yehan's head. He had no obvious injury, but parting his hair revealed a series of fingernail cuts behind his ears.

Cassie signalled to Bran. "We can put him back as he was."

Opening Yehan's mouth would mean cracking his jaw. Fortunately, Cassie had brought a fine pair of tweezers. She pulled a small piece of sand-covered waterweed from inside Yehan's nose.

Cassie held it in the lamplight. "That's interesting. He did drown after all."

"But you said..." Bran's voice faded in confusion. "Do you mean it wasn't murder?"

"Oh no. Someone definitely held him down in the river. The fingernail marks are from his head being forced underwater. There's no other explanation. Once he was dead, the murderer pulled him out and lay him on his back. But a few hours later, they returned and tried to make his death look like an accident."

"They sobered up and realised what they'd done?"

"That's one explanation." Cassie replaced the lamp and stood up. "But we're finished here." She went to the doorway,

Bran stayed looking down on the body, then turned to the shrine. In front of the decorated skull was a small bowl. Bran dipped his fingers then touched his throat, his forehead, and finally his lips. He stood a moment in silence before joining Cassie. Neither spoke until they were back in the courtyard of their house.

"You offered up a prayer for Yehan?" Cassie asked.

"The water at the shrine, it'll be from the sacred spring. I just wanted to promise the ancestors..." Bran shrugged awkwardly. "I don't know if they'll be offended by us being there, but I wanted to promise we'll avenge Yehan. I guess, something of the tribe hasn't let go of me. I'm sorry."

"You don't have to apologise."

"You don't mind?"

"Of course not. I'm very happy if your ancestors talk to the gods on our behalf. I'll never turn down divine help."

Another log landed on the pyre in centre of the meeting ground, close by the bier where Yehan's body lay. The priest continued his song, flicking water over the growing tower of wood. The threatened cloudburst had swept through before dawn, soaking everywhere, before blowing away. The pyre had the rest of the day to dry out, but lighting it might prove tricky. Cassie could not see that it needed to get any wetter, regardless of the water's sacred source.

"When will the funeral be?" Cassie asked.

"At dusk. The dead get a full night and a day for everyone to say their goodbyes, then their body leaves this world with the sun." Bran pursed his lips. "In theory, at least. My family would've been dumped together on a fire whenever somebody got round to it, if they weren't eaten by wild animals first."

Onlookers dotted the edge of the meeting ground. Was one the murderer? Surely some knew more than they were letting on. Cassie tapped Bran's arm. "Let's go somewhere quieter."

On their way out of Breninbury, they passed more wood bound for the pyre. It was going to be quite a fire. Cassie stopped atop the outermost embankment, with a clear view of the surroundings. No one was within earshot.

"Has anyone raised doubts about Yehan's death being an accident?" Cassie asked.

"One or two. But I get the feeling even they don't believe what they're saying. They just enjoy stirring things."

"Is anything else being said?"

"People are pleased Arian's summer-born son will be king one day. Some go so far as to say Yehan's death was a blessing from the gods."

"Poor Merial." Hard enough to lose your child, without others taking it as good news.

"Who do you think murdered Yehan?"

"Ah. Now that's the question." Cassie marshalled her thoughts. "The least serious option is the boy he had the fight with. He could have followed Yehan. Snuck up and pushed him in when Yehan knelt to wash the blood off his face. He'd fit the scenario of faking an accident after he'd had time to sober up."

"Why's that least serious?"

"Because it's a juvenile squabble with no implications for anything else. The fight may have sprung from hostility to the empire, but that's as far as it goes."

"Except he's getting away with murder."

"That happens." Cassie shrugged. "Arian's another suspect. Yehan's death puts her son on the throne."

"Everyone knows she loves her sister, and she's backed Yehan all the way."

"I can't risk ignoring her. She could be acting a part. Though if that's the case, I might as well pack up and go home, because she's got me outclassed."

"I'd still put my money on you, my lady."

"Flattery won't get you a pay rise." Cassie smiled at him. "There's Nelda and her brothers. Maybe even Gethryn. As things stand, the baby hasn't got a claim on the throne, but with Yehan out of the way, it's just a couple of young children in the way. There's plenty of time for more accidents."

"Nelda's brothers won't benefit. If Gethryn goes against the law and claims the baby as his son, it'll cut them out."

"They'll be uncle to the king, which is a big step closer to power."

"Any other suspects?"

Cassie shrugged. "Anyone who can't stomach the thought of a black-haired, empire-born king."

"You mean most of Breninbury?"

"There's not liking the idea, and then there's being angry enough to commit murder."

"Warriors don't need much of a push to start killing people."

"True. I'd like to put Leirmond on the list."

"Any reason why him?"

"He's an arrogant jackass. I know that's not much of a reason, but he did get involved in the spat with Yehan. But we can discount anyone who was on the meeting ground when the murder took place."

"Do we know when that was?"

"Very soon after he left the meeting ground. The rigor mortis was starting to ease when I examined him, which means he'd been dead for just over a day. Yehan could have washed his face in a bucket, but he went down to the river. I guess he wanted time alone to calm down or plot his revenge. Whatever made him happiest. The murderer followed him, then pushed him in and held him under. It's the only timeline that makes sense."

"What will you do when you've worked out who it was?"

"Nothing, probably. But I'd like some idea of the who and why of it."

"Don't you…" Bran's voice faded.

"Supposing Gethryn's the murderer and I tell him what I know. That'll be a shortcut to my own funeral. If it's someone else, once Yehan's a pile of ash, it'll be my word against them, and I still might end up dead."

"If you can't do anything, why do you want to find out who it is?"

"I didn't say I couldn't do anything with the information. If I know who murdered the king's heir, I'll know someone who takes risks. If I know why, I'll know a flame I can fan or dampen, as needed. And I'll know who to be careful of. If they murdered Yehan, they won't hesitate to murder me."

Bran rubbed the back of his neck, then let his hand drop. "Can I ask a question, my lady?"

"Yes."

"Why are you really in Breninbury?"

"What makes you think I'm not here for a trade deal?"

"Because Gethryn isn't going to give you one. I know it. You know it. And you're not the sort of person who'll sit around, wasting time on a lost cause. You're after something, and you think you can make use of a murderer to get it."

"You were wasted as a slave." Cassie could not restrain a smile. She was willing to overlook any impertinence on Bran's part. He was asking the right questions. Agents who could think for themselves were hard to come by. Mother would approve. "The empire really does want the iron and tin. If Gethryn gives me an acceptable deal, I'll take it. But you're right, he won't do that willingly. I have to get access to the metal with the minimum fuss and bloodshed."

"The empire will invade?"

"If I'm really clever, the empire will be invited in."

Bran's eyes fixed on the opposite side of the valley. "It's strange. Part of me knows it'd be the best thing for the common folk. The legions would stop the raiding. Miners would make a better living. But then, part of me thinks, this is our land, and I've realised I care about it more than I knew."

"The land won't change. As for your people, we'll keep them safe." Cassie risked a smile. "After all, dead people don't pay taxes."

"Do you care if they're happy?"

"Happy means less trouble." Cassie shrugged. "Of course, after enough time has passed, they'll grumble, and tell stories about how wonderful it used to be, and how much they all loved good King Gethryn. Then they'll pour themselves a mug of beer, fill their stomachs, and sleep soundly in their beds."

Bran's frown twisted into a wry pout. "It's not like I want to stay here." He drew a deep breath. "So. You want me to ask around. Who saw Yehan last? Where everybody was?"

"Yes. While you do that, I'll take a look at the river."

"Do you think you'll find anything there?"

"No. But it doesn't hurt to look."

The river below the main gate was at least forty feet across, and reddish brown after the rain. Leaves and other debris rushed past, swirling in eddies. Even the tributary joining from the sacred grove lacked its usually crystal clarity.

A muddy track led to where the crumbling bank gave easy access down to the water. If Yehan had wanted to wash his face in the river, this was where he would have come. It was the place to start looking for clues.

As she reached the bank, Cassie saw she was not the only one with an interest in the location. Arian stood below on a gravel beach. She had obviously come back to where she found the body. Or was it the spot where she had committed the murder?

The idea felt absurd, which was all the more reason not to dismiss it out of hand. It was far too easy for sexual attraction to overwhelm common sense. And Arian was certainly attractive enough to make a fool of anyone. With a murderer at large, keeping a guard up was essential. Putting too much trust in your gut was a mistake. Putting any trust in even lower parts of your body was fatal. Cassie had no intention of joining the ranks of those who had let a pretty face beguile them to their death.

"Good morning, Arian."

Arian jerked around. "Er…yes. Good morning."

It was the most civil greeting Cassie had yet received from her, but Arian would doubtless revert to her usual hostility once she got over her surprise. Cassie half scrambled, half slid down to the beach, while fighting to maintain her balance. Mud squidged over the top of her sandals and got between her toes.

Arian took a step back, but then stopped. "You've got soot on your nose." She spoke in Lycanthian.

Cassie kept her expression neutral and replied in Kavillian. "Pardon? What did you say?"

The attempt at entrapment was endearing in its artlessness and answered one question. Arian had overheard her encounter with Leirmond at the naming feast, Cassie was annoyed at herself. There was no excuse for the lapse, even if the self-proclaimed stud had rattled her more than she cared to admit.

Arian now suspected she could understand Lycanthian, though it probably did not go beyond suspicion. Otherwise, Arian would not be looking for proof. However, Cassie was not about to be caught out by such a childish ploy—unless it was a double bluff. Maybe Arian was one step ahead and had deliberately botched a trap, so as to seem inept at intrigue.

Or maybe not. It was Mother's fault. The trouble with being brought up by the sharpest mind in Kavilli was you could end up tying yourself in knots.

"It was nothing." Arian switched to Kavillian.

Cassie stepped past her to the water's edge. "Was this where Yehan died?"

"Yes."

"I heard you were the one who found him." When she got no response, Cassie looked around.

Arian was biting her lip, but then nodded.

"I'm sorry. I know it's horrible blow for your family. Especially your sister. Please pass on my heartfelt condolences."

Again, Arian nodded. Her expression said, as clearly as words, that she wanted Cassie to leave but, having failed at subterfuge, she was unsure of her next step.

Cassie turned back to the river. "He was lying here, face down. I'm sorry. I don't mean to be insensitive, but it's hard to imagine. The water is so shallow."

"I know." Surprisingly, Arian came to stand beside her.

Cassie's insides gave a kick. Her pulse sped up.

"He wasn't far out." Arian pointed. "He was up against that rock. He'd got tangled in his cloak. But he ought to have been able to crawl back onto dry land."

But not with someone kneeling on his back. "I guess his arms were trapped against his body."

"Yes. They were crossed over his chest."

And it had not raised suspicions? "I saw him just now, up on the bier. I assumed the priest had laid him out that way."

"No. When we got the cloak off him he was like that. He was so stiff. We couldn't have moved his arms. It's…" Arian swallowed.

"It's tragic when someone dies that young. Alcohol is responsible for so much trouble. I saw the fight beforehand. Do you know what it was about?"

"Nothing important."

"It rarely is with men that age."

How far could she push Arian? How far should she push Arian? It was another trap. A very different sort of trap, and one Cassie also had no intention of falling into, even though it was far more fun to play with. For now, a small prod should get her the beach to herself.

Cassie continued. "They aren't much better when they're older. Like that man who had accosted me. Leirmond's his name, isn't it?"

"Yes."

"He strikes me as the sort of man who thinks he's a gift from the gods to womankind."

"You could say that."

"So is he?"

"Is he what?

"A gift from the gods? Is he a good lover?"

"I wouldn't know."

"Really? I'm surprised. I can't believe he's never shown an interest in a woman like you."

"Like me?"

"Leirmond might be full of himself, but he's not blind." Cassie let her eyes travel down to Arian's feet, and then back up. She was rewarded with a blush. "Or has he tried his luck with you, and you turned him down?"

Arian gave an awkward shrug in response.

"I'm not used to beards, so it's hard for me to judge, but I'd have said he was a good-looking man."

"Some might say so."

"But you don't agree?"

"Yes, he's…" Arian swallowed. "I mean. He…"

Cassie laughed. "Of course, speaking for myself, good-looking men have little appeal, as I told you before I prefer—"

"I have to go." Arian fled.

Cassie watched her hurry up the hill, toward Breninbury. If Arian was acting the part of a naive, too honest for her own good ingénue, then she was making a remarkably convincing job of it. It was so tempting to imagine breaking through the hostility, of teaching Arian the truth of her own nature, showing her what it was her heart wanted. Arian was…

Cassie sighed. Arian was not worth the risk. Not quite.

The fun was over. It was time to hunt a murderer, not that she expected to find much. The beach was pitted with footprints. Half of Breninbury must have visited the spot and the rainstorm had washed away any remaining evidence. Anything that had fallen in the river would have been carried on the current. Was it worth checking downstream?

The water was higher than usual, but finding a path between the high bank and the river should be possible. She might get her feet wet in places which would not be a bad thing if it washed the mud from between her toes. Cassie picked her way over the rocks, on the lookout for anything of note.

The river rounded a bend while the bank rose yet higher. Soon the beach was out of sight. Another curve and Cassie reached a pool where a loop in the river had undercut the hillside. The bank was now a thirty-foot-high cliff. Brush and saplings overhung the top. The foot was piled with fallen rock.

Cassie recognised the spot as seen from above. The locals called it the lower pool. She and Bran had followed the river downstream one day and stood at the top of the cliff. After the pool, the river funnelled through a steep-sided gorge and the flow became a torrent. She had gone as far as she could.

Cassie was about to turn back, when she spotted a glint of copper between two rocks up ahead. Getting to it would be tricky. If she fell in, the current could sweep her into the gorge, with fatal consequences. She inched her way over the boulders at the foot of the cliff, carefully shifting her weight between hands, knees, and elbows. Thankfully, nobody was around to witness her inelegant scramble. Normally, it took two bottles of wine before she was this ungainly.

Finally, she was able to slip her fingers between the rocks. The object was long, thin, and smooth to the touch. Cassie strained a little more. The rock beneath her wobbled. A last effort, and she pulled out a six-inch copper pin, identical to what everyone in Breninbury used as a cloak fastening. Even if it had belonged to Yehan or his killer, it told her absolutely nothing.

Cassie braced herself for a repeat of her awkward scramble in reverse. A scattering of gravel landed by her hand. Grinding sounded overhead, barely audible over the river. Without time to think, Cassie threw herself backwards, landing sprawled on the rocks, half a wobble from ending up in the water. A boulder the size of a cow's head crashed down where she had been.

Frantically, on heels and elbows, Cassie scuttled away from the overhanging cliff. A few more loose pebbles bounced on the rocks. One landed in the water with a splash. And then there was silence, apart from the roar of the river in the gorge and the pounding of Cassie's heart.

Nobody was visible at the top of the cliff. Either the assailant was hiding or had left—if they existed. It could have been an accident. The stones piled at the bottom was proof of previous rockfalls. Rain could have loosened soil holding the boulder in place. A foraging sheep might have kicked a pebble, setting off an avalanche. Maybe she was just there at the wrong time.

Cassie did not believe it.

She got to her feet. She was wet and covered in mud. Splinters of rock had peppered her face and arms, drawing blood. Her best dress was ruined. But she was alive. The would-be killer had missed. She could not count on being lucky again.

Arian

"It is time." The kindness in Tregaran's voice did not detract from its finality.

"I…" Merial brushed the hair from Yehan's forehead. She straightened her shoulders as if to stand but did not move. Her hand fell into her lap, while tears rolled down her face.

Arian knelt and put an arm around her sister's waist. "Come, Merial. The ancestors are waiting to greet him."

She urged Merial to her feet. Their place was taken by six warriors who lifted the bier and adjusted its weight atop the tower of crisscrossed logs. Leirmond, as leader of the warband, placed a shield over Yehan's legs, then laid a sword and war-axe beside him. Yehan would enter the afterlife equipped as a warrior.

Tregaran raised his voice in the chant for the dead. At his side, Gethryn held up a burning torch, for all to see. The acrid smoke carried on the evening breeze. Three times, Tregaran walked around the pyre, calling on the ancestors to guide Yehan's path.

Watchers lined the edge of the meeting ground. The heavy clouds of morning had gone, leaving only orange and pink wisps on the horizon. The first stars appeared overhead. Tregaran's chant reached its end. The echoes faded.

Gethryn stepped up to the pyre. "Farewell, kinsman, blood of my blood, until we meet again, beyond the stars, in the Hall of Heroes." He thrust the torch into oil-soaked kindling stuffed between the latticework of logs.

For a moment, it looked as though the torch had gone out—the worst of all possible omens. But then a flicker showed. The glow strengthened by the heartbeat. Merial gave a low moan and lurched forward, catching Arian by surprise. Most likely, Merial would not have tried to join Yehan on the pyre, but Arian tightened her grip. And then, as the flames blossomed, Merial's knees buckled, and the strength seemed to slip from her body. It needed all Arian's strength to keep her standing.

Arian looked up. The column of smoke rose into the darkening sky, twisting on the breeze. Sparks danced among the stars, just as they had a few months earlier, for Yehan's rite of passage. Such a short time ago. All Yehan might have become was now gone, lost to the Lycanthi. What sort of king would he have been? Nobody would ever know.

Tongues of flame lapped around the pyre, first snaking between the logs, then flowing up and over the top. The heart of the tower glowed white hot. Cracks and pops from the damp wood were loud enough to scare away any evil spirit hoping to feast on the soul of the dead. Tregaran need take no further steps on that account. Merial pressed her face into Arian's shoulder. Her body shook with sobs.

Night deepened while the moon rose overhead. The flames grew hotter, the column of smoke was now invisible against the night sky, except for distortions in the field of stars. Watchers broke into groups, talking in low voices. Merial's sobs faded, although she still clung to Arian. Her eyes were glazed, inward looking.

A small figure toddled into the firelight. A very recognisable figure, to Arian's horror. Even in silhouette, Feran was unmistakable. He made a throwing action, possibly adding a twig to the pyre. Where was Hertha, the teenage cousin who was supposed to be looking after him? Knowing Merial would need her support, Arian had made arrangements for Feran and Eilwen. Odella was looking after her young siblings.

"Are you all right for a moment?"

Arian did not wait for Merial's reply. Quite apart from the danger should the tower of burning logs collapse, a funeral was not a game for children. Feran's actions could be seen as disrespectful. Arian swept him up and carried him to safety.

Hertha, appeared, looking suitably shamefaced. "I'm sorry."

"You shouldn't have let him run off."

"I know. I'm sorry. I just turned around and he was gone. It won't happen again."

Did she give Hertha a second chance? Merial was calmer, but it might not last. Arian glanced back, but the spot where they had been standing was empty.

She pressed Feran into Hertha's arms. "Keep hold of him this time, please."

Arian hurried back. "Did you see where Merial went?"

The aunts broke from their conversation and looked around in obvious confusion. No need to wait for an answer. Arian went from group to group. Few had noticed Merial leave, and none had more than a hazy idea of her direction. Was it worth looking at home? The latrine?

At the edge of the meeting ground, Cassie and Bran stood apart from the mourners, observing the funeral like foxes, scouting out a hen coop. Cassie's expression was sombre, yet still gave the impression of witnessing something faintly absurd. Arian almost turned away, she was in no mood to be patronised, but concern for Merial came first.

"Have you seen my sister?"

"Yes. She went that way." Cassie pointed.

Merial was not heading for home. "Thank you. I'll—"

Cassie stopped her with a hand on her arm. "Is something wrong?"

"No. I… She isn't…"

"That didn't sound convincing. I'll help you look for her."

Cassie's aid was neither needed nor wanted, but Arian did not have time to waste arguing. She hurried off.

"Shall I come as well, my lady?" Bran asked.

"No. Stay here. Come find us if Merial returns." The rapid beat of Cassie's footsteps followed Arian.

Away from the meeting ground, the town was deserted. The buildings stood stark in the moonlight, painted in faded greys etched with hard black shadows. Sounds from the funeral faded. The palisade came into view.

Cassie caught up. "Do you know where she's going?"

"I've got an idea." And no reason Arian could think of was good.

The main gate was shut and barred at night, with a sentry posted, but the small side entrance was easily opened from inside. As children, they would sneak out at night for a dare. But this was no children's game. Merial had fled Breninbury. The latch bar was out of its socket and the gate ajar. Arian stepped onto the hillside. It took a moment to spot Merial, two hundred yards away, heading to the river.

"There she is." Cassie had seen her as well. "She's going to where you found Yehan's body."

But Cassie was wrong. Merial turned aside halfway down the hill.

"She's going..." The air solidified in Arian's throat, and the words would not come.

"Hurry." Cassie clearly picked up on the urgency and broke into a run, though her dress and sandals were unsuited to the open hillside.

Even in boots, Arian tripped over hassocks, and slipped on mud. The long grass and heather grabbed at her feet. She gained ground slowly, but too slowly to overtake Merial before the cliff, overlooking the lower pool. Merial stood at the edge, staring down. Arian stopped a few yards away.

Twice during her lifetime, bodies had been pulled from the river beyond the rapids, after falling from this spot. Arguments still continued on whether they had been suicide, murder, or accident.

"Merial?" Just saying the name meant forcing air through the tightness in her throat.

Merial did not move. Her eyes were fixed on the water below her feet. The lower pool was as black as the sky, but where the river entered the gorge, sprays of churning surf gleamed white in the moonlight.

"It was my fault. All my fault."

"No." Arian sunk to her knees. *Please, step back.*

Neither voice nor legs would obey her. And it was no longer just about Merial. The death of a child was so hard. Arian fought back the memories hiding in the deepest corners of her mind, snapping at her heart whenever she was at her weakest. Little Olin, ten days old, crying and coughing, and then never crying again.

Cassie arrived. She circled around Merial, moving casually, as if on a midnight stroll with all the time in the world. "Are you seriously thinking of jumping?" By her tone, Cassie might have been asking about the weather.

"I killed him." Merial switched to speaking Kavillian.

"Really?" Cassie sounded genuinely surprised.

"I brought him here. We shouldn't have left Verina. It's my fault."

"Oh, that. It's silly and you know it. What if you'd stayed? From what I saw, Verina isn't a safe town. Who knows what he might have got caught up in?"

Moving only her head, Merial looked at Arian. "You've never asked why I came back."

"I..." Arian's voice would not obey her.

"Yehan's father, I wanted to leave him. But the children...he said any judge would side with an empire man against a barbarian woman."

Merial swayed, sobbing. Regardless of how serious she was about jumping, she could fall. Arian tried to move, but her legs were frozen.

Cassie had no similar problem. She reached Merial's side and put an arm around her. "You didn't want your husband to take the children from you."

Merial nodded. "He was out of town for a few days, so I took my chance. It was all about me. I never asked the children what they wanted. That's why Yehan was angry all the time. He loved his pa. And I've lost him anyway. He's gone and it's all..."

Cassie eased Merial away from the edge. "It's hard for children when their parents separate. Yehan was torn. But that's only because he loved you too."

"Yehan could have stayed. Been a blacksmith. He'd still be alive."

"You don't know that. Accidents happen. And do you truly think he'd rather be a blacksmith than a king?"

Merial was crying too hard to answer, but with Cassie holding her, the risk of falling was gone.

Arian's legs were tight, but she managed to scramble forward. "You mustn't blame yourself."

"But if you feel you have to, remember you have other children." Cassie's unsympathetic tone had the effect of stopping Merial's tears.

"What if I fail them too?"

"You can think of a worse failure than letting them think Yehan was the only one you cared about? That you didn't love them enough to want to stay with them?"

Merial flinched, as if dowsed with cold water. "I do love..." She was silent, then drew a deep breath and allowed herself to be coaxed back another step. She looked at Cassie. "Thank you."

"We should go back," Arian said.

Cassie leaned out to look over then edge, before meeting Arian's eyes for a moment, as if she had a question. However, she then merely took Merial's other arm for the walk back to Breninbury.

By the time they returned to the meeting ground, the pyre had collapsed in a white-hot mound. It had a while left to burn, but Yehan was gone from this world. Merial gave the pyre a final look, then went to reclaim Perri from Odella.

Arian stayed with Cassie. She ought to say something. "Thank you for helping."

"It's hard losing a child, as we both know." Was that a quaver in Cassie's voice?

"You've lost children?"

"Two daughters. They—" Cassie clenched her jaw. "They're gone."

For a moment, the firelight glittered in her eyes. Then Cassie turned and walked away.

"Riders in sight." A shout from the lookout.

Arian put down her needle, giving up any pretence of doing something useful. Kendric had arrived half a day too late for Yehan's funeral. He was also two days too late to meet Yehan face-to-face, and five years too late to have an effect on his life.

Kendric was a man Yehan should have known. Someone to admire and emulate. Then maybe Arian would have memories of her nephew that added up to more than a sullen pout and arrogance. Sighing, she left the bench outside her house. It was all too late, and wishing otherwise was pointless.

Arian took a place with those lining the palisade. Two dozen riders had come over the hill opposite, and were trotting down the road, followed by a supply wagon. Excited whispers skipped back and forth between the watchers. She was not the only one happy to see the old warrior back in Breninbury, even though his return would be brief. Gethryn was wrong to have sent Kendric away, but it was not a mistake he showed any sign of putting right.

The wagon pulled into a fallow field, north of the village. Four warriors on horseback continued on, leaving the attendants on their mules to set up camp. With Kendric in the lead, the warriors forded the river upstream of the tributary from the sacred spring. Arian fought a childish impulse to wave as he drew close. She stayed in place, craning her neck until he was out of sight around the curve of the outer defences, So what if she looked like an abandoned puppy, waiting its owner's return.

Arian left the palisade and joined the drift to the meeting ground. She arrived at the same time as Kendric. The years were taking their toll. His hair and beard were white, and his face deeply lined, yet he sat straight in the saddle, and the hands holding the reins revealed no hint of tremor. His eyes were as sharp as ever. Kendric dismounted, leaving care of his horse to one of his warriors.

Gethryn should have been there. He must have heard the lookout's call. Making Kendric wait was childish. Arian did not doubt it was deliberate, and as such, totally in keeping with her brother. But just because Gethryn wanted to act like a spoilt toddler did not mean she had to.

Arian walked over. "Well met, cousin."

"Well met, cousin." Kendric's smile of welcome faded. "I heard about Yehan. It's a sad misfortune for one so young. How is Merial?"

"Upset."

"Understandable. I hope to speak with her later."

"She'll be pleased to see you."

Kendric's smile returned. "And you. How are you faring?"

"All the better for seeing you."

Kendric had been her guide, her mentor, her favourite adult—far more so than her uncle, King Maddock. Kendric was the one she had gone to with scraped knees, childhood feuds, broken toys. And somehow he had been able to make everything right. *Damn Gethryn and his pathetic feud.*

Arian took a step forward and wrapped her arms around Kendric. "I've missed you."

He patted her back. "Likewise."

A murmur rippled around the meeting ground. Kendric gently disentangled himself. Gethryn had finally decided to show his face, with Leirmond at his shoulder.

Kendric bowed his head. "Greetings, my king."

"Greetings, my beloved kinsman." Any love in Gethryn's voice was buried under ice. "The journey can't have been easy for a man of your advanced years. And I fear I've wasted your time. I doubt there's much you can add to the matter at hand."

It was typical infantile small-mindedness. Apart from suggesting Kendric was infirm with age, Gethryn admitted dragging him all the way from Yanto's Leap on a fool's errand.

Kendric did not react. "It's always my pleasure to fulfil my king's commands."

"As soon as you have finished setting camp, I'll summon the Council of Elders, so you may speak with the imperial envoy."

"I'll be happy to offer what help I can. But, regarding the camp, my warriors—"

Gethryn cut him off. "Will, I'm afraid, have to remain in the valley with the rest of your attendants. We don't have room for you in Breninbury."

"Of course, my king." Kendric's voice and expression remained calm.

However, many of those watching showed their shock. Gethryn wanted Kendric and his warriors to stay with the farmers, as if they were serfs. It was a planned insult. Even if the absurd claim about lack of space were true, Kendric, as former leader of the warband, should have been allowed to sleep in the Warriors' House.

Kendric raised his fist to his chest in a salute. "I'll be back as soon as I can."

"Do that."

Kendric sent a last smile in Arian's direction, then mounted his horse and rode out. Behind him, Gethryn and Leirmond were laughing and slapping each other's backs, as if they had just won a bet. And as ever, Cassie was in the background, looking on with interest.

Assuming Cassie could understand Lycanthian, how well had she followed the undercurrents in what had just taken place? Her expression gave nothing away. Which, now that Arian thought of it, was not so different from Kendric. Both wore the face of a master swordsman, whose eyes never revealed where the next strike was coming. Both would have their opponent off-balance and outfoxed before the fight started.

Cassie was dangerous. She had schemes afoot. She was plotting and planning, gathering information, playing games, while Gethryn was looking the wrong way. What was she after? Arian caught her lip in her teeth, certain Cassie's true goal was not the one she claimed. Merely in sending a woman, the empire had baited its trap. Men found it so hard to take a woman seriously. Arian shook her head. If Kendric had taught her one thing about combat it was the only enemy you could safely disregard was a dead one.

Gethryn and Leirmond disappeared back into the Great Hall. Did they have any idea just how much they needed Kendric's help?

The rhythmical action of spinning was calming. The sight of the spindle twirling on the end of the yarn let Arian's thoughts wander free.

Yehan's death had been a shock, but with the funeral over, the hardest part was past. Merial would be able to grieve and move on. Kendric's arrival also helped. Despite the stupid conflict with Gethryn, he was a source of strength and comfort, just like when she was a child. Kendric would always know what to do.

A shadow fell across Arian's lap. Emlyn, the steward, stood over her. "Do you know where Lady Cassilania is? The Council of Elders is about to start."

"No, I d—" She broke off as Cassie came into view. "There she is. Someone else has found her."

"Thanks." Emlyn strode away.

Arian put down her spinning. How would Kendric handle Cassie? That was, if Gethryn and Leirmond gave him a chance to speak. Their feud was worse than childish. The empire was the true enemy, and Kendric was one person Cassie could not run circles around.

Unexpectedly, Nelda also wanted to observe the meeting. Her interest in politics was generally even less than her understanding of it. She tried to follow Cassie into the Great Hall.

A warrior at the door blocked her way. "You're not allowed in."

Arian hung back, wanting to see how things would go between Nelda and the guard.

"Why?" Nelda asked.

"It's the Council of Elders. Women aren't allowed to attend. You know that."

"You're letting her in. The slut from the empire."

"The envoy has been declared an honorary man for the duration of the meeting."

"What? Don't be stupid. She's a woman. And if she can go in, I can too." Nelda's voice rose in outrage.

The warrior did not budge. "The king made the decision. Go argue with him."

Nelda stormed away. Arian could not imagine Nelda's interest in the meeting was anything other than a whim, but there was no doubt that she was furious at being barred.

She latched onto Arian. "Did you hear that? Honorary man!"

"Yes." Arian shrugged. "I guess there was no point having the Council meeting without her. They had to get around it somehow."

"Next they'll be saying it's all right for her to drag women into her bed, and play at being a man there as well. Filthy pervert."

Arian worked at controlling her expression. The idea was shocking. Utterly shocking. And Cassie's total lack of concern on the subject was just another game. Cassie was toying with her, putting thoughts in her head, images in her dreams. Arian's stomach knotted, as it had taken to doing, every time she saw Cassie. *Damn her to hell and back.*

But yet, if Cassie had not been there last night, would Merial have jumped? Arian bit her lip. Would she now be mourning her sister as well as her nephew? She owed Cassie gratitude. She did not trust her, did not like her, and wanted nothing to do with her. But did she still hate her? Everything was becoming more confusing.

Nelda continued her rant. "That slut has everyone running around like headless chickens."

"It's what she's good at." That was for certain.

"I bet she thinks she can flash her tits at the men and get anything she wants."

"I can name a few who'd fall for that."

"I've seen the way Gethryn looks at her."

"Gethryn? I was thinking more of Leirmond."

"Why do you say him?" Nelda was instantly defensive.

"She's female. That's all it takes."

Nelda turned and glared at the Great Hall. "They don't need to talk to her. Just tell her to fuck off back to where she came from. But Gethryn won't. She's got everyone trying to crawl up her arse."

Exactly what Merial said we'd do. Arian could only shrug and turn away.

Cassie

They had barely covered the opening formalities and already Cassie's face ached from the effort of hiding her smile. "Would it be possible for our engineers to visit the mines?"

"If the king says yes, I've—" Kendric did not get a chance to finish.

"Wait for the translation. We all need to know what's being said." Leirmond's voice snapped like a whip.

Bran duly did his bit. Even then, Kendric was not given a chance to speak.

Gethryn jumped in. "They should make a direct appeal to me, giving their numbers."

"How many miners are employed in the region?"

This time Kendric waited for Bran to finish. It did him no good. "When I la—"

Leirmond cut him off. "Who bothers counting slaves and serfs?"

Keeping a straight face was getting harder by the minute. Bran was also struggling, clearly unsure whether to translate the remark.

"Did Leirmond just say how many miners there were?" Cassie asked, in feigned innocence.

Kendric and two others smiled—the ones whose Kavillian was good enough not to need Bran's translation. Useful knowledge in its own right.

Gethryn said, "On his return, Earl Kendric will ask the mine overseers and have the information sent directly to the guild in Verina."

Cassie nodded. "Thank you."

The farce continued. Gethryn remained seated, while Leirmond stalked the length of the hall, like a caged animal. Apart from them and

Kendric, the fourteen elderly men who formed the council were present, including the high priest, Tregaran. A dozen younger warriors stayed in the background, playing no part in the meeting—not that the others contributed much. Kendric was not allowed to answer any questions, and nobody else had anything worthwhile to say.

This did not mean it was a waste of time. Far from it. Gethryn should have let her visit the mines. Nothing she might have seen there would have been half as beneficial as the display he and Leirmond were putting on.

Their eagerness to push Kendric aside resulted in a few revelations. Gethryn displayed a basic grasp of Kavillian, and Leirmond did not—which came as no surprise after his abysmal attempt at seduction. In the rare opportunities granted him, Kendric displayed more fluency than either, although he was not as proficient in the language as either Arian or Merial.

Apart from this, with every slight sent Kendric's way, most of the young warriors looked amused, while the disapproval on other faces grew more marked. Most interesting of all, Tregaran was foremost among those backing Kendric, and he made no attempt to hide it. A rift between the nobility and the priesthood had so much potential. Cassie could not have asked for more. Yet, Gethryn was oblivious to the gift he was laying before her.

Cassie dragged the meeting out long enough to bolster a pretence of seriously seeking answers and information. But eventually, she stopped asking questions, and Gethryn signalled an end to the meeting. A couple of councillors immediately homed in, keeping him pinned on what was referred to as his throne, although Cassie had thrown out better chairs as junk. Judging by their questions, they were upset over what had just gone on. Gethryn looked forlornly across to where Leirmond was embedded in a group of his supporters. Kendric marched from the hall, accompanied by the warriors who had come with him.

Leirmond sneered, watching him go. "Go on. Run away, you old fool."

"Earl Kendric has served our people for many years. It would be fitting to show him more respect." Now that the meeting had finished, Tregaran was not biting his tongue

"He'd let our enemies ride over us."

"When has he ever done that?"

Leirmond scowled but made no answer.

Tregaran strode across the hall to join a cluster of councillors. The battle lines could not be more obvious if they all wore uniforms to show their allegiance. Cassie bit the inside of her lip. This was getting better and better.

"Go stand by the rear door and act as if you're waiting for me," she whispered to Bran.

He headed off. Cassie started to follow but stopped near Leirmond. She shuffled her foot as though trying to dislodge a stone trapped in her sandal.

"Look at the bitch. Swanning around like the sun shines out her arse. She's got the old farts shitting themselves." Leirmond's voice was pitched too low for the old farts on the other side of the hall to hear. He was, though, clearly relying on Cassie not understanding Lycanthian.

His friends agreed. "Jumping at their own shadows."

"No wonder the empire thinks we'd roll over for them."

Cassie continued her performance, slipping the sandal off her foot and picking it up to shake. She pretended not to notice the way Leirmond glared at her.

He turned back to his friends. "We must take the fight to the empire."

"What does Gethryn think?"

"He'll think what I tell him to. But I swear, I've seen worms with more backbone." Leirmond gave a humourless laugh. "We need to hit the empire hard and show them what we're made of."

"Send them running home with their tails between their legs."

"They haven't got anything else there." Laughter greeted the jibe

Cassie put her sandal on and joined Bran at the doorway. She looked back at the gathering. The battle lines were clear. Gethryn had finally escaped from his throne and gone to Leirmond's side of the hall, not that it had been in doubt.

"Let's go for a walk." Cassie waited until they were alone before stopping to massage her cheeks. "Oh, my face. How did I stop myself from laughing?"

"You found that amusing?" Bran asked.

"Didn't you?"

"I doubt I read it as well as you did, my lady."

"And I doubt you missed much." Cassie continued walking. "What do you know about Kendric?"

"He was leader of the warband under the previous king, Maddock. I think they were related somehow. Maybe cousins?"

"Find out. It might be relevant."

"Yes, my lady." Bran's nose wrinkled in thought. "Kendric wasn't hated as much as most other lordly folk. Some saw him as a hero."

"He still commands respect from the older people, including the priest. And Arian doesn't share her brother's opinion of him. Do you have any idea what's at the root of the trouble between him and Gethryn?"

"I'll dig around. There've been hints about a clash with Leirmond."

"That sounds likely. Leirmond's leading Gethryn by the nose. And at the moment, he's trying to steer Gethryn into a war with the empire."

"That's..." Bran was speechless for a dozen paces. "Do you know why?"

"I hurt his pride when I turned down his offer of a night of passion. I can't believe that's the reason, but it might explain dropping the rock on me, yesterday."

Bran shook his head. "No. It can't have been him. After we separated, I went back to Breninbury. They were holding funeral games for Yehan."

"Funeral games?"

"A competition to honour the dead. For a king they'd go on all day. Yehan just got a few sparring matches beside the pyre. I joined the audience, chatting to people to see if I could find out who last saw Yehan alive. Leirmond was one of the fighters taking part."

"The whole time? Right up till I returned?"

"Yes. I'm sure of it." Bran frowned. "He might have slipped away for a few minutes, but he couldn't have got down to the river and back."

"Damn. There goes my favourite suspect."

"Do you have others?"

"Arian." Not that Cassie could take the idea seriously.

"Why her?"

"I'd just needled her into running away. Although dropping a rock on me because of it would be touch extreme."

"What did you say to her?"

"I was flirting." Cassie smiled at Bran's reaction. "Don't look shocked. Arian is easy on the eye, and she's so naive it's adorable. Or she's a first-class actress who's got me outfoxed." Which was highly sexy in its own way. "But I'm not going to do anything stupid. I'm not so desperate for a romp I can't wait until I'm home. Life is quite dangerous enough."

Bran twitched his shoulders and looked away. "It's strange being back. I knew I didn't want to stay here, but I hadn't realised how much I'd changed. You and Arian…"

"Isn't going to happen." *Unfortunately.* "But no. I don't really think Arian dropped the rock. Last night, she showed no reaction to standing above the lower pool with me. Given the drama over Merial, no matter how good an actress Arian is, she'd have let something slip."

"Do you think Merial would've jumped, if you weren't there?"

"I doubt it. She was suffering from guilt and felt the need for atonement. But she'd have come to her senses. She didn't want to die."

They walked in silence for a while.

"So you've no idea at all about who tried to kill you?" Bran asked.

Cassie shrugged. "The same person who murdered Yehan. As for why…" It was a trickier question. "Possibly they saw Yehan as a tool of the empire. Having got rid of him, I'm number two on their list. More likely, I was careless. The murderer left a telltale marker in the Warriors' House, to show if anyone disturbed Yehan's body. They knew someone examined him, then saw me searching the riverbank, and put two and two together."

"Do you think they'll try again?"

"Probably. I need to be more careful in the future."

"You're very calm about it."

"Assassination is part of everyday life in the Senate." Which was a slight exaggeration, but letting fear rule her was a sure path to failure.

Cassie stopped and rested her arms atop the palisade. Kendric's campsite was a collection of tents on the other side of the river, north of the village. Kendric and his riders must have returned by now, although there was no sign of them. "I need a private chat with Kendric."

"You won't be allowed."

"I wouldn't have been allowed to examine Yehan's body either." Cassie shrugged. "I'll watch out for telltale traps this time."

❖

Cassie lifted the bar on the side gate. A haze of cloud covered the moon. Muted light made the mud and rough vegetation challenging, but unlike the previous night, there was no need for haste. Cassie and Bran kept low, using bushes and shrubs to hide from the lookout over the main gate.

They skirted the sacred grove until reaching the river. A short way upstream was the ford where Kendric and his riders had crossed. Here the water came just below mid-calf, rushing over smooth stones. Cassie lifted the hem of her dress to keep it dry, which she was largely successful in doing, although her toes had turned to ice before she was halfway across. Water squidged from her leather sandals as she climbed the bank on the other side.

The farmers' hovels were slouched mounds in the night. No lights shone, though whiffs of smoke carried on the breeze. A dog barked once but made no attempt to approach. Kendric was camped in a field to the north. A fire burned in the middle of an area marked out by the wagon and tents. Horses and mules stood hobbled nearby.

Cassie was almost at the wagon when a challenge came.

"Who goes there?" An armed warrior held out a spear. "Come forward into the light and show yourself."

"My lady wishes to talk with Earl Kendric," Bran answered for her.

"And who is y—"

"Let them through." Kendric stood in the opening of the largest tent. He lit a lamp, using a splint of wood, then gestured for Cassie and Bran to follow him inside.

A saddle and weapons were stacked on one side of the tent, and a bed roll was laid out on the other. Judging by the thrown back cover, Kendric had been asleep when they arrived, and had woken and reacted quickly. More useful information. Two logs served as benches. Kendric waved Cassie to one, while he sat on the other.

"What can I do for you?" He spoke in careful Kavillian.

"I fear I was daydreaming in our meeting today. There were questions I meant to ask you, but I can't remember your answers. I came, hoping you could prod my memory."

Kendric stroked his beard thoughtfully while studying Cassie's face. "I think you asked about mines, miners, and roads, but I wonder why you've come here at night to ask again, since we both know you'll not be allowed to make use of my answers."

Cassie shrugged. "Call me hopeful."

"I'd have said you were…" He looked at Bran and switched to Lycanthian. "What's the word? Someone who sees things as they truly are?"

"A realist?"

"Thank you." He reverted to addressing Cassie in Kavillian. "I'd have said you were a realist."

"Maybe. It still leaves the issue of my lapse in memory. Do you know why I have so much trouble recalling your answers?"

"You want to play games?"

"No. I'm giving you the chance to say problems with my memory are no concern of yours and then send me away."

"Yes. Of course you are." He laughed. "If I refuse to talk with you now, you'll go, and let that be the end to it?"

"I'll go, but no, it won't end there."

"So you do sometimes say what you think."

"As long as you understand me."

"Yes, I do. You want to know why Gethryn didn't give me a chance to speak." Kendric shook his head. "I'm the king's loyal subject. You'll not get me telling tales."

"Loyalty shouldn't only go one way."

"Maybe not, but Gethryn is the one who'll have to explain himself to the ancestors."

Cassie nodded. "Fair enough. But there's one thing I'd like to ask."

"Ask. But I might not answer. I owe you nothing."

"Why does Leirmond want war with the empire?"

"Why do you think? It's because he's a fool. He…" Kendric paused, then nodded. "All right. Here's a scrap for you. He wants to fight the empire because I told him it was a stupid thing to do, and he'd lose, badly. He wants to prove me wrong."

"I see."

"You do?"

"I think so. Leirmond wants everyone to agree he's the greatest warrior of all time. But you're a problem. His big rival. He got Gethryn to banish you, but it hasn't stopped some folk thinking you were a better leader to the warband. That hurts him. Leirmond can't even bear the thought of you knowing more than he does about mining in your domain. That's why he shut you down at the meeting. Gethryn goes along with him, because that's what Gethryn does." Cassie met Kendric's eyes. "Can I take it you've encountered the imperial army?"

"Yes. Once. It didn't go well for us."

Everything dropped into place. "Leirmond wants to beat the empire in battle, because it will prove to everyone that he's a better warrior than you. He thinks he can find victory where you failed."

"He'll lose."

"I know."

"But Gethryn…" Kendric clenched his jaw.

"May be the only person who loves Leirmond nearly as much as he loves himself." Cassie finished the sentence for him. Kendric was happy to vent his feelings about Leirmond but, for now, his loyalty to his king was holding up. She got to her feet. "But I must go. Thank you. You've been very helpful."

Kendric also stood. "I'd ask you to leave our land. The empire does not need us, or our iron and tin. But I'd be wasting my breath."

"Yes. You would."

Cassie and Bran again forded the river. On the opposite bank, Cassie stopped and looked back. "Find out everything you can about him. Absolutely everything."

"You think he's important?"

"Oh yes. He's the man we want on our side."

By the time they reached the courtyard of their house, gaps were appearing in the cloud. Breninbury lay silent, the paths between houses deserted. Even the lookout in the watch tower was missing. Was he sneaking a quick nap?

"Good night, my lady." Bran whispered, so as not to wake the others.

"Good night." Cassie hesitated. Her mind was racing. Sleep was unlikely. "Actually, I'm going to take a walk."

"Do you want me to come with you?"

"No. I need to mull things over. Walking helps me think."

"I'll see you tomorrow then."

"Yes. Tomorrow."

Cassie paced the hillfort's perimeter. The meeting with Kendric had gone to plan. Her goal had been to gauge the man, rather than obtain answers to particular questions. Kendric had turned out sharper than expected, although stuck with notions of honour and duty to a king who did not deserve it. No wonder he and Arian got on well, as demonstrated by the hug she had given him.

How to gain Kendric's support? How would he respond to the news Yehan had been murdered? Of course, his reaction might depend on the identity of the murderer, and feeding him the information would require careful handling. Cassie sighed. It would also require proof which was now a pile of ash.

She could aim for a better relationship with Arian, who might influence Kendric. The incident with Merial ought to translate into goodwill, though it would not be enough on its own to swing Arian and Kendric behind the empire.

Leirmond was driven by arrogance and rivalry, which made him easy to provoke into making mistakes. And as long as she steered Leirmond in the right direction, Gethryn would present no problem. If Leirmond told him to dance naked in the snow, Gethryn would do it without a moment's hesitation.

Tregaran wielded considerable power, which he preferred not to use. He would clearly be happier if Kendric was king rather than Gethryn. Although Kendric on the throne would be a far trickier obstacle to manage. However, the high priest was deeply hostile to the empire and, in Cassie's experience, regardless of which god was followed, trying to change a priest's mind about anything was impossible. In all the lands conquered by the empire, there had been countless gods of love and war, but not one of indecision.

And on top of this, there was a murderer on the loose, and she had no clue as to their identity or motive.

The full moon floated clear of cloud as Cassie completed her circuit. She paused for a last look over the serene hills surrounding Breninbury, then left the palisade and wound her way through the sprawl of houses. The concept of town planning had not caught on with the Lycanthi. Beyond a tendency for houses' entrances to face south, nothing in the hillfort lined up with anything else.

A crunch of gravel was so faint as to be almost inaudible, though too loud to be a cat or mouse. It came from somewhere close at hand. Cassie froze. Someone had trodden on loose stones. She was not the only one out of bed and moving around.

Cassie pressed herself against the nearest wall and looked back the way she had come. Nobody was in sight, nothing was moving, but she was not alone. Silver moonlight cast stark shadows on the ground. The outlines of houses were crisp and clear, as was the unmistakable shape of someone crouched behind a wall. Someone moving slowly, stealthily. Someone stalking her. Another instant and the shadow vanished.

At first, the thud of her heartbeat was all Cassie could hear. She concentrated on her ears. The clink of a kicked stone, the squelch of soft mud, the rasp of cloth against dry stone as the stalker slipped around a building, getting closer. Cassie had to move. She had to get to the house, and safety.

She did not remember the shadow holding a bow, but could she rely on a fleeting impression? Was the stalker ahead of her or behind? Was it safer to run or sneak through shadow? She could scream for help and wake everyone in earshot. It would do nothing for her popularity, especially when she could say no more than, "I think one of your fellow tribesmen was following me." Any hope of presenting an image of calm authority would be gone, and diplomacy was nine-tenths acting. She might as well give up and return to Kavilli.

Cassie inched along a wall, listening and looking. She hitched up her dress and scurried across a patch of bright moonlight. The footsteps mirrored hers, breaking into a run, and then silence. Where was the prowler?

Another house to slink around. Another patch of moonlight she must cross. How had Breninbury become so large? At last, her goal was in sight. Cassie braced her hands against the wall, ready to push off for a final sprint.

Sudden quick movement, close at hand. Far too close. The rustle of clothing. A rush of air. Cassie threw herself to the ground, landing face first in the dirt. Something smashed into the wall above her, hitting the stones with an explosive crack. Loose grit and splitters of wood rained down. Cassie rolled onto her back, just in time to catch the briefest glimpse of a figure disappearing around the side of the house.

A baby's wail rent the night. A dog barked.

Adult voices rose. "What's that?"

"Who's making noise?"

Cassie scrambled to her feet and fled in the opposite direction to her attacker. Hanging around to explain things was not a good idea. She could imagine the sort of rumours it would prompt. A circuitous route took her around the back of another three houses. She hurried across a last patch of open ground and into her house. All was quiet.

Placing the hurdle over the courtyard entrance was purely symbolic. It would be of no use in keeping a murderer out. Waking Massillo and Palonius would be far more effective. The bodyguards could take turns keeping watch over her. It was the job they were paid for. However, the attacker would surely not try again so soon. Tomorrow would be soon enough to consider her options, after a chance to calm down and think.

Tullia was asleep in their room and thankfully, for once, not snoring. Cassie slipped under the covers. The blankets were comforting in a childish way, although they offered no more protection than the hurdle over the entrance. Cassie closed her eyes and forced herself to take slow, even breaths, but it was a long time before sleep claimed her.

Bran brushed the wall where strands of bark clung to the stone. More splinters littered the ground. "It was a rough branch. Might even have been a piece of firewood someone picked up."

"An improvised club, which fits the pattern."

"It does?"

"Yes." Cassie started walking. Bran kept pace beside her. "The attacker did not come armed. We're looking at an opportunist. None of the three attempts were planned in advance."

"Three?"

"Including Yehan. The murderer took their chance when they saw him kneeling by the water. They pushed the rock off the cliff when I obligingly crawled beneath it. And last night they spotted me wandering around and grabbed the first weapon that came to hand."

"Umm, I don't mean to disagree, my lady, but…"

"I don't mind. Go on." Only a fool employed someone with brains and knowledge, and then refused to listen.

"The way Yehan was killed might not mean anything. Nobody is allowed to carry a weapon at feasts or other gatherings. They make out it's to do with holding a sacred truce, but mainly it's to stop folk from getting drunk and stabbing each other. And last night, surely your attacker hasn't been hanging around every night, on the off chance you'd go out alone." Bran had a point.

"They've been spying on me." It was not a comforting thought.

"You must be more careful."

"I know. But that might just mean the murderer will become more proactive. I wish I'd got a better look at him…or her."

"You think it might have been a woman?"

"They were on the small side."

"Gethryn isn't a big man."

"True. And I had a spilt second, with my face covered in mud, in the dark. I'd say the person was shorter than either Leirmond, or Kendric, but I wouldn't want to stake my life on it."

"And your life is at stake." Bran started a sentence three times before saying, "I wouldn't want anything to happen to you, my lady."

"I wouldn't want anything to happen to me." Cassie shrugged. "Politics is a high stakes game. But it's the one I've been brought up to play. I need to back myself to win."

"Do you think the odds are on your side?"

"I'm my mother's daughter. There aren't many in the Senate who'd put money on the opposition." And, no matter how things went, panicking would not help. Cassie switched subject. "Have you found out anything of interest?"

"I chatted to the bondservants making breakfast."

"And?"

"They had a lot to say about Kendric, once I got them going. He and King Maddock were cousins, as I thought."

"He's Arian's cousin once removed?"

"I guess so, though we don't keep count like that. Maddock never liked Gethryn as his heir, but he didn't have a choice. There had been a couple of older nephews by another sister, but both were killed in battle. Maddock would taunt Gethryn and tell him he needed to grow up to be more like Kendric."

"So Gethryn started with a grudge, even before Leirmond."

Bran nodded. "On his deathbed, Maddock made Gethryn swear to keep Kendric as leader of the warband. Which he did, for a while, though he wasn't happy about it. It took Leirmond a couple of years to talk Gethryn into shunting Kendric off to Yanto's Leap. A lot of folk were surprised Tregaran let him get away with it. Oath-breaking is a serious thing. Gethryn was taking a chance."

"Can the high priest overrule the king?"

"Yes. When it comes to sacred law."

"How long ago did this happen?"

"Eight years. It was while Merial was gone. She might have talked Gethryn out of it. She has influence with him, or did before Leirmond took over."

"How do people feel about it now?"

"They call Gethryn an oath-breaker behind his back. Leirmond has his supporters, and nobody disputes he's a good fighter, but he rubs people the wrong way. Not much gets said in Breninbury, but word from traders is that even the lordly folk in other hillforts hate them both."

Which was easy to believe. Cassie stopped by the palisade. Despite bright sunshine, the weather was cooler than of late. Autumn was drawing on. People moving about in Kendric's camp were clad in thick cloaks. As yet they showed no sign of taking down their tents, but they would be leaving soon. If not that day, then surely the one after.

"So what now?" Bran asked.

"Kendric. I need to keep him around for a while longer. As well as an excuse for me to stay."

"What sort of excuse?"

"I've got an idea. Come on."

From Gethryn's expression, he was getting ready to say no. The trap was primed and ready.

Cassie continued speaking. "I know it would be a huge imposition on Earl Kendric. I'm certain he must be eager to return home. For a man of his standing, to spend yet more time camping in the valley, is a lot to ask."

And she had won. She saw the switch in Gethryn's eyes. Leirmond was just as keen, once he heard Bran's translation. The flimsiness of her story was irrelevant. She had given them another excuse to heap humiliation on Kendric.

"Do you have it ready?" Gethryn asked.

"Yes." Cassie held out the sealed letter.

He signalled to his steward. "Emlyn will see that a courier is found."

Cassie passed the letter over. Most likely it would be opened and read before leaving Breninbury, but its contents were as she claimed, a request to the guild of blacksmiths for estimated production quantities on assorted metalwork. It would cause confusion in Verina, since she already had the information, but Gethryn was not to know.

"Thank you, and please apologise to Earl Kendric for me. It was a gross oversight on my part."

Cassie left the hall, with Bran following. They stopped a short way off, where there were no listeners around.

Bran smiled. "That went to plan."

"Yes. It gives us nine or ten days for the message to get to Verina and back. Depending on how fast the courier is."

Ten more days to sound out Kendric. And ten more days of him being reminded just how much he disliked his king. Cassie could count on Gethryn doing half her job for her.

"What next?"

"We need more information. Talk to the bondservants again. Take your time. Gain their trust." The Breninbury servant's rumour mill might not run at the same breathless pace as the one in Kavilli but was still worth tapping into.

After Bran left, Cassie spotted Nelda, feeding her baby on a bench outside the house she shared with Arian and Merial. Could she be last night's assailant? It seemed unlikely, not least because Nelda would have had to leave her newborn son alone. However, if getting him on the throne was the motive for killing Yehan, Nelda might be in league with the murderer.

"Good morning," Cassie said in Lycanthian. After twelve days in Breninbury it would be suspicious if she had not picked up the simple greeting.

Nelda pulled her cloak over, to cover any hint of breast. "Filthy pervert. Ogling women."

Cassie pretended not to understand, merely smiling in response. She switched to Kavillian. "What a good-looking baby you have there."

"Why don't you ??????? back to the shithole you came from? Somebody should smash your head in." She had come up with a new word. Cassie would need to ask Bran.

Nelda glared at her then stood and stomped into the house. Was the bit about a smashed head merely coincidental? Clearly Nelda would not be shedding tears if the makeshift club had connected with its target. Why such a heated reaction?

Cassie was about to go when Arian appeared. "Good morning, Arian."

"Good morning." Arian sounded more nervous than friendly. But then she indicated the bench and said, "Would you like to sit?"

This was promising. "Thank you." Cassie waited until Arian was also seated. "How's Merial? I haven't seen her around."

"Better." Arian licked her lips. The sight was mesmerizing. "I wanted to thank you for helping to calm her down when we were by the lower pool. I don't know if she would have jumped but..."

Cassie gave her warmest smile. "Don't mention it. As I said at our first meeting, I'd really prefer it if we were friends."

"We aren't on the same side."

"It doesn't mean we have to be enemies."

"I don't kn—"

"Whaaaaaa." Arian's daughter came running up, holding her ear.

"What is it?" Arian held her arms out.

"Linna hit me."

"I'm sure it was an accident."

The girl buried her face in Arian's shoulder. "Wasn't."

"I tell you what. Let's go find Linna and see what she has to say." Arian stood and picked her daughter up. She looked down apologetically. "Maybe we'll talk later."

"Of course."

Cassie was about to go in search of another target, when movement sounded inside the house. Rather than Nelda returning, Merial came out. Her eyes were red, and her face puffy.

Merial gave a weak smile "I thought I heard your voice."

"How are you feeling?"

"Not good." She sat down, for a while picking at lint on her clothing.

Cassie waited until she was ready to speak.

"I keep remembering the first time I held Yehan. I was happy and in love. I told you about his father, didn't I?"

"Yes."

"He was such a sweet natured baby." Merial's face crumpled. "Do you know the worst thing of all?"

"What?"

"I'm the only person in the whole world who misses him. Even his sisters don't." Tears rolled down her cheeks.

Cassie took her hand. "I'm sure…" What did you say to that?

Merial answered the question for her. "It's all right. You don't need to lie. I shouldn't have brought him here. His father named him Jehanus. I changed it when we arrived, hoping it would make a difference." She freed her hand to wipe her eyes. "It didn't. Now I've got to work out what's best for my other children."

"What options are you thinking about?"

"Whether to stay."

"You think you might go back to Verina?"

"Not there. The girls' father will be around. But the empire's a big place. There's a lot to choose from." Merial indicated their surroundings with a wave of her hand. "But look at it. Would you want to spend the rest of your life here?"

Cassie could not help grimacing. "Not without hot baths and a proper heating system."

"Or olives, honey coated dates, and red wine." Merial shook her head, sadly. "It's Perri I worry about most. Growing up, I took it for granted men had to fight. But they don't. And my daughters… Women get the short end of the stick everywhere. In some ways we have it easier here. You don't have a man calling you his wife and thinking he owns you. But money talks in the empire, and women can be as rich as men. They're bright girls. They could go to school, learn to read and write. They'd have the chance to make more of their lives."

"There's benefits and drawbacks on both sides."

"Is it wrong to want the best of both worlds?"

"Not wrong, but unrealistic."

Merial sighed. "Can't you talk the imperial army into invading?"

The question was so unexpected Cassie was caught off guard. "Would you want it to?"

"Why not? Empire legions enforcing the peace, so Perri won't be forced to become a sword wielding oaf. A school for the girls. Money from trade to build bathhouses. Shops selling honey coated dates and red wine. "

"The tribe would lose its independence."

"To do what? Launch raids on our neighbours?"

"Your brother wouldn't be happy."

"My brother's a fool."

While Merial was undoubtedly right about that, just how serious was she? Cassie stared at the clouds drifting overhead. What should she say?

"Cassie?"

"Yes."

"I was joking just now."

"I guessed."

"But…is the empire planning on invading?"

"Why do you ask?"

"Because that's what the empire does."

"Not always. We have trade agreements with neighbouring states."

"The empire really does want access to the mines?"

"Yes."

"Then it's going to get it. One way or another."

"Not—"

"No. We both know it's true." Merial's tone allowed no argument. "You being here. You don't send someone from a leading senatorial family to haggle over iron ore. You send a couple of merchants."

"I have authority to accept a range of conditions on behalf of the Senate. A merchant couldn't."

"Conditions? If Gethryn agreed to become a client king, giving full access to the mines, and let the imperial army take care of border security, you'd accept those terms?"

"Yes." That would be easy to sell to the Senate. "But what chance he'd agree?"

"Small enough. It's his best option, though, isn't it?"

"I doubt he'd see it that way."

Merial stood up and rubbed her face. "I need to think."

Cassie watched her go. The question was, what would Merial do when she finished thinking?

Arian

The tables on either side of the Great Hall were crammed with warriors gathered for the evening meal. Firelight tinted the scene in warm colours but could not pierce the layer of smoke beneath the roof. Mud-soaked rushes covered the floor where hounds scavenged for scraps. At the high end of the hall, Gethryn sat with his closest friends. Laughter and shouts cut above the roar of banter. The bard singing before the king's table was struggling to be heard.

Two bondservants tended the deer carcass, roasting in the middle of the hall. One turned while the other carved. Boys scurried in and out, bringing supplies from the kitchen, bread, baked leeks, cheese, eggs, and fruit. Women moved between tables, refilling tankards while swapping jokes with their brothers and cousins.

Arian returned from the hearth with a wooden platter, piled with venison. Leirmond speared the largest slice with his knife but otherwise ignored her. Merial moved behind the men, leaning over their shoulders to pour mead. It was the first night since Yehan's death that she had taken part in the nightly ritual, serving their menfolk.

Her return was welcome. Not only did it mean she was starting to recover, but Arian did not have to rely on help from aunts. It was fitting that the king's sisters should have the honour of waiting on Gethryn's table.

What would have been even more fitting was if Kendric and his warriors had been there. They had not been invited, of course. Did Gethryn not realise he was the one shamed? Dishonouring a guest reflected only on the ill-mannered host. Kendric should have been eating in the Great Hall, not alone in his tent, like a woman or a serf. Gethryn was desperate for Leirmond's approval, but did he not care how he looked to everyone else?

The snub to Kendric was certainly not due to oversight. Gethryn was talking about him as if it was a joke. "I told Kendric he'd have to hang around until the reply came back."

Leirmond laughed. "How did he take it?"

"Like someone had stuck a stick up his arse." Gethryn took a swig from his tankard. "I've sent the bitch's letter off."

"I hope you told the courier not to run." Both men snorted with laughter. "It's not like the old fart has anything else worth doing."

Arian's insides knotted in anger. In his prime, Kendric could have beaten either man. Merial also looked unhappy. Would she say anything? Gethryn still cared about her opinion.

Leirmond signalled to Arian for more venison. "I've got an idea. Why don't you hold games while he's here?"

"Why? Won't it look like I'm calling them in his honour?" Gethryn sounded as surprised as Arian felt.

"Who cares? It'll give me the chance to challenge him. Man to man."

As if a warrior could win renown, fighting someone twice his age. However, Leirmond's followers laughed and pounded the table with their fists.

Leirmond grinned. "Besides. It'll be good for the empire slut to see. The men she's used to are half-arsed cowards. She should see what warriors look like, the sort of man the empire will face when they come up against us."

The cheers of approval were cut short. Merial slammed the flagon on the table. Mead splashed over the brim. "You think a rabble of drunken oafs, thumping each other, is going to worry anyone who's seen an empire legion?"

Leirmond leaned back and sneered. "I'm saying she's never seen real fighters in her life. Just a bunch of bedwetters who think they can win a battle by wearing pretty clothes, so they all look the same."

"The legions will cut you to ribbons. Try running face first into the side of a house. That's what it'll be like when you hit their shield wall. Except houses don't carry swords."

"I'm not scared of them. Not now. Not ever."

"That'll be true, soon enough. The dead no longer fear anything."

"It won't be me lying dead when the battle's over. And that time is coming. We all know it."

Merial turned to Gethryn. "Please, don't pay any heed to him."

Leirmond stood. Around the hall, conversation stilled. The bard stopped his song, mid-verse. Arian placed the platter of venison on the table to free her hands, with no clear idea of what to do.

"You think your brother needs your advice?" Leirmond spat out the words.

"He needs to listen to people who know what they're talking about." Merial was not backing down an inch. "I lived in Verina for ten years. I saw the soldiers drilling. Just one legion, in one town. It's a fraction of their army. The empire could wipe us out so totally nobody would ever know we'd existed."

"Typical woman to be frightened of nothing. We need to lure them onto our land, in the sight of our ancestors." Leirmond slapped his chest. "Real men will not lose."

Things were getting heated. Arian moved to stand behind Merial, in a show of support. Regardless of whether Merial was right, Arian would always back her sister, but it might be wiser to let the matter drop.

However, Merial was not finished. "They'll mow you down like grass. Use your brains."

"No woman tells me what to do. Keep your mouth shut. Your brother doesn't need to hear your wittering."

"I'm the king's sister, the keeper of his bloodline. I'll talk to him whenever, and however I want." Merial put a hand on Gethryn's shoulder, twisting him round so their eyes locked. "You're my brother, and I love you. It's because I love you that I don't want you doing anything stupid. Leirmond doesn't have a clue about the empire. He doesn't see what a powerful ally it could be. You think you're playing games with Cassilania, making a fool of her, pretending to listen. But she'll win in the end. You need to take whatever you can get. Start with asking the empire to build a villa for you, with hot baths and water that flows whenever you want it. If you're sharp, you can have the legions push the Endridi back. Go on. Ask Leirmond that. If he's so great, how come the Endridi still hold the land they took from us fourteen years ago?"

Gethryn's mouth flapped, like a dying fish. He looked between Leirmond and Merial, clearly unable to see his way forward.

Leirmond slammed his fist on the table. For a moment it looked as if he might upend everything. Men on either end grabbed the top and held it steady. An empty tankard fell over and rolled onto the ground. Leirmond stepped around Gethryn's chair and loomed over Merial.

"Shut your mouth. What right have you to speak?"

"Cadryn's blood flows in me, in a line unbroken since the goddess Alwyni gifted this land to our people. That all the right I need."

"You're a traitor to your people."

"And you're a fool."

Leirmond's hand lashed out, catching Merial across the face and knocking her sideways. Leirmond drew back his hand for another blow. Arian was frozen in shock. And she was not the only one. A gasp sounded across the hall.

"STOP." Gethryn got to his feet.

"A woman should know her place."

"You will not strike my sister in my hall." Fury added strength to Gethryn's voice. It was the first time Arian had heard him sound like a king.

She was not alone in being stunned speechless. Only the crackle of flames broke the utter silence. The bondservant stopped turning the meat over the fire

The anger on Leirmond's face slid into sullen defiance. His head dropped. "My king, I mean no disrespect, but…"

But what? A moment before, Merial had invoked the linage in her blood. Had Tregaran witnessed the blow, things would be even more serious.

"I'm sorry." Leirmond's apology was to Gethryn, not Merial. "I also have your best interest at heart. I want you remembered as a hero, not a coward, frightened of your own shadow."

Merial's hand was pressed to her cheek. She dropped her arm. Even in the flickering firelight the red imprint of Leirmond's slap showed like a beacon. "I'm n—"

"No. Both of you. Enough. I will hear no more." Gethryn looked at Arian. "Take care of her. Go."

Arian put an arm around Merial and steered her from the hall. But at the doorway, Merial shrugged herself loose and looked back. "Gethryn, you must think this through. The empire can be our ally. Don't let Leirmond push you into a fight you can't win."

"We'll talk tomorrow. For now I…It's not…" Gethryn mumbled to a stop. Already, the confidence had left his voice.

Arian urged Merial from the hall. As they walked away, Leirmond's voice drifted after them. "Ignore her. Women get frightened over nothing. You should act like a man."

The person who Gethryn would listen to tomorrow was not in doubt. Arian's main surprise was that he had sprung to Merial's defence. She had never before heard him take a stand against Leirmond. But clearly, somewhere deep inside Gethryn was still the little boy, clinging to his big sister's skirt.

They reached the courtyard of their house. Merial was shaking.

"Are you all right?" Arian asked.

"Yes. I'm angry. Not hurt." Merial took a deep breath. "And scared."

"Leirmond won't dare strike you again."

"It's not that. It's him dragging us into war with the empire."

"Leirmond isn't that much of a fool. He—" Did she believe her own words?

"Yes, he is. Maybe, one on one, a Lycanthian warrior could beat an empire legionnaire. But it won't be one on one. It won't even be one against ten. It will be one against a hundred. And if that isn't enough, it'll be one against a thousand."

"You really think we stand no chance?"

"I don't think. I know. Cassie isn't…"

"Isn't what?"

"She isn't on our side."

Arian gave a humourless laugh. "That's not news."

"But just because she isn't on our side doesn't mean we can't join hers." Merial straightened her shoulders. "I have to win the argument with Gethryn."

"I don't think you'll do it."

"Neither do I. That's what frightens me."

Leirmond caught the other fighter in the gut. The man staggered back, only to fall victim to a flurry of punches. He collapsed to his knees, blood streaming from a cut over his eye. It ran over his tattoo and vanished into his beard. A final roundhouse kick sent the man sprawling on the grass. Leirmond raised his fists in the air, inviting cheers from the crowd. Blood—mostly from his opponent—splattered his bare chest. He made no attempt to wipe it away, instead wearing the red smears like a badge of honour. Which was, no doubt, the way he saw it.

Was Cassie impressed? Arian spotted her, deep in conversation with Merial. They were on the embankment with a clear view of the contests but, judging by their lack of attention, the answer for both was a definite no.

"Come on. Who's next?" Leirmond shouted the challenge. He paced the ring of onlookers lining the dip on the hillside where boxing matches took place. He stopped in front of Kendric. "How about you? I've heard you're good with your fists."

"Once. Those years are long passed."

"Something else then? Name it." Leirmond's expression changed to a sneer. "But not hunt the thimble, or hopscotch."

"How about a horse race? Around Wolf Tor and back."

Leirmond's grin soured, but then he shrugged. "All right."

Boys ran to fetch horses, while the crowed moved up the embankment for a better view of the course. Gethryn stood at the finishing point, in front of the main gate. Soon, seven riders were ready, milling around, waiting for the signal. Gethryn held the ceremonial spear over his head then drove it, point first, into the ground. The riders set off at a wild gallop.

People cheered and whooped. The horses were briefly out of sight behind the sacred grove, before reappearing, crossing the river. The race continued, up the opposite hillside towards the lonely outcrop of rock.

"Come on, Mama. Play." Feran tugged on Arian's hand, and pointed to where his friend Wenda was poking something with a stick

"Wait a moment." Arian wanted to see how the race would end.

The riders were on their way back. The breakneck pace had slowed as the horses tired. The lead rider hitting the ford looked like Kendric, though Arian could not be sure. The horse at his shoulder stumbled on the steep descent of the riverbank, pitching the rider into the water. Another horse balked at the drop, forcing the rider to circle round and try again, and that one was certainly Leirmond. His bare chest made him easily identifiable.

Kendric held a clear lead as the horses pounded up the hill. Bending low in the saddle, he snatched up the spear, without slowing. The applause from the crowd was louder than anything heard so far that day. Kendric dismounted and handed the spear back to Gethryn.

Leirmond rode up last, looking furious. He jumped down, stalked to his horse's head, and pulled back his hand as if to punch it between the eyes. An immediate chorus of jeers erupted. Leirmond froze, then slowly mimed a punch that changed to a friendly pat at the last moment. Was anyone convinced? Arian had no doubt he would have struck the horse, were no one watching.

Arian went to congratulate Kendric. "Well done."

"Thank you."

She glanced around. Nobody apart from Feran was in earshot. "Did you know Leirmond would have trouble?"

"It was an easy guess. I've ridden the course enough times. You need to let a tired horse pick its own path on the return. Leirmond's the sort who wants to hammer everything to his will. So, no. I wasn't surprised with how it turned out."

"Play, Mama, play."

Kendric smiled down at Feran. "And it looks like you have your own headstrong young warrior who isn't ready to compromise."

Arian sighed. "I'll talk to you later."

"Yes. Later."

Normally, Arian would be happy to let Feran play unsupervised, but not with potentially dangerous games in progress.

Gethryn called the next contest. "Archery. Set the targets."

That was definitely one Arian did not want Feran anywhere near. Wherever Eilwen was, she and her friends ought to have enough sense to stay clear.

Wenda and her mother, Becca, were a safe distance away, yet close enough to keep an eye on the contests. Arian did not let go of Feran's hand until she joined them. Becca, a distant cousin, smiled a greeting.

Feran and Wenda were soon holding their own version of the games, seeing who could roll down the embankment quickest, and jumping over a mud puddle—or attempting to. Feran, and his clothes, were going to need a wash. Meanwhile, roars of encouragement along with cheers and groans marked the progress of the events.

"The boys' race." Gethryn's announcement was greeted by whoops.

Becca looked over. "Oh, poor thing."

"Who?" Arian asked.

"You sister. She's…" Becca shook her head.

Of course. The last full games had been at midsummer, the day of Yehan's rite of passage. Arian was annoyed at herself. She should have been more thoughtful. Everything must be dredging up memories for Merial, but nothing more so than the footrace for boys who had not yet passed into manhood.

That day was the last time Yehan had been eligible to take part, and he had won. He had always been quick on his feet. The image was easy to call to mind. Yehan running up the hill, his arms raised in triumph, people calling his name. It was Arian's only memory of Yehan where he had truly seemed one of the Lycanthi.

Merial was close to the main gate. Her face was buried in her hands while her body shook with sobs. Odella was holding Perri. Everyone else standing nearby looked awkward, except for Cassie, who had a supportive arm around Merial's shoulders. Odella nodded to Cassie, then rejoined her friends, taking her baby brother with her. Together, Merial and Cassie walked back through the gate. Nobody joined them. The vultures in the crowd were clearly looking forward to a fresh round of gossip. Yehan's tragic death had entertained people far more than anything that had happened during his life.

"Can you keep an eye on Feran for a while? I'll be back soon," Arian said to Becca.

"Of course."

The vultures did not need more to peck over. Rather than draw attention to herself, Arian slipped away in the opposite direction, around outside of the palisade. Once out of sight of the crowd she broke into a trot. As was normal during daytime, the side gate was unbarred. Inside, Breninbury was deserted. The lure of the games was too much to ignore. Even the elderly and infirm had been helped to a good vantage point.

Arian spotted Merial and Cassie rounding the end of the Great Hall but did not catch up until the courtyard of their house.

"Merial? How are you?"

"I'm..." Merial shook her head.

Cassie retreated tactfully, leaving them alone. Arian wrapped her sister in a hug. For a while Merial clung to her, then stepped away.

"I'll be fine. But..." Merial ran a hand over her hair, pulling it back from her forehead. "I'd rather be alone."

"You're sure?"

Merial did not answer. Her face held a mixture of pain and emptiness.

"I'll stay if you want."

"No. Go watch the games. We'll talk later. I want to lie down." Merial brushed Arian's cheek with a sisterly kiss, then ducked into her room.

Cassie was waiting outside the house. "Is she all right?"

"She will be. Let's go back."

"You go ahead. I want to grab a thicker cloak."

"I'll come with you." The words were out before Arian had time to think.

Cassie nodded in reply.

Arian waited in the courtyard of Cassie's house, the one that had been Nelda's and presumably would be again, after the Kavillians left. As befitting the Royal Quarter, it was well built, with stout walls and large rooms. But for the first time, the thought struck Arian, of how it might look in Cassie's eyes. Merial spoke of empire homes with hot baths, flowing water, wooden floors, and tiled roofs. Was it possible the houses in Breninbury were no more impressive than watching Leirmond batter his opponent?

"I'm ready." Cassie returned, pulling a long blue cloak around her shoulders. The material glistened with a sheen, as though wet. The colour was richer than anything made locally.

"Thank you for..." *Not acting like a bitch.* "...taking care of my sister."

Though, to be fair, Cassie and Merial had always got on well. Arian caught her lower lip in her teeth. Did she want her own relationship with Cassie to improve? Merial had said they could be on the same side. But could you trust a word Cassie said?

"It's a cruel hill to climb. Merial was telling me about Yehan winning the last race, and suddenly it was all too much for her." Cassie sounded sincere.

"Getting over a lost child takes time." How much longer before little Olin was not a raw wound in her heart?

"True."

"You said you had lost a child."

"Yes. Two. Both daughters." The words were clipped, emotionless. Cassie took a step to leave.

Yet here, surely was something raw, honest, and genuine, without games or half-truths. If she and Cassie were to build any level of trust, it was a place to start. "How old were they?"

"I..." Cassie stopped and took a deep breath. "Little Marci was just a couple of months. She was weak from the start. But Della? She was nearly six. I'd hoped...thought..." Cassie shook her head. "My boys. I'd known from the day they were born I'd be seeing them off before they were half grown. They were always bound for the army. If anything, I was lucky to keep them as long as I did. Mother got the upper hand in the divorce settlements. Della, though, I'd..." Cassie looked away. Were there tears glinting in her eyes? "A sickness swept through Kavilli one winter. Most survived. She didn't."

"I'm sorry."

"And I'm sorry for your son."

"You heard about Olin?"

"Finding out things is part of my job." Cassie tugged the cloak more firmly around her shoulders and again stepped towards the courtyard exit.

Arian stopped her with a hand on the arm. "What is your job, truly? What are you hoping to achieve here?"

"What I've said. I want a trade deal for iron and tin."

"Gethryn is never going to allow it."

"I'm hopeful. We're still talking and—"

"Talking will get you nowhere. You know that. You're far too smart not to."

"Thank you for your vote of confidence." Humour had returned to Cassie's voice.

"Merial says the empire will get what it wants. One way or another."

"Merial…" Cassie paused. "Obviously, she's more familiar with everyday life in the empire than most of your people. But that doesn't mean she's right about everything."

"She says we need to work with you. That the empire would be a better ally than enemy."

"I'd agree with her there."

"So what can the empire offer?"

"For your people as a whole, or you personally?"

"There's nothing I want."

Cassie laughed. "Ohhhh. I'd be envious, except that's not true."

"Nothing the empire has the power to grant."

"Such as?"

"I'd like to live forever and be able to fly. Those sort of things. You're not going to say the empire can give me that."

"No. You have me there. But there's other benefits for a woman like you." The last two words were delivered with a subtle emphasis.

"Like me?"

"You don't know what I'm talking about?"

"Should I?"

"We've discussed it before, admittedly very briefly, but I'm positive you won't have forgotten." Cassie was back at her games, teasing, taunting.

Arian's pulse kicked, but she was determined not to back down this time. "Remind me."

"Are you sure?" Cassie's eyes danced with amusement. "Did I tell you the story of why Mother picked me for this mission?"

"Is that what you think I won't have forgotten? Because…"

Cassie shook her head. "No. Not that bit. I'm digressing, but it is relevant. I seduced the wife of a rival senator. By bad luck, he came home unexpectedly and found us in bed together. Mother thought it would be better if my face wasn't seen around Kavilli for a while."

"I…" The air stuck in Arian's throat.

She should not have started this conversation. The only sensible thing—the only sane, prudent, virtuous thing, was to go. She had to put as much distance between herself and Cassie as possible, physical, mental, emotional, and everything else. But it was so hard. Like watching a snake slither through the grass. Deadly, dangerous, gut-wrenching. Yet so hard to look away.

"What's it to do with me?" Arian forced the words out.

"Come on. Are you telling me it's not something you've thought about? Dreamed about? The stirring of desire that sneaks up when you let your eyes linger too long on another woman?"

Arian's face burned. She shook her head in denial but could not speak.

Cassie took a step closer. "Has there never been a woman who's made your heart beat faster? You hear her voice and your knees grow weak? She walks into a room and the rest of the world fades away? Every day can be counted by the seconds that have passed since you last saw her?"

"Not you." The words came out as a squeak.

"Maybe not. But I'm the woman who's here now."

Cassie was so close the folds of their dresses brushed. She raised a hand and stroked Arian's cheek. The touch was so soft, yet so forceful, a lightning bolt through Arian's soul. Cassie's hand slipped behind her head and pulled their faces together. Their lips touched. At first the lightest butterfly caress, and then stronger, harder, moving with passion.

Arian wanted to pull back, but her body was in rebellion. Nothing worked. Her legs would not move. Her arms stayed glued to her sides. Only her mouth moved. Her treacherous, traitorous, disloyal mouth. The air squeezed from her lungs in a moan. Arian's lips parted, inviting in a wild, outrageous chaos, that could sweep her away, and take her to a place she could never escape from, yet was the only place she was supposed to be.

Time flipped through a loop, and then surged back. Arian's body returned to her control. She backed away, a hand held to her lips. Lips that felt more alive than ever before. Blood pounded in her veins, each heartbeat bringing with it a raw ache. Shock, surprise, and, to Arian's utter confusion, an urge to throw herself back into Cassie's arms.

And all the while, Cassie stood there, smiling at her. Knowing. Confident. Amused. That was the worst part. Cassie was playing games.

How dare she!

In the riot of emotions, anger was the only one Arian could trust. Cassie had tricked her, making her feel things she did not feel, and could never feel. It was all a lie, a trap. Arian pressed her hands against the sides of her head. If her skull burst open, that would be an end to it. She spun away, her knees loose as though she were drunk. But it was anger, not alcohol. Anger, and nothing else.

Arian stopped at the courtyard entrance and braced a hand on the wall. She needed to get herself under control, take a few moments to gather her breath and her composure, then rejoin the crowd watching the games, and act as though nothing had happened—act as though her life had not just upended itself.

A high-pitched shriek ripped through the air. A moment of silence, and then another scream. Had someone seen them kiss? But no. Although the person screaming was close at hand, they had no clear line of sight into the courtyard, and the timing was wrong. Arian stumbled outside, dimly aware of Cassie following.

A third scream. Nelda was backing away from the entrance to Arian and Merial's house. Her hands were fists, pressed against her cheeks, but that did not stop her giving one more, ear-piercing, shriek.

Arian forced her legs to move. "What's up? What's wrong?"

"Merial, she…she…" Nelda's lips quivered. She held out a hand, pointing. Her fingers were painted red.

Arian raced into the house and through the courtyard. She burst into Merial's room.

Merial lay on the bed, silent, unmoving. Her blank face stared at the rafters. The blanket pulled up to her neck was soaked in blood. Arian dropped to her knees and put a hand on Merial's forehead. The flesh was still warm to her fingers, but Merial was dead.

Odella sat on her bed, holding her sobbing younger sisters, one on either side. Aunt Ireni walked back and forth, rocking Perri in her arms, but with no hope of calming him. He was too young to understand what had happened but could not fail to pick up on the grief. His wails filled the room. Other relatives dithered in the background, wanting to help, but only making things worse. Arian finally managed to shoo them out.

"Would you like me to go as well?"

Odella nodded. "Thank you. The fewer people, the more chance of getting Perri to sleep."

Which was as Arian had thought. "If I can help, let me know."

"Of course."

She bent to plant a kiss on Odella's tear-streaked face, patted Aunt Ireni's shoulder, and left the house.

Fewer people were in sight than expected, given that the games had been abandoned. Or maybe she should not be surprised. It was hardly a normal afternoon. Arian walked the short distance to her own home, the one she had shared with Merial. Tears filled her eyes, blurring the scene.

She hesitated in the courtyard. Sitting alone in her room would only make things worse, but she did not feel up to talking. Even dealing with Feran and Eilwen would be a strain. Fortunately, a cousin was looking after them. It left her free to…do what?

Another sob shook her shoulders. Arian dashed a hand across her eyes. Merial was dead.

The sound of soft murmuring came from Merial's room, a soothing rhythmic chant. Tregaran was reciting prayers for the dead. He was someone she could talk to. Someone to make sense of it. He might even help her to feel better. Arian lifted the hanging over the door and entered the room.

Merial still lay on the bed, her position unchanged, although her eyes had been closed and the bloody blanket swapped for a clean one. Two lamps, one at her feet, one by her head, lit the room. Tregaran knelt beside the bed.

He stopped his chant and looked up. "Arian, how are you doing?"

"Awful."

"That's to be expected."

Arian sat on the ground beside Tregaran. "Why? Who'd want to hurt her?"

"The why remains to be seen. As for who…." Tregaran's tone held a grim satisfaction. "The guilty party has been named."

"Who?"

"The imperial envoy."

"What? No. It can't be."

"There's no doubt of it. We have a witness. The envoy was seen, running from this room, just before the body was discovered. I knew no good would come from the Kavillians' presence in our land, but I hadn't expected murder. She has shed Cadryn's blood."

Arian stared at Tregaran in confusion. "Who says they saw her?"

"Nelda."

"No. She's mistaken. Whatever she thinks she saw."

"You can't know that." Tregaran was sceptical

"I…." Arian swallowed. "Where is she?"

"In the Great Hall. Gethryn has summoned a court to try her."

Arian lurched to her feet. "I've got to go."

"It might be better if you don't…"

Arian did not stay to argue.

The crowd blocking the door was three deep. Arian shoved her way through. Inside was just as crowded. Some stood on benches for a better view. The only clear space was a ten-foot circle in front of Gethryn's throne. In the middle stood Cassie, with a warrior grasping either arm. Bran, looking bewildered and anxious, stood behind her, where he could deliver his translations directly into her ear.

Nelda was midway through her evidence. "…wondered what it was. Then I saw her—" She pointed at Cassie dramatically. "Running from our house. I went in and spoke to Merial. But she didn't say anything. Then I saw the blood. It was awful. She'd murdered poor Merial. Cut her throat." Nelda finished with a sob.

Gethryn looked stunned, a lost little boy. He made an effort to speak, but nothing came out. Leirmond took over. "Does anyone have something to add?"

"I do. Quite a bit, in fact." Cassie was surprisingly calm. How did she manage it? Bran gave the translation.

Leirmond glared at her. "You're going to deny it, of course."

"Actually, I was going to ask what possible reason I had for murdering Merial."

"Who cares? You did it." Nelda screamed the words.

Arian squeezed to the front of the crowd. Cassie glanced at her, and for an instant, a flicker of doubt showed, but it did not seep into Cassie's voice, which remained firm. "Whoever killed Merial has blood on their hands, quite literally." She held up her hands, palms out. "Blood sprays out when you cut someone's throat."

"You'd know that," Leirmond sneered, once he had heard the translation.

"I know many things."

"You washed your hands before you were caught."

"I'd have to scrub the blood from my fingernails and change my clothes. I didn't have time since I was detained immediately."

Arian had missed that part of the drama, being too caught up with Odella and the other children.

"You're trying to be clever. I know you did it." Yet Nelda's confidence was slipping.

Leirmond took over. "You're the only one it could have been. Everyone else was outside, watching the games."

It was time to speak up. "No. Not everyone. Whoever Nelda saw, it wasn't Cassie."

Leirmond turned to Arian. "How would you know?"

"Because I was with her."

The hall had been abuzz, people agreeing and conferring with their neighbours. Now there was silence.

Arian continued. "I saw Merial leave the games and wanted to make sure she was all right. I found her and Cassie talking in the courtyard of our house. Merial went inside to rest and…" Tears flowed down Arian's face and for a moment her voice faltered. "Cassie and I were coming back, but we stopped at her house while she picked up a cloak. We were still there talking, when Nelda screamed. Cassie can't have murdered my sister. She was with me the whole time."

"You weren't in Breninbury. We'd have seen you enter."

How dare Leirmond accuse her of lying. Anger kicked in. "I used the side gate. If you want, check with Becca. She was keeping an eye on Feran for me and saw me go."

Leirmond looked as if he had been slapped. "You'd swear to this?"

"By my ancestors and all the gods, at the sacred spring, if you want."

The stunned silence was broken by Nelda. "It wasn't the envoy. It was her maid."

"Can't have been her either," someone shouted. "She was getting frisky with that Kavillian fighter she hangs around. They went off to the woods together. Me and my friends were watching them, between keeping an eye on the races."

"You wanted to know who'd come first." Another shout was greeted by laughter.

Despite the seriousness, the situation was descending into farce, and Nelda continued to make it worse. "No. It was the other one I saw. Him." She pointed at Bran, who, despite looking surprised still gave the translation.

Cassie laughed. "You definitely, positively saw me, or someone six inches taller with short, blond hair, dressed as a man."

The warriors holding Cassie released her and shuffled back into the crowd, clearly sensing their role was over.

Gethryn slammed his hand on the arm of his throne. "Who murdered my sister?" His roar silenced the hall. He got to his feet, swaying like a drunk man. Tears rolled into his beard. "My sister's dead, the holder of my bloodline. She will be avenged."

"There's one possibility," Cassie said.

Gethryn turned on her. "What?"

"A spy from a rival tribe. The Endridi, perhaps. The side gate was open. The spy came in, thinking to cause trouble while Breninbury was empty. Maybe set fire to your grain store. They found Merial alone and chose another way of settling old scores. They might even have used a disguise. Perhaps that's who Nelda saw."

Nelda barely waited for the full translation.

"Yes. That's wh—" Leirmond elbowed her.

Gethryn looked around the hall, wild-eyed. "Go. Search the countryside. Leave nowhere unchecked. I will have my revenge. GO!" He bellowed the words.

People emptied from the hall, like sand from a bottle. Gethryn joined the outpouring. Leirmond shouted, calling the warband to grab their weapons and join the hunt. Before long the voices had faded, leaving only a few old folk and women behind.

Arian approached Cassie. "Do you really think it was an enemy spy?"

Cassie gave a humourless half laugh. "No. Of course not. Someone in Breninbury murdered Merial."

Wind rustled over the roof of the house. Mournful whispers. Arian shivered at the sound. Merial's body was washed and dressed in her best clothes. She lay on the bed that had once been their mother's. It was the bed where she and Merial had been born. The bed where their mother had died, and now the bed where Merial had been murdered. Tradition dictated it be so. Tradition could be cruel.

The blood-soaked bedding was gone, but phantom sights and smells tormented Arian. She stroked Merial's hair. Tomorrow would see another funeral pyre in the meeting ground. Who would have thought one might be needed again so soon?

The rustle of the door hanging made Arian look back. Lamplight wavered in the draft. Outside was dark. Night had fallen. Cassie stood in the doorway.

"What are you doing here?" Arian asked.

"I wanted to pay my respects to Merial. I'll come back later if you'd prefer."

"Do what you want. I'm not going anywhere."

Cassie entered the room. Her eyes glittered in the lamplight. Were imperial envoys trained to cry to order? Her manner had lost all its teasing, and a little of its assuredness. Or was this just another ploy in the game?

"Do your people believe in the afterlife?" Cassie asked.

"Of course."

"Then I hope your gods look on her kindly, and she's reunited with her son."

"Do you really care about her?"

"We got on well. Had time and place been different, we might have been close friends."

"Would you have tried to seduce her too?"

"No. She had no interest in women that way."

"And you think I..." Denying it was pointless. Cassie had seen through the facade. That was the most galling part. *She knew me better than I knew myself.*

Even now, sitting by Merial's dead body, the memory of kissing Cassie made her lips tingle. Easy to ignore what you have never acknowledged. But Cassie had forced her to face the demon inside, and it might never release her from its claws.

"I owe you my thanks," Cassie said.

"For what?"

"Speaking up for me. I'd wondered if you'd go along with Nelda's absurd attempt to frame me."

"You thought I'd lie?"

"I thought you might stay silent. Especially after what had just happened."

"You think honour means so little to me, or any of the Lycanthi? We do not lie or allow a lie to go unchallenged."

"Have you told that to Nelda?"

"She was mistaken."

"Oh, Arian, are you truly that innocent?" Cassie laughed softly. "Though I can't complain, since I've good reason to be grateful for your innocence and honour. If you hadn't spoken, Gethryn would have found me guilty of Merial's murder."

"He'd have taken your head from your shoulders."

"Is that your peoples' preferred method of execution?" Cassie's tone was back to its normal light-hearted nonchalance. "There are worse ways to die."

"Does honour mean nothing to you?"

"Of course it does. I have to take it into consideration when dealing with people. You and Kendric, Tregaran as well, I think. You need far more work. My job would be much easier if everyone was like Nelda, or…"

"Or who?"

Cassie shrugged. "Whoever it was who murdered Merial."

A fresh avalanche of grief struck Arian. "Why? Of all people, why Merial?"

"I wish I knew. But I'll leave you alone." Cassie got to the door then stopped and looked back. "Goodbye, Merial. I hope the afterlife has red wine and honey coated dates for you."

The door hanging fell back into place behind her.

Cassie

Bran tossed a stone into the river. The ring of ripples spread and twisted until they were lost in the current. "Who else could the murderer be, other than Nelda? She was right there, like you said, with blood on her hands. Why would she accuse you, other than to shift the blame from herself?"

"She hates me passionately, and I don't have a clue why." Normally, Cassie could at least make a guess. "I don't suppose you've heard anything?"

"She did get kicked out of her house to make room for us."

Did that deserve a laugh or a groan? "She could keep it. I'd be happier over there, in the tents. Cassie indicated Kendric's campsite on the other side of the river.

"I admit it's not much of a motive."

"Certainly not if she murdered Merial purely for the chance to frame me. If she had another reason, the house might put my name at the top of the list. But I don't see Nelda being able to work out the scheme on her own."

"It didn't need much planning."

"The murderer had to be quick off the mark. They couldn't have known in advance Merial would leave the games early, or I'd be alone with her, as they thought. Even if Nelda just happened to find the body, she isn't sharp enough to think, *Here's my chance to get back at the bitch who stole my house*. The idea wouldn't tunnel its way into her head until the next day, at the earliest. You saw her attempt at thinking on her feet."

"Claiming she could have mistaken me for you?"

"Exactly. However, if she didn't work out the plan for herself, it means someone put her up to it."

"She knows who the murderer is."

"She must." Cassie continued walking along the riverbank. The afternoon was cloudy but dry. Workers were carrying the final few logs up the hillside for Merial's pyre. "The question is, who would she be willing to cover up a murder for?"

"Her brothers?"

"They have to be high on the list. Except for lack of a motive. Why would they want me dead? Moving Nelda's son closer to the throne ties in with killing Yehan, but not the two attempts on my life. It's not even a strong motive for Merial. Her son and Arian's are the ones in the way."

"They grabbed the chance when it was there. Without Merial to protect her son, he's more vulnerable."

"Killing the king's sister is a big risk, especially one he's fond of. I don't think the benefit justifies it."

"What other motive could there be?"

"Money, power, sex, secrets. They're the usual reasons. You can add war with the empire. We know Leirmond would like that. Having Gethryn execute me would be a sure way to start one. And he's still upset I turned down his offer of a romp. He's done nothing but scowl at me since."

"Neither of those reasons work for Yehan's murder."

"True. And why Merial? Though, according to Arian, she wanted the Lycanthi to ally with the empire. If anyone could get Gethryn to agree, Merial would be the one. Which would wreck Leirmond's dreams of glorious carnage."

Cassie looked up. Seen from below, the embankments were intimidating. In practice, they would not stop a legion, especially when the hillfort was so vulnerable to siege. The main problem lay in the land itself. Mountains and forests were suited to ambush, which played to the Lycanthi warriors. She had to find a way to tip the balance in Quelin's favour.

"Merial and Leirmond had an argument a few nights ago," Bran said.

"What about?"

"I don't know. It was mentioned in passing. I wasn't able to dig deeper. All anyone wanted to talk about back then were the upcoming games."

"The murder will have changed that."

Bran nodded. "I'll see what I can find out. And if anyone else argued with Merial recently."

"Do that. I'd love to put Leirmond at the top of the list of suspects."

"Why him?"

"Because he's an obnoxious, arrogant, idiot. Although if being one was a crime, we'd need gallows all the way from here to Kavilli."

"And back again." Bran was not wrong.

"It's not just personal dislike, there's some marks against Leirmond. He was definitely trying to control Nelda's testimony, as though he'd schooled her in what to say. Then he got angry when it fell apart. But…" She glanced at Bran. "You're certain he was on the meeting ground, when the rock was dropped on me?"

"Yes. I checked with others who were there. They all agree."

"And I guess he's too tall to be the one who took the swipe at me. Though he does have his share of followers. Are there any names you can think of? People who'd carry out murder for him?"

"I'm sure there's some."

"It'll mean adding to the list of suspects." Things were not getting easier. "Is there anyone we can rule out now, apart from Arian?" She definitely could not have killed Merial.

"Gethryn. He was calling the games. Anyone else might have snuck off for a few minutes, but not him."

"That's some sort of progress. Not that he was much of a candidate. Whatever he might have felt about Yehan, he'd never harm Merial."

The light was fading. Behind the blanket of cloud, the sun was close to setting. No stars would show that night. On the opposite bank of the river, a group were heading to the ford. Kendric and his followers were coming to pay their last respects to Merial.

"We should go back for the funeral. We'll talk more tomorrow." Cassie started up the hill.

Gusts of wind whipped up the pyre. Flames snapped at the night, all the brighter without competition from stars or moon. Nothing broke the cloud cover. A mist of rain fell, as if the sky itself was weeping for Merial.

As usual at massed gatherings, Cassie stayed well back, observing the people, with Bran beside her, offering explanations and analysis. An overhanging roof provided shelter from the worst of the wind and rain.

Gethryn stood nearest the pyre, so close the heat must sting his skin, though he showed no sign of retreating. Firelight washed over him, reddening his face. Leirmond had tried talking to him, but left after being ignored.

Arian was a few yards back, surrounded by female relatives. Her young nieces clutched her skirt, watching the fire take their mother. Odella stood beside Arian, holding the baby. Aunts and cousins formed a supportive ring. The hillfort inhabitants were bound in a web of family relationships.

Cassie leaned towards Bran. "What's happening with Merial's children? Will Arian or Odella look after them now?"

"Odella. Siblings stick together. When Perri grows up, his sister's children will be his heirs. If anything happens to Arian's son, it will affect who gets to sit on the throne, after Gethryn." For now, though, the baby's main concern would be finding a wet nurse.

Cassie's eyes kept returning to Arian. Kissing her had been fun, but very unwise. Why had she given in to the temptation? Admittedly, talking about her daughters had left her uncomfortably vulnerable, but that was not an excuse. Cassie forced her eyes to move away. She dared not let her emotions lead her into even greater slips.

Kissing Arian could so easily have proved fatal. Luckily, Arian had not fled until after Merial's body was discovered, and so could provide the alibi. Arian's sense of honour was also fortunate, and intriguing.

Arian would not lie, except to herself. She was intelligent but could not see what was before her. She was proud and confident but refused to back her own judgment. And, for a dozen heartbeats, she had returned the kiss with passion. Despite the appalling lack of wisdom, the thought of kissing Arian again was dangerously enticing. A warmth flowed through Cassie at the memory, setting off a deep ache inside. Without intending it, she found herself again staring at Arian.

The wind gusted hard, then eased, and the crackle of flames died down. The sudden lull allowed Cassie to hear the sound of cautious footsteps, drawing closer. Someone was sneaking up behind her. She immediately moved forward into the circle of firelight, then turned to look round.

Two men were edging around the side of the building. Neither was known to her. For their part, both men were clearly caught by surprise. One moved to follow Cassie, but his companion grabbed his arm and jerked him back into the shadows.

Bran was also aware of them. He moved into position between the men and Cassie. However, rather than retreat or attack, they gestured for Bran to come close. After a moment of hesitation, he joined them in the shelter of the eaves.

Bran beckoned to Cassie. "It's all right."

"Who are they?"

"They came with Kendric."

"They work for him?"

"Sort of, but…" Bran looked around. "We should go somewhere less public."

"You trust them?"

"Yes. And I think you'll want to hear what they have to say. But they'd rather not be seen talking to you."

Bran's judgment had been sound. And, since Kendric had arrived after the first attempt on her life, the men could not be responsible. Cassie let herself be led to the deserted kitchen. The bondservant cooks would not be back until dawn. She stood close to the bread oven, enjoying the heat given off by the thick clay walls. Bran lit a lamp, using the last red embers. In its light Cassie noted neither man had blue warrior tattoos, but their beards were neatly braided. Presumably, this meant they were neither warriors nor serfs.

"This man is a mine overseer, and his companion works for Kendric's quartermaster." Bran's introduction confirmed their social class.

"Do they have names?"

"They prefer not to say."

"What are they willing to say?"

The quartermaster's assistant licked his lips nervously before speaking. "There's a trader who visits the mines, bringing stuff from Verina. He also brings news. And he says…" The man licked his lips again. "The empire wants to expand the mines. Do more business with the miners."

Cassie made a show of waiting for Bran's translation. "That's why I'm in Breninbury. I'm negotiating on behalf of the empire."

"My boss, the quartermaster, he says the king's never gonna agree."

"What makes him think King Gethryn won't let the mines expand?" The quartermaster was right, but his reasoning would be interesting

"It's a question of who gets their hands on the money."

"Who is the king worried about?"

"Us." The overseer was more forceful than his companion. "My family have worked the mines for generations. The ore's in our blood. We're down there from dawn till dusk, crawling in spaces barely big enough for our shoulders, just to dig out a few piddly pounds of rock. Everyone knows empire mines are as big as streets, with donkey carts hauling ore by the ton. And the miners get to live in fine houses and drink as much beer as they want every day."

This might not be strictly true, but there was no need to correct him. And it was all relative. Compared to Breninbury, the average empire hovel was a huge step up, and getting drunk was a common hobby for large sections of the working population.

"You think the king wants you to stay poor?"

"I know he does. All them lordly folk, getting fat off our hard work, and thinking they're so much better than us. They want us under their boots. Earl Kendric's the only one worth a fart in a barrel."

Bran translated the phrase literally, without explanation. Clarification could wait, and even without it, the sentiment was clear. "You approve of your lord?"

"He's fair, maybe a bit set in his ways. But he's another reason the king won't let the mines get bigger. They made Earl Kendric lord of Yanto's Leap, thinking he'd be out of the way. But he's done all right by us. More ore and fewer accidents. Nobody's gone hungry. The king would be pissed off if he knew, 'cus the two of them hate each other." The man gave a one shoulder shrug. "The king wouldn't want Earl Kendric sitting on the richest part of the kingdom."

"If all this is true, why are you talking to me?"

"The trader I told you about, he says the empire won't take no for an answer. And well…we all know what that means."

"And?"

The nervous companion took over. "We're not fighters. We can't help that way, but we've got eyes and ears. We've got family out in the farms. We know what's going on, and who's where."

"You'd pass this information on to the legion commander?"

Both men nodded in response to Bran's translation.

"How would you contact us? Or we you?"

"There's a token we use. The people who deal with the trader. So we know who to trust."

"Ah. That sort of trader." Otherwise known as a smuggler.

"You take a sprig of white heather and stick it in the top of your left boot, so it just shows. If you see someone with that token, you know he's from us and has things to tell you."

"Then in turn, I promise the information will be rewarded with gold coin. The more useful it is, the more gold." The broad smiles were a promising sign. People who were keen on money were always easy to work with. "Is there anything else?"

"When the empire's in charge, we don't want the lordly folk giving orders, grabbing all the money, and leaving us with nothing."

Certainly nobody would want either Gethryn or Leirmond in charge. "It'll need agreement from all parties, and I can guarantee, whatever happens, someone will be unhappy. But you say Earl Kendric is fair, and from what I've seen of him, I agree. I'll seek his approval for any arrangements made."

The men exchanged a look and nodded. "Deal." They slipped away into the night.

Bran looked at Cassie. "Was that useful?"

"Oh yes. Very. My cousin Quelin will have a much easier time if he knows where the enemy is, and doesn't need to worry about ambushes, or being outmanoeuvred." If nothing else came of her time in Breninbury, it was one positive development to take back.

"Are you sure you can get Kendric to go along with this?"

Cassie laughed. "I said I'd seek his approval. Regrettably, I expect to be disappointed. But I'm not ruling it out. Either way, it's an issue for tomorrow. Come on. Let's go back to the funeral."

Cassie strolled between the houses, smiling and nodding at everyone she passed. Some smiled back, most did not. During her time in Breninbury, the percentage of people who smiled had shifted her way, but not by enough to get excited about. Certainly nothing as significant as meeting the miners' representative the night before.

Divide and conquer had been Mother's advice. She had a division. Commoners and nobility were not on the same side. Even if the lower orders could offer little help in a war, they would be a docile, compliant population post-conquest. All the empire had to do was offer them a better life than their own lords had done. It was not a high bar to get over.

Snippets of overheard conversation added nothing of note. Everyone was horrified at Merial's death, had no idea who was responsible, but were pleased the funeral had gone well. Cassie headed back to the house for lunch. She rounded the end of the Great Hall into the Royal Quarter. Both names still made her smile. In the empire, the hall would serve as a cow barn. The houses would be pigsties.

The thought shot straight out of her head. Arian was a dozen steps away, coming in the opposite direction. They saw each other at the same moment. Arian took a hitch step, as if her legs tried to stop walking without first asking her permission. Her face darkened in a blush, and her eyes fixed somewhere over Cassie's left shoulder.

Cassie hoped she covered her own reaction better, despite the flutter in her stomach. Kissing had been a huge mistake, opening the flood gates. The risk of becoming besotted was a real concern. Despite Arian's innocence and artlessness, there was a strength to her. An inner resolve. What would she look like if that resolve was breached? What would she look like, in the heat of passion, naked on a bed? The image was so tempting to play with.

"Good morning, Arian."

"Good morning, Cassie."

They passed each other and carried on walking. Or Cassie assumed they both did, since she did not look back, but the temptation to stop and check on Arian was overwhelming. She clenched her teeth and concentrated on putting one foot in front of the other.

The harder she tried not to think about kissing Arian, the harder it became to think of anything else. There was a murderer on the loose, and war on the horizon. She needed to keep a clear head. She had to stay in control. Mistakes could be deadly. And yet, every time she let her guard down, her mind would drift into fantasies of Arian. It was fun. It was also very dangerous.

Bran was waiting in the courtyard of the house. "I've got information about Merial's argument with Leirmond."

"Good." Cassie beckoned for him to join her in her room. They sat on the three-legged stools. "What have you found out?"

"I tracked down a bondservant who was working in the Great Hall that night. Like you said. Merial wanted Gethryn to throw his lot in with the empire. Leirmond got more and more angry. In the end he slapped her across the face."

"Really!"

"Gethryn was furious. He ordered Leirmond never to strike his sister again. Nobody has ever seen him stand up to Leirmond before."

"That must have come as a shock for Leirmond."

"It did. He was overheard muttering about it later."

"Any details?"

Bran shook his head. "Just a lot of rude words."

Massillo stuck his head around the door hanging. He held out a wooden bowl. "Tullia sent lunch for you, my lady." He looked at Bran. "Sorry. She didn't know you were here."

"It's all right. I'll get my own."

A wise decision. Even when roast meat was unavailable, the Lycanthi produced passable bread and cheese. Yet Tullia had a knack for finding the most unappealing combinations of food.

"I'll eat outside." Cassie wanted to see what it was before putting anything in her mouth.

But for once the meal was reasonable, sliced meat, rye bread, and vegetables mashed with yoghurt and herbs. She tore off a corner of crust to use as a scoop. The vegetables were cold, with a savoury aftertaste Cassie half recognised, but could not place. Overall, it was far from the worst thing she had eaten in Breninbury. Had Massillo played a part in choosing it?

"Where's Tullia?" she asked.

"She's got laundry on the racks. She wanted to check if it was dry. She asked me to bring you lunch." Massillo shuffled towards the exit. "And, um…I said I'd go meet her."

Cassie noted the soft leather flask hanging on his belt. Massillo was known to have a fondness for drink. His meeting with Tullia would doubtless involve alcohol and limited clothing, dry or otherwise.

After he had gone, Cassie ate her lunch while mulling over Bran's story. What would have upset Leirmond more, Merial urging a compromise with the empire, or the fact she had the power to get between him and Gethryn? Would either be a sufficient motive for murder?

Cassie finished off the meat and took another scoop of mashed vegetables. Who else would want Merial dead? What was she missing? Leirmond could not be the person who dropped the rock on her, but might he have more accomplices? He clearly had Nelda dancing to his tune. And, beyond this, was there any way she could get Arian into bed?

Bran returned with his own lunch at the same time as Tullia appeared, carrying a bundle of clean clothes. Had Massillo not found her at the drying rack, or did they have an arrangement to meet elsewhere? Either way, Tullia seemed in no rush to join him and began folding the clothes.

The vegetables were almost gone. Cassie tore off another piece of crust. The first scoop was now soggy and not up to the task. She was about to wipe up the last mouthful when the tingling in her lips grew to the point of claiming her attention. How long had it gone unnoticed? Immediately, the tingling turned to numbness, spreading over the roof of her mouth. Now she recognised the savoury aftertaste. Why had she not noticed it before?

Please. By all the gods, let it not be too late.

Cassie hurled the bowl aside. She stumbled across the courtyard, dropped to her knees, and grasped the water bucket in both hands. Between breaths, she gulped down as much as she could, then stuck two fingers down her throat. The vomit landed where it would.

Shouts from Bran and Tullia. "My lady?"

"What are you…"

More water. Repeat the process. Pray she was in time. The numbness was spreading, forming a hand around her throat. Her heartbeat raced. Her lungs were tight. Blackness and stars swam around the edges of her vision. Her stomach heaved, no longer needing encouragement to empty itself.

Sounds in the courtyard were muffled. Even Tullia's high-pitched shrieks were coming from a long way off. The darkness was winning, bringing with it silence. Her body no longer belonged to her. The water bucket dropped from hands not strong enough to hold it. Night flowed in, devouring the world.

The pounding of hoofbeats. Wild horses, tearing through the night. They were going to trample her. She had to move, get out of their way, but the beating was so loud she shook with each hammer blow.

Cassie opened her eyes. At first, the blurred shapes refused to shift into focus. She blinked, surprised at the effort it took. Wavering lamplight danced on a ceiling of woven branches and grass roots. She lay in bed, dreaming, and still the pounding continued. Her heart beat to a staccato rhythm. It was trying to break out of her chest. She gasped, taking in air like a diver emerging from the depths.

"Here. Drink this." Arian's voice, close by.

Cassie rolled her head to the side. "Huh?"

"You were poisoned."

Yes. Of course she was. Mother would be furious. The plant was common enough, flowering across the empire and beyond. It was one of many she had been taught to recognise—a drop of sap on her tongue just long enough to learn the taste before washing it away.

"Widows' nightcap." Cassie's mouth fought her.

"What?"

"Widows' nightcap…its name."

Arian was kneeling by the bed. She slipped an arm around Cassie's shoulder, urging her to sit. It was not fair. She and Arian were alone in her bedroom, and some bastard had poisoned her. Cassie could have cried.

"Drink this." Arian held up a beaker. "Tregaran prepared it. He knows more about herbs than anyone."

Mother could surely match him when it came to poison. Cassie sniffed cautiously, except her nose was not behaving. Nor were her lips. She managed a sip without too much running down her chin. The numbness in her mouth lifted a little. But her heart was the critical thing. Would it give out before morning?

"Where's Tul…" A wobble of nausea took over.

"Your maid?" Arian said. "She's still hysterical. She says if she'd had any idea what he intended, she'd never have let him near the food."

"He?"

"Her bedfellow…Massalon. Something like that. The man who gave you the poisoned food."

"Massillo." Cassie gestured for another mouthful of Tregaran's potion. "What's he say?"

"We don't know. He's vanished. Run away before he could be questioned."

Yet the idea of Massillo trying to kill her was absurd. He had been with the family since he was old enough to work. Cassie remembered playing with him when they were children. He was only a year older than her. First, he had been in the stables, before being put forward for the years of training as a bodyguard.

"Why..." *are you here?*

"We don't know why he did it. It'll have to wait till he's found. Gethryn has warriors searching for him."

Arian had not guessed the right question, although it was a safer one to answer.

Cassie took another sip then signalled to lie down. Her mouth and throat were better, but her heart thumped in a wild, off-kilter drumming, as if every beat might be its last. And it might. Widows' nightcap could make the strongest hearts burst, and the weakest give up. But if a victim survived the initial attack, there was little long-term harm. Death either came within a day, or not at all.

Cassie closed her eyes. The next few hours were the critical ones. If she was still alive in the morning the worst would be past. If not, then it would all be someone else's problem.

Arian

Arian watched Cassie slip back into a restless sleep. She put down the beaker with Tregaran's potion. What was she doing there? The question circled in her mind with a persistence matched only by her refusal to look inside herself for an answer. She needed to be there. That was all. Tomorrow she could dig through her thoughts and emotions and dredge up an excuse. But not now. Not tonight.

Cassie mumbled nonsense between laboured gasps. Arian closed her eyes. Was she imagining the sound of erratic beats? She brought an ear close to Cassie's chest and concentrated. Yes. A faint patter, skipping and jumping, which suddenly stopped. In panic, Arian grasped Cassie's wrist, but even before she could put her finger on the pulse, the beats resumed, racing at double time to make up for the lapse.

Cassie might yet die. Tregaran had said as much when he examined her. His potion could ease the symptoms but not cleanse the poison from her body. Cassie's life lay in the hands of the gods. Did it matter she was no longer in the homeland of her ancestors? Would they still speak for her? Did distance matter in the afterlife?

Arian reached out to stroke the hair from Cassie's face, just as the door hanging was pulled back. She froze guiltily, though the action could be seen as that of an attentive nurse. When she was sure her expression was under control, Arian turned, expecting to see Tregaran. Instead, Tullia stood there, looking confused. Her hysterical crying had stopped.

"I…er…it's good of you to take care of my lady. I'll look after her now." Tullia found her voice.

Arian got to her feet. She did not want to leave, but now had even less reason to be there. "If you need anything, please send for me."

Tullia gave a weak smile. "Yes. Thank you."

Night was falling. The last purple of sunset painted the clouds in the west. Arian wandered over to the palisade. The hills, woods, river, and valley were the same as always. Yet everything had changed and could never go back.

Demons were supposed to lose their power when you named them, yet hers had strengthened a thousandfold—the demon that had always been there, hiding in the deepest recesses of her heart.

Cassie's challenge echoed in her head. *"Has there never been a woman who made your heart beat faster? You hear her voice and your knees grow weak? She walks into a room and the rest of the world fades away? Every day can be counted by the seconds that have passed since you last saw her?"*

Yes. There had been. Of course there had. But unnamed could be ignored. Then Cassie had kissed her. Now Arian knew the name of her demon and would never be free of it.

Even if Cassie died, she would never be free.

"Damn her. Damn her to the deepest pit of hell." But that was unfair. Cassie had not given life to the demon. She merely dragged it into the light and given it a name. Desire.

Arian left the palisade, heading back to her home, although there was no point going to bed. She would not sleep. A long, wearisome night lay ahead.

As she passed the Great Hall, a surge of excited voices broke out. Something had happened. Arian entered through the rear door. In the glow of the fire, a group of warriors were huddled around Gethryn, talking and pointing. More people arrived as word spread. Tregaran stood in the shadows to one side, his expression sombre.

Arian approached him. "Do you know what's going on?"

"Yes. They've found the fugitive."

"Has he confessed?"

"No. Nor will he. He's dead. Presumably from the same poison he tried to kill his mistress with. They found him in the woods overlooking the lower pool. His body has been dragged back and is outside."

"So we'll never know why he tried to kill Cassie?"

"He certainly cannot tell us." Tregaran frowned. "Of more concern to me is knowing why he murdered your sister."

"You think it was him?"

"I was certain from the start it was one of the Kavillians. None of our people would dare shed Cadryn's blood. The only question is whether he worked alone or had an accomplice." Tregaran paused. "Has the envoy woken?"

"Only briefly. She took some of your potion."

"She was able to drink it? That's good."

"Do you think she'll live?"

He shrugged. "Did she say anything?"

"Not much. She wasn't awake long."

"Hmmm." Tregaran stroked his beard, looking troubled. "I wouldn't count on her speaking the truth, anyway."

Arian stared at him. "You don't suspect her of being involved, do you? She was the victim."

"When conspirators fall out, they don't value their former associates' lives any higher than their other victims."

"No. I'm sure Cassie is innocent."

Tregaran sighed. "You may be right about the murder. But you cannot deny the Kavillians' influence. We need them gone, and the sooner the better. This envoy will spread her corruption. None of us, not even you or I, will be safe."

The memory of their kiss swept over Arian. She looked down, praying the darkness would hide her burning cheeks. She was saved by the sound of movement. Gethryn and the warriors had finished talking and were going to inspect the body lying outside. They carried torches, lit from the fire.

Tregaran patted her shoulder. "I must attend to my duties. Even murderers require their due rites. We can talk more tomorrow." He followed Gethryn from the hall.

Arian slipped out through the rear door. She had no need to look on yet more death. Far more vital, before seeking her bed, Arian had to see Cassie again. She had to confirm Cassie was still breathing, because the other possibility was unbearable.

Tregaran's words had also given birth to a worm of doubt, crawling in her gut. There was a reason the dead man had not been a suspect in Merial's murder. He had been with his lover, the maid. Arian could not share Tregaran's certainty in the Kavillians' shared guilt, but, at the very least, Tullia had questions to answer.

True night had fallen. The waning moon had crept over the horizon, sending cold beams to light the world in silver, blue, and black. Nobody was moving between the houses. Those not in their beds would be at the meeting ground, viewing the body. Murderers were rare in Breninbury. People would want to see the man who had killed Merial.

The hurdle was across the entrance to Cassie's house. As quietly as possible, Arian shifted it out of the way and went to the inner doorway. She stopped, bracing her hands against the stone wall on either side. This was stupid, ridiculous. Talking to Tullia could wait until tomorrow, and no matter what Cassie's condition, nothing she could do might help. For the sake of her own self-esteem, she should not play the part of a lovelorn fool.

Arian was about to turn away when she heard scrabbling. Was it rats? Then came the rustle of bedding and a muffled groan. The mumble turned into the stifled, desperate whimpers of someone caught in a nightmare. The scrabbling became frantic.

Arian tugged the door hanging aside, letting moonlight spill into the room. Cassie was lying on the sleeping platform just as before, except Tullia sat astride her chest. For the barest instant, Arian thought she was interrupting a moment of intimacy. But no. Her eyes adjusted to the darkness. Tullia had a bundled blanket, pressed hard over Cassie's face.

"What are you—"

Even before Arian spoke, the sound at the door had alerted Tullia. She turned her head, yet she did not move away. And still she held the blanket in place. "I..."

Cassie's legs were twitching, her heels scraping the bed, in a weak attempt to squirm free.

"GET OFF HER." Arian bellowed the words, lurching into the room.

"No, it's not—" Finally, Tullia scrambled off Cassie and skittered away backwards across the room on elbows, arse, and heels, crablike.

Cassie sucked in a breath, then another. Each wheeze sounded as though it was dragged from the bottom of her lungs. Arian dropped to her knees beside the sleeping platform.

Bran burst into the room. "What's up?"

Another Kavillian, the second fighter, was in the doorway behind him, a huge shape, blocking the moonlight.

Arian pointed. "Her. She was trying to smother Cassie."

"No, I…no." The maid stumbled over the words, in helpless denial. Her back was pressed against the far wall.

"I saw her. She's the one. She's the murderer."

"Bring in the prisoner." Emlyn's cry cut through the clamour filling the Great Hall.

Immediately, noise and motion stilled, but did not cease completely. Excitement was bubbling over, sweeping even the wisest heads along in a tide of speculation. Two elderly councillors sitting behind Arian continued the conversation between themselves in hushed tones.

"You think she murdered Merial as well?"

"There's no doubt."

"Why would she do it?"

"I'm sure Gethryn will ask her. But it's what Kavillians are like. Murder is in their blood. The envoy will be behind the plot, mark my words. She'll have…um…" The councillor's assertions ground to a halt, as he grappled with finding a plausible reason for Cassie organising a double attempt on her own life. "Anyway, Nelda told the truth. She did see a dark-haired woman run away. She got them confused. It's easily done. Kavillians all look the same."

Arian shook her head in disbelief. As if you could mistake Cassie for her maid. Even without seeing their faces, Cassie's vibrant satins could not be confused with the neutral woollens Tullia wore. At most, Nelda had caught a glimpse of someone and made a lucky guess.

Gossip in Breninbury had been on fire. The councillor was not alone in his assumptions. Everything Arian overheard was a variation on the lovers, maid and bodyguard, conspiring to murder Merial, while providing each other with an alibi. Tullia had then duped her lover into poisoning Cassie and disposed of him. When the poison did not work, Tullia tried suffocation. And had Cassie been found dead in the morning, she might have got away with it.

Best of all, as far as the gossip went, the Kavillians were responsible for everything. Being able to lay the blame on outsiders was comforting. Arian battled a twisting knot of doubt. It was too convenient. This did not make it untrue, but she would be happier once she had answers. The foremost was why? What reason did Tullia have for wanting Cassie and Merial dead?

The Great Hall was full, but more orderly than for the previous farce of a trial. The tables were pushed back, and no one was standing on them. The benches were arranged to provide seating for councillors and witnesses. Tregaran was on the right of the king's throne. Leirmond was inconspicuous in the background. Other spectators lined the walls. The steward, Emlyn, stood alone in the middle of the hall.

A stream of daylight through the open doorway leached colour from the fire in the hearth. The rest of the population were gathered outside on the meeting ground, trying to peer in. Their voices formed a background rumble. Suddenly, the sound grew into a chorus of jeers and angry shouts. All heads turned as prisoner and escort entered the hall.

Tullia's wrists and ankles were tied. She was half-dragged, half-carried into the centre, then thrown to the ground. She barely managed to break her fall with her bound hands. One guard grabbed her shoulder and hauled her up until she was sitting on her heels.

Streaks of tears lined the dirt on Tullia's face. Her dress was torn at the neck and her feet were bare. Bruises and scrapes on her exposed skin spoke of rough handing. Her terror was easy to read. Her eyes were open wide, giving an impression of seeing little and understanding less. Arian might have felt pity, were it not for the twin memories of Merial's blood-soaked body and Tullia astride Cassie's chest, trying to smother the life out of her.

True silence fell. No one spoke. No one moved. Gethryn's face was fixed in a snarl of animal rage. His hands locked on the arms of his throne, clenched hard enough to turn his knuckles white. Finally, he signalled to Emlyn, but before the steward could open the trial, a fresh disturbance rippled through the crowd.

People near the rear door shifted aside to make way for Cassie. Her face was drained and her movement unsteady. She shuffled from foot to foot, leaning heavily on Bran's arm, but she was alive and back on her feet. Arian clamped her hand over her own mouth to hide her disproportionate reaction. People would surely wonder at the idiotic smile. Fortunately, all eyes were on Cassie, as space was made for her at the end of a bench.

"I call on all present, to witness the justice done here today." Emlyn began the trial. "Prisoner, what do you have to say for yourself?"

Tullia gaped at him blankly. Cassie nudged Bran, who stood and gave the translation. Tullia's eyes widened and she opened her mouth, but no sound came out, until prompted by a guard's foot.

"No. No. It was a mistake. I didn't mean it. I wouldn't. It was all Massillo's doing."

Bran made a heroic effort to translate the inarticulate string of denials.

"Are there any here to bear witness?" Emlyn continued.

Arian stood. "I am."

"Step forward and speak."

Arian moved to the middle of the hall and faced Gethryn. "I saw her, with my own eyes. Tullia was trying to smother Cassie. I was on my way to bed but stopped off to see how Cassie was doing."

Bran's translation produced a squeal from Tullia. "No. It wasn't how it looked. I—" Her protest was cut off by another kick from a guard.

"When I got to the house, I heard a disturbance. I went into the room and saw Tullia pressing a folded blanket over Cassie's face. I called for her to stop, which she did, but only when others arrived. She was trying to murder Cassie. I saw her. I..." *I couldn't bear it if Cassie had died.* "I'm certain, if I hadn't stopped her, Cassie would have been found dead in the morning." Arian battled the urge to look in Cassie's direction. They needed to talk, but it would have to wait.

"Do you have more to add?" Emlyn asked.

Arian shook her head. "Unless anyone has questions."

Nobody spoke. Emlyn motioned for Arian to sit. "Do others wish to bear witness?"

"I do." For once, Bran spoke on his own behalf. "I'd just gone to bed when I heard shouting. My first thought was that my lady had died from the poison. I rushed in. I wasn't in time to the see the assault, but Tullia still had the folded blanket in her hands. I took it from her and examined it. The imprint of my lady's face was clear to see in its folds. There's no doubt Tullia had been trying to suffocate her."

"And you, Lady Cassilania, do you have anything to add?"

Cassie waited for translation. "No. I woke from a nightmare, but my state of mind was confused. I couldn't say what part was true and what part was a bad dream." Her voice was quieter than normal, but steady.

"Is there anyone else?"

Tregaran stepped forward. "I questioned the bondservants in the kitchen. They confirm the accused and her lover were there together. He selected the food for his mistress while the accused filled a leather flask with mead. She was acting furtively, presumably since she's aware it isn't for everyday consumption."

"Why didn't they stop her from taking the mead?" Emlyn asked.

"She's done it before. She hides behind her inability to speak our language."

"Go on."

"The bondservants are certain nobody other than those two could have added poison to the food." Tregaran paused. "The only thing in doubt is whether the man took his own life or was murdered by the accused to ensure his silence."

"Is there anyone else who wishes to speak?" Emlyn looked around the hall.

"Yes." Gethryn's voice cracked like a whip. "This is none of my concern. Who cares why Kavillians murder each other? The fewer of them left, the better. But what about my sister? Why did you murder Merial?"

Tullia stared at Bran as he gave the translation. "No. Not her. I…No."

"You're lying." Gethryn launched himself from his throne and stood, stabbing a finger towards Tullia. "You murdered her."

"I saw her running away." Nelda piped up from the edge of the room.

"No. It was Massillo. It was all his doing. He did it. Not me. I…" Tullia's mumbled stream of denials continued until her voice choked off in sobs. She hung her head, surely knowing her situation was hopeless.

"Get the truth from her." Gethryn gave the order.

The guards grabbed Tullia's shoulders and dragged her backwards so she ended up flat on the ground. One knelt across her legs while another took a branding iron from the fire. The end glowed dull red.

"No. No. No—" Tullia's cries ended in shrieks, loud enough to lift the roof. The screams went on and on while the stench of roasting flesh drifted through the air. A third guard joined his comrades, holding the writhing woman.

Arian tore her eyes away. Faces around the Great Hall reflected the usual range of reactions, everything from excitement to revulsion. Only Cassie appeared disinterested. Some of the women, Nelda included, pressed their hands over their ears to dampen the sounds. Tempting though it was to copy them, a member of the king's family should not show such faintheartedness. Arian fixed her eyes on the rafters over the doorway until the screams abated.

The guards had moved away. Tullia lay alone, curled on her side, whimpering high and sharp with each ragged breath. Three black lines, oozing blood, marked the soles of both feet.

Gethryn signalled for the guards to haul Tullia back onto her knees. "Did you murder my sister?"

All spirit was gone. Tullia nodded even before Bran translated the question. "Yes."

"Why?"

"She…she…" Tullia's voice choked off in sobs. "I don't know."

"WHY?" Gethryn bellowed.

"It was…it was because she found out I was going to poison Lady Cassilania. She was going to warn her. So Massillo and me. We sneaked away from the games. And killed her." Tullia spoke between gasped breaths.

Gethryn lowered himself onto his throne. His eyes never left the sobbing woman. "Carry on. What else?"

"Massillo cut her throat. He did it. Then after we poisoned Lady Cassilania, he must have mixed the bottles up, and…" Tullia's voice died. Her whimpered sobs and the crackle of the fire were the only sounds.

"Does anyone else wish to speak, before the king passes judgment?" Emlyn asked.

What more was there to say? Neither verdict or sentence were in doubt.

"I have some questions for her," Cassie said.

Emlyn frowned at Bran's translation. "You have her confession. Is that not enough?"

"I'll need to make a report, on my return to Kavilli. There are family matters to resolve. None of it concerns anyone here, and I wouldn't take up this court's time, except I assume Tullia won't be available to answer at a later date."

Emlyn waited for Gethryn to nod, before saying, "Go ahead."

"Thank you." Cassie gave a gracious smile. "Tullia." She waited until Tullia raised her head. "My first question, who paid you to kill me?" Bran started to translate, but Cassie stopped him with a hand on his arm. "It's all right. Nobody here will be interested."

Which was true enough. The reason why one Kavillian might murder another had not attracted much curiosity. A few teenage girls had speculated about a love triangle between maid, mistress, and bodyguard, but that was all. Most gossip assumed it was to do with money, which Cassie's question seemed to confirm.

"Senator Flavinus Ennius pars Avitae dom Tribonae." Another of those ridiculous long names.

Cassie smiled. "The man with the floppy sausage."

Sausage? Tullia did not respond, yet she did not look either confused or surprised.

"Mother was right. As usual. Out of interest, how much did he offer you?"

"Forty gold dracos."

"That little! I'm shocked. You should have held out for twice as much. I'm worth it." Cassie's laugh turned into a cough. It took a while to get her breath back. "Was that why you volunteered to come with me?"

Tullia nodded.

"And you roped Massillo into helping you?"

Tullia's eyes darted to the fire, before again nodding.

"You were going to split the money with him?"

"Yes."

"What was his share?"

"Five…no, ten. Ten dracos."

"He didn't want to split the money evenly?"

"Yes. Yes, he did."

"So twenty dracos each."

Tullia nodded.

"Right." Cassie looked thoughtful, as if the exact amount was particularly relevant. "Was it you who pushed the rock off?"

What rock?

However, Tullia clearly understood. "Yes."

"And took the swipe with the log?"

"I woke and saw you were gone. I went looking for you. When I found you alone, I…I'm sorry."

"I'm sure you are. But it's too late for regret."

Around the hall, people were showing signs of impatience. Even for those like Arian, who understood Kavillian, the questions and answers made little sense.

"A few last points." Cassie gave Emlyn an apologetic smile. "Why not kill me before getting here?"

"I thought it'd be easier to get away with in the Shadowlands. I hoped the barbarians would be blamed."

"You brought the poison with you from Kavilli?"

"Yes."

"Why not use it to start with? Why the other attempts?"

"Senator Flavinus warned me you'd recognise the taste. He told me not to try. But it was easy." Tullia shook her head. "The rock and the log, I didn't have time to think. Not like the nights when you were asleep. I'd pick up a dagger and stand over you, but I couldn't—I just couldn't make myself do it. I've never killed anyone before."

"A novice. Senator Floppy Sausage wasn't taking me seriously." Cassie sighed and turned to Emlyn. "Thank you. That's all I need to know."

"Is there anyone else?" This time, Emlyn's question was met with silence. "King Gethryn will give his judgment."

Gethryn rose and pointed dramatically to the open door. "She is guilty of murder. Take her to the place of execution and strike her head from her body. Then throw her into the pit, to shorten her journey to hell."

The guards grabbed Tullia and dragged her away. The audience streamed along behind. Tullia screamed when her burnt feet scraped the ground, but her cries were less piercing in the open air and covered by cheers and whoops from the waiting crowd.

Arian started to follow, but Cassie remained seated. Of course, even if she wanted to attend the execution, in her current condition, the trek to and from the hawthorn grove was out of the question. For herself, Arian was in two minds. The entertainment others got from watching a bloody death was a mystery to her. Yet, it was unthinkable for her not to bear witness to justice done and Merial avenged. She had to go, but first she must talk to Cassie.

"How are you feeling?"

Cassie smiled up at her. "Like a herd of elephants jumped on me."

"What are elephants?"

Cassie laughed, then pressed a hand to her chest. "Something you don't want jumping on you."

"The questions you asked Tullia, the man with the floppy sausage. Who is he? Why does he want you dead?"

"He's the husband I told you about. The one who turned up unexpectedly. His wife complained his sausage wasn't firm enough."

"Oh. Him." Arian felt the heat rise on her face. Fortunately, only she, Cassie, and Bran remained in the hall. "The other stuff, the rocks and how much she was being paid?"

"I was not satisfied with her confession. There were too many gaps."

"But you're happy she confessed."

"As would everyone else in Breninbury, if you burned their feet long enough."

"Do you th—"

"I'm sorry." Cassie signalled for Bran to help her stand. "I need to go and lie down."

"Will you be all right?"

"Oh yes. Another day or two and I'll be back to normal."

Sounds of the crowd were fading. Everyone had left for the hawthorn grove, a half mile beyond the lower pool. Arian glanced at the door. "I must go."

"Of course." Cassie patted her arm and turned away. "We'll talk later."

Arian hurried to catch up.

Spindly hawthorn trees were scattered across a hillside of broken stone. None grew taller than a man. Their black, wind-ravaged limbs were twisted, like souls in torment. They surrounded the chasm, a gash in the rock, twenty feet across and three times that in length. Sheer sides plunged into the depths. The bottom, if there was one, was lost in darkness. Legend held that the chasm went all the way to hell. None who entered it had ever returned to say otherwise.

It was a fitting site for executions. A rock ledge projected over the abyss on one side, where an executioner's block was carved from an ancient stump. Old blood stained the wood black. Knotted roots clawed the rock beneath.

Arian arrived in time to see Tullia shoved into place, with her head hanging over the edge, forcing her to look into the depths. So far, she had put up no resistance, accepting her fate, but now she gave a low wail, rising in a final plea, "No. Please, no."

Leirmond had claimed the role of executioner. He stepped forward, axe in hand. The blade flashed through the air.

"N—"

Tullia's head bounced off a protruding root, and then tumbled into the darkness. Streams of bright red blood ran down the side of the block and dripped over the edge. A collective gasp rose from the crowd, as if the act of violence came as a surprise. Arian wrapped her arms around her waist. She hated it. She always had, since the first time she had been judged old enough to attend an execution. For now, Feran and Eilwen were being looked after elsewhere, but she could not shield them forever. Other, older children were present.

Two warriors picked up the headless corpse and swung it over the edge. Tullia would join her lover, who had already been consigned to the depths. The sound of her body hitting the chasm's sides grew ever fainter, until the only noises were the wind through the hawthorns and a dry whisper of loose gravel trickling between the rocks.

The crowd began drifting away, while Gethryn remained fixed in the same spot, staring into the abyss. Arian thought about talking to him. Merial was her sister as well, and they both had loved her. But, in truth, she wanted to get away from the place. The hawthorn grove held a grim, mournful air. No honest oak would grow on the spot.

Kendric joined her. "Walk back with me?"

Which was as good an excuse to leave as any. Arian fell into step beside him. "Any reason?"

"The pleasure of your company." He smiled at her. "I also wondered what you made of Lady Cassilania's questions to her maid. Your Kavillian is better than mine."

Tregaran was a short way ahead. He stopped and waited for them. "I can guarantee you both understood far more than I did."

Kendric laughed. "Don't count on it. I could have sworn at one point she was asking about sausages."

"A floppy sausage. It's umm..." Arian picked her words. "Cassie's pet name for the man who paid Tullia to murder her."

"Ah. Right. No need to explain. I can guess what it refers to." Kendric's smile shifted to curiosity. "Why was she so interested in how they were splitting the money? Do you know?"

"No. But I spoke to her briefly after the trial and I got the feeling Cassie doesn't think Tullia was guilty."

"Was the confession not enough for her?" Tregaran asked.

"No. In fact that was the thing she questioned. Cassie said anyone could be made to confess if you burned their feet."

"There was more than a confession. What about the witnesses? Does she doubt you found the maid trying to smother her?"

"I don't know. Probably not. We didn't mention it. There was only time for a few words." Arian dug into her memory. "But the questions she asked Tullia, the money, the rock. I think Cassie knows more than she's saying."

Kendric gave an amused snort. "I'd say that's a very safe bet."

"I'll talk to her when she's recovered and see if she's willing to say more." And hope it was the truth.

"Be careful. Her words cannot be trusted." Tregaran clearly shared her doubts. "I still would not rule out this…what do you say her name is… Casanilia?"

"Cassilania," Arian said. "Cassie is easier."

"I still wouldn't rule out her playing a part in your sister's murder."

Arian shook her head. "If that were the case she wouldn't have needed to question Tullia."

"She will construct a maze out of words, to hide her true purpose. I predict you'll end up no wiser after talking to her. Quite the opposite. She sows doubt and confusion, and we have reaped a sad harvest. She'll seek to shift the blame."

"I'm sure Cassie has no responsibility for Merial's death." Or Arian desperately wanted to believe it.

"She's responsible just by being here. Murder comes as naturally as breathing to the Kavillians. As with this rival paying the maid to kill her mistress. One of them murdered your sister. I've always known it."

Kendric said, "I wish I could share your confidence."

"None of the Lycanthi would dare shed Cadryn's blood." Yet a trace of doubt tinged Tregaran's voice.

Kendric must have heard it too. "Do you truly believe that, in your heart of hearts, or is it what you want to believe?"

"And what do you want to believe?" Tregaran challenged him.

"Like you. I want to believe our people are always brave, and honourable, and trustworthy. But I fear my faith has been tested too often. There comes a point when you must open your eyes to the truth. I'll happily face any foe, but not one who strikes at my back."

"I understand your bitterness. I…" Tregaran drew in deep breath and let it out in a sigh. "Your point is well taken. These are difficult times."

"The air's so much cleaner at Yanto's Leap. In truth, I'd forgotten what Breninbury was like." Kendric stopped and looked back at the hawthorn grove. Gethryn had not moved. "It's cause for great sorrow that Maddock died so young."

Tregaran nodded slowly. His eyes were also on the solitary figure by the chasm. "Indeed. Maddock was a wise and noble king."

And Gethryn isn't.

Tregaran did not need to say it. Arian had never heard either man come so close to sharing criticism of Gethryn, even in a roundabout way. Her uncle had died in the prime of life, from an infected wound. Gethryn had become king when scarcely more than a boy. But would another decade or two have made much difference? Arian thought not.

They carried on walking up the path to Breninbury in silence, until Kendric gestured to his camp across the river. "Our ways part here." He looked at Arian. "If you find out anything of interest, let me know."

"I will. I'll speak to Cassie when she's better. And I'll remember to take anything she says with a pinch of salt."

"You will do what you must." Tregaran sounded resigned. "But please, don't end up making me regret the health potion I made for her."

Cassie

Cassie pressed her signet ring into the soft wax, then returned her writing case to the travel chest. Thankfully, she had thought to bring paper, ink, pen, and wax with her. The Lycanthi's only form of writing was runes carved in wood or stone. While this was fine for inscriptions, it would not work for anything substantive. And, despite the amusement value in picturing Mother's face as she received the report inscribed on half a tree, the report's contents were not a matter for jest.

There was a spy in the Passurae household. Or there had been. Mother suspected Senator Flavinus would resort to assassination to sooth his hurt pride. Hence the mission to Breninbury had been arranged quickly and in secret, hoping Cassie would be long gone before Senator Flavinus had time to react. Yet news had reached him before the party left Kavilli. Tullia had proved herself open to bribery, and was the likely source of the leak, unless she had been recruited by the true spy. Either way, Mother needed to be aware.

Senator Flavinus had shown horrendously poor judgment. Assassination was best left to professionals. More than this, infiltrating the Passurae household must have taken months of planning. Was he so thin-skinned as to throw his agent away over such a trivial matter? Mother would be forewarned if he tried inserting a replacement for Tullia

Cassie stood. Her heartbeat raced briefly, then settled. Yesterday had been spent resting, apart from the brief attendance at Tullia's trial. Today, she was feeling better. Maybe not yet ready to run up stairs, but fit enough to continue her mission.

Bran was sitting in the courtyard. He sprung up when he saw her. "Do you need anything, my lady?"

"Yes. I'm going for a short walk. I want you to come with me."

Cassie took his offered arm. Accepting his assistance was less embarrassing that falling over in public. She waited until they were away from prying eyes before handing over the sealed document.

"Take this. Should anything happen to me, you must see it gets to my mother in Kavilli. You will be well rewarded." Among other matters, the report contained a strong recommendation to make Bran a permanent family employee.

He slipped the document inside his tunic. "Are you worried something might happen to you? Tullia was the one who tried to kill you."

"Unfortunately, she's not the only murderer in the picture. Someone else killed Yehan and Merial."

"Leirmond? He's always been your favourite suspect."

"Except we're totally lacking evidence." Gut feelings did not count. "As for motive, me being executed was a sure way to start a war with the empire, and Merial was trying to talk Gethryn into making a deal. But Yehan doesn't fit in."

"You don't think Leirmond's hatred of the empire is enough?"

"Does he hate the empire? I know he's contemptuous, but that's not the same thing as a motive for murder."

"He wants a war."

"Only as a way to prove what a heroic fighter he is." Cassie stared at the distant hills. "I suppose he might worry Yehan would follow his mother's advice about making a deal."

"I've heard they argued a lot. Yehan didn't show Merial much respect."

"He was a teenage boy. That's what they're like."

"I'd have got a clip round the ear if I'd been a brat with my mother. Wouldn't matter how old I was."

"Good for her." Cassie's laugh turned into a cough. "But his age is significant. Yehan was years from being in a position to make deals. There has to be more to it."

"What'll you do if we get proof?"

"Depends on who the murderer is."

"You're not convinced about Leirmond?"

"In my gut, yes. But guessing is dangerous. Nobody's gut is infallible." *Not even Mother's.* "One thing we can be sure of, Nelda knows their identity. Somebody put her up to that nonsense about seeing me run away."

"You or Tullia."

"Or you. Don't forget how adaptable she was." A tremor started in Cassie's legs. Not enough to prevent her walking, but there was no need to force things. "Time to go back. That's enough exercise for now"

"Are you all right, my lady?"

"I'm fine." A slight exaggeration. "I want to mull things over. We need a plan. If Leirmond is the murderer, pushing Gethryn into doing anything will be a challenge. He may have loved his sister, but…"

Bran was shaking his head. "Gethryn won't have an option. It's serious, really serious, shedding the blood of the king's sister."

"More than anyone else he's fond of?"

"It's not up to him. The king's sisters hold the royal bloodline. Shedding their blood is the worst crime. Even the king isn't allowed to do it. It a sacred bond. Cadryn's blood is what binds the people to the land. Leirmond was taking a huge risk when he slapped Merial."

"I doubt he was thinking."

"He can't have. If he'd cut her lip and shed just one drop of blood…" Bran sucked a breath in. "Doing it by accident would be bad enough. But striking her? Gethryn would have no choice but to exile him for a year or two. Tregaran would insist on it."

"What if Gethryn refused?"

"The high priest has the authority to outlaw anyone."

"Even the king?"

"Yes. And it's everyone's sacred duty to kill outlaws on sight. If Tregaran outlawed Gethryn, even a serf like me would be allowed to stick a knife in his back."

"What if one sister hurts another? Arian must hold the bloodline as well. What if she'd murdered Merial?"

"She'd be drowned." Bran shrugged. "No blood shed."

"Just as well she's innocent, then."

They reached the house. Cassie slipped her arm from Bran's. "We must be sure we're on the right scent. We've spent too long chasing false trails."

"I'll see if I can dig up anything new about the night Yehan died."

"Do that." Cassie smiled at Bran. "I need to lie down for a bit."

Alone in the room, Cassie stretched out on the bed. She must regain her strength before events overtook her. It was another gut feeling. Trouble was on the way. She stared at the smoke-stained ceiling. She needed answers, and soon.

❖

"I heard you were out walking." Arian dithered in the doorway. "How are you feeling?"

Cassie sat up and beckoned her in. "Much better."

"That's good." Arian plonked herself down at the far end of the sleeping platform, then looked as if she wished she had sat closer. She was endearingly unsure of herself.

"I'm pleased you've called by," Cassie said.

"You are?"

"I wanted to thank you for saving my life. If you hadn't turned up when you did, I wouldn't be here."

"Oh, that. I couldn't not…um." The dim light did not hide the flush of colour on Arian's face.

"I also remember you looking after me, giving me medicine to drink."

"Tregaran asked me to. He's the one you should thank."

"Then I owe you both my gratitude."

Arian picked hay stalks off the blanket. "I shouldn't have left you alone with her."

"You had no reason not to trust Tullia. I'm the one who slipped up. I missed clues."

Arian raised her eyes. "The reason I'm here…one of the reasons. I wanted to ask about what you said."

What are the other reasons? Cassie kept the question to herself. Guessing the answer was more fun. "What I said when?"

"After the trial. You don't think Tullia murdered Merial."

"Did I say that?"

"Maybe not in so many words."

Cassie hesitated a moment, but she needed to shake things up. "No, Tullia wasn't the murderer."

"How can you be sure?"

"Because Merial and I had spent the afternoon talking. She wanted to return to the empire and was worried about her former husband. I offered to help. My family has enough influence to handle anything he might try. We were making plans for her future. Don't you think Merial would have said something to me if she had any idea Tullia intended to poison me?"

"Why didn't you say that at the trial?"

"What would've been the point? Executing her for Merial's death made your brother happy. She certainly murdered Massillo and tried to murder me. No matter how many crimes someone's guilty of, you can only cut their head off once."

"You think she murdered her lover?"

"I'm sure of it. Tullia had to think quickly under pressure. She was sharper than she'd been letting on, but she still slipped up. Not just with the excuse she invented for killing Merial. She knew exactly how many coins Flavinus had promised her but was vague when it came to Massillo's share. Tullia was the sort of person who never forgets about money." And, presumably, she had not heard of Flavinus's reputation for reneging on payments. "Massillo played no part in the plot. Not intentionally."

"He gave you the poison."

"Tullia had him select food while she filled the flask with mead. I'd guess she'd already put a dose of widows' nightcap in it before getting to the kitchen. Once outside, she distracted him by giving him the flask to hang on his belt. While he was doing that, she poured more poison over my food. She told him to give me the bowl because she had to check the laundry. Massillo thought they were meeting afterwards, for a game of hide the sausage. Instead, Tullia stayed in the house. Maybe to make sure no one else ate my lunch. Maybe she wanted to watch the poison do its work."

"How did she get him to take the poison?"

"Left him alone with the flask. Massillo wasn't the sort of man to sit around looking at a drink. Tullia would've known that. She may have enjoyed fooling around with him but, in hindsight, I suspect she had lined him up as a stooge from the day we left Kavilli." A shame. Massillo had deserved better.

"What was that other stuff you asked her? The rock?"

"She'd tried to kill me before. She dropped a rock on me, down by the lower pool. She also took a swipe at me with an improvised club one night. She missed both times, obviously."

"You didn't know it was her?"

"Of course not."

"Why didn't you say anything?"

"Because I assumed it was one of your people. Making unsupported accusations wouldn't have won me any friends. And, I admit, I had no faith in your brother's ability or willingness to help. The empire isn't popular. I didn't want to put ideas into people's heads."

"If Tullia didn't kill Merial, who did?" Arian had pinpointed the most crucial question.

"I don't know."

"They've got away with it?"

"For now."

"Don't you have any idea?"

"Nothing more than suspicions. But I can tell you someone who does know."

"Who?"

"Nelda."

"Why her?"

"The nonsense she spouted about seeing me run away. Me, or Tullia, or Bran, or whoever. It wasn't her own idea. She'd been told what to say. It was obvious from the way her story fell apart when she tried to improvise. Someone got her to lie, and my money's on that person being the murderer."

Arian jumped to her feet. "I'm going to talk to her."

"Wait. She'll simply deny everything."

"I've got to do something."

"Yes. But you ought to do something sensible."

"Such as?"

"To start with, don't accuse her directly."

"Why not?"

Arian and Jadio really must meet sometime. They had so much in common. "Because it won't help. We can't prove anything. It would simply put her on her guard. In Nelda's case this won't amount to much, but she'll tell the murderer, and that's somebody we don't want to warn." Although it did suggest an idea. Even without the language barrier, Nelda would refuse to talk to her. But Arian would be perfect in the role.

"So what do we do?"

"You speak with her, but be oblique."

"What?"

"Act as though you're not doubting her, but equally, you're not completely certain the murderer was Tullia. Ask what the woman she saw was wearing. How tall was she? Then throw in some odd stuff. Was there a smell of lavender? Did the woman step in a puddle? Has she noticed fewer cats around than usual? Don't give any reason for why you want to know. If she asks, you can even insist you don't have a reason."

Arian looked bewildered. "Lavender? Cats? What have they got to do with it?"

"Nothing. That's the point. You want to get Nelda confused. It won't take much. As soon as you leave her, she'll run straight to whoever she's in league with, looking for reassurance."

"You want me to follow her?"

"No. If she spots you, even Nelda might realise it's a trap. Bran and I will take up position where we can watch from a distance."

"Right." Suddenly, Arian's expression became pained, and she collapsed back on the bed

"What is it?"

"Nelda. If she's involved in Merial's death, Gethryn will be…" Arian went back to picking hay off the blanket. "I know he's a…" She shrugged. "But he's still my brother."

Unless Gethryn is the one she's working with. Something best left unsaid. Gethryn could have remained at the games and sent Nelda in with instructions to kill Merial. Although, in his shoes, Cassie would never entrust a murder to anyone so scatterbrained. Of course, it was arguable whether Gethryn was much better. They were a well-matched couple.

Arian continued. "They've been bedfellows for ages. He's been so happy, ever since Nelda finally got pregnant. People had been saying she was barren. After seven years, you'd have thought she'd have a couple of children."

"They've been together that long?" An idea hopped into the back of Cassie's head.

"Yes."

"And no children before now?"

"No. I said that."

"Stillbirths? Miscarriages?"

"Not that I know of." Arian looked at Cassie. "What are you getting at?"

"Did she and Gethryn have an argument shortly beforehand?"

"Yes. But what's that got to do with it?"

"Nelda kicked Gethryn out of her house?"

"Of course not. He's the king. She went back to her family at Drusbury for a while."

"And suddenly got pregnant. Really? Did nobody question it?"

Finally, Arian caught on. "You think she took another bedfellow while she was away?"

"Yes." *Of course.* "I think Nelda's not the barren one." How could fatherhood be such a blind spot? "Has nobody said anything?"

"Not in my hearing."

Maybe not, but Cassie would love to hear what the old women had to say about it. Possibly Nelda was lucky, and the baby a little overdue—common enough for a first child.

Arian's was clearly running the same sums through her head. "There's nobody I can ask. Nelda's brothers have gone back to Drusbury. The only other person who might know..."

"Yes."

Arian grimaced. "He wouldn't say anything to me, even if I asked."

"Who?"

"Leirmond. Gethryn was so miserable after Nelda left, Leirmond went to see her. He talked her into returning to Breninbury. If he knows anything about Nelda having another bedfellow while she was away, he's not saying."

No. He wouldn't. Suddenly, everything was much clearer.

Apart from the watchtower over the gate, the palisade had three lookout points. The raised platforms were only a few feet above ground level and not normally manned. The ladder had only eight steps. Even so, Cassie was wheezing by the time she reached the top and her heart was pounding. She bent forward and rested her forehead on the palisade, waiting for the dizziness to fade.

Arian put an arm around her shoulder. "Are you all right?"

Now Cassie had two things to worry about. Arian's touch set off a riot of sensation, flowing up her spine and down her legs. Her stomach flipped. Had she been feeling better, her knees might have given way. As it was, she did not have the strength to react forcefully enough to fall down.

"Just a little out of breath." Which really was one of her bigger lies.

"You should have said. We could have waited. Tomorrow would've been fine."

"No. We both want answers." Time was not on their side. Cassie knew it in her bones.

She raised her head. On the opposite side of the hillfort, Bran was already in position on the watchtower over the gate. Between the two viewpoints, they had the entirety of Breninbury in sight. Nelda was in her favourite spot, the bench outside her house, nursing her baby. Leirmond was on the other side of the Great Hall, surrounded by a gaggle of warriors on the meeting ground.

"Are you sure you'll be all right, on your own?"

"I'll be fine. Go. See if you can rattle Nelda."

"I'll try." Arian was too innately honest to be comfortable playing a role. Luckily, her acting ability was not an issue.

"Remember, you don't need to sound convincing. We want her to think you're up to something and not telling the whole story."

Arian nodded and climbed down the steps. Cassie watched her walk away, drinking in the sight of her. The weakness from the poison was undoubtedly playing a part, but Cassie could not remember the last time any woman had so totally entranced her. *Typical murderer, spoiling a perfectly good romantic situation.* Being surrounded by a hillfort full of barbarians did not help either.

Arian arrived at her house and took a seat beside Nelda. The ensuing conversation lasted far longer than expected. Either Arian needed time to gather herself or Nelda was nattering so much Arian had trouble getting a word in. From what Cassie knew of them, both possibilities were equally likely.

Eventually, Arian stood and went into the house. As soon as she was out of sight, Nelda bounced to her feet and scurried straight to the meeting ground, where Leirmond stood with his fellow warriors. She had taken the bait. As a co-conspirator, Nelda could only be classified as a liability.

She waved to attract Leirmond's attention, gesturing for him to join her in a quiet spot, behind a storehouse. They stood, heads together, deep in a heated debate. Without hearing a word, it was obvious Nelda was upset and Leirmond was irritated.

Cassie was satisfied. It was not the sort of proof that would convince Gethryn, but she had the murderer. And, as luck would have it, Leirmond and Nelda were directly between Cassie and her house, offering an opportunity for discreet eavesdropping. The steps were easier going down and then, despite a temptation to rush, she set off across Breninbury at a casual stroll. Nothing she might overhear was worth the risk of alerting Leirmond.

However, the conspirators had not moved by the time Cassie reached them. She continued her slow amble, playing the part of an invalid concentrating on her feet. Leirmond's temper was clearly fraying, which was doing nothing to calm Nelda. With luck they would carry on talking, assuming she could not understand. However, both fell silent when Cassie drew near.

She nodded at them. "Good afternoon."

Neither responded. However, as soon as she was passed, Nelda burst out, "Stop ogling the bitch."

"Don't be stupid. I'm not," Leirmond snapped back.

"You are so. I've seen the way you watch her. You want to hammer her."

"Be quiet. You don't—" Leirmond's voice rose.

The tone and volume were such it was only reasonable for Cassie to stop and look back. Tears glinted in Nelda's eyes. Her lips were set in a hard line. The emotion was not hard to read. Jealousy. Simple, blatant jealousy.

Cassie gave a bland smile and continued her stroll. As she passed out of earshot she caught one last retort.

"Fucking man-stealing, bitch." Nelda spat out the words.

So that was it. The source of Nelda's hatred for her. How ridiculous could life get? It did not even count as a bad joke. Of all the things in Breninbury that Cassie wanted even less than Nelda's house, her lover headed the list.

Cassie stood atop the embankment outside the palisade. Light from the sinking sun cast horizontal beams across the opposite hillside. The first hints of autumnal reds and browns coloured the trees. Summer was on its way out. The evidence against Leirmond, such as it was, marked a step forward, but time was running out. The courier with the delaying message to the Verina blacksmiths would soon return.

Bran stood beside her. "It's certain then. Leirmond's the murderer."

"Yes. I have no doubt. I can even add a motive. Leirmond is the father of Nelda's baby."

"Where did you hear that?"

"Putting one and one together, when they shouldn't, and getting three. Has nobody spoken about it?"

"Maybe hints Nelda had another bedfellow. But it's a personal thing. Women's gossip, and I wasn't included. Fatherhood never gets mentioned."

"Even with Gethryn acting like he wants to name Nelda's son as his heir?"

"Even then. As far as the baby goes, his supporters wouldn't question whether he's the father. And the traditionalists won't care about other bedfellows Nelda has taken."

"That still leaves Leirmond, who backs Gethryn, while knowing the truth."

Bran wrinkled his nose. "I'm not sure it would bother him. With his reputation, he's probably responsible for more than his share of the children running around Breninbury."

"I still think Leirmond would prefer a child he'd sired on the throne, rather than a black-haired spawn of the empire."

"Maybe. But I can give you another reason he had to kill Yehan."

"Go on."

"I found someone who knows the background to the fight Yehan had with the other youth. One of the cooks overheard others in the group talking afterwards. It started with jokes over the way Gethryn was acting. As if he wanted to be the baby's mother."

"Making jokes about the king's masculinity?"

"Put it down to youngsters who'd had more to drink than they could handle. Things shifted to sneering the empire and ideas about fatherhood. I don't know how much was directed at Yehan personally. Nobody owned up in the cook's hearing. But Yehan got angry."

"Not good when you're drunk."

"Yehan said only bastards can't name their fathers. Another lad challenged him to name his, if it was so important. Yehan said his father was legion commander in Verina."

"That'll come as a surprise to my cousin." And nearly as much of a surprise to his wife. "But I have it on good authority his father's a blacksmith."

"Nobody knew that at the time, so the lad settled for saying why didn't Yehan fuck off back to his father then? Yehan started boasting about how the empire would take over Breninbury. He just had to say the word and his father would send the legions in."

"He was being a stupid, young idiot." And a worthy heir to Gethryn. But was it really so surprising if a boy who aimed to be king did not want a common blacksmith as a father? Yehan had been caught between cultures. "You're suggesting Leirmond heard this and thought he'd found a way to start a war. Then he changed his mind and decided to make it look like an accident. Why?"

"Because as soon as Yehan left, someone thought to ask Merial. They were all ready to have a go at Yehan when he came back. When he didn't, they assumed he knew his lie would be found out, and he didn't want to face them. Which is why nobody went looking for him."

Filling in the gaps was easy. "Leirmond returned from killing Yehan, only to learn the truth. After a night of agonising, and a chance to sober up, he decided to stage an accident."

"That was what I was thinking."

Cassie stared at the distant horizon while mulling everything over. Dusk was thickening. A trail of smoke from Kendric's campfire flowed into the sunset. Overhead, an arrowhead of geese were going south. Livestock ambled across the valley. The peace and calm gave no hint of the metaphorical storm clouds gathering.

"It could have been a combination of things for Leirmond. He was drunk. Yehan had just insulted him in front of everybody. Don't forget the scattering like sheep bit. Gethryn was laying claim to his son. I'd turned him down. And he thought he'd found a way to start a war. Maybe it was all too much."

"Can we prove he did it?" Bran asked.

"No. The most we can do is show Yehan's death wasn't an accident."

"You can't admit to examining his body."

"True. However, Arian knows the truth, even if she doesn't know that she knows it." She also knew Leirmond killed her sister, which was enough to put her in danger.

"What do we do?" Bran asked.

"Two options. We return to Verina. I've made contact with the smugglers. A network of native spies will make all the difference to my cousin. Or…" She had all the cards. How best to play the game?

"Or?"

"We play a high stakes game. We see if we can split the Lycanthi wide open and pick up the pieces."

Bran broke into a laugh.

"What is it?"

"I'm sorry, my lady. But is there's any doubt which option you'll take?"

No. None at all.

Arian

Feran gulped down the last of his breakfast and trotted off to play with Wenda. Arian sat alone in the courtyard, pushing food around the bowl. Her stomach was unsettled. It matched the rest of her. Thankfully, Nelda was out of sight, although she could still be heard, crooning a lullaby to her baby. The normally soothing sound grated on Arian's ears.

Did Nelda not know Leirmond had murdered Merial? She might be gullible, but what possible story could he have told her? And, even if she was being duped by him, what about Gethryn? Leirmond was supposed to be his closest friend. Nelda was his bedfellow, yet they were making a fool of him.

Arian could bear it no longer. Hiding away was not going to help. Another verse of Nelda's lullaby and she would be unable to contain herself. She put the bowl on the ground for the dogs to enjoy and left the house. Nelda was sitting in her favourite spot, the bench outside the entrance. Arian mumbled a greeting as she hurried by.

Cassie was finishing her own breakfast when Arian arrived. "Ah, good, you're here. I was about to come find you." By the smile, you would have thought her completely free from worry. Maybe she was.

The calm self-confidence and sarcastic humour were not a mask. Arian now knew it went far deeper. Cassie would face death with an off-hand quip, showing courage any warrior might envy. The games she played were focused on a goal, not a display of childishness. She was dangerous, and determined, and the sight of her threw all coherent thoughts into disarray.

Arian took a seat. She had to keep a grip on herself. "What do we do about Leirmond?"

Bran stood to one side, listening. The remaining Kavillian, the fighter, was nearby, cleaning and sharpening his weapons.

"We must find evidence we can present to Gethryn. Something putting Leirmond's guilt beyond doubt," Cassie said.

"What sort of evidence? How do we get it?"

"We need others involved. Kendric is a good person to start with. His word counts for a lot."

"Not with Gethryn. He won't listen to Kendric, any more than he'd listen to you or me." Although his support would be comforting.

"Gethryn's the one on weak ground. Most people respect Kendric, including some who can't be ignored. And…" Cassie caught her lower lip in her teeth. "There's more I need to tell you. A lot more. I've been holding back about some things."

As if that was a surprise. "What sort of things?"

"It'll be quicker if I tell you and Kendric at the same time."

Arian stood. "Then let's see him now."

"Unfortunately, I'm not allowed to cross the river. At night, I could sneak over to his camp, but not at the moment."

"You want to wait until dark?"

"No. We don't want to waste time. You go. Arrange a meeting." She paused. "Where would be a good place?"

"Here?"

Cassie shook her head. "We can't risk being overheard."

"My lady?" Bran said.

"Yes?"

"How about the hawthorn grove? It's usually deserted. It's about a mile away. Will you be up to that?"

"Yes. I'm much stronger after another night's sleep. Though I might not run there and back." Cassie looked thoughtful. "Isn't it where Tullia's execution took place?"

"All executions do." Arian tried not to grimace. The grove was not somewhere she would choose to go, but nor would anyone else. Bran was right, the risk of running into other people was slight, and there was no way for an eavesdropper to get close without being seen.

"Perfect. If anyone asks what we're doing, you can say I wanted to see where my poisoner met her end. You were showing me as a favour."

A grim favour. "All right. We'll meet you there."

Even on a sunny day, the hawthorn grove held a sinister air. Bright red berries clung to the branches like drops of blood. Dead leaves lay curled on the ground, rattling in the chill breeze. A shiver ran down Arian's back, yet Cassie looked unconcerned. She stood by the execution block and peered down.

"A good place to hide a body. I wonder how many have ended up there unofficially."

Kendric gave an amused snort. "Have you a plan to kill someone?"

"Not right now, but it's good to be prepared." Cassie moved away from the edge. "Arian has told you we suspect Leirmond of murdering Merial?"

"Yes. I wish I could say I'm surprised."

"But you're not."

"No. When Leirmond has his eyes on a goal he'll not care about those he tramples on the way."

"You said you had more information." A dozen ideas had been tying Arian's head in knots.

"Yes. I do." Cassie paused, clearly considering her words. "It wasn't his first murder. Leirmond killed Yehan as well."

None of Arian's guesses had been close to the mark. "What? No, he didn't. It was an accident."

"The scene you found was staged."

"Can you back that up?" Kendric asked.

"Arian can."

"Me? No, I…" What did Cassie mean?

"When you pulled Yehan from the river, his body was in full rigor mortis."

"In what?" The phrase was not one Arian knew.

"The stiffness that comes after death."

"Oh, that. Yes."

"Temperature is important. If Yehan died soon after leaving the meeting ground, and lay on the ground, by dawn his body would be as you described. But if he'd been in the cold river all night, the process would not have been so advanced. You'd have noticed the difference."

Kendric nodded. The old warrior would have seen enough of death to know such things.

"Secondly, you said how pale his face was. And for this we can find any number of witnesses. When someone dies, their blood sinks, like water in a sponge. It makes large bruises on whatever part of the body is lowest. If Yehan had died as you found him, his face would have been purple, not pale. And finally, his position." Cassie raised her arms, crossing them over her chest. "He was like this, correct?"

"Yes. His arms were trapped by his cloak." The image was imprinted on Arian's memory.

"And you thought it was a coincidence he looked like a body ready for his funeral?" Cassie gestured to the ground. "Here. Try it out now. Pretend you're kneeling beside the river and you slip. Your hands will go out to save yourself. Even if they get caught up in a cloak, they'll be around your head and twisted awkwardly. There can be no doubt. After Yehan was dead, somebody laid him out on his back. But just before Arian found him, the body was repositioned in an attempt to make it look like an accident."

Kendric pursed his lips thoughtfully, and then asked. "If he didn't drown, how did he die?"

"I don't know. Apart from being willing to bet Leirmond murdered him."

"Why him?"

"In the space of a few days, a mother and son were murdered. Do you really think their deaths are unrelated? And Leirmond has the same motives in both cases. Both Yehan and Merial had publicly insulted him shortly before their death. Yehan likened him to a frightened sheep, and Merial called him a fool. Even worse, Gethryn supported Merial and stood up to Leirmond on her behalf."

"Others have insulted Leirmond and lived to tell the tale. Myself for example," Kendric said.

"Yes. But you're also an example of how badly he takes it. And though it might not have been enough on its own, resentment provided the spur when he saw a chance to achieve something he wants. A war with the empire. He thinks it will be a game where he can show off his prowess."

Kendric grimaced. "He's been wanting it ever since I told him he stood no chance of winning."

"But killing them wouldn't start a war." Arian did not want to believe it. Surely Merial could not have died for something so stupid.

"In Merial's case it was a means to an end," Cassie said. "If I'd been executed for her murder, Leirmond would have had his war. And Yehan had been imaginative with the truth. He claimed his father was the army legate in Verina. The implications of fatherhood must have been at the front of Leirmond's mind that night, given that he's the father of Nelda's son."

"Leirmond is what?"

Cassie smiled at Kendric. "The baby was born nine months after Nelda and Leirmond had some time alone together. Have you never done the sums?"

Kendric shook his head. "It's not something we worry about."

"As I've come to realise." The humour in Cassie's voice was unmistakable. Although maybe this time it was deserved. Arian could not believe she had never thought about the dates before.

Cassie continued. "He could see how emotional Gethryn was over the baby. And hoped the legate would be just as attached to Yehan. Except of course, the legate has no idea who Yehan is, or was. But it explains the body being moved. Leirmond killed Yehan by the river, and laid him out, making it obvious he'd been murdered. Then Leirmond learned Yehan was no relation to the legate. He went to sleep, woke up sober, and realised he had to do something."

Arian dug into her memories. "Leirmond can't have been far away. He was one of the first to arrive. He arranged carrying Yehan up to Breninbury."

"To limit the people who saw the body as it was found. Rigor mortis meant Leirmond couldn't arrange Yehan in a more natural position for an accidental death."

Silence drew out on the hillside. A gust of wind skittered dry leaves across the ground. Eventually, Kendric blew out his cheeks. "Can you prove any of this? Gethryn isn't going to take your word, simply because Nelda rushed to speak with Leirmond."

"Not at the moment. But I have an idea."

"I thought you might."

"It's to do with timing. Leirmond saw Merial and me enter Breninbury and assumed we'd be alone together. He wouldn't trust Nelda to kill Merial, even if she was willing. So they slipped in together through the side gate. Leirmond murdered Merial and then Nelda started screaming to attract attention."

Even Cassie's matter-of-fact recounting could not dull the pain. Tears filled Arian's eyes. She turned away and stared across the hawthorn grove. Unexpectedly, Cassie reached over and squeezed her shoulder.

"If we're lucky, there's one piece of evidence that might be available."

"What?" Kendric asked.

"The knife Leirmond used. They didn't have much time. I'd already left Merial before they got to her. For all they knew, I was on my way back to join the crowd. Nelda couldn't claim she'd seen me running away if I had dozens of witnesses to being outside the gate. She had to start screaming the moment Merial was dead."

Of course she did. It ended any hope, for Gethryn's sake, that Nelda was an innocent dupe. She must have witnessed the murder. But what was Cassie trying to prove?

Kendric was also mystified. "I don't see where you are going."

"Leirmond didn't have time to get back to the games. He had to hide out of sight and pretend to arrive with everyone else. Given the uproar, no one would notice which direction he came from, but not if he was holding a bloody knife. He was conveniently splattered from his boxing matches. But he wasn't supposed to have stabbed anyone. He had to hide the knife. And the only safe place is Nelda's room. Possibly they've removed it by now. It'd be the sensible thing to do, but Nelda's not the most sensible person, and Leirmond lacks attention to detail. I think there's a good chance the knife is still in her room. If we find it there, would that go some way to convincing you?"

"It would be a start."

"Then let's go."

Before leaving, Arian took another look at the gaping hole in the land. *A good place to hide a body.* Had anyone ever disposed of a victim that way? The thought had never crossed her mind before. Breninbury was her home. It was safe.

Had the world changed, or had it always been the same, and she had been too naive to notice? The comforting blanket of innocence was stripped away. Nelda and Leirmond were bedfellows who had conspired to murder Merial. How many others harboured guilty secrets?

Of course, she had her own guilty secret. Her shoulder still tingled from Cassie's touch.

❖

Arian sat with Kendric on the bench outside her home, chatting about events from her childhood. Or, more accurately, Kendric talked while Arian tried to smile in the right places.

Nelda appeared at the entrance. She looked surprised to see them, but then gave a weak smile. "Tolred's having his afternoon nap. I'm going for a walk."

The announcement was unnecessary. It was what Nelda did every day. Before, it had seemed mundane. Now, Arian suspected she was meeting with Leirmond. But regardless of where Nelda was going, on past form, she would be gone long enough to search the room. Nelda wandered away on a meandering route between the houses of the Royal Quarter. Arian gave a sigh of relief. They could stop the pretence of making small talk.

Arian had not entered Merial's room since the funeral. She found herself staring at the empty bed. It was so hard to drag her eyes, or her memories away. But it would be better to mourn Merial when she was properly avenged. She joined Kendric at the back of the room.

The curving passage chamber, built into the thickness of the outer wall, was long enough for an adult-sized bed. The narrow space had been Odella's. Merial had put Nelda there when she first moved in. From the undisturbed state of the bed in the main room, Nelda had not taken advantage of Merial's death to swap over. Was it due to guilt, superstition, or a basic sense of decency?

Daylight struggled to reach the end of the passage chamber. Kendric lit a lamp. Tolred lay swaddled in the middle of the bed. The sight of him, asleep and utterly unaware made Arian flinch. Would he also grow up without a mother? How would this end for Nelda?

The flame wavered in a draft as Cassie joined them. "Bran's keeping watch outside. He'll signal if he sees Nelda returning." She looked around the chamber. "If the knife is here, there aren't many hiding places."

"The bed?" Kendric suggested.

"She did say about keeping a knife under her pillow in case…" *Cassie tried crawling into bed with her.* Arian prayed her blush did not show. "But that was before Tolred was born. I doubt she'd leave him alone, within reach of a sharp object."

Cassie remained by the opening. "My guess is Leirmond was the one who disposed of the knife. He murdered Merial, then signalled to Nelda to start screaming. He hid in this cubbyhole, until the main room was hectic enough to slip out and join the general commotion. He had a bit of time to find somewhere to put the knife, but not a lot."

"Leirmond, you think?" Kendric lifted the lamp and examined the ceiling. He reached up and teased apart some of the interwoven branches. "Here it is. Too high for Nelda." He pulled out a small dagger.

"That was easy," Cassie said. "I'm impressed."

Kendric smiled at her. "Leirmond is not noted for his imagination. It's where swords are hidden in the sagas."

They moved to the brighter light of the courtyard. The blade was twice the length of Arian's middle finger and smeared in blood. Merial's blood. Arian's jaw clenched so tight it hurt. The pommel was carved in a beast's head, though it was hard to say what sort. The handle was worn leather, also stained, except for the clear part where it had been gripped.

"The hand's too big for a woman." Cassie looked at Kendric. "Are you convinced yet?"

"Halfway."

"Enough to work with me on a plan?"

"What are you thinking of?"

"The one person Gethryn can't ignore—Tregaran. We need to get his backing."

"How?" Kendric asked.

"We draw Leirmond into betraying himself with Tregaran as a witness."

"Again. How?"

"By setting a trap with the right bait."

"Which is?"

"Me."

Kendric gave a half laugh. "You want to be tied to a stake in the middle of the forest?"

"Done the right way it might just get Leirmond's interest. But no. I want you to talk to Tregaran. Tell him everything. He'll listen to you. Then you both must go to Leirmond and let him know I've accused him of murdering Yehan and Merial. Ask for his side of things."

"Leirmond will simply deny it."

"Of course he will. But say I claim to have proof. I'm going assemble it and put it to Gethryn tomorrow."

"What proof?"

"The proof is in what Leirmond will do next."

"You mean, apart from getting angry and swearing?"

"Yes. He'll try to kill me."

"No. You can't. It's too dangerous." Arian cursed herself for speaking before thinking. Cassie's smile only made it worse.

Kendric took longer to reply. "Are you sure it'll work?"

"Yes. He knows he's guilty. He'll be flogging his brains trying to work out what I could have found by way of proof. He won't come up with anything. To be honest, I can't think of anything either. But he won't be able to risk it."

"You being murdered will look suspicious."

"True. But it's still his best option. Without proof, he can depend on Gethryn's support, and events will be on his side. If Tullia's attempt to poison me had succeeded, just maybe it could have been passed off as a natural death, but not if I have my throat slit. My cousin, the legate, will be forced to take retaliatory action. The Senate will demand he levels Breninbury as a warning to all. With empire legions on the way, people here won't have either the time or the appetite to investigate my death properly. And if Leirmond ends up as a war hero, who'll want to dig around in what went before?"

"He'll be dead, not a hero." Kendric said.

"You and I know that, but Leirmond doesn't." Cassie tilted her head to one side. "So, do you think you can talk Tregaran into going along with this?"

"I'll try. But I can guarantee he won't like it." Kendric studied Cassie thoughtfully. "Aren't you worried Leirmond might succeed?"

An icy fist clenched Arian's stomach. However, Cassie merely smiled. "No. Leirmond will only have tonight. He'll wait until I'm asleep, thinking I'll be alone now that Tullia's gone. But you and Tregaran will be lying in wait, as well as my bodyguard."

Kendric held up the knife. "Should I put this back?"

"No. Show it to Tregaran. It's the best evidence we have. You might want to show it to Leirmond as well. His face should be interesting. He doesn't cope well when he's on the defensive."

"I'll find Tregaran right away. It might take some time to persuade him." Kendric went.

Once they were alone, Arian paced the length of the courtyard, trying to untangle the knot of emotions twisting inside her. Which thread to pick loose first?

She stopped and faced Cassie "Are you sure this is a good idea?"

"Yes. Gethryn won't be able to brush Tregaran's testimony aside."

"No. About making yourself the bait in the trap. Supposing Leirmond attacks when you're not expecting it?"

"I need to make sure I'm never alone."

"You'll be alone in your room. And that's when you expect him to strike."

"Others will be on hand." Cassie's obvious amusement did not help. "We don't need—"

Bran interrupted with a polite cough from the courtyard entrance. "Excuse me, my lady. Do you still need me to keep lookout?"

"No. We've finished. Unless…"

He cleared his throat again. "Yes, my lady?"

"It's nothing. You can go." Cassie watched him leave, then returned to Arian. The teasing edge on her face increased. "Now, where were we? Oh yes. Me sleeping alone. You weren't offering to keep me company, were you?"

"I don't think…" Another thread slipped free from the knot, a very different one than before.

"Trust me. Very little thinking will be required." Cassie ran the tip of her tongue along her upper lip. "It's months since I left Kavilli. I haven't gone this long without bedroom company since…well, forever. Not even an offer, except for Leirmond, and I don't count him. You were there, weren't you, when he tried to get my interest?"

Cassie was playing games again. A strand of anger pulled loose. Why did she do it? What was so hard about being honest and open? "Yes. I was there. And I do remember." Arian switched to Lycanthian. "I remember you understood what Leirmond was saying."

Cassie hesitated, then she dipped her head in acknowledgment. "Yes. I confess. I did." She spoke Lycanthian with a heavy accent, but quite clear.

"You've been able to understand what people are saying, all the time you've been here?"

"I've got better, though I wouldn't claim to be fluent. I'm sure my accent is awful. I've not done any speaking. Only listening."

"You've been listening a lot."

"It's the best way to learn. Should I take this chance to practise? If you're sure you can understand me." Cassie pronounced each word slowly and with emphasis. In truth her accent was passable. "What was I talking about? Ah, I remember. Leirmond." Her smile broadened. "Is there nothing else you would rather talk about?"

"Such as?"

"Kissing me maybe? I'm sure you have not forgotten it."

Arian felt her face burn. "What's there to say?"

"Did you enjoy it?" Cassie laughed. "No need to answer. I can see it on your face. So, would you like to kiss me again?"

Arian's stomach bounced around like a spring lamb. Her mouth was dry and she could not tear her eyes from Cassie's lips. She did want to kiss again, denying it would be a lie, and a pointless one at that. But she was not going to give in, because Cassie was playing games. Arian would not let herself be anyone's toy.

She stepped back. "Yes. I do. But I'm not going to."

"How about if I try to make you change your mind?"

"How?"

"I could talk about what we might do after we kiss. Would you like to hear about that?"

"No."

"Come on. You and me. Naked. Together. Tell me that you haven't thought about it. In secret. In your dreams."

"I…I…" The words stuck in Arian's throat.

"Is it suitable for one woman to speak of hammering another? I think that's your phrase." Cassie advanced slowly across the courtyard, closing the space between them.

No words would come. All Arian could do was shake her head. Then, just when it seemed their lips would meet again, Cassie stopped and returned to the far side of the courtyard.

"No. I can wait." She reverted to Kavillian. "A willing woman is so much more fun."

"I'll never be willing."

"We'll see." Cassie's smile did not change. She pressed her fingers to her lips and sucked an overblown, dramatic kiss, which she then blew across the courtyard. "We'll see."

Cassie swept from the courtyard, leaving Arian behind, shaking, hot, and flustered. "I'll not be her toy. I'll not." She muttered the words under her breath. But who was she trying to convince?

❖

An owl hooted as it swept over the rooftops. Its call was matched in the distance by the howl of a lone wolf. Tregaran stood by the door hanging, peering out. Moonlight through the gap showed the outline of his face but did not touch the rest of the room. She and Tregaran were the only occupants. Kendric, Bran, and the Kavillian fighter were in Cassie's room on the other side of the courtyard, hiding in the passage chamber.

Arian went to stand by Tregaran. She whispered, "Can you see anything?"

"No."

"Do you think Leirmond will come?"

"I fear so."

"Why fear?"

"Because…" Tregaran closed his eyes. "Because I was sure the murderer was Kavillian. I wanted it to be so. It's a far more comfortable conclusion."

"But you now think it was Leirmond?"

"I don't think. I know. I recognised the knife Kendric showed me."

"From where?"

"The day of the games. A young man had brought a knife with him. He said it was an oversight on his part. He'd forgotten to leave it behind. I confiscated the knife, put it with the ceremonial spear, and thought no more of it. Then later the knife was missing. The only person who'd gone near it was Leirmond, a short while before Merial's murder was discovered."

The source of the knife had not occurred to Arian before. As with all sanctified gatherings, no one would be carrying a weapon. Yet the murderer had found one quickly. "You knew Leirmond had taken the knife?"

"I thought he had. I wasn't certain."

"You said nothing? Even after Merial was murdered?"

"I had no reason to think there was a connection. Nelda swore she saw a woman run away." He sighed. "But Leirmond's face when we showed him the knife. There's no—" Tregaran stopped sharply and put a finger to his lips.

Seconds rolled by. Straining her ears, Arian caught the faintest whisper from the courtyard. Leirmond had brought someone with him. Then more silence. Hard, remorseless, nerve-shredding silence.

Light from the quarter moon flowed in as Tregaran quietly pulled back the door hanging. Arian followed him into the courtyard. The hurdle across the entrance was pulled aside, and a woman stood in the opening with her back to them, keeping watch over the Royal Quarter. It had to be Nelda, which meant Leirmond was in Cassie's room.

Arian wanted to rush in, but Leirmond was better left to the armed men. If Kendric and the Kavillian fighter could not handle him, with Bran's assistance, then she would be worse than useless.

Tregaran patted Arian's arm and pointed to Nelda. Together, they slipped across the courtyard. Nelda still showed no sign of looking behind her. They waited, one on either side of the doorway.

Then came the shouts.

Nelda turned just as Tregaran reached out and wrapped his arms around her.

"What." Nelda shouted. "Leir—"

Tregaran's hand clamped over her mouth. Arian grasped her wrists. Not that it mattered. Leirmond knew they were discovered.

Voices rose from surrounding houses, as the group emerged from Cassie's room, Kendric and the Kavillian holding Leirmond prisoner between them. Bran followed on with Cassie. A wave of relief overwhelmed Arian. She tottered to Cassie's side and flung her arms around her in a hug.

"Don't worry. I'm fine." The amusement in Cassie's voice was obvious.

Tregaran raised his voice. "Summon Gethryn. He needs to hear of this. Now."

Indeed he did. They had evidence, from a witness nobody could ignore.

Gethryn sat slumped on his throne. He squinted at Nelda through bleary eyes, and largely ignored everyone else. He was one of the few people in the Great Hall making no sound. Even Tregaran was unable to get his voice heard over the chaos. Leirmond shouted loudest of all.

Emlyn arrived, hastily buckling the belt at his waist and straightening his shirt. The bands around his leggings were twisted, but the steward was better dressed than the elders who tottered in. Most were relying on long cloaks to cover their lack of clothing.

"Silence for the king," Emlyn bellowed.

The noise subsided. Last to shut up was Leirmond. "You're going to regret this." He was still defiant. The sneer on his face held no trace of doubt or unease. "You'll see." He mouthed the words at Arian.

Surely he could not get out of this. He had murdered Merial. He had shed Cadryn's blood. There was only one way this could end, yet he looked so confident.

Tregaran stood before the throne. "King Gethryn. I have shocking news to tell." The last whispers quietened around the edges of the Great Hall.

"Not as shocking as mine," Leirmond shouted.

"One at a time," Gethryn snarled.

Emlyn glared at Leirmond before turning to Tregaran. "High priest, please speak."

"Earl Kendric came to me today with a serious accusation. He claimed Leirmond was the one who murdered your sister Merial."

Shouts erupted around the hall, quickly fading to excited mutters. Expressions varied between surprise, confusion, and anger. Nelda looked terrified. Only Leirmond and Cassie appeared unconcerned. She maintained her usual dispassionate calm, while his arrogant smile grew ever broader. He was up to something. Anxiety turned to a lead weight in Arian's gut. Her heart started to pound. She could not concentrate on Tregaran's words, not that she needed to. She knew what he had to say. But what about Leirmond? How did he hope to explain himself?

Tregaran finished his account. "We've brought him here to face your justice. I regret waking you like this. But the matter was too serious to wait until morning."

While he had been speaking, Gethryn's expression changed from confusion to dismay. He did not wait for Emlyn. "Leirmond. What do you say?" His voice was pained, pleading, desperate. He wanted his friend to make it right. He wanted someone to cling to. Yet surely he could not doubt Tregaran's testimony?

Leirmond, on the other hand, looked like a man who has just listened to a childish joke—one in poor taste and without humour. He looked around the Great Hall slowly, milking the moment. Then nodded slowly.

"Yes. I was going to kill the slut. Any man might have done the same, had he just learned what I had. I was wrong. I admit it. I should have brought it before you, in a proper court. But if you knew what that fiend in female form has done—" He flung out his hand, pointing at Cassie.

She did not react, waiting for Bran's translation before speaking. "I've done nothing, apart from being the victim of yet another murder attempt."

"You say that. But I know better." Leirmond puffed out his chest. "She's the one who murdered Merial. Nelda was right all along. She did see her running away from the scene."

"No. I—" Arian did not get the chance to speak.

"Be quiet." Gethryn thumped his fist on the arm of his throne.

Silence gripped the Great Hall.

"Continue, Leirmond." Emlyn made a belated bid to regain control.

"Arian gave her an alibi. Arian lied. And do you know why she lied?" Leirmond let the question hang in the air. "She lied to protect her lover. The two of them. Two women. That's what the imperial slut has done. She's brought her depravity into the heart of our land. She's spread her corruption in the king's own family. She's polluted Cadryn's bloodline."

"No." Arian could not let that go. "No. That's not true. We—"

"You were overheard. I have my own witness." Leirmond pointed to Nelda. "She heard you."

Nelda nodded. "Yes. I—"

Leirmond had clearly learned from his previous mistake and did not let her say more. "Nelda was outside your house today and heard you talking with that fiend. You are…no. I won't call you lovers. That debases the word. You are joined in your perversion."

"Arian. Do you deny this?" Gethryn turned to her.

Before Arian could find her voice, the silence was broken by the last sound she expected—Cassie's laughter.

She indicated Bran, standing beside her. "I'm sorry if I'm behind the conversation, but I'm relying on translation. And that's the point. How did Nelda overhear us? Can she speak Kavillian?"

"She doesn't need to. Because you can speak our language. She heard you. You've been playing tricks. Spying on us. You're a two-faced deceiver. And if that's not bad enough, you murdered the king's sister. You will pay for it." Leirmond turned on Arian. "She can speak Lycanthian, can't she? Admit it."

How could she lie? Arian nodded, helplessly. "Yes, she can. And if Nelda was outside the house, she could have overheard us. But she misunderstood. We—"

It was no use. The hall was engulfed in chaos. Everyone was shouting at the same time, apart from Cassie who had her eyes closed and was slowly shaking her head. Denial? Despair? Tregaran and Kendric were also subdued, speaking together urgently in low tones.

"SILENCE." Emlyn bellowed for calm.

Leirmond held up his arms, claiming the floor. When the hall had quietened, Emlyn signalled to him. "Continue."

"Tregaran and Kendric came to me with the nonsense. The imperial slut dared accuse me of her own crime. I don't know if Kendric was duped or if he's in league with her. Somehow, they dragged Tregaran in. Of course, I wasn't worried. I knew it was nonsense. But, later, when I was asleep, Nelda came to talk to me. She didn't know who else to turn to. She'd overheard those two…" He pointed at Cassie who was listening to Bran's translation, still with her eyes shut. Leirmond shouted at him, "Stop the game. We all know she doesn't need you."

Cassie opened her eyes and nodded to Bran. "It's all right." She switched to Lycanthian. "It…I know a few words. Who…no…we have many days been here. I have a little…little knowing of words. I was to learn, with Arian. Me…I use wrong word. That it is what Nelda hear." It was a convincing show which did not fool anyone. That much was obvious from the faces around the hall.

Leirmond continued. "Nelda told me what she'd overheard. She didn't know what to do. The king's own sister! How could she tell him? She was shocked. Disgusted. And suddenly everything made sense. The slut murdered Merial, got Arian to lie for her, and was now trying to frame me. I wasn't thinking clearly. I was furious. I rushed to her house. I was going to kill the bitch. Who wouldn't in my shoes?"

"Why me want killing Merial?" Cassie kept up the show of limited fluency.

"Maybe because she'd found out what you'd done to her sister."

"Me and Arian not have done the wrong thing. We are friends. Is all."

"You said you'd kissed her." Nelda squeaked out the line.

Leirmond turned on Arian. "Do you want to deny that as well?"

Before Arian could summon her voice, Cassie said. "No. Women kiss here." She patted her cheek. Technically, it could count as the truth. Most women did.

"You don't ca—"

"No. Enough" Once again, Gethryn slammed his fists on the arms of his throne. "I…I…" He hit the throne again. "No more. This can wait. Tomorrow. We will have a full hearing. Tomorrow. Not now. Not when it's all so…" He looked like a little boy, lost and alone. "We should all go back to bed. In the morning. When I've had…"

"You'd leave her unguarded?" Leirmond sounded incredulous.

"No. We'll set guards." Gethryn turned to Emlyn. "I want armed warriors in the courtyard of the Kavillian house, and confiscate their weapons."

"I'm not sharing a house with her." Nelda piped up, pointing at Arian. "Now that she's got the taste for it. I wouldn't feel safe."

"There'll be guards in your house as well." Gethryn already sounded less sure. "Somebody see to it. We'll sort everything out in the morning." He huddled down in his throne, until Nelda came over to his side.

Arian challenged Tregaran. "The knife? Remember?"

"I feel I've not heard the full story. I must think." Tregaran shook his head and wandered away.

"Do you believe what Leirmond has just said?" Arian made a last appeal to Kendric.

He stared into her face for the space of a dozen heartbeats. "No. Not a word of it. Except that Cassilania knows more of our language than she's let on." He gave a half smile. "I'm going back to my camp. I'll see you tomorrow. And no matter what, I'm on your side."

Sleep was impossible. Arian lay, staring into the darkness. No moonlight entered her room. How had it gone so wrong? Beyond any hope of a doubt, by tomorrow, Gethryn would have persuaded himself that Leirmond was telling the truth. And then? Arian put a hand over her eyes. Not that that it made any difference to what she could see.

A crunch. A soft grunt. The sound of something hitting the ground. Arian rose on an elbow. The door hanging rustled, and a draft wafted across her face. Somebody had entered the room. Then a hand touched her shoulder.

"Arian?" The whisperer was Cassie.

"Yes. How…"

"No time for explanations."

The sound of a flint striking was followed by the glow of an oil lamp. Cassie was kneeling beside the bed. "We have to leave. Grab any essentials for you and your children."

"But the guards…"

"Have been taken care of."

"Nelda?"

Cassie grinned. "I'm sure her face would be most entertaining if you and I went to her room to ask if she's interested in a threesome. However, I think it's wiser if we leave her to sleep."

Arian sat up and fumbled for her outer clothes. "We're running away?"

"Unless you want to stay here and see how things turn out tomorrow."

"Where do we go?"

"Kendric's our best bet. I trust him far more than I do your brother."

It was not a hard call. Arian shoved a few items into a bag—her comb, a favourite shawl, a knife, needle and thread. If Kendric was willing to help them, he had all the supplies necessary for a journey. And if he was not willing, she would not be needing anything for much longer.

The children were asleep at the end of the bed. "Do we bring them with us?"

"Yes. Otherwise they'll be used as hostages to make you return. And of course, Feran is at risk on his own account."

"Why?"

"He stands between Nelda's son and the throne."

Arian wanted to argue, to insist the world had not turned upside down. But if Yehan had been murdered, what guarantee was there for Feran?

Eilwen mumbled as she was woken.

Arian urged her out of bed. "Hush, darling. We need to be quiet."

"Wha…"

"It's a game." Cassie put a finger on her own lips. "Shhh. You don't want to spoil the fun."

Eilwen nodded and took Cassie's hand. Feran did not wake as Arian picked him up.

Two warriors were supposed to be standing guard in the courtyard. Instead, they lay crumpled in a corner, either dead or unconscious.

Arian stared at them. "How?"

"Palonius is an elite senatorial bodyguard." Cassie kept her voice low. "They weren't. He dealt with the guards in our house using his bare hands. These had no chance once he'd got his weapons back."

"They were overconfident." Palonius flexed his shoulders. "A mistake."

"Are all your soldiers like that?" Maybe Merial was right to say the empire would win any war.

Cassie shook her head. "Legionnaires fight in formations. Anyone with enough arms and legs can do it. Bodyguards are skilled individuals. Their training is brutal, and very few make the grade. That's the hardest bit about Massillo being poisoned. He deserved a fighting chance."

Bran stood at the courtyard entrance. "It's all clear."

Cassie nodded. "Now the fun starts."

They set off across Breninbury, slipping from shadow to shadow. The quarter moon was high overhead. Houses were silent hulks, familiar shapes that had turned into sleeping monsters. The alarm might sound at any moment. Arian's heart was trying to crawl up her throat. The dryness in her mouth eased a little once they were through the side door, although swallowing took an effort. They were still not safe.

The scramble across the hillside was a nightmare. Shrubs grabbed at Arian's feet, trying to ensnare her. Halfway down, Palonius took Feran from her arms. The boy looked so small curled against the man's huge chest. They forded the river and approached the silent campsite. But not everyone was asleep.

Kendric sat beside the fire, poking it with a branch. He stood when they entered the ring of firelight. "I've been half expecting you. And trying to work out what to do if you appeared."

"Have you reached a decision?" Cassie asked in Lycanthian.

"You're not going to pretend a poor grasp of our language?"

"The situation is too serious for games."

Kendric gave a half laugh. "Does it ever reach that state, with you?"

"It has now. Leirmond's outplayed me. He invented a story Gethryn will believe."

"How much of it is invention?"

"When you and Tregaran spoke to him. You saw his reaction. Tell me, do you have any doubt about his guilt?"

"No." Kendric shook his head. "And nor did Tregaran."

"Priests are usually a good judge of character."

"It's more than that. Tregaran recognised the knife and knew Leirmond had it before Merial was murdered."

"Really?" Cassie looked surprised. "That's interesting."

"Was none of Leirmond's story true?"

"The part about me speaking Lycanthian is. Though I'd point out I've never denied it. I used a translator and people made assumptions. As for the other…" Cassie faced Arian. "Have you and I ever been bedfellows, or whatever word you want to use? Have we ever lain naked togeth—No. We can go further than that. Have we ever been anything less than fully dressed in each other's presence? Have I as much as touched your private parts, or allowed you to touch mine?"

"No. Never." Arian felt the heat rise on her cheeks.

Cassie turned back to Kendric. "There you have it. Have you ever known Arian to be anything other than utterly truthful?"

"Never."

"Tomorrow, they'll drown her for a lie, and cut off my head. Then Leirmond will have his war with the empire. If he survives it, he'll come for you. Because you're next on his list. You know that, don't you? He won't forgive you."

Kendric nodded. "Yes. I've got that far in my calculations."

"So?"

His sigh sounded like a groan. "Gethryn isn't respected the way a king should be. He's made enemies, or allowed Leirmond to make them for him. There've been men, heroes of the tribe, who've begged me to rise against him. They've pledged their support. I guess now's the time to see if they'll stand by their word."

"It's going to be war?" The answer was obvious, even as the words left Arian's mouth.

What else could it be, when the king was willing to break the sacred bond between the people and the land? The shedding of Cadryn's blood had to be avenged. Yet Gethryn would let Leirmond get away with murdering Merial. That Cassie's and her own life were at stake was a secondary issue. Or it should be. But the world was fracturing around her. Nothing was as it should be.

Kendric raised his eyes to Breninbury, perched atop its hill. "I've swallowed so many petty insults, hoping it would never come to this. But I think I've always known, one day, I'd have no choice. I just didn't expect it to come about to save the life of an imperial agent."

"Not just my life," Cassie said.

"Your execution would bring devastation upon us. I know it, even if Leirmond doesn't."

"Then since my life is the one at issue, let me send word to Verina. I can offer a full empire legion to fight on your side."

Kendric gave a wry smile. "Much as I'd like to tell you where you could stick your legion, I'm not that sort of a fool. I'll take whatever help you can give."

"Then one more thing...no, two. I'll send Bran as messenger, with Palonius to ensure he gets there in one piece. One of your men as a guide would be welcome. We don't want them wandering around in circles. And..." Cassie turned to Arian. "You and your children should go to Verina with Bran. The three of you will be safe there, until this is resolved, one way or another."

"What about you?" An unexpected chill went through Arian at the thought of them being separated.

"You should both go," Kendric said. "The middle of a war is no place for women and children."

Cassie shook her head. "The empire is involved in this. I'm the only person who can speak on behalf of the Senate."

"Can't your army commander do that, when he gets to us?"

"He's a soldier, not a diplomat."

"He says what he means and means what he says?"

"Yes."

"Then I look forward to meeting him," Kendric said. "But keeping you alive is at the root of this. I cannot guarantee your safety."

"There's a difference between me being executed by your king for something I haven't done, and me getting caught up in a civil war when I've made the conscious decision to stay. And the legions will already be committed to attacking Gethryn, who they'll treat as the guilty party." Cassie paused and glanced at Arian. "In my family, we're expected to accept the risks that come with the job. But I'd be happier if Arian and the children were somewhere safe. For myself, I'm not afraid."

And you think I am? Arian bit back the retort. Cassie's tone had held a patronising edge.

Cassie continued. "Also, I carry some of the responsibility for the bloodshed to come. I didn't kill Merial or Yehan, but my presence in your land has been a spark. If I'd been more open about my knowledge of your language, things would have turned out differently. I'd be ashamed to run away and hide while good men died putting out a fire I'd started."

That was too much. Arian's hands formed fists of their own accord. Cadryn's blood flowed in her veins, and it was not the blood of cowards. "If Cassie goes with you, I will too. If it wasn't for me, my brother would have no excuse to support Leirmond." She held up a hand to forestall objections. "I have a death to avenge. That gives me the right to invoke the spirit of Rigana, Cadryn's sister." She swallowed as tears stung her eyes. The next part was harder. "But Feran and Eilwen? Yes. They need to be somewhere safe. They should go with Bran. When will he be leaving?"

"As soon as possible."

Arian nodded. "Let me say goodbye to them."

Cassie's expression softened. "Of course. I need to give full instructions to Bran. Take your time."

"Then it's agreed." Kendric raised his voice, loud enough to wake the men sleeping. "Strike camp. We ride for Yanto's Leap."

Cassie

It all went just like you said it would." Bran sounded as though he could not quite believe it. "Leirmond swallowed your bait."

"And the fence post it was tied to." Cassie glanced over her shoulder. They stood a short way beyond the campsite perimeter, with no risk of being overheard. "It was like herding blind sheep."

The rising moon's light was supplemented by torches. Kendric's people were halfway through preparing for departure. The men moved with practiced efficiency, clearly having done this many times before. Haste was crucial, and non-essential items would be left behind.

Bran stared at the ground. "I'd have liked Leirmond to pay for his crimes, though."

"Don't worry. I can't see any way he's going to come out of this alive. Once he'd walked into the trap, he was finished, whichever way it went. Even if he'd been too slow to grasp the lure we dangled in front of Nelda, he'd have been executed. As it is, he's on the losing side in a war. Which is a much better outcome for us. Everything went to plan. If anything, it went too smoothly." Something Cassie would normally be suspicious of, but given the quality of the opposition, it was not so surprising.

Bran nodded. "Like being lucky with Nelda returning when she did? I was about to go looking for her, when there she was, wandering back to her favourite seat. Leirmond must've been too busy to talk to her."

"All my ingenious plans to manoeuvre us into position, and we didn't need any of them. I could hardly believe it when you gave the signal. I wondered if you meant it."

"That's why I coughed again."

"I appreciated the confirmation." She and Bran made a good team. "Everything worked perfectly. I just needed to say Leirmond's name loudly a few times to get Nelda's attention on the other side of the wall, then remind Arian of her suspicions about me speaking Lycanthian." In truth, it was a little disappointing Arian had been quite so easy to manipulate.

"Are you bothered Tregaran didn't continue backing us?"

"He was always a long shot, even with the surprise twist of him recognising the knife." A gift that would work in their favour. "Regardless of what he believes about Arian, he knows Leirmond is guilty. The thought of Merial's murderer avoiding punishment will tear him apart. As a sop to his conscience, he'll put more effort into arguing with Gethryn than supporting him. That sort of conflict among your enemies can't be overstated. Then, when it's all over, Tregaran will be well placed to play the role of neutral party in the peace negotiations. Whereas he'll actually be bending over backwards to make up for not doing the right thing at the start."

"That'll be helpful."

Cassie nodded. "A scoundrel would double down and refuse to admit he'd been wrong. Tregaran is honest, so he'll go to the other extreme."

The clop of hooves came as the first of Kendric's messengers departed, carrying news and requests for support. The riders trotted away into the night.

"You need to be off," Cassie said.

"Are you sure you won't come to Verina with me, my lady? Won't things play out on their own now?"

"I want to be on hand in case of the unexpected."

"Then shouldn't I stay with you? Palonius can take your letter."

"My cousin might have questions that aren't covered by it. There isn't time to explain everything to Palonius." If it were possible. Palonius was skilled in combat, and his loyalty was unquestionable, but he had never been the sharpest knife on the rack. "When you get to the legionary fort at Verina, you need to ask for an audience with Legate Quelinus Regulus con Cavionae dom Passurae. You can talk to him freely and tell him anything he wants to know."

"Will he be ready to take the word of a native ex-slave? Supposing he won't see me?"

"Palonius is a long-time family employee. He knows the passwords to get you a face-to-face meeting. Once there…" A memory popped up.

"Tell Quelinus you're speaking on behalf of the girl who dropped a worm down his neck. He'll know you come from me."

"A worm?"

"He'll remember."

Palonius joined them. Arian's young son was still asleep, cradled against his chest. "We're ready to leave for Verina, my lady."

Arian had an arm around her daughter's shoulders. Two of Kendric's men and a mule for the children to ride completed the group.

Bran glanced at them, and then back to Cassie. "Take care when the fighting starts, my lady. From what you've said of your mother, I wouldn't want to be the one to tell her you'd been killed."

"Then make sure you get back quickly. It's, what? Four days to Verina, and then another two to muster the legion? I believe Yanto's Leap is a little closer to Verina than we are here."

"It's north, where the terrain is more rugged. The journey might take a day or two longer."

"So, I'll expect to see you in eleven days or so."

"Stay safe until then, my lady."

"I aim to."

Arian hugged her daughter, then lifted her onto the mule. Bran took the halter. Wordlessly, Arian stood at Cassie's side, watching until the small group had vanished into the night. A chill wind blew across the starlit farmland.

Kendric rode over. "We're all set."

He reached down and offered a hand to Arian, then helped her up to ride pillion behind him. She wrapped an arm around his waist for stability. Of course, no side-saddles. This was not going to be the most comfortable of journeys. But it would be worth it.

Cassie gave a last look up at the dark silhouette of Breninbury, crouched atop the hill like a sleeping beast. The Lycanthi were split. There was a civil war, with one side willing to accept help from the imperial legions. On top of this, the heir to the throne would be safely in empire hands.

Divide and conquer. Mother might even be impressed.

❖

The afternoon sun was sinking as the riders emerged from the path through the trees. Cassie shielded her eyes from the glare. The path left the forest halfway up a hillside of scree and low scrub, heading for a jagged peak. Down to her left was a fast-flowing river. Sprays of white surf glittered as it cascaded over boulders. Cassie squinted for a better look at the rocks crowning the hill. They were not natural formations. The outlines of walls and roofs were silhouetted against the skyline.

"Is this Yanto's Leap?" she asked Nyle, the warrior she was riding with that day.

"Yes. Gethryn gave it to my lord because it was the most remote of the holdings, and he wanted Earl Kendric as far away as possible. I don't know whether the king gave any thought to it being the best stronghold in the land." The amusement in Nyle's voce was clear.

"Probably not." Gethryn was not prone to thinking things through.

"And that was before Earl Kendric made improvements. The palisade has been rebuilt in stone. The ground's too rocky to dig deep foundations. The old timbers would've fallen over if an attacker as much as spat at them."

"Good move." Stone was so much harder to set fire to.

Cassie shifted her position, trying to ease tired muscles. After five days, she would not be sorry to get off the horse. Kendric had favoured stealth over speed and picked a circuitous route to elude pursuit, should Gethryn have set his warband on their heels.

They were on the final stretch of the journey, zigzagging up the steep hill. Eventually, the track passed through a gateway. They were now in the shadow of the peak, allowing Cassie to look around without being blinded by the sun in her face. The outer wall was ten feet thick, and double that in height, topped with a walkway and parapet. Wherever possible, use had been made of natural rock outcrops to increase the strength and height of the defences.

The path climbed to a second gateway through another, even higher, stone wall. Inside was a maze of buildings balanced on irregular steps in the rock. These homes were identical to those in Breninbury, with turf covered rooms opening onto an inner courtyard.

However, there was a marked difference in inhabitants. Men outnumbered women by twenty to one, few were elderly, and children were completely absent. Non-combatants had obviously been evacuated. The men cheered as Kendric rode by and shouted his name. The more enthusiastic brandished swords and spears.

They reached a flat area before the largest building. This was, presumably, the local version of the Great Hall and meeting ground, although both were smaller than the equivalent at Breninbury. Kendric jumped down from his horse and passed the reins to an attendant.

With a hand from Nyle, Cassie gingerly slipped down from the horse. She shook her legs, trying to get the blood flowing again, not that it helped much. Walking was not going to be fun. Arian also looked tired, although she was doing a better job of hiding whatever discomfort she might feel. Cassie forced herself to stand straight. This was no time to show weakness.

An older man greeted Kendric. "Welcome home, my lord."

"How are things going?"

"Earl Halgor and his warband got here a short while ago. He asks to speak with you as soon as possible."

"Of course. I'll go now. Where is he?"

"In your hall."

Kendric took a step, then paused. "Can someone see to my cousin and the imperial envoy? Make sure they know where the important things are."

"I can do that myself, unless you need me with you."

"No. I'll be fine. But I'll want a full update before going to sleep."

"Yes, my lord."

Kendric strode away.

The man dipped his head to Arian. "Welcome to Yanto's Leap. I'm Talfryn, Earl Kendric's steward. You would be Arian." He smiled at her. "You probably don't remember me, but we met at your uncle's funeral. Maddock was a good king, who died far too young."

Arian's polite smile said he was right about the state of her recollections.

Talfryn turned to Cassie. "And you would be the imperial envoy."

"Cassilania Marciana pars Vessiolae dom Passurae, representing the imperial Senate in Kavilli."

Talfryn's lips moved, as if practicing the name to fix it in his memory, then he smiled again. "Please, follow me."

Before leaving the meeting ground, Cassie stopped and looked back. Thickly wooded hills rolled away into the gathering dusk. The climb to Yanto's Leap was even steeper than she had realised on the way up. The ground dropped sharply, giving a clear view over roofs and walls, down to the river. Beside it, an area of meadowland was cleared of trees to provide grazing, although no livestock were currently visible. It would be a perfect site for a trebuchet, and the hillfort was well within range. Fortunately, the Lycanthi had demonstrated no understanding of siege machines.

Trying not to hobble, Cassie followed Talfryn around the hall, to where a half dozen houses were clustered. At Breninbury, this area was known as the Royal Quarter. If a similar pattern followed at Yanto's Leap, this would be where the most important families lived.

Talfryn pointed out the largest of the houses. "That has been put aside for women."

"All of us?" Arian asked.

"Normally, two hundred folk live here. In the next few days, we're expecting over five thousand fighting men. Most women have left with the children, but a few remain, healers and bondservants. Elona is senior wise-woman. She'll find space for you." Talfryn gestured for them to continue walking. "I'll show what else you need to know."

At Breninbury, the encircling palisade was always visible whichever way you looked. But here, Cassie had the unsettling impression of the world ending. Nothing but sky could be seen behind the houses ahead.

Talfryn wound between the buildings, and suddenly, the ground vanished. They stood atop a sheer cliff, two hundred feet or more in height. Far below, the river cut through a gorge. The view was stunning.

The river flung a loop around the crag. It had not been obvious on their approach, but Yanto's Leap was virtually an island. The steep hill they climbed on their arrival was the easy way up. Back here, an attacker would have to ford the angry river, before scaling the rock face.

"Nyle wasn't exaggerating when he said it was the best stronghold." Cassie was impressed.

"Yanto's Leap has never been taken by force of arms." Although Talfryn's claim left out the possibilities of treason and subterfuge.

They were at the highpoint of the cliff. Cassie peered cautiously over the edge. The river was a long way down "Can I take it this is where Yanto leapt from?"

"Or so the saga claims."

"It also claims he made it safely to the other side of the river." Arian joined Cassie.

"Have any tried to repeat this feat?" It was not just a question of distance; the opposite side was much lower.

"What do you think?"

"I think drunk men do very stupid things at times."

Arian laughed. "In that case, their surviving friends have remained tactfully silent about it."

Talfryn also smiled as he led them farther along the cliff, towards the apex of the loop and away from the Great Hall. Immediately, the ground began dropping in a series of crumbling tiers. Steps were hacked into the rock, taking them down to a wide ledge, thirty feet below the highpoint of the cliff.

Talfryn pointed to where the path continued on, disappearing over the edge. "That leads down to the river. Water for drinking is brought up daily. But you'll need to go down to bathe. I hope you won't mind if I don't show you. My knees aren't as young as they were."

Cassie had no wish to go a step farther than necessary. "Is there any danger of enemies attacking through this back entrance?"

"None have dared try. You'll see why when you get to the bottom."

Which could wait until she had recovered from the journey. It was, though, one more advantage to the location. The absence of a well at Breninbury meant it could not withstand a siege. Yanto's Leap had no such weakness.

On the inward side of the ledge, a stone hut abutted the rock wall. What was clearly the flue of an oven stuck out at the side, although currently no smoke was coming from it.

"This is the kitchen and stores. Are you hungry?" Talfryn asked.

Arian shook her head. "Not me. We ate on the journey. Though I wouldn't mind water to clear my throat."

Despite the need to sit down and rest, Cassie nodded her agreement. She could hold out a while longer, if she must.

The hanging over the kitchen door was hooked back. Inside, three bondservant cooks were clearing up after the day's work. One pointed to a water jug. While Arian filled a beaker, Cassie grabbed a chunk of bread from a basket in case she got hungry during the night. Although the fire in the bread oven was out, the thick walls still radiated heat, and the kitchen was pleasantly warm, compared to the growing chill outside.

The interior was far larger than Cassie had expected. The kitchen was built over the entrance to a cave, extending deep underground. Heaped sacks and storage jars disappeared into the darkness, beyond the reach of the failing daylight. Its usefulness as a storeroom was obvious. The position at the rear of the hillfort was secure from a surprise raid, and food kept there would stay good for longer.

"These are the main stores. Any domestic supplies you need will be here," Talfryn said. "Blankets, lamp oil, soap, and so on."

"Is the cave natural?" Cassie asked.

"Originally. It's been enlarged over time and the floor smoothed. This whole region is riddled with caves. That's how the mining started."

Cassie put her hand on a protruding nodule of rock. Mining. What the whole game was about. "There's iron here?"

"Not any more. It was worked out long ago. Other caves, farther down the river, hold plenty of iron ore, and some lead."

"Gold and silver too," one cook added.

"Gold?" That was something people had kept quiet about, and it explained how the smuggler got paid.

"Not a lot." Talfryn shrugged.

Still, precious metals were a nice bonus.

They left the kitchen and Talfryn lead the way back to the cliff top. Dusk had thickened while they had been inside. "I must speak with Earl Kendric. We'll go by the latrine on the way to the women's house. Elona can help you with anything else you need."

The latrine turned out to be a wooden structure overhanging the cliff. While smelling far better than the equivalent at Breninbury, it was not as sturdy as Cassie would have liked. Thoughts of the sheer drop beneath the seats did not help her relax.

Talfryn bid them good night in the courtyard of the women's house. As expected, the building was crowded. It was larger than the one Cassie had occupied in Breninbury, but instead of the five Kavillians, over three dozen women were squeezed in. The room allocated to free women was marginally less jam-packed than the one for bondservants, but not by enough to get excited about.

Elona was an elderly, rotund woman. She coupled a sweet smile with a voice to make a centurion jealous. One barked order, and space was cleared for Arian and Cassie at the end of the sleeping platform. In the cramped conditions, women had to lie crosswise on the platform, with their feet sticking over the edge. Despite the noise and bustle, some were already asleep, and at least one had a rasping snore.

Gratefully, Cassie shoved at the hay to even out the worst lumps and lay down, squashed against the curved outer wall. Even so, she was grateful. Her legs were at the point of giving out and rest was essential. She felt the platform shift and heard the rustle as Arian settled behind her.

It was hard to keep back a sad smile. Of all the scenarios in which she had envisioned sharing a bed with Arian, this had most definitely not featured among them.

❖

"Lady Cassilania, a council of war is about to start. Would you be interested in attending?"

It was a silly question. Cassie smiled at Talfryn. "Yes. Of course."

All morning, a steady stream of men had been flowing into Yanto's Leap, either singly or in small groups. Messengers had come and gone. Yet news was in short supply. Cassie had settled for finding a bench where she could view traffic through the gates and listen to the clamour of rising activity as her best way to gauge the state of affairs.

She carefully levered herself to her feet and followed Talfryn, trying not to wince with each step. Her body felt worse now than it had on the journey.

Clusters of armed men were gathered in the Great Hall, interspersed with white-haired elders. Kendric stood by the fire, talking to Nyle. Another, older, man was with them. His bearing suggested this was the other earl, named the night before. Arian was also there, standing behind Kendric. She gave a smile of welcome.

Kendric looked over as Cassie entered. "This is the imperial envoy. I'd give her full name, but it's a bit of a mouthful."

"Lady Cassilania Marciana pars Vessiolae dom Passurae. But I'll answer to Cassie."

"Just as well, we don't have all day," a warrior muttered under his breath

"This is Earl Halgor." Kendric gestured to the man beside him. Cassie's guess had been correct.

"A pleasure to meet you."

Halgor settled for a sharp nod in reply.

Cassie smiled at the meeting. "Thank you for inviting me to attend. I'm here to offer whatever support the empire can give."

Nobody appeared overly hostile, but it was not hard to see that, like Kendric, the people would rather not have an imperial legion on their land. However, they also knew they had little choice.

Kendric signalled to Talfryn. "Sum up the current status, for the benefit of everyone here, so we'll all know how things stand."

"Yes, my lord. Most of your thanes have now arrived. The exceptions being those from the Weol Valley, who're staying to guard against raids from the north."

"Wise. It'd be just like the Endridi to take advantage," Halgor said.

Talfryn continued. "Earl Halgor has brought his warband, as well as twenty-six thanes, with partial quotas. We have promises of support from Earls Dallwyr and Osric. They and their warbands should get here either today or early tomorrow. Several of their thanes have arrived already, and more are coming in by the hour. The housecarl numbers are good, although we're short on freemen."

Kendric nodded. "Understandable, given the short notice."

"Have we heard from Ranvald or others to the east?" a voice asked from the back of the hall.

Talfryn shook his head.

Halgor frowned. "That's not good."

Kendric also looked concerned. "I admit, I'd hoped for more. Tregaran's intervention has had an effect."

"What has Tregaran done?" Cassie asked.

"He's nominally supporting Gethryn. But he's called on everyone to lay down their arms and attend truce talks. He wants the Council of Elders to sit in judgment on Leirmond."

"Has Gethryn agreed to this?"

"Of course not." Kendric folded his arms. "He's backed Leirmond and declared you and Arian guilty of murdering Merial. He's sentenced you both to death."

Little surprise there. "I don't get to present my defence?"

"No. Gethryn's demanding you both be handed over to him."

"Was that one of the messengers who arrived this morning?"

"Yes. Don't worry, we're not about to do it." Kendric's voice held no hint of compromise. "But some are taking Tregaran's call for a truce as an excuse to sit on their hands. We've got less than half the forces I'd hoped for."

"Won't Gethryn be hit just as badly, if not more so? If I heard you correctly, Tregaran wants Leirmond tried for murder, not me or Arian. I'd have said there was a clear message to be had."

"Maybe. But that doesn't mean people want to hear it. They're more comfortable believing Merial was murdered by a foreigner than one of our own. And once Gethryn gets to Yanto's Leap, he can block reinforcements from reaching us, while browbeating more thanes into ignoring Tregaran and joining him."

"Until the legion arrives."

"Yes. Until then."

"How big is a legion?" Halgor asked.

"Five thousand heavy infantry, with auxiliary cohorts of cavalry, archers, and skirmishers. The legate will leave enough troops to keep order in Verina." Cassie weighed up the numbers. "I'd expect around four thousand in total."

"Which should tip the scales in our favour. Until then, we'll have four warbands and nearly a hundred thanes with their quotas." Kendric nodded. "It could be worse. We'll be outnumbered, but we're in a good defensive position." He turned to Talfryn. "What's the state of our supplies?"

"Good. In fact, better than good, given the reduced numbers."

The meeting turned to details that held little interest for Cassie. The food would last for a month, and if the legion had not arrived by then, finding something to eat would be the least of their problems. More debate went into fanciful suggestions for improving the defences, and a pointless roundabout digression over sending a messenger to Tregaran.

By the time the meeting broke up, Cassie's legs were trembling from the strain of standing. She barely made it out of the hall with a semblance of dignity. Arian fell into step beside her.

Cassie hoped the smile she gave did not look too much like a grimace. "If you have time, I've got questions for you."

"You have?"

Cassie returned to the bench with its view down to the riverside meadow. The hills beyond were turning amber with autumn colours. Puffy white clouds drifted across the blue sky. It could be worse, Cassie told herself. She had something nice to look at while waiting for the fighting to start, a sentiment which applied to Arian even more than the scenery.

"What did you want to ask?" Arian's voice was hesitant.

What sort of question was she anticipating? But, tempting though it was to tease Arian, business came first. "The talk of warbands, thanes, and quotas. Everyone else clearly understood, so I didn't want to slow things down."

"Warbands..." Arian looked adorable with her forehead furrowed in thought. "They're what you saw at Breninbury. Every earl has his own band of warriors, though there're only half the size of the king's. No more than sixty men. They live in the hillforts and spend all their time training."

When not getting drunk and trying to bed as many women as possible. If Gethryn's warband was anything to go by.

Arian continued. "Thanes live in their own steading."

"A steading?"

"A fortified homestead. There's one for every village, if there isn't a nearby hillfort. The thane is responsible for maintaining order for his overlord."

Order, as in, keeping the peasants in their place. "And the quota?"

"When an earl calls a weapontake, every thane is required to attend and bring a quota of two score fighters with him."

"Who are these men?"

"The housecarls are members of the thane's family and his trusted followers. They'll be armed with swords, axes, and spears. The best of them will be as good as members of the warband."

"And the rest won't be?"

Arian shrugged in answer.

"So that's forty housecarls of varying ability."

"They won't all be housecarls."

"Who are the others?"

"Freemen."

"And the freemen are..." Cassie made a guess. "Anyone who isn't a slave or bondservant?"

Arian nodded. "They don't have any training and make do with whatever weapons they can find."

"Just to be clear, we're talking about farmers with pointy sticks?"

"They'll be better than that." However, Arian did not sound convinced.

"What's the proportion of freemen to housecarls?"

"It depends. Thanes select their housecarls first, then use freemen to reach the quota."

"What would be a typical breakdown?"

"Roughly even numbers, or thereabout."

"How many earls are there?"

"Sixteen."

"And how many thanes?"

"It varies. I don't know the total. Each earl has thirty or so under his command."

Cassie run the numbers through her head. "So, if Gethryn summoned his entire army, it'd be about twenty thousand strong."

"Probably."

Of whom half would have minimal fighting value, and there were questions over the rest. No wonder Quelin gave himself an even chance of conquering the territory with just a single legion. And if Tregaran's intervention was keeping most people away, the numbers were looking very good indeed.

"Was that all you wanted to talk about?" Did Arian look disappointed?

"No. It's not all I want to talk about." Cassie let her eyes roam deliberately over Arian's body and was rewarded by a blush. "But, given the circumstance, I think it's all that's wise."

Once the fighting was over, there would be opportunities for more interesting conversations.

Of all the things Cassie missed about the empire, hot baths came top. Or maybe good food and wine, smoke free central heating, proper beds, water flushed latrines. The list went on. She braced herself before emptying the bucket over her back.

No. Hot baths.

Definitely hot baths.

The icy water was made worse by the wind whistling through the gorge. Any source of warmth would have been welcome, but the sun's rays did not reach the bottom. This was not a bath time to savour. The Lycanthian version of soap was made from animal fat and ashes and smelt exactly as might be expected. It was, though, marginally better than nothing.

Cassie scrubbed herself dry with a square of sheepskin and pulled on her clothes. These were also in desperate need of a wash, but she was unwilling to walk around in them wet. She had not dared to prepare in advance of leaving Breninbury. Kendric was quite sharp enough to pick up on such things, if when the time came to flee, she had just happened to have a bag of clothes and toiletries ready to hand.

This was the first time Cassie had come down to the river. After three days, her legs finally felt up to the task. She took a moment to steady herself for the climb back. The stone platform at the foot of the path was large enough for a dozen people to stand on. Swirling water had undercut the cliff, providing minimal privacy against being watched from above. The roar of the river drowned out all other sound.

Little wonder Yanto's Leap had never been attacked via this route. Crossing the river here would be suicide. The rush of water had threatened to rip the bucket from her hands, which was undoubtedly why the handle was chained to a rivet driven into the rock. How many buckets had been lost before someone thought to do this?

Cassie started on the climb, praying she would not meet another bather coming the other way. Despite having a good head for heights, there were few places where she would feel safe in passing. The narrow, precipitous path was a further safeguard against an invader.

Fortunately, she reached the top without encountering anyone. In fact, Yanto's Leap seemed unusually quiet. The everyday rumble of voices was silent. Even the cooks were absent when Cassie went to return the sheepskin towel and soap to the cave behind the kitchen. Something was up, and she could make a guess as to what.

Cassie hurried between the houses. Now, she could hear excited voices, punctuated by occasional shouted threats. She rounded the hall. Groups were clustered on the meeting ground, gossiping and pointing to the meadow. More people lined the walls below.

Ragged columns were emerging from the trees and spreading out beside the river. A knot of riders galloped up the path in a show of bravado before wheeling around and joining their comrades. Ox-drawn supply carts rumbled over the rough ground to form a line backing onto the trees. As Cassie watched, a city of tents was growing. Already, trails of smoke from cooking fires drifted skyward. A banner fluttered over the largest tent. And, all the time, more and more were arriving, spilling out over the grass.

Gethryn and his army had arrived.

Arian

Trying not to look at Cassie was becoming harder and harder. Arian concentrated on the logs burning in the hearth, but the temptation was overwhelming. She risked a quick peek, and there was Cassie, smiling at her from just a few feet away. Arian's stomach flipped in a way that was becoming far too familiar. *Dammit to the deepest pit of hell.* Why could Cassie not leave? Or stay forever? Or never have existed? Or be someone different?

Which option did she want? Arian returned to staring at the fire, yet she could feel Cassie's eyes on her, making her skin tingle, making her legs grow weak, setting off a torrent that threatened to sweep away any hope of hanging on to caution.

And all the while, Kendric was talking. She really ought to listen, but her mind would not follow, until he slapped his hands together and said, "It's agreed then."

Was it? Arian nodded along with everyone else, hoping no special role had been assigned to her.

Kendric left the hall, with Earls Halgor, Dallwyr, and Osric at his shoulder. Several of the more senior thanes followed on, along with the elders.

Cassie moved closer and dropped her voice to a whisper. "It's good you're included. I'll need someone to explain things to me." So that was the plan. As long as they stayed together, she ought to be in the right place. She just needed to concentrate on something other than the awareness of Cassie beside her.

They tacked on the end of the small procession, following Kendric down between the houses and out through the two sets of gates. He led the way for another dozen yards before raising his hand in a signal to halt.

The weather had changed overnight, and now a thick blanket of cloud hung low overhead. The wind was cold and damp. A babble of voices filled the air behind Arian. She glanced over her shoulder. The top of the wall was crowded. Packed rows of faces peered over the parapet.

Cassie leaned over. "Why are we outside the walls?"

"We need to meet on neutral ground."

"Will it be safe?"

"Nobody is allowed to bring any weapons with them."

"You trust Leirmond and Gethryn not to break the rules?"

"A truce is sacred. A priest will call on the gods as witnesses. If anyone breaks the truce, they'll be immediately outlawed, doomed to eternity in hell. Nobody would dare. It's..." Arian tried to find the words.

"Like shedding Cadryn's blood? And the way Leirmond didn't dare murder Merial?"

What had happened to the world? A month ago, Arian would have staked her life that no one in the tribe would violate the sacred blood-bond with the land. Such things could never happen. She had been wrong. She would have lost the bet, and her life was truly at stake. For a moment, the ground beneath her feet seemed to soften. The sky darkened in her sight.

Cassie touched her arm, anchoring her back in reality. "I'm sorry. I'm sure Leirmond won't break the truce. Not with a thousand people watching."

And that was it. Leirmond would do whatever he could get away with, while Gethryn, her brother, would let him.

A harsh wind pushed layers of cloud across the sky and sent angry waves through the treetops. One strand of Arian's hair came loose and fluttered across her face. She tucked it behind her ear, hoping it would stay in place. Somewhere behind the clouds, the sun would have risen, but it gave no warmth to the day. How much longer must they wait?

Finally, a group emerged from the disorderly city of tents, wagons, and cooking fires on the riverside meadow. They climbed the hill, led by a solitary figure, slightly detached from the others. Rumbles from the wall grew louder, then hushed as the party came close.

The leading figure was a priest, one of Tregaran's subordinates. Judging by his wispy beard and pimples, he was barely into manhood. He held the ceremonial spear, with the sprig of mistletoe tied around its shaft.

"The priest looks young." Cassie had noticed as well. "Do you recognise him?"

"No."

"Would he be here against Tregaran's orders?"

"No. Of course not. Tregaran would have picked him to accompany Gethryn."

Cassie laughed under her breath. "Right."

"What?"

"Unless you can tell me otherwise, I'd say Tregaran won't defy Gethryn outright, but he's sent the most junior neophyte he has to represent him. It says he's giving Gethryn the bare minimum of support. It could even count as a rebuke."

Maybe Cassie should be the one explaining what was going on.

Gethryn and Leirmond were close behind the priest, followed by several earls Arian recognised, along with a selection of thanes and white-haired elders. They stopped the required two arm spans away—close enough to talk without bellowing, far enough to be out of striking range, just in case a flare of temper briefly overcame someone's better sense.

The priest attempted to drive the point of the spear into the ground. However, rocks defeated his first effort. A flush brightened his cheeks as he caught the spear before it fell. That would have been a terrible omen. Three attempts were needed before the spear stayed upright without a supporting hand.

He stepped back nervously. "We stand in the sight of the gods. I call on them to witness all that is said and done here. If any defile this sacred truce, then he will be outcast, and all men's hand shall be against him, for now until the end of time." The priest's voice squeaked through the octaves. Was he old enough to have passed the ordeals? "I call on King Gethryn to speak first."

Gethryn glanced at Leirmond, either wishing his friend could stand in for him, or trying to remember what he had been told to say. "As your king, I demand you lay down your arms and submit to my judgment. I say this as Cadryn's heir, blood of his blood."

Kendric answered him. "You forfeited the right to call yourself Cadryn's heir when you allowed the man who spilled his blood to walk free. Leirmond killed Merial, your sister."

"That's a lie."

"We both know it isn't. Have you spoken with Tregaran? What does he say?"

"You've deceived and confused him."

"So you admit it. He agrees with me. He knows who the true murderer was."

Gethryn clenched his fists, while his mouth opened and shut without any words coming out. Then he straightened his shoulders and pointed at Cassie. "We know who killed my sister. It was her, the fiend from the empire. I demand you hand her over, and the woman I once called sister. The two of them are..." He swallowed. "She's...she shouldn't. I...I won't—"

"Do you in your heart, really believe that?" Kendric was calm and strong, cutting through Gethryn's incoherent rambling. "Because you're the only one. Everyone else here knows Leirmond murdered your sister. Go home. Let Tregaran hold his investigation. And come back when you have his verdict."

The men behind Gethryn looked increasingly uneasy.

Leirmond could stay silent no longer. "If you want to claim I killed Merial, why don't you put it to the test? I challenge you to single combat. Let's sort this out, man to man, in the sight of the gods."

"All that would prove is you're thirty years younger than me. But if you want to decide it by combat..." Kendric turned to the priest. "Would you be happy for me to name a champion to fight on my behalf?"

"That's acceptable if—" The priest did not get a chance to finish.

"It's not acceptable to me," Leirmond shouted.

Kendric laughed in his face. "You're only happy to lift a blade against old men and sleeping women. There's a name for people like you."

Leirmond took a step, as if about to launch himself at Kendric.

Gethryn caught his arm, holding him back. "As your king, I demand you surrender."

"You've broken the oath you swore when King Maddock named you his heir. You've defiled the sacred bond between Cadryn's blood and the land. You're no king of mine." Kendric turned to the priest. "Is there anything else?"

"Do you have more to say?" the priest asked.

Gethryn only scowled in response.

Kendric shook his head slowly, like an adult exasperated by a toddler tantrum.

The priest pulled the spear free. "Go in peace. The truce will last until the sun reaches its zenith."

Kendric led the way back up the hill. No one spoke until after the inner gateway.

Cassie gave a long sigh. "That was a waste of time. Why did we bother?"

This was one question Arian could answer. "Leirmond wanted to draw Kendric into single combat but didn't anticipate him asking for a champion."

"Obviously. But why did Kendric agree to the truce in the first place? We could have saved ourselves the walk. Or is it a rule that you can't refuse?"

"It is when the king calls the truce. It's about precedence. But there was no need for you and me to be there. Did Kendric say why he wanted us?"

"I can make a guess."

"What?"

"To annoy Gethryn. Angry men are easier to outwit."

"They are?"

"They spout whatever's on the top of their head and give too much away. Not that Gethryn needs much prompting."

Cassie turned round and looked down at the siege camp. Gethryn had reached his tent. "The truce lasts until noon?"

"It allows time for people to return safely."

"No shooting someone in the back as they walk away?" Was Cassie joking? Arian could not be sure.

"What do you think Gethryn will do now?"

"Whatever Leirmond asks him to. As for what that will be…" Cassie looked thoughtful. "If he's sensible, he'll wait until all their forces have arrived. But from what I know of Leirmond, I'd expect an attack as soon as he's sure midday has passed."

Arian stood on the highpoint of the cliff, staring at the trees clinging to the opposite wall of the gorge. Everyone else was on the other side of the Great Hall, watching the siege camp for signs of an attack. She could join them, except the pointless vigil merely inflamed the tension in her gut. Or was she hiding from Cassie? Or hoping Cassie would join her, so they could exchange a few words without being overheard? And if Cassie did join her, what did she want to say?

More importantly, how much longer would she be tying herself in knots over stupid questions like these?

Arian closed her eyes and groaned. She half hoped Gethryn would attack. Then she would have something else to think about. The sun was still hidden behind cloud, but surely it was past noon. Maybe Gethryn would hold off after all, until more troops joined him.

The distant blare of a war horn carried on the sullen wind, immediately drowned out by other, nearer voices. She shook her head. Cassie was right. Of course. The battle was starting. Arian hitched up her dress and broke into a run.

Women, elders, and other non-combatants stood in huddles on the meeting ground. The walls below were lined with armed men.

Cassie stood alone to one side. "There you are. I wondered where you'd gone." She looked completely unconcerned.

"What's happening?"

"See for yourself." Cassie pointed downhill.

Gethryn's troops had left the camp and were spread across the bottom of the hill, crowded into an uneven formation between the river and the trees. Their shouts and whoops were matched by defenders on the walls. The line was many men deep, tightly packed at the front, but less well defined towards the rear. Warriors on horseback rode back and forth behind them, in the manner of sheepdogs.

Another long blast on the war horn startled a flock of crows from the trees. The black dots wheeled under the grey sky, while Gethryn's army began to advance, slowly at first. The shouting on both sides turned into a roar. Urged on by the mounted men, the attacking line sped to a trot. Ragged gaps appeared between the quickest and slowest. Someone on the wall loosed an arrow, more in anticipation than anything else, since the nearest attacker was still far out of range.

"There." Arian pointed to the wolf's head banner in the middle of the line. "That's the king's standard. Gethryn will be with it. Or…" *Or was he?*

"What is it?"

"Something's wrong."

"In what way?"

"The men around the banner. That should be the royal warband. A few might be warriors but…" The feeling of wrongness increased. "It's as you said. They look like farmers armed with sharpened sticks."

"They certainly lack discipline." Cassie did not sound impressed.

"It's a fake attack, to pull defenders out of position." It had to be.

Cassie gave a snort of derision. "And if you and I have worked it out, I think Kendric should be highly insulted anyone might think it'd fool him."

Arian scanned the walls, until she spotted him, standing in the centre of the inner wall. His warband were clustered behind the gateway. Even at a distance, their eagerness to join the impending battle was obvious. Yet Kendric was holding them back, neither signalling to open the gate nor sending them to join those manning the wall.

Meanwhile, on the outer wall, defenders were drifting right, towards where the attacking forces would arrive, leaving gaps at the other end.

"Kendric's voice won't carry over the racket, to get them to move back," Arian said.

"The legions use trumpet signals to send commands. Unless, of course…"

What was Cassie thinking?

Unless? It would be a step beyond the obvious. An idea came to mind. "Unless Kendric wants Gethryn to think the ruse has succeeded?"

"Maybe."

The front of the wave got within arrow range, although few defenders on the outer wall carried bows. Some attackers fell, others faltered. Those at the back looked as if they would retreat, were it not for riders urging them on. Even so, the pace of the onslaught slowed. Screams were mingled with the shouts.

By now, the outer wall was denuded of defenders on the left. Suddenly, a fresh barrage of war cries erupted. More of Gethryn's men charged from the cover of the trees at the closest point to the wall on that side. Even to Arian's eyes, these were different from the first wave—warriors, along with the best of the housecarls, rushing forward, eager to engage the enemy.

"They've even brought ladders," Cassie said.

More accurately, teams carried tree trunks with notches hacked to provide foot and handholds. It showed more forethought than for the first wave, but then, there had never been any hope of the decoys reaching the wall.

Everything moved so much quicker than before. The new wave had barely left the forest, and already they were at the outer wall. Defenders, realising their mistake, were scurrying back along the walkway, but too few would make it in time. And still, Kendric did not send in his warriors.

The first of Gethryn's men appeared over the parapet. The few defenders who had stayed in place were cut down in seconds. More attackers appeared, flowing over the wall. Some moved along the walkway, however, the width allowed at most three abreast, preventing the attackers from bringing numbers to bear. The rest of Gethryn's men dropped into the space between the walls. By now, at least half of his warriors were inside the outer wall.

"Archers." Even at the distance, Kendric's roared command could be heard.

Every man on the inner wall lifted a bow. Kendric had not merely spotted the decoy attack, he had foreseen it, and placed his archers accordingly.

Cassie shook her head. "Like spearing fish in a bucket."

For observers on the meeting ground, the area between the walls was hidden from view. But Arian did not need to see to know Gethryn's men would be helpless targets until the makeshift ladders were brought forward. Attackers on the outer wall were attempting to pull the logs up, but they were heavy and cumbersome, and the walkway gave little room to manoeuvre. A team almost made it, until an arrow felled one of the lifters.

"There's Leirmond and Gethryn." Arian finally spotted them.

Leirmond was still on the outer wall, with Gethryn at his shoulder. He was attempting to clear the walkway of defenders, but Kendric's men had made a hedge of spears

Finally, Kendric signalled to his warband. The heavy bar on the inner gate was hefted off, and the warriors surged through to join the battle. The tumult of war cries made Leirmond look around. For a moment, he looked ready to leap down and join the fight, but then he must have seen that the battle was hopeless. Too many of his warriors had been lost. He spoke briefly with Gethryn, then raised his sword in a signal. A horn sounded from the trees. Three short blasts. A retreat.

Leirmond and Gethryn vanished over the parapet, followed by as many of their warriors who could make it back to the outer wall. Figures reappeared, running for the cover of the trees, still showered by arrows. In the final reckoning, the attackers had left maybe a third of their number behind, dead or wounded.

The decoy wave was also in full flight. Cheers rung out from the defenders. All around, the women and old men began laughing and clapping their hands. The battle was over. They had won.

"Your people don't have much experience of storming strongholds, do they." By her tone, Cassie might have been inquiring about the weather.

"It doesn't happen often. Battles usually take place on open ground."

"I might have guessed."

"Why?"

"Because there's no well in Breninbury."

"What does that have to do with it?"

"You really need to ask?" Cassie laughed and patted Arian's shoulder. "Strategy and tactics. And Leirmond fails at both."

Rain started to fall as the first of the wounded arrived at the meeting ground, helped by their comrades. Some moaned in pain. Some did not move. One young man staggered past, still on his feet, although blood soaked his chest. Another was missing half his hand. One had red froth bubbling from mouth and nose while he gurgled like a baby, then suddenly the sound stopped and his body sagged lifeless. Elona moved to take charge, marshalling the healers with the same authority Kendric had shown with the fighters.

Kendric and Halgor arrived on the meeting ground.

"You anticipated the decoy attack then?" Cassie was clearly unconcerned by the blood and broken bodies around her.

Kendric gave a disgusted snort. "They don't have the numbers they need. It was obvious they'd try a ruse. Gethryn should have waited for more troops."

"Gethryn will do whatever Leirmond asks." Cassie shrugged. "Leirmond didn't want to share the glorious victory."

"Now he's got the ignoble defeat all to himself."

"I imagine he's never been confronted by a double palisade before."

Kendric looked down at the siege camp. The rain grew heavier. "Gethryn will have to wait until the numbers are on his side." He turned back to Cassie. "How long before your legion arrives?"

"Three days, at a guess."

Kendric shouted, "If Gethryn requests safe passage to collect his fallen, tell him it's granted." His voice dropped again. "Let's hope the legion isn't delayed." He left.

"We should get out of the rain," Cassie said.

But the sight of the dead and wounded was not something Arian could turn away from. "When the warband returned from a raid, sometimes they'd have lost men, and..." She struggled for words. "Their mothers, sisters, bedfellows. It was so hard to watch them. This war. It's not going to be just one or two. There'll be so many grieving. And it's our fault."

"What?"

"You and me." Arian glanced around. Nobody was near enough to hear. "If we had never kissed, Leirmond wouldn't have been able to accuse us, and this wouldn't be happening."

"If Leirmond hadn't murdered your sister, this wouldn't be happening."

"You can't—"

"If you think you can equate a kiss with murder, your moral standards are badly out of kilter. Do you really think they're remotely comparable crimes?"

Did she? Regardless of what others might say, how did she feel in her heart?

Cassie continued. "Anyway. You heard what Kendric said. This war would have happened regardless of you and me. It's not because we kissed. It's because Gethryn isn't fit to be king."

Rain fell in sheets from rolls of low hanging cloud, as it had for the previous four days. Dawn had passed an hour ago, yet the day showed no sign of brightening. The ground was awash. Arian's feet were so wet she had given up dodging puddles. Mud caked her legs to mid-calf. She spared a thought for those in the siege camp. Small comfort conditions there must be even more miserable, especially for people caught out when the river overflowed its banks.

Arian reached the door of the Great Hall, then turned and walked away. Her attendance at the meeting would serve no purpose. She had nothing to add and could make no use of whatever information might be shared. She went a dozen yards before changing her mind and backtracking towards the hall. Halfway to the door, she came to yet another halt and turned around. This time she took a single step before stopping.

This was stupid. Beyond stupid. Arian pressed a hand against her forehead. What chance anyone watching the absurd display might think she had a headache?

Cassie would be at the meeting. Seeing her would drive any coherent thought from Arian's head. Then Cassie would smile in a way that made it clear she saw though any pretence. On the other hand, staying away merely gave Cassie a different message to interpret. And there was no doubt Cassie would draw the right conclusions.

Arian could not hold back a groan. It was a sad fact, Cassie understood her better than she understood herself, and had since the day they met.

Dammit.

An icy blast of wind pelted Arian's face with sleet. Water dripped off her hair and ran down the back of her neck. Of all the foolhardy signals she could give Cassie to decode, what could be more idiotic than standing out in the rain? Arian turned back and marched into the hall, where a group of elders, thanes, and earls were gathered around the hearth. Cassie smiled as she entered, and all the previous turmoil vanished. But it would be back. That much Arian was sure of.

The meeting had already started, and those present were midway through querying the troop numbers.

"How many fighters has Gethryn got now?" Halgor asked.

"From the look of his camp, four times what we have, and growing, despite the weather." Kendric turned to Cassie. "Have you any news from the legion?"

"I'm afraid I left my crystal ball behind. I'm as much in the dark as you."

"They should be here by now."

"The storms will have slowed them down, but…" Cassie shrugged. "I expect them any day."

"Expect. Supposing they don't come?" Earl Osric snapped. The mood in Yanto's Leap had fallen as the army outside the walls had grown.

"They will, I assure you."

"But if they don't?" Osric persisted.

Kendric answered for Cassie. "Then we'll lose. Gethryn has more than enough troops to overrun the walls. He has for a while now."

"Why hasn't he attacked then?" someone asked.

"The weather is against him. And he may be overestimating our numbers. He won't know whether the earls he's not heard from have joined us, or are sitting on their arses, using Tregaran as an excuse."

"Can we get a messenger out?" Another voice from the back of the group.

"To who? To say what?"

It was pointless. Arian could see that. But then Cassie smiled at her again.

"When do you think Gethryn will attack?" Halgor asked.

Kendric's expression was grim. "As soon as the rain stops."

The evening was drawing on. Already some women were preparing to sleep. Cassie was standing by the door, looking at the sky. The last of the pale daylight picked out her high cheekbones, the length of her throat, her delicate lips. Arian could not drag her eyes away. They were lips she had kissed. The memory made her pulse race and her stomach flip.

"What's the weather doing?" one of the women called out.

"Easing." Cassie extended an elegant hand to test the rain. "It might even have stopped." Her accent, speaking Lycanthian, sounded rich and lyrical.

Elona joined her at the door. "It'll be back before dark." She sniffed the air, like a hound on the scent. "But the wind's changing. The rain'll be gone for good by dawn."

So this was it. The end was close. Tomorrow Gethryn would attack. By reputation, Elona was as good a guide to the weather as she was about herbs and medicine.

A man appeared outside. "Lady Envoy, Earl Kendric wants you and Arian to join him in the hall. Do you know where she is?"

Cassie indicated the room behind her. "She's here. What's it about?"

"Gethryn has asked for another truce, but..." The man gave an apologetic smile. "My lord will tell you more. Please, I must find others." He trotted away.

Arian got to her feet. She could sense the eyes on her as she went to the door. This was serious, and everyone knew it. "What do you think Gethryn wants?"

"Let's find out." Cassie waited until they were out of earshot of the other women before adding. "But I imagine he wants to give Kendric a last chance to surrender."

"Do you think he'll accept?"

"No. Regardless of what Gethryn promises, Leirmond will make sure Kendric doesn't live to see next spring." They separated to go around opposite sides of a large puddle. "And of course, you and I won't even last that long."

In the hall, tempers were fraying. "I'm not going to make wild guesses." Kendric shouted at a thane.

"Guesses about what?" Cassie asked.

"Some of Gethryn's forces marched away a few hours back, and now he's asking to talk to us."

"He's suffered a desertion?"

"It didn't look that way. There was no attempt to stop them. But as for what it means…" Kendric shrugged. "I don't see any point guessing, when Gethryn's sure to drop hints."

"Even if he doesn't mean to."

Cassie's words brought the ghost of a smile to Kendric's face. "Precisely. So, now that everyone's here, let's go talk to him."

This time, Gethryn's party was waiting for them outside the walls. The people appeared to be the same as before, yet something had clearly changed. Halgor stiffened then whispered urgently in Kendric's ear. For his part, Gethryn's smile could only be described as smug.

After all the rain, the priest had an easier time impaling the mistletoe adorned staff in the ground. His voice was more confident, reciting the traditional opening to sanctified truce talks.

Gethryn did not wait to be asked to speak. "You know our numbers are increasing daily, including some unexpected additions." He indicted a man standing behind him. "We not only have new warriors, we also have new information."

With a shock, Arian recognised one of Halgor thanes, someone who had been at the meeting in the hall earlier that day.

"You've found yourself a fellow oath breaker. So?" Whatever Kendric might be thinking, his voice gave nothing away.

"So I know your strength. I know your plans. I know you've sold out to the empire dogs. And their bitch has you kissing her arse. You hope the legion will get here to save your skins." Gethryn's smile changed to a sneer. "We'll have them pissing themselves and running back where they came from—those who make it. Their route has to pass through Blackstone Gorge, and you know what can happen there, don't you?"

Of course they did. Who had not heard the tragic saga of King Ceolwulf? Of how the king and his army were massacred, after Ceolwulf was betrayed by his brother. The steep-sided valley lay a short march downriver. As a spot for an ambush, Blackstone Gorge could not be bettered. It explained where Gethryn's missing troops had gone.

Gethryn continued. "You stand no chance. This is my last offer. Surrender. We'll grant mercy to those who've committed treason…" His eyes shifted to Cassie. "But not murder."

Kendric had been listening with his arms folded and his head down. Now he stood straight. "I treat your offer of mercy with the contempt it deserves. You're a disgrace to your lineage. You stand there, talking about treason. Cadryn's blood has soaked the land, yet you connive with that murderer." Kendric pointed at Leirmond.

"He's not—"

"Tregaran, keeper of the sacred law, has demanded Leirmond be put on trial. Not Arian. Not the imperial envoy. Leirmond. Because Tregaran knows the truth. If you win the coming battle, you might call it a victory, but in the years to come your name will be counted among those who have shamed the Lycanthi. I guarantee, when you draw your last breath, whenever that might be, the ancestors will not be there to welcome you. And I have nothing more to say." Kendric stalked away.

"Come back. I'm your king and I demand it."

Kendric did not turn his head.

"Yes. I..." The priest was again out of his depth. "Go in peace. The truce will last until sunset."

Not that there was any risk of fighting breaking out that day. Apart from the failing light, at that moment, the heavens again opened. Arian was soaked to the skin before she reached the inner gateway.

They trudged up the hill. The mood was sombre. Nobody in the group was speaking, but murmurs from those who had watched from the walls followed them. Hope had gone. Would that night see more desertions? Elona was sure the rain would stop tomorrow. Gethryn would have no reason to delay. Arian bit her lip. Was this to be her last night in the lands of the living?

They reached the meeting ground while the rain fell relentlessly. People began to disperse in search of shelter. However, Earl Halgor planted his feet and crossed his arms. His voice boomed over the pounding rain. "I swear by the blood in my veins, the sky above my head, and the ground beneath my feet, by the gods and all my ancestors. None shall ever say Halgor was a coward. None shall ever say Halgor turned his back on his friends. Gethryn's lackeys will pay for each step with blood. We'll make the battle of Yanto's Leap a story to set the bards singing for a thousand years."

Kendric took a place beside him. "Blood is our bond. It is the price we pay willingly. The ancestors are ready to welcome us into the afterlife. And I will not be shamed in their company. We may lose the battle, but we will never lose our honour."

Men cheered, punching the air, while Kendric and Halgor hugged each other. Those who had started to leave turned back. Others emerged from their house, heedless of the rain. More men joined Kendric and Halgor, shouting their refusal to be cowed, pledging their loyalty to death and beyond.

The cheering went on and on, while rain ran down Arian's face and back. Her clothes clung to her, but it did not matter. To leave this world fighting. That was how true Lycanthi met their fate. Arian could not help joining in the outpouring of enthusiasm. Ridiculously, she felt an urge to laugh.

The rain, if anything, grew harder. But nobody seemed to notice, apart from Cassie who stood on her own under the eaves of the Great Hall. She alone was not cheering, but she was not of the Lycanthi. Her blood was not bound to the land. Yet neither did she look concerned. From the familiar sardonic smile you might have thought her only concern was the weather. And perhaps it was. Who could say what people from the empire felt, when they looked death in the face?

Cassie briefly met Arian's eyes, then turned and sought shelter in the hall.

Women drifted back to the house in ones and twos. The mood was high as they prepared to sleep. Someone had picked up sheepskin towels from the stores and coaxed the fire back to life. One of Kendric's nieces offered a loan of dry clothes, which Arian gratefully accepted. She changed and hung her wet things by the fire, but there was no sign of Cassie. Was she still in the hall?

Arian went to the door and pulled back the hanging. After the final deluge, the rain had stopped, and a stiff breeze sprung up, tearing holes in the cloud. For the first time in days, stars peeked through the gaps. The quarter moon appeared briefly, casting cold light over the empty courtyard. Where was Cassie?

Arian glanced over her shoulder. The room was warm, filled with women, chatting, laughing, even singing, while others snuggled down on the sleeping platform. Her place was with them, but she could not stay. Arian slipped out, letting the door hanging fall into place behind her. If this was to be her last night on earth, she needed to talk with Cassie.

The hurdle had been placed over the courtyard entrance. Arian pulled it aside far enough to squeeze past, then replaced it after her. The sound of male voices was a rumble from the Great Hall, overlain by bursts of laughter and song. Arian stopped just inside the door.

Undoubtedly, the scene of chaos owed much to the flagons of mead. Mostly it was young warriors, turning the eve of battle into a celebration, although older folk and a few women had joined in.

A man dropped his arm over Arian's shoulder. "You come to give me a proper hero's send-off?" He slurred the words.

Arian wormed her way free. "I'm looking for Cassie, the imperial envoy. Have you seen her?"

"She's...she's." He peered around in confusion. "She was here. Didn't want to spend the night with me either." He sounded sorrowful, but then smiled. "Guess, I'll have to get drunk instead." He staggered away.

"You want the envoy?" another man asked, then carried on without waiting for an answer. "You've just missed her."

"Do you know where she was going?"

"To bed, I'd have thought."

"Thanks."

Arian escaped before other drunk warriors accosted her.

The distance between the hall and the women's house was too short to have missed Cassie on the way. So, where could she have gone? Surely Cassie would not be attempting to flee and abandon everyone. Even if she wanted to, both the main gates and rear path would mean certain death.

Another ragged tear in the clouds allowed moonlight to flood the scene in blue and silver. The wind chased ripples over the surface of a large puddle, distorting the sinking moon's reflection. Arian was about to check on the meeting ground when she spotted a figure standing on the high point of the crag, peering down into the gorge.

A sudden fear gripped Arian, she approached cautiously. "Cassie?"

"What?"

"You aren't thinking of jumping, are you?"

"No. Not at the moment. Though I won't let myself be taken alive, if it comes to that. This would be easy and mostly painless." Cassie gave a soft laugh. "As long as I avoid hitting the side on the way down."

"I wondered where you were."

"I was in the hall, hoping to dry out before going to sleep. But it was getting far too rowdy."

"Are you coming back to the women's house?"

"No. I intend to get dry and warm. Death I can face, but I don't want to do it chafed raw from sleeping in wet clothes. And I'm sure at least one woman would think I was making a sexual advance if I spent a night naked in the same room as her."

Arian felt a blush rise on her face, but she pushed the image aside. "Where are you going?"

"The kitchen. The oven will still be warm, and there are towels in the store."

"Do you mind if I join you?"

"You're free to go where you want." Cassie sounded amused. "But yes. I'd welcome your company."

Somewhat surprisingly, Cassie was the only one to have the idea, and the kitchen was deserted. The fire in the oven had gone out, but the thick walls gave off waves of heat. Arian found an oil lamp, which she lit using the glowing embers.

By the time she finished adjusting the wick, Cassie had stripped, and replaced her clothes with a large blanket draped around her shoulders as a cloak. The pulse kicked in Arian's stomach, and a tingle flowed over her skin. Fortunately, Cassie was occupied, arranging her dress so the folds dried evenly, but as she did so, the blanket slipped, briefly exposing a breast. The kick in Arian's stomach turned into a hammer blow. Her knees threatened to buckle.

Arian lurched to the doorway and braced her shoulder against the wall. She pulled back the hanging and peered out. More of the cloud had blown away, leaving tendrils behind. Moonlight etched the scene. The view was beautiful and calming.

She sought a safe topic. "Where did you learn to speak our language?"

"Bran gave me lessons on the road here."

"Just that?"

"I've always had a way with languages. There's at least a hundred spoken across the empire. I'm fluent in six and can get by in several others, which covers the most common ones. Yours has similarities with Alvaeric, enough to help me pick it up. And after a month here, listening to you all day, my ear has improved."

And she had been listening. Arian felt her face burn, remembering some of the things she had said, assuming they would not be understood.

Cassie continued. "The accent in Yanto's Leap means I have to concentrate more. But I understood when Elona said the rain has gone for a while."

"Do you think Gethryn will attack tomorrow?"

"It'll depend."

"On what?"

When Cassie did not reply, Arian risked a glance back. Cassie had pulled over a sack to sit on and was finishing drying her hair. She moved to her legs and feet. Arian could not drag her eyes from the sight of Cassie's smooth skin, the delicate turn of her ankle, the clean definition of her calf muscle.

Cassie looked up and smiled, clearly amused to have caught her staring. "I'm sorry, you asked a question?"

"Um…You said whether Gethryn attacked tomorrow would depend. What on?"

"Whether he waits for the troops to return from the ambush."

"Do you think he will?"

Cassie paused a moment, then shook her head. "No. He now knows Kendric is short on numbers. And after all the rain, a river might have become impassable. The legion might not get here for days, or even longer."

"So, tomorrow?"

Cassie nodded. "Midday, I'd say. Maybe a little earlier. Mud won't be too much of a problem for his troops, even coming uphill. The ground is mostly rock. But he might wait for the largest puddles to drain away."

"I would never have…" Sudden tears threatened Arian's eyes. The kitchen wobbled. "Never have thought it. My brother leading an army here to kill me."

"I can't imagine my brother wanting me dead. But then Jadio isn't…" Cassie stopped drying her feet. "For us, family is everything."

It was just about the last thing Arian expected to hear. But why should she be surprised? "Blood counts for you too?"

"Oh, blood's irrelevant. Half the people I call family are related by marriage or adopted. And many of my blood relatives are in rival families."

"How does that work?"

"Power, politics, and money. I know the length of my name amuses you, but I could easily treble it, describing my links to various other families."

"Your brother, is he a blood relative?"

"Yes. Jadio and I actually share both parents. Though Father's dead now."

"Jadio is head of your family?"

Cassie laughed. "Jadio? No. Mother's in charge."

"That's something that gets said here a lot. Men in the empire let women rule them."

"Not true. There are even slightly more men than women in the Senate. But I imagine just a single woman in a position of power would get your people's attention." Cassie put the towel down. "It's the army. In the leading families, boys are sent to the academy when they turn seven, and then the legions. They're gone for at least twenty years. While they're away, their sisters learn to manage trade and navigate political mazes. It evens things up. My brother has chosen to stay in the army. He likes the life and, apparently, he's good at it. He can look at a valley and spot how to turn it into a tactical advantage. Whereas I can walk into a room full of people and spot how to turn it into a political advantage. Though I'm not up to Mother's standard, which is why she's Doyenne."

"Is that the same as holding your family's bloodline?" Arian tried to understand.

Cassie laughed. "No. She wasn't even born into our family and her elder sister is Doyenne of one of our main rivals. She married my father when she was young. My great-uncle was Doyen back then. When he saw Mother's talent, he made sure our family kept hold of her."

Arian gave up. None of it made sense. But then, how much about Cassie did? How much could be believed? "Why are you here? Why are you really here?"

"You don't mean right now, sitting in the kitchen?"

"Why are you in our land?"

Cassie's expression lost its teasing edge. "Politics, family, and the governorship of an obscure province you'll never have heard of."

"It's a game to you."

"Some might see it that way."

Arian moved away from the door and sat cross-legged on the floor. Despite the shared danger, they were not on the same side, and never had been. She could not afford to forget it. "I can't trust you."

Cassie met her eyes with a steady gaze. "Not if you've got any sense."

"Do you expect me to credit you for your honesty?"

"Oh no. I'm probably the best liar you've ever met. But for now, I'll be open with you. If you stay here in the kitchen, I'm going to try to seduce you. Because there's a good chance we'll both die tomorrow, and I can't think of a better way to spend my last night. And for you, if you're going to die for a crime, you might as well be guilty of it." Cassie allowed the blanket to slip, revealing the ridges of her collar bones, and the curve of her shoulder.

Arian could not drag her eyes away. Her body would not obey her. Even the act of breathing was an effort. She tried to force out a word. "I…"

Cassie's smile broadened. "I know you pride yourself on telling the truth. But, when you said you'd never be willing, I don't think you were being entirely honest. Though I'm not sure whether the lie was for my benefit, or yours." The blanket slid completely from Cassie's shoulders.

Arian thought she had faced her inner demon. She thought she understood what it was, and what hold it could have on her, the strength and nature of the beast, its power to drag her into its maw.

She had understood nothing.

She was gripped by desire. A raw ache, a need, spreading through her. Her breath grew ragged. Her pulse hammered between her legs. Every inch of her skin was more alive than she had thought possible, desperate to touch and be touched.

"It would be better if we have some warning, should anyone come in for warmth, or supplies." Cassie smiled and stood up. "I'll find a spot where we'll be out of sight. It's your choice whether to follow me or not." She pulled the blanket over her shoulders and strolled away.

Arian's hands were shaking. Her whole body was shaking. Getting to her feet required three attempts. Her knees were almost too weak to take her weight. *Dammit.* Cassie was playing games. But it was a game she could not resist.

Arian picked up the lamp and followed Cassie into the darkness.

Cassie

Cassie woke from a light sleep. The sound of voices echoed through the cave, the words too mumbled to make out. Someone had come into the kitchen. Cassie pulled a blanket up over her arm to shield the glow from the lamp and waited. After, a few garbled sentences, whoever it was left the kitchen again. Cassie lowered the blanket and studied Arian, sleeping beside her.

She was beautiful. And naive. And a whole jumbled mess of wisdom and gullibility and misplaced certainty. Cassie stretched, feeling the way her muscles shifted, and the deep sense of contentment and relaxation within.

As was to be expected, Arian had been awkward and unsure of herself, sometimes too hesitant, sometimes too abrupt, her lack of experience evident. She had, though, not been guilty of selfishness, and there was an intensity in her lack of pretence, which more than compensated for any shortfall in skill. Who knew earnestness could be so arousing?

Cassie reached for Arian's shoulder, about to shake her awake. Much as she would have liked to spend the night in further rounds of lovemaking, it would be better if they were not caught. They ought to leave and hope the future gave them more opportunities, however unlikely that might seem.

She froze, staring at Arian's face. A wave of tenderness swept over her, along with the awareness that she could not bear to see Arian harmed. The surge of protectiveness was like nothing she had felt since the day Derry left for the academy. Whether or not Arian was happy mattered. Currently, Cassie's insides had the warm, golden glow from lovemaking, but there was more to it. She was adrift in a strange, deeper emotion that was so unlike her. Cassie shook her head. She had not touched the mead in the hall, so could not blame the maudlin sentimentality on drink. But equally, she was not sure if she wanted to blame it on anything other than the effect of lying beside Arian.

Cassie put a hand on her shoulder. "Wake up. We need to go back to the house before anyone notices we're missing."

Arian reached up, wrapped an arm around Cassie's shoulders and pulled her down into a long, searching kiss. Her hand slid down Cassie's back to her hips, pulling their body into hard contact. A soft moan escaped Arian's lips. When a dam breaks you can expect a flood, but this was not the right time.

Cassie disentangled herself and pulled away. "Believe me. There's nothing I'd like more than to make love to you for the rest of the night, and all tomorrow as well. But we have to go."

Arian drew a deep breath, then sat up. "You're probably right." She sounded resentful.

"There's no probably about it."

Cassie reclaimed her clothes from beside the oven. They were now dry. With luck, whoever just came in had been too lost to drink to notice or wonder about them. Outside, the clouds had gone, and the moon had set. The paths between the buildings were deserted, although a few voices from the Great Hall were raised in snatches of song. Cassie guessed many warriors would be fighting a hangover as much as the enemy tomorrow.

Nobody stirred as they settled on the bed in their usual spot, with Cassie facing the wall. Arian's hand slid around her waist, then wormed its way up to cup her breast. Cassie was about to peel it away, but let it stay. With the blanket over them, the chance of another woman in the room spotting them was slight enough to ignore. The risk was worth it, given the likelihood she might never sleep in Arian's arms again.

"Won't be long now." Halgor paced the meeting ground like a caged beast.

It was not speculation on his part. Something was happening in the siege camp. Gethryn's forces were leaving the tents and forming an untidy horde on the meadow. Cassie looked around the meeting ground, hunting for sight of Arian, with no success. Where was she?

"Do you think they've worked out how to deal with the second wall?" a white-haired elder asked.

"With their numbers, they could make a ramp out of bodies and walk over," another replied.

And as long as the bodies belonged to farmers, or equally unimportant people, Cassie was sure Gethryn would not care. It explained much about Bran's attitude to his former rulers.

Kendric stood nearby, on a natural stone dais, where he could see, and be seen, by everyone. "This day, we'll show the world the iron in our souls. We will show what courage, and honour mean." His voice was loud enough to be heard as far as the outer walls. "This night, we'll feast with our ancestors in the Halls of Glory. I'm proud to know you, each and every one here. I'm proud to live and die by your side."

Cheers resounded across the hillfort, but then, as they started to fade, a new sound started from by the Great Hall, a growing rumble that turned into song.

Dark the hall, and cold the hearth.
Grim the foe, and hard the path.

More voices joined in singing, until they were drowned out by whoops and shouts.

Cassie turned around as Arian arrived on the meeting ground. Instead of her normal shapeless smock and chequered shawl, she was dressed in male leggings, cross-wrapped with cord. Her loose shirt came to mid-thigh. Even more surprising was the sword strapped to her side, and the round shield in her hand. The look suited her even better than Cassie would have expected, especially when combined with the resolute expression on Arian's face. Cassie's knees threatened to betray her.

Arian joined Kendric on the stone dais. From people's reaction, it was obvious they had not anticipated her switching clothes, but neither were they incredulous nor confused. For her part, Cassie would have liked a warning. Clearly, something was at work, and Bran was not on hand to explain.

Although Arian was the only woman dressed as a fighter, both the names "Arian," and "Rigana" were called out, along with the term "Sword Maiden." Arian waited for the shouting to cease. The rustling and murmurs faded away.

"I stand here with my body as testament to the bond between our people and the land. Cadryn's blood flows in my veins. Cadryn's blood beats in my heart. And when I die, Cadryn's blood will again soak our land." Arian's voice did not carry as strongly at Kendric's but in the quiet all would hear her. "My sister, Merial, was murdered. And so I follow my foremother's example. Like Rigana, when Cadryn was killed by treason, I take up arms to seek vengeance."

Obviously, Arian had invoked a Lycanthian legend, and people were responding as though she was her mythical ancestor reborn. But she was only flesh and blood, and no matter what the story said, nothing Arian did in the forthcoming battle would make any difference to the outcome. Yet people were acting as though Arian could win it single-handedly.

Arian held out her hands for silence. "With my last breath I'll name Leirmond a murderer, accursed for all time. And I call my brother a coward for shielding him. In breaking his blood oath, Gethryn has shown himself to be no true king. In fighting him, I may die, but I'll never surrender."

Arian drew her sword and thrust it upwards, as if hoping to pierce the sky.

"Arian. Arian." The chant went up all around, resounding over the hillfort. This time there would be no silencing them.

It was awe-inspiring. It was also completely insane.

Arian looked horribly exposed on the inner wall beside Kendric. Logically, it made little difference where she stood. Once Gethryn's troops overran the defences, even hiding in the depths of the cave could only put off the inevitable for a short while. Yet Cassie would have preferred Arian beside her. Or better still, somewhere far, far away.

Cassie was not immune to an occasional niggle of guilt, nipping at the edge of her mind, but the gut level remorse churning inside her was both unfamiliar and unwelcome. Too late now to wish she had played things differently. Rather than taunt Arian into staying, she should have persuaded her to go with Bran and the children. But of course, she had wanted to keep Arian close, in the hope of a night like the one just past. The irony, now that her wish was fulfilled, was to realise the thing she wanted, more than anything else, for Arian to be safe. Regrets were always pointless, and this time even more so than normal. Soon it would be over.

The drawn-out blast of a tribal war horn sounded over Gethryn's camp, a strident, primeval braying, echoing off the surrounding hills. The horn was answered by a roar from the horde below as they started up the hill. The difference from the previous attack was immediately obvious, and not just in terms of numbers. There would be no decoy attack. No tactics. No subtlety. Just an all-out, frontal assault.

Poorly armed conscripts still formed the majority on the wings, but the fighters surrounding Gethryn's banner in the centre were unmistakably warriors, several hundred strong, the combined warbands of the king and those earls supporting him. The elite warriors soon outpaced the weaker troops on either side.

To a deafening roar of shouts and war cries, the attackers broke into a headlong charge. The leading edge of the massed fighters was halfway up the hill when the first volley of arrows struck. Men fell, but nowhere near enough to affect the onslaught. Already, they were closing on the outer wall. More arrows. More men crumpled to the ground, to be trampled by those following.

Defenders on the outer walkway surged back and forth, preparing to fend off ladders. The leading attackers were briefly lost from sight behind the wall, and then reappeared, struggling over the parapet. Some were struck down with sword or spear, but more took their place. Always more, while fewer and fewer defenders remained. The odds were hopeless. Archers on the inner wall made little impact.

Bodies were strewn along the walkway. Others lay crumpled lifeless on the ground below. Meanwhile, teams of attackers hauled up the makeshift ladders using ropes. Someone had learned the lesson of the first failure. They swarmed down the stairways and disappeared into the space between the walls. The second stage of the battle was about to begin. Kendric had kept most of his warriors in reserve for this last defence. Not that it would have any effect on the outcome.

Cassie desperately tried to spot Arian on the inner walkway. If they could share one last conversation, what would she say? Cassie fought back uncharacteristic tears. It did not matter. With luck, they would meet again in the afterlife, otherwise—

Another horn sounded, with a very different tone compared to the first. The clean, pure, bugle note made Cassie's heart leap. Like everyone else, she had been too intent on the battle for the walls to spare a glance for the valley floor.

Unnoticed by all, legionaries had arrived at the far end of the meadow. Two full cohorts were forming up in close order, four hundred men wide and five rows deep. The back line took shape as the last few soldiers appeared on the riverbank. Quelin and the legion had arrived. To another bugle command, they began their advance, shields raised.

Excited shouts broke out across the meeting ground. People pointed, cheering. Defenders on the inner wall roared, even as the first attackers appeared over the parapet. Possibly, these foremost troops were unaware of the legion's appearance behind them, but those who had not yet made it over the first wall were faltering. The flow of attackers over the outer parapet stopped. Kendric seized the moment to bring his warriors into play. The inner gate was flung open and his warband surged out, cutting the attackers on the inner wall off from their comrades.

The weakest of Gethryn's troops, the freemen farmers, had made slow progress up the hill and were yet to reach the outer wall. Someone with a loud voice was trying to marshal them into a defensive order, although several had already cast aside their improvised weapons and run for the trees.

The legion bugle again rang out. As it faded, a soft sound took its place, at first a low rumble, growing by the second, turning into the thunder of hooves. An auxiliary unit of cavalry burst from the road through the forest. The horses swept around in a wide arc, taking form as a narrow wedge, an arrowhead of mounted lancers. The ill-disciplined freemen stood no chance. They scattered, like leaves in the wind, and fled. Meanwhile the infantry cohort passed through Gethryn's siege camp, barely breaking stride as they smashed the tents aside. They reached the bottom of the hill.

In the battle between the walls, Gethryn would still have numbers on his side, but his troops were in retreat. Then Cassie spotted Leirmond, standing on the outer walkway. She could not hear his voice over the uproar, but he was clearly pulling back his warriors.

It was a mistake. His only hope was to continue the assault, take control of Yanto's Leap, and force Quelin to lay siege to the hillfort. But Leirmond had got what he wanted, the chance to fight an imperial legion, and like the fool he was, he could not resist the challenge.

Most of Gethryn's warriors made it back over the outer wall. Those who could not get to the ladders either surrendered or were killed. Of Gethryn himself, there was no sign, not that he would have argued against Leirmond. A small group of his warriors, surrounding the royal banner, headed for the cover of the trees.

The cavalry unit had wheeled around, ready for another charge, but would not reach the fleeing group in time to prevent their escape. The dense forest would work against both mounted cavalry and heavy infantry formations. However, the departing warriors represented a small fraction of Gethryn's better troops. The majority of warriors and housecarls had gathered just beyond the outer wall.

To a renewed barrage of war cries, Leirmond launched himself down the hill, followed by his troops. At first, Cassie was able to make out him in the lead, but then he was lost amid the swarming mass. They crashed against the legion's shield wall like storm-driven waves against rocks. And like the waves, they broke.

The cohort's first rows buckled under the initial weight of the onslaught, but then recovered and held firm. The advance continued, step by step, unfaltering, until they were halfway up the hill, cutting down everyone before them.

The cavalry auxiliaries returned for a second run and the battle became a rout. Gethryn's troops were plunged into a desperate race to escape, each man for himself. Some made it to the safety of the trees. Many did not. The fighting was over.

But where was Arian? Surely she would not have done anything so stupid as follow the warriors out through the gate. Would she? She was not a warrior and did not have the training or the strength, no matter what the childish legend might suggest. Panic knotted Cassie's gut. Neither Arian nor Kendric were on the walkway. But then a group of warriors appeared, marching up the hill to the meeting ground with Arian hoisted aloft on their shoulders. Other warriors cheered and shouted her name, as if Arian, rather than the legion, had swung the course of the battle.

It made no sense, but Cassie did not care.

Cassie caught up with Kendric near the outer gates. Halgor was propped against the wall, coated in blood, although still alive and conscious.

Kendric crouched beside him. "I'll get Elona to look at you."

"It's nothing." Which was possibly not quite the truth.

"There'll be surgeons with the legion," Cassie said. "I'll ask them to help with the wounded."

"I'm not having some arse-fucker of an empire pox merchant poking around at me." Halgor continued with a string of phases even Bran's coaching had not equipped Cassie to translate.

Kendric patted Halgor's shoulder and stood up. "I guess a man who can swear like that is not yet ready to meet his ancestors."

"You shouldn't be so quick to dismiss empire medicine. Army surgeons get a lot of practice."

"As do our priests and wise-women," Kendric said. "But I assume you've come to suggest we talk with your legion commander."

"Legate Quelinus Regulus con Cavionae dom Passurae. He's a relative of mine." Cassie smiled at Kendric's bemused expression. "Don't worry. He'll be happy to answer to the title of Legate."

"My lord, riders are coming," a man on the wall shouted down.

"And that will be my cousin. Shall we go?"

"Yes." Kendric raised his voice. "Open the gate."

Arian had been released by her bearers and joined them, along with several others. Cassie risked a few sideways glances. The male attire really did suit Arian, far more so than the horrendous smock she normally wore. It set off a whole slew of ideas that had nothing to do with the upcoming meeting, and Cassie needed to focus her thoughts. So far, everything had gone to plan. A clear head for the next phase was essential.

Quelin and his officers dismounted, leaving the horses in the care of their adjutants. Behind them, the legionaries stood like statues, eyes front, heads up, feet square. Their shields rested on the ground, and their swords were sheathed. Yet, if anything, the stillness only increased the aura of menace. The cohort was a killing machine that could spring into life on a command.

The two groups met at the midway point between the legion's front rank and the outer wall. Cassie stayed beside Kendric, rather than join her fellow Kavillians. A display of switching sides would not give a good visual impression.

The amusement in Quelin's smile when he saw her was easy to decipher. Despite the care taken in drying her clothes, Cassie knew her appearance would shame a common street whore in Kavilli. Her standard of grooming had taken a hit over the previous month. Her gown was stained, and her hair felt like a haystack glued to her head. The absence of proper mirrors in Yanto's Leap was a blessing.

"I'm pleased to see you again, cousin," Quelin said.

"As I am to see you." That much was certain. "Can I introduce Earl Kendric, overlord of this region."

Quelin gave a formal bow. "May the gods bestow their blessings upon you."

"I welcome you as an honoured guest." Kendric spoke in Kavillian. "I never thought I'd be happy to see an empire legion arrive outside my gates, or wish it might have happened sooner."

"I apologise for the delay. The weather was against us. One ford was impassable, so we had to detour around it."

"I'm grateful you arrived at all. We had been told an ambush was planned for you."

"We were told about it as well. Farming folk in a village warned us, and a local trader showed us an alternate route."

"I'm glad my commoners were able to help." Kendric probably had suspicions about what sort of trader it was. He was too astute to be ignorant of smuggling in his region.

"You arrived without a second to spare," Cassie said.

"The timing wasn't as tight as it might have seemed. Normally, I'd have tried ambushing the ambushers, but we were told the situation here was critical, so we pressed ahead." Quelin smiled "The trader's route wasn't ideal for a large scale overnight march, so I only brought half my cohorts and the cavalry. We reached position on the hill overlooking the river just before dawn. I was finalising my plans to attack the camp, when they beat me to it. When I saw them obligingly leave the meadow free, I took my chance to get into formation."

"Which is something I've told our young warriors," Kendric said. "Once your men are lined up, attacking them is a shortcut to a fool's death."

"You've seen empire legions in battle before?" Quelin asked.

"Yes. Once. It didn't go any better for our warriors back then than it did here."

"Then may I say I'm happy we're on the same side this time."

"Not as happy as I am." Kendric laughed. "I'm glad you got here in time. Forced marches are never easy, even more so with a battle to fight at the end of it."

"Better to fight now, with your help, than fight alone and pick up the pieces afterwards."

The men were clearly feeling each other out, as two military commanders. So far, the signs were good. They understood each other and were prepared to give due respect. It would serve them well in the future, but it was time to move on.

"We must think about our next step," Cassie said. "The king's banner left, so I assume Gethryn went with it. Which leaves the question of why he didn't join Leirmond in attacking the legion."

"He may be dead," Kendric said. "An honour guard could have taken his body away for a proper funeral."

"Then the first thing we need is information." Cassie looked around the battlefield. "We need to question the wounded."

"Agreed. Someone will know what happened to Gethryn."

"Either way, we should take control of Breninbury. I suggest sending messengers asking people to meet us there. The earls who failed to join you before won't be so hesitant now." It was a sad truth that the less need there was for support, the easier it was to find it. "We should also send word to Tregaran. We want him to first hear about this from us. He'll have a role in bringing things to an end with a minimum of bloodshed."

Kendric nodded. "I'll see to it."

"Time is on our side. Even if Gethryn is alive, his support will melt away, and we know where to find him. For now, we should tend to the wounded and summon the other cohorts."

"And deal with the would-be ambushers, if they're still around," Quelin added.

"I'd enjoy helping you with that." Kendric took a step forward. Quelin met him in the middle, and the two clasped each other's forearm in the universal gesture of camaraderie.

"I look forward to getting to know you better," Quelin said.

"And I you."

The meeting ended. The Lycanthi returned to Yanto's Leap, while army officers bellowed orders at their men.

Quelin approached Cassie. "I'll speak with you later. I've got matters to attend to right now."

"Of course."

"Your man, Bran, thought you might appreciate a few bits and pieces from Verina. He persuaded me to bring a pavilion for you. I'll have it set up in camp."

Cassie mentally added a bonus to Bran's salary. "Thank you. Is Bran with you?"

"He wanted to come, but I left him with the two children. They needed a translator, and he was a familiar face."

How could she have forgotten them? Cassie turned, preparing to shout. However, Arian had not left with the other Lycanthians. She stood a short distance away, staring across the hillside.

"Arian."

She looked around. "Yes?"

"This is my cousin Quelin. He's the one I sent your children to."

"You're the mother." If Quelin was surprised at Arian's attire he gave no sign.

"They're safe?" The eagerness in her voice was both understandable and unmissable.

"Yes. Your son's of a similar age to my youngest. When I left, they were playing together with a set of toy soldiers. However, I regret to say you may have trouble getting your daughter out of the bathhouse. She's taken an extreme liking to it."

"Thank you. I can't wait to have them back."

"I imagine so. But I must go. I hope to see you soon." Quelin went.

Arian took two steps away but then stopped with her back to Cassie, scouring the hillside. Gethryn would not be there. Regardless of what condition he was in, he would have left with his banner. So what was she looking for?

Battlefields never made easy viewing. The ground was smeared with red. Bodies lay scattered, eyes wide open, seeing nothing. They would never see anything again. Smashed heads. One severed arm. An early crow, helping itself to eyeballs. From somewhere near at hand came gurgling, the unforgettable sound of a man choking on his own blood. Farther away, a voice screamed, "Mama, Mama."

Healers emerged from Yanto's Leap, led by Elona, to tend to those who could be helped and provide a quick release for those who could not. The cries of Mama ended abruptly. Soon, the mother in question would be getting the worst of all news.

Nobody living was close enough to overhear, even so Cassie lowered her voice. "Are you all right?"

"Yes. Why shouldn't I be?" Yet, Arian would not face her.

Rather than answer directly, Cassie switched tack. "I was surprised to see you dressed like this."

"It's my right."

"Your right?"

"I'm the king's sister. It's traditional. When Cadryn was betrayed and murdered, his sister, Rigana, took up arms to avenge him. She was the first Sword Maiden. Ever since, women of my bloodline have copied her when there was a death to avenge. My great-grandmother did it three times."

"Wasn't she running out of brothers?"

"First it was her uncle, then a nephew, and finally her son." Arian turned around but would not look up. "It's said no battle has ever been lost with a Sword Maiden fighting on their side."

Which explained why everyone had gone crazy. "You've kept up the winning record. But you could have told me what you were planning."

"Why?"

"Because, when I saw you dressed for battle, I wondered if you were suffering an attack of guilt and were looking to get yourself killed in an extravagant display."

"Guilt? About what?" For the first time, Arian met Cassie's eyes.

"About indulging in shameful empire perversions." Cassie keep her tone light, but was still rewarded with a scowl.

"No." The denial came too quickly.

"Something's upset you."

"Why do you say that?"

"Because it's obvious. Are you concerned over Gethryn? He might be alive. It's pos—"

"No. He's brought this on himself."

"Then what?" When no answer came, Cassie continued. "Quelin is putting up a tent for me. Why don't you join me there? We can talk. Maybe I could make you feel happier."

The attempt at charm failed. Arian's expression twisted, as if she was either about to cry or be sick. "No." She snapped the word and stalked up the hill.

Cassie groaned. The battle was won, but she could not claim an unqualified success all round.

Cassie put down the comb. Her hair finally felt as though it was not merely following her around out of habit. She nibbled on a cheese and almond pastry and followed it with a mouthful of sweet red wine. The cook had apologised for the standard of the food. If he only knew!

A junior officer poked his head into the tent. "Lady Cassilania, there's a representative of the tribesfolk to see you."

The flare of hope that Arian had changed her mind died. One of Kendric's thanes entered. He looked around with naked curiosity. If he was expecting a display of empire decadence, he would be disappointed. The folding table and chairs were probably the most noteworthy items. The oil in the lamp did not give off rancid smoke, if he thought to sniff it. Cassie had washed in a basin of hot water, and steam was still coming off, but there was no bath. The camp bed was far more comfortable than hay, however, this would not be apparent without lying on it.

"Earl Kendric sent you?" Cassie prompted him after the gawking had gone on long enough.

"Err, yes. He wanted you know what he's found out from the prisoners."

"Please, go ahead."

"Leirmond is dead." Which gave little cause for either surprise or sorrow. "As are two earls. Gethryn was wounded fighting on the outer wall. Leirmond was arranging for him to be taken to safety when the legion arrived."

"Ah. That's why Leirmond wasn't leading the attack on the inner wall." It had been surprising not to see him in the forefront of battle. Whatever his faults, Leirmond had never been accused of ducking a fight. "Do we know how badly Gethryn was injured?"

"He was alive when he was carried away, but that's all anyone can say."

"Is there anything else?"

"Yes. My lord invites you and the legate to feast with him in his hall tomorrow night. You will be accorded honorary male status for the evening."

"Thank you." Cassie smiled. They meant well. "Please tell Earl Kendric we'll be pleased to attend."

The thane left. Cassie was pouring herself another glass when the tent flap opened again.

Quelin entered. "How are you doing?"

"Fine. Here, have some wine."

Quelin sat in a chair. "I'd better not. I need to keep a clear head, in case somebody decides to do something stupid."

"Such as?"

"If you knew soldiers the way I do..." He let the sentence tail off. "You've done an amazing job. I don't want it thrown away because a grunt hasn't seen enough fighting for one day, or decides a local woman owes him a favour." He smiled at Cassie. "Even after talking to your man, I'm not sure how you did it. A ready-made spy network. The heir to the throne in our keeping. The legion invited inside the territory. And we're about to lay siege to the main stronghold with half the tribesfolk fighting on our side."

"I was lucky."

"You're being modest."

Cassie shrugged. "Anyway, it's not over yet. We still need to get the right deal with Kendric."

"What are your thoughts about him?"

"He's sharp. Quite sharp enough to know that having let us into their land they aren't going to get us out easily. But he's a sensible man, and I'm sure we can reach a compromise acceptable to both him and the Senate. As long as we have full access to the mining, we can offer autonomous client kingdom status. They have troublesome neighbours to the north, so we'll need to permanently station troops there to protect the trade route." Cassie pursed her lips. "Some folk won't like it, but I think Kendric will be happy to let us deal with their traditional enemies for them."

"Do you want to make him king?"

"No. But for the right reason. He's got a strong sense of honour. He wouldn't usurp the throne even we begged him to. And that's what will make him acceptable to the various factions. Everyone knows they can trust him not to abuse the role of regent for Arian's son."

"How about the current king? Do we know if he's still alive?"

"I've just had a message from Kendric." Cassie quickly ran through the information. "However, even if Gethryn lives, he's not someone we can work with. He's too weak. He'll latch on to a favourite and turn himself into their pawn. With Leirmond gone, he's a straw in the wind."

"We can't blow him into our hands?"

"It would only last till the next draft. Within a year or two, someone would talk him into being stupid."

A head appeared through the tent flap. "Sir, Centurion Vitus dom Gavinae wants to speak with you."

Quelin sighed and got to his feet. "I'd better see what it's about. I'll talk to you tomorrow." He nodded at the wine bottle. "Have a drink for me."

Alone again, Cassie stared at the glass. If only Arian were there to share it with her. Images kept swirling though her head, along with memories, making her entire body ache. She wanted Arian with an intensity she had not felt since leaving adolescence behind.

Cassie drained the glass. The pieces were falling into place. Victory in everything she had set out to achieve lay within her grasp. And yet, the one goal she now wanted most might slip through her fingers. They had enjoyed each other for one night.

Cassie emptied the bottle into her glass and groaned. One night. She wanted more.

Without looking, Cassie knew where Arian was. She could feel a prickling on her skin, a ray of warmth, a bone deep ache, calling to her. Cassie rested her chin on her hand and let her gaze travel around the gathering, trying to make it appear like an idle scan of the hall.

With the meal over, the food servers had gone. At one end of the hall, a ring of young men were enthusiastically cheering on an arm-wrestling contest. More were gathered around the harper, beside the central hearth. A knot of white-haired elders clustered at the table where remains of the food were laid out.

And there was Arian, exactly where Cassie had known she would be, back turned, listening to the song. Arian had been the only woman, apart from herself, to sit and eat. Did the title of Sword Maiden come with automatic male status? She was still dressed as a man, and it still suited her.

The clothes might have been designed to show off the length of her limbs, with a tightening over her breasts and waist. The hip-level sword belt perfectly balanced the width of her shoulders. Putting her in one of those shapeless smocks should be made a crime. All that remained was to swap the awful boots for something more…

Cassie was staring. She dragged her attention back to Kendric and Quelin, who were deep in conversation about the rival tribe, the Endridi. If she remembered correctly, they were the ones who had butchered Bran's family and sold him as a slave. It was the sort of thing the empire would put a stop to. She tried to pay attention to the talk of choke points, supply lines, and flanking opportunities, but the sense of Arian's presence suddenly spiked beyond her ability to resist.

She peeked over, and this time caught Arian, looking her way. Their eyes met. Immediately, Arian turned and left without a backwards glance. Cassie returned her attention to Quelin and Kendric. With Arian gone, concentrating should be easier.

It was not.

Why was Arian acting this way? She said she was not feeling guilty, which might not be the entire truth. Yet, there had to be more. Where had she gone? Would talking to her help or make things worse? Cassie bit back a groan. This was stupid. She could not stay at the table. It was not as if she had anything useful to add to the military analysis.

"Back soon." Cassie mouthed the words to Quelin.

Although night had fallen, a few people were around. Most of the thanes had gone to their steadings to repair and replace items damaged in the battle. They and their followers would rejoin Kendric in a few days for the march on Breninbury. Their place in Yanto's Leap was taken by the returning civilian population. For the first time, children were in evidence.

Had Arian gone to bed? The latrine? Somewhere else? There was, though, one obvious place to check. If Arian had gone there it would mean something, although possibly not something good.

The kitchen was empty. Cassie passed the oven and heaped sacks, heading deeper into the cave. Even before reaching the alcove, the sound of movement let her know her guess was correct. She turned the corner. Arian was standing in the spot where, just two nights before, they had made love.

"Why are you here?" Arian was clearly not happy.

"Isn't it obvious? I followed you."

"Why?"

"That ought to be obvious as well. Do you really need me to explain?"

"I don't want to talk to you."

"Now it's my turn to ask why. And you can't say it's obvious. I'm very good at picking up on things."

Arian did not reply.

"You're upset, and I'd like to know why."

"I don't care what you'd like."

"So it's personal." Cassie tried to hide how much that hurt. "You blame me for what happened here. And if that's the case you aren't being honest with yourself. I gave you the choice."

"It's not that."

"Then what?"

Arian turned her back and pressed her hands against the wall, as if drawing strength from the stone. "It's what Merial told me, months ago. She said the empire was a seductive monster. One way or another, we'd end up inside it. If it didn't swallow us, we'd crawl up its arse. That's what I've done, haven't I? I've crawled up your arse."

"That's not the nicest of images."

Arian spun to face her. "I don't give a fuck about being nice. It hit me yesterday, after the battle. Everything Merial said came back to me. She'd been right, all along. She said our warriors stood no chance against the legions. I didn't believe her." Hard to tell in the darkness, but it looked as if Arian was crying. "When Leirmond led the charge, I didn't want him to win, but…"

"What's there to say 'but' about? He murdered Merial."

"I KNOW THAT." The shout was loud enough to be heard outside the kitchen. Fortunately, no one came to investigate.

"You didn't want Leirmond to win. But you still wanted the legion to lose?"

"Something like that." Arian's shoulders slumped. "The first battle didn't upset me. It was awful, but the dead and wounded brought back to Yanto's Leap were strangers. Not like the men from Gethryn's warband who died with Leirmond. I know them. They're boys I played with, growing up. I saw them every day of my life. I know their mothers, their sisters. Then I saw them lying on the ground. Your damned legion wasn't even scratched, and they were dead. They were heroes. Their death should have meant something other than…" Arian was definitely crying.

"A pointless waste?"

"One of your games." Arian stepped closer until they were face-to-face. Tears streaked her cheeks. "Ever since you got here, you've had us running around, like children wearing blindfolds. How much of this did you plan? Have we walked into your trap? Without you, we wouldn't be killing each other."

"I promise you, I did nothing to make Leirmond murder anyone. Even if I'd never set foot in Breninbury, I'm sure he'd still have killed Yehan. Probably Merial as well. You can't lay the blame for their deaths on me."

"But you've been pulling strings. Did you plan this war?"

"Do you really want the truth?" And would she give it if asked? Cassie felt dangerously close to the brink. Reckless words crowded onto her tongue. However, Arian moved away.

Cassie closed her eyes, willing herself to think before speaking. "Maybe, if I wasn't here, you wouldn't be at war right now. But that would mean Leirmond getting away with Yehan's murder. I don't know how bothered he is about the child he sired on Nelda becoming king. But she wants it, and you know who else is in the way, don't you? How long would it be before Feran had an accident? Leirmond killed one heir to the throne. It wouldn't take much for him to do it again."

Arian shook her head in denial. "No. We don't…we aren't. It's…"

Cassie forced her tone to soften. "Not all of your people see things the same way you do. My being here has been the spark, but the fire would have come regardless. Leirmond wanted war with the empire. He'd have found a way eventually. All I've done is strip away your illusions. You're upset and want to blame me because the world isn't the way you'd thought it was. But that's not my fault."

Arian slumped against the wall. "I don't trust you."

"I've never asked you to."

"But you're still working on your schemes. What do you have planned for us?"

"Us as in you and me, or us as in your people?"

"Either. Both."

"For your people, I plan on unfettered trade in mining, and your land becoming a prosperous, peaceful, autonomous, empire protectorate."

"Ruled by you."

"Ruled by Feran, when he's old enough."

"Truthfully?"

"Of course."

"Do you want me to trust you about that?"

"You don't need trust, just common sense. If we impose a king who your people don't accept there'll be trouble, and trouble is bad news. Your people see Feran as the rightful king. We've got from now until he's grown to persuade him that working with the empire is best for everyone."

"What's the catch?"

"Why do you think there is one?"

"Because I don't trust you."

"All right. This is the catch. Right now, Feran is too young to rule, so I want Kendric to act as regent. I want Feran to grow up to be a friend to the empire, and I don't want him murdered by an idiot with a grudge." This would be the tricky bit. "The best place for him, the safest place, is in Kavilli. There he can learn how to be a bridge between the empire and the Lycanthi."

"You'd keep him from me? Won't let me see him" Arian's voice cracked. "You—"

"No. I want you with him. He needs his mother. If he's to be a bridge, he'll have to understand the ways of his people, which means not just you with him, but a priest, and others as well. And somewhere in there is the answer to my other plans, those I have for you and me."

"What if I refuse to leave here?"

"Then we'll have a problem to resolve. At the moment, it's all up for negotiation." No need to point out who held the stronger hand. "But I've been away from the hall long enough. I must go back." She left Arian leaning against the wall.

An owl hooted. Cassie stared at the flame dancing over the lamp. She had said more than she had intended to Arian, though it was no bad thing to have sown the seeds of a final resolution. But, for one daredevil moment, she had been on the brink of saying too much—far too much. Arian had dragged her to the precipice. If Arian had pushed harder, challenged with sharper edge, how much more of the truth would she have revealed?

Cassie let out a deep sigh. Just as well she would never find out. The question was, how would Arian respond? If she wanted to cause trouble, how much support could she gather? Equally, after time to think, would she recognise it as being for the best? Not least from the viewpoint of Feran's safety.

The next few years would have their bumps. Describing Feran as a client king would ruffle feathers. Gethryn's friends would resent his dethronement. Young hotheads would see empire troops in the land as an insult or a challenge. Entrenched nobles would grow uneasy as the miners and merchants became richer. And, as ever, old folk would get upset over everything that was not as they remembered from their youth.

The environment was not safe for a young child. Yehan's murder was all the evidence needed for that. There would be fanatics who saw killing Feran as a justifiable first step in overthrowing the empire. They would fail of course, just as Leirmond had failed, but not without the loss of life.

Cassie yawned. Time for bed. She was about to blow out the lamp when the tent flap opened. A legionary stepped in, presumably a sentry from the perimeter. By now everyone else would be asleep.

He snapped a salute. "Lady Cassilania. There's a messenger from the hillfort. He says he has to speak with you. Will you see him?"

"Yes. Send him in." What did Kendric want at this time of night?

The sentry left and a man entered. His cross-tied leggings and loose shirt were covered in a heavy cloak. His hood cast deep shadow over his face, and then he threw it back.

The messenger was not a he. The possibility she was dreaming hopped into Cassie's head. She went as far as glancing at her bed, in the thought she might already be lying there asleep.

She turned back to Arian. "I hope you're not here to assassinate me."

Arian looked pained. "I've tried persuading myself I don't want you. I can't do it. You're in my head, every moment of the day. You've turned me into someone I don't recognise anymore. I flip from mood to mood. I can't work out whether I love you or hate you. Either way, I just can't stop thinking about you."

Cassie stood and walked over. She slid her arms around Arian's waist and pulled her close. One of them was shaking, Cassie had no idea who. It might have been them both.

Arian laid her face on Cassie's shoulder. "Fuck you."

Not the most romantic of offers, but it would do for now.

Arian

The air chilled as evening advanced. A light rain misted Arian's face. She paused and looked up at Breninbury, crouched atop its hill. How could such a familiar sight feel so strange? But of course, before, it had been her home, a sanctuary. Now, the gates were barred to keep her out. Her, and the thousands gathered below.

She continued walking. The male clothing no longer felt so strange around her legs. In fact, she was coming to enjoy the increased freedom of movement. She might even miss it when she resumed her normal dress. For now, Kendric had asked her to maintain the role of Sword Maiden. The morale boost of thinking your side could not lose was worth a thousand extra men to him.

Wafts of wood smoke and roasting meat carried on the breeze, as men prepared their evening meal. The siege camp spread on both sides of the river, noisy and ominous. Grass was trampled in the mud, the water fouled with discarded waste and the passage of countless boots across the ford.

Their numbers grew by the day. Most of the earls had answered Kendric's summons. Cassie said people were always quick to throw their lot in with the obvious winner. Kendric blamed Gethryn and his erratic behaviour over the years of his rule. He had made enemies or allowed Leirmond to make them for him.

Arian had known Gethryn was not popular, but the strength of anger against him had not breached the cocoon of Breninbury. She had not before heard of Gethryn's demands for extra tribute, earls exiled, ignored pleas for help, and ill-planned raids. When there had been shortages, they were blamed on the weather, rather than poor protection for farmers and their crops. The current gossip around camp was giving her a different picture.

How many of those besieged in Breninbury genuinely supported Gethryn? Feeling sympathy with them was easy, remembering the growing dread and despair as enemy numbers had increased outside Yanto's Leap. Folk in Breninbury would have additional cause to fear. They must have heard the story of Leirmond's last charge and how it ended.

The imperial army was camped north of the village, where Kendric had been before. In stark contrast to the Lycanthian side of the river, their tents lay in arrow-straight rows, each line the same distance apart, the same size and shape, each man identical in red uniform, helmet, and banded breastplate.

The empire troops represented four infantry cohorts, not even a full legion. The cavalry remained at Yanto's Leap. Horses were less useful against a hillfort but could respond quickly should the Endridian warband attack while Kendric's thanes were away. How many legions did the empire possess? No wonder Merial had said if the empire wanted their land, no one could stop them.

Did Cassie want their land? She said Feran would be king, but what could they do if she was lying? Cassie said not to trust her, yet Arian so desperately wanted to. When they lay together, surely there was truth in that? Touch she could trust, and taste, and scent, and the shared honesty of bodies. Passion sated, she could stare into Cassie's eyes and see the reflection of her own soul. Arian mentally shook herself. Or she was simply crawling in, ever deeper, as Merial had said?

The siege camp stretched as far as the sacred grove, but had not, would not, intrude farther. Arian passed between the ancient oaks, emerging beside the pool. Here at last was peace. Nothing disturbed the deep solemnity. Water bubbled up, pure and clean, unsullied by doubts, or half-truths, or games. Here she was in the presence of the divine. Arian knelt and dipped her fingers, then touched her head, throat, and lips.

She stopped.

Would the ancestors listen to her? She was conspiring with the empire. The gods had given the land to the Lycanthi. Yet Feran would be a client king, a king on the sufferance of outside forces. Would he still rule in the eyes of the gods? Worse than this, the ancestors would know she had willingly taken a woman as bedfellow. Arian closed her eyes. As ever, thoughts of Cassie swept all other ideas from her head. Memories made her heart race.

The old prayers would not come. Arian tried to force out the words, tried to turn herself back into the person she had once been. But it would be a lie. It had always been a lie. That person had never truly existed. She could fool herself no longer. How had she ever thought to fool the gods?

❖

"Arian," a voice called as she returned to camp.

"What is it?"

The young warrior was barely into manhood, his beard no more than fluff. "Kendric wants to see you."

"Where?"

"By his tent."

The usual people were gathered around the campfire, including Cassie and several earls. There was, though, an unexpected addition. Tregaran had come to speak with them. It was the first time Arian had seen him since the night she and Cassie fled Breninbury.

Tregaran looked up as she arrived. "Good. Now we can begin."

This was also unexpected. She was rarely anything other than an observer at these meetings, yet they had been waiting for her. Even more unusual, normally either Kendric or Cassie took the lead, but apparently that role was hers.

"Have you come from Gethryn?" Arian asked.

"No. Your brother doesn't know I'm here."

"Then what's this about?"

Tregaran moved in front of her and stared into her eyes. "I have questions for you."

"Me?"

"Yes. Is it true you armed yourself for battle, taking the mantle of Sword Maiden?"

This could not need confirmation, given what she was wearing. Arian answered anyway. "Yes."

"Who bid you do it?"

"Nobody. It was my decision."

"You swear to that?"

"Yes."

"Why?"

"Why would I swear to it? Or why…" What was Tregaran getting at?

"The gods will judge you, but I stand here to give them voice. To be a Sword Maiden is to place your life in their hands. It cannot be for personal gain, or private feuds, no matter how deadly. Nor may it be at the bidding of others. It is sanctioned by nothing other than the avenging of royal blood. Do you swear you have acted in accordance with our laws?"

Tregaran was testing her, but his question was easy. "Yes. I'm avenging royal blood. Leirmond murdered my sister and my nephew. I've had to take the step because my brother was shielding him, rather than doing as he should."

"You're certain Leirmond was the murderer?"

"Yes."

"And you'll b—"

"Oh, come on, Tregaran," Cassie interrupted him from the other side of the campfire. "Are you seriously going to pretend you have the slightest doubt?"

"I haven't come here to speak with you." He glared at her.

"And I haven't come here to waste time while you try to find a salve for your conscience." Cassie moved around the fire to challenge Tregaran, face-to-face. "You knew Leirmond was guilty. You knew it as soon as Kendric showed you the knife. You didn't need to see his face when you confronted him. You didn't even need the proof when he tried to silence me with yet another murder."

"I'm not answerable to you."

"No. But one day you'll have to answer to your ancestors. Have you thought about how you're going to explain your actions to them?"

Shocked faces ringed the campfire. Nobody should challenge the high priest in such a manner. Yet Tregaran seemed more defensive than Arian would have guessed.

"You dare invoke the ancestors." Despite the defiant words, his voice lacked fire.

"Yes. And I think it's a sad day for the Lycanthi when an agent of the empire shows more respect for your traditions than the high priest does."

"I am the keeper of the sacred law."

"Then you should have performed your duty better."

That provoked a response. Tregaran's eyes narrowed in anger. "I'll not have you lecture me on my duty. I'll do whatever I must to stop your empire from destroying us. You throw your shadow over us. You deceive the gullible. You spread discontent and false dreams."

Cassie gave a small shake of the head, as if in rebuke. "And there you have it. You're so blinded by fear of the empire, you've lost sight of all else. Tell me, of all possible ways your people could betray your gods, what could be worse than the high priest colluding with a man who had shed Cadryn's blood?"

"I…" The blood drained from Tregaran's face. "I did not collude with him."

"Really? You knew Leirmond was guilty, but you wouldn't throw your support behind Kendric. You hoped some of the blame for Merial's death might still attach to me, even though you knew it would be a lie. But you should know better than any that the gods require the truth. Arian took up the mantle of Sword Maiden because you had turned your back on your duty. And now you've come here to see if you can find a way to twist the story and shift your share of the guilt onto another's shoulders."

Silence hung in the air. Tregaran seemed shrunken, far older than before. At last, he said, "I cannot deny some of what you say. I admit, with hindsight, I wish I'd done things differently."

"Believe it or not, I sometimes feel the same." Cassie gave a wry smile and returned to her original position by the fire. "Now tell us what you came here to say and stop trying to make it seem as if Arian is the one with questions to answer."

Tregaran nodded slowly. "Gethryn isn't of sound mind. He's taken a fever from his wound." Which was serious, given Gethryn's character, even when healthy. "I've begged him to seek peace. Leirmond is dead. A compromise can be reached. But he refuses. He insists you must submit to his authority, without conditions. I don't want more bloodshed. Arian has claimed the name of Sword Maiden. I had to be certain she was acting in good faith, and not because…" Tregaran bit his lower lip. "I'm satisfied. If Arian calls for truce talks, she'll have my support. Gethryn cannot refuse to meet her."

Exerting the rights of a Sword Maiden was not going to sit well with Gethryn. "You think anything I say will have an effect on him?"

"Gethryn is easily swayed. At the moment, he listens to his own dark thoughts. If he faces you…" Tregaran sighed. "I don't know how he'll react. But it's the only chance I see for a peaceful resolution."

Was it worth pointing out Gethryn was more likely to dig his heels in? Arian had no illusions about his feelings for her. Merial might have made Gethryn see sense. She could not. But nor could she deny Tregaran's request.

"If that's what you want. With Cadryn's blood to avenge, I claim the name of Sword Maiden and demand King Gethryn meets me, on neutral ground, under a sign of truce."

"I'll take your message to him."

An icy lump settled in the pit of Arian's stomach. This was never going to turn out well.

Arian stood beside Kendric and his supporting earls, including Halgor, who had struggled up the hill on a crutch, refusing all help, even when Kendric called him a "Stubborn old fool." A short way back, close enough to hear all that was said, Cassie and Quelin were discreetly buried amid a gaggle of thanes. Arian resisted the urge to glance over her shoulder and draw attention to them. Tregaran had felt an empire presence would inflame Gethryn. Arian doubted he would react any more favourably to herself.

Knowing Cassie was close at hand was a source of support. Of more practical benefit were Cassie's lessons the previous night, schooling her in what to expect and how to respond. They had taken turns, acting out the roles. It had been silly at times, and fun. But the fun was over. She needed to put the lessons into effect.

The palisade was lined with faces on either side of the gate, staring down at her. It was easy to read the fear, excitement, hostility, and suspicions. More people were crowded on the watchtower. They would hear all that was said and were the subject of Cassie's first lesson. *Forget that you're talking to Gethryn. Your real audience is Tregaran and people in Breninbury. They're the ones you need to win over. Gethryn's a lost cause.* What did the audience want to hear? How did she gain their trust?

The gates opened and Gethryn emerged, followed by several thanes and a half dozen members of his warband. His face was flushed, and his movement stiff. As he got closer, Arian could see Gethryn's breath was quick and shallow. He was making an effort not to wince with each step. Gethryn stopped the required two arm spans away and glared at her. Whatever physical weakness he might have, it did nothing to sap the strength of his anger.

Tregaran stood to the side, holding the ceremonial spear with its garland of mistletoe. He thrust the point into the ground. "We stand in the sight of the ancestors and the gods. I call on them to witness all that is said and done here. If any defile this sacred truce, he will be outcast, and all men's hand shall be against him, for now, until the end of time. I call on Arian, Sword Maiden, to speak."

"Why her first? I'm the king." Gethryn spat out the words.

Tregaran did not bother to answer. No explanation should be necessary. The truce had been called in her name, and it was for her to set the terms. "Your position is hopeless. Too much of our people's blood has soaked the ground. I ask you to surrender befo—"

"Never."

"Before there are more deaths to mourn. You swore to protect your people, not to sacrifice them pointlessly." Arian was rewarded by faint nods from several people standing behind the palisade.

"I swore to lead them."

"You cannot lead if they won't follow. Look at how many have rejected your leadership." Arian indicated the camp behind her.

"They're all traitors, and they'll die for it."

Which took her effortlessly to Cassie's second lesson. *Provoke him into making threats he can't carry out. He'll think it makes him sound strong, but it does the opposite. Show everyone he's living in a fantasy world, with no grasp of reality.* "You've brought them to this point by your actions. The people who've risen against you have done so in sorrow."

"It's nothing to the sorrow they'll feel when I crush them. They'll see their families' blood drench the land."

"Even if you could win. You'd turn your kingdom into a wasteland."

"It's my kingdom, to do with as I see fit. Not yours, or that empire bitch you follow. You want her to rule over us."

"I want you to abdicate in favour of Feran, my son and your rightful heir. Kendric, a hero of the Lycanthi, will serve as regent until Feran is old enough to rule in his own right."

"Do you think I'd agree to this?" Gethryn's voice shrieked with outrage.

No. It was Cassie's third lesson. *No matter what you offer, Gethryn won't agree, even if it includes my head on a spike. Make him look unreasonable.* "You won't be exiled. You'll take the honourable title of Earl, and—"

"And I'll be dead within the month."

"Each earl and thane will swear, by the sacred pool, to vouchsafe your safety. If any harm you, their life will be forfeit. You can take your pick of hillfort as your domain. You'll be foremost of our people, second only to Kendric and Feran."

"No. I'm king, and I'll take no lesser rank." He thumped his chest.

Next lesson. *Don't forget to talk about Merial. He'll get upset and emotional and lose the thread of his argument—if he has one.*

"You lost the right to call yourself king when you didn't avenge Merial's death. She loved you, raised you as a mother would. And you let her murderer walk free. How will you face her in the afterlife, knowing you failed to avenge her?"

"I didn't fail her. I know who her murderer is. It was that fiend from the empire. I've already sentenced her to death, and I'll take the bitch's head off myself, after I've dealt with the rest of you rabble."

"Leirmond murdered Merial. Not Cassilania. You let him play you for a fool."

"You're the fool. Worse than a fool. You've become a depraved freak. You and that pervert from the empire. I know what you've let her do to you."

Cassie's final lesson. *Never, ever, let the argument become about you, even if it means not defending yourself from accusations. Ignore them and go on the attack. Hit him hard enough and everything else will be forgotten.*

"You put too much faith in what Nelda says. You always have. You think you're responsible for the child she bore? Have you never thought to count months on your fingers? You've got enough. You only need nine. Her son was born that many months after she and Leirmond were alone together. That's why she's willing to lie on his behalf." Arian paused, as if being hit by a new idea. "Or was that the arrangement? Nelda couldn't get pregnant with you, so Leirmond helped you out?"

Gethryn flapped his mouth open and shut but made no sound. However, a few sniggers came from the onlookers.

Back to lesson one. Arian turned to Tregaran. "This is a waste of time. I'm sorry for the people of Breninbury. None of us bear them ill will and would happily grant them safe passage, if my broth—"

A blur of movement caught the corner of Arian's eye. Shouts erupted all around. Something smashed into her, knocking her down at the same moment as fire burned a line across the top of her right arm.

Arian rolled over and sat up. The fire turned to pulsing waves. Her shoulder was wet to the touch and her fingers came away covered in blood. She shook her head in an attempt to clear it.

She was sitting on the ground, with Kendric standing defensively in front of her. The ceremonial spear lay close by, minus its garland of mistletoe.

Gethryn was a few feet away. The fury on his face changed to confusion, then horror. He backed away. "No. I didn't mean it. It wasn't what…" Hearing him over the cacophony of shouts, screams, and howls of outrage was almost impossible

"SILENCE!" Tregaran bellowed the command.

A hush fell.

Tregaran pointed at Gethryn. "You have defiled the sacred truce. You have shed Cadryn's blood. In the name of the ancestors and the gods, I declare you outcast. May all men's hand be against you, for now, until the end of time."

"No. I…I…"

Gethryn turned and stumbled towards the gates of Breninbury, making what haste he could to reach the safety that no longer existed. He got no farther than five steps. A bowstring twanged, and then more. Gethryn fell with three arrows in his chest, all shot from within the palisade.

In the final analysis, he had few friends.

Arian opened her eyes and stared at the ceiling, although it was too dark to see anything. Out of habit, she listened for the soft sounds of Feran and Eilwen sleeping. They were not there, of course, but soon would be reunited with her. Their absence was a constant, low-running ache, cutting more deeply now that she was back in what had been their home.

The only noise was wind over the roof and the distant bleating of sheep. Her shoulder was sore, which was what had woken her. It could have been worse. Luckily, Kendric had been quick to push her out of the way, and Gethryn was too weak for better aim. The spear had struck no more than a glancing blow, The cut was the length and depth of her little finger. It would be tender for a while to come, but leave no lasting damage.

Despite everything she knew about her brother, the level of insanity he had shown defied belief. Maybe his fever had played a part. Either breaking the truce or deliberately spilling her blood could mean a death sentence. To do it with the ceremonial spear left Tregaran no other option, even if he had wanted one.

Arian rolled onto her good shoulder, but she was not going to fall back asleep. This was the last time she would wake in Breninbury for years—maybe forever. The future was always uncertain. There could be no guarantee she would return. She rolled off the sleeping platform and fumbled in the darkness for her boots, then grabbed a warm cloak.

The courtyard was dark and silent. Dawn was still some way off. Arian stopped outside what had been Merial's room. Currently, it was empty. Nelda's current location was unknown. Her capture and punishment for the part she played in Merial's murder was a matter for Kendric and Tregaran.

The barbs about Nelda's faithlessness must have cut even deeper than Arian expected. When Gethryn's army returned from Yanto's Leap without Leirmond, Nelda had immediately left for her family in Drusbury. Whether or not Gethryn had worked out the truth about her son, the way Nelda abandoned him could only have added to his turmoil.

Arian reached for the door hanging, tempted to pull it aside. A wave of childhood memories rolled over her—Merial telling stories at bedtime, her crying after Merial left for the empire, whispered secrets shared, sunny days and snowball fights, and then Merial's blood drenching the bed, her throat slashed open. Arian stepped back. She did not need to enter the room. The memories would follow her always.

She removed the hurdle from the courtyard entrance. Her meandering route took her to the palisade, with a view down into the valley, just as the first light brightened the eastern horizon. Autumn was advancing and the dawn air was cold. The Festival of the Ancestors was mere days away, but she would be gone. Thankfully. In the past it had not seemed an issue, as long as she was drunk enough. But after having Cassie as a bedfellow, her feelings had changed. Eilwen would just have to accept there would never be a summer-born sister for her to play with.

Arian stared across the distant hills. The scene was so familiar, she could almost imagine herself stepping back in time. But the illusion faded when her gaze dropped to the valley. The sacred grove was unchanged, but there were no longer any easy prayers. Even so, she would make a last offering before she left.

Elsewhere, changes on the ground were less significant than those in her head and heart. The once green riverbank was churned mud, but grass would return, unlike the dead. She could see where Yehan's body had lain in the river. Closer was the spot where Gethryn had fallen.

The Lycanthian army had gone, but the imperial legion still occupied the far side of the river. Most would accompany her and Cassie to Verina that day. Automatically, Arian sought out the large pavilion. Cassie was in there, asleep. Or might Cassie be lying awake, thinking about her? Despite all the doubts, Arian felt her insides melt and suspected a soppy smile had spread across her face. Just as well nobody was around to see. Because she now needed to hide what she was feeling.

Arian's mood hardened as she acknowledged the biggest change—the one that had taken place inside her. She had stopped lying to herself, which meant she now had to lie to everyone else. Each day she spent in Breninbury would be a lie, and she could not live like that. Arian turned east to where light was strengthening on the horizon. Merial had wanted to return to the empire. She would go in her sister's place.

Her feelings for Breninbury had changed. It held too many memories, too many ghosts—betrayal, deceit, and lost illusions. It was no longer a home where she belonged. In truth, it never had been. Even without Cassie's plans and plots, she could not stay.

Why did you come back? The question she had never asked Merial. But, even if their reasons were not the same, she no longer needed to ask why Merial had left.

Cassie

The supply cart crossed the bridge and rolled along the dirt road, following the column of soldiers. They were back in the empire. At first, the outskirts of Verina amounted to little more than shanties, but as they approached the centre of town, buildings on either side became more substantial, with whitewashed walls, tiled roofs, and wooden window shutters. Cassie shook her head in bemusement. Who could have imagined her finding the sight of raucous bars and shoddy brothels so comforting?

They turned onto the main road. The gates of the legionary fort were just a couple of hundred yards ahead. Cassie was more than ready to get out of the cart. The busier the route, the deeper the ruts, and suspension was nonexistent. The wheels hit another pothole, making her joints crack. Arian winced and put her hand to her injured shoulder.

"Are you all right?" Cassie shouted over the clamour of street life, although Verina was quieter than normal, with most of the legion away.

"Yes. I..." Arian's eyes were wide. She leaned closer to be heard. "Are all your towns like this?"

"Most aren't this trashy. It's a border town. It's here to service the army. And you know what soldiers are like."

"No, what?"

"Like your young warriors would be if they didn't have to worry about their mothers seeing what they were up to."

"Right." Arian laughed and stared up at a three-storey brothel. Half-dressed women hung from upstairs windows, shouting to the passing soldiers.

"How does the building not fall down?"

"The mortar, I guess." Cassie had never felt the need to find out.

The wagon passed through the gates of the fort leaving the chaos behind. The three cohorts marched onto the parade ground and formed up, ready to be dismissed. The other cohort had joined the cavalry at Yanto's Leap. The temporary arrangement would need formalising, along with everything else necessary to get the mining trade running efficiently and safely.

First thing in the morning she must dispatch her report to Kavilli by fast courier, detailing the agreement reached with Kendric. Cassie had no doubt the Senate would approve it. Mother would ensure that. The terms met or exceeded all demands.

The supply cart stopped outside the legate's house.

"Mama, Mama." Feran burst from the doorway, running on his chubby toddler legs.

Arian jumped down and lifted him in an enthusiastic hug. Eilwen was not far behind. She wrapped her arms around Arian's waist, threatening to upend them all.

Bran followed the children. "It's good to see you again, my lady."

"It's good to see you too." Cassie alighted more sedately.

"I trust everything went to plan?"

"A few tight spots. But it worked out all right." They had much to discuss, but it could wait.

Meanwhile Feran had squirmed free and was jumping up and down in excitement. Eilwen took the chance to grab Arian's hand and tug on it. "Mama, you must come with me, now. Right now. You must see the bathhouse."

Cassie's first impression of Arian had been right. She did scrub up well, and from a very high starting point. Her blond hair now flowed in waves and revealed natural highlights. Her face held a heightened blush from the hot bath. The satin robe shimmered in the right spots to accentuate her body perfectly. In fact, the only thing that would improve it was removing the robe altogether, which was definitely an idea worth pursuing.

Arian was staring at the window, although it was too dark to see anything outside. "What's this?" She tapped a square.

"What's what?"

"Like hard green water."

"You mean glass?"

"I thought glass was black rock."

"That's volcanic glass. The windows are man-made."

"Not all the houses in Verina have it."

"It's expensive. Most people can't afford it."

"And the heat. It's cold outside. How does the house get warm without a fire?"

"There's a furnace attached to the hostel. Hot air is drawn under the floor. If you took your sandals off, you'd feel it with your feet."

"Does your home in Kavilli have glass, and a furnace?"

"Of course." Cassie patted the daybed. "Why don't you join me here?"

Arian faced her but stayed by the window. "I've been wondering. Did you know how Gethryn would react? Did you know he'd try to kill me?"

"No. I'd never risk you being hurt." Cassie was shocked Arian could ask. But was it really unjustified? "When I saw him grab the spear, I..." How to put into words the stark, raw terror of the moment?

"How did you think it would end?"

"I thought someone in Breninbury would assassinate him that night, as their best bet for saving their own skin."

"But you planned most of what happened, didn't you?" Arian held up her hand." Don't bother denying it because I won't believe you."

"I didn't plan everything. To be honest, some things turned out better than expected. And some were worse. One thing you must believe is that I had nothing to do with Merial's death." Quite apart from any personal feelings of friendship, Merial was far too useful alive. "I'd have saved her, if I'd had any clue it might happen."

Arian turned her head away. Warm candlelight lit her face in profile. Cassie's pulse ticked up a notch. Any artist would die to carve a statue half as sublime.

"Supposing everything now goes as you expect. How do you see things working out?" Arian asked.

"In what way?"

"What does the future hold for my people?"

"At a guess?" Why not play at being an oracle? "Kendric will sort out all the things Gethryn screwed up. He'll have to rely on Quelin's help more than he'd like, but they're both reasonable men. Kendric won't do anything stupid, unlike some of your young hotheads who'll still want to fight. Quelin will entice any overeager warriors to join the army, so they can go far away, meet strange new people, with strange new customs, and fight them instead. Your common folk will be richer and safer, but they'll still complain, because they'll be living longer, and after a certain age, complaining becomes a hobby."

"And Feran?"

"He'll grow up expecting glass windows and heated floors. Eventually, he'll return to Breninbury. Hopefully, while Kendric is still alive to set a good example. But Feran won't want to live in a smoky hut with a dirt floor and shit covered walls. He'll build a villa in the valley. Before long, all the earls will copy him and move into their own villas. He'll probably start a fashion of shaving his beard as well."

"You mean, our land will become identical to every other part of your empire."

"All the regions have their own distinctive style. Your people will be free to pick and choose the bits they want." Best not to point out neither Arian nor Tregaran would get to decide for them.

"What about us? You and me?"

"We'll get a private carriage and set off for Kavilli. The journey will take two months. Winter's on the way, but the roads ought to stay open. We shouldn't get snowed in anywhere."

"I didn't mean that. Will we stay together?"

"As lovers?" That was the hard one. Cassie forced her voice to stay light. "If we want. Nobody will be upset about it. Eventually, I'll have to marry whichever man benefits my family the most, though that needn't put a stop to anything. We'd just have to be less blatant about it." She shrugged. "It might not be for a while. By then, you'll be tired of me."

"Never."

Cassie shook her head. "I'm your first true lover, and you might think I'll be your one and only, but life's not like that. You'll be overwhelmed by the temptations Kavilli can offer. You'll be an exotic, barbarian sensation, with your blond hair, green eyes, and pale skin. You'll make a new life with new friends, and you'll want to see less and less of me. All the men and half the women will try to bed you. It'd be a wasted opportunity if you don't let a few of them succeed."

"I love you." Arian blurted out the words.

A knot formed in Cassie's guts. Somehow she kept control of her expression. "No, you don't. I'm merely the first woman who's given you what you wanted. That's all. What you feel won't last. Believe me."

"And believe me, I know my own heart."

"Do you? Because I don't think you had the first idea about your heart before you met me."

"I was lying to myself back then. I'm not lying anymore. I'm in love with you." Arian left the window and loosened the sash on her robe. The front fell open, revealing the fullness of her breasts, and the triangle of golden hair between her legs. She reached the daybed and put a hand under Cassie's chin, raising her head so their eyes met.

"Don't doubt me."

Cassie awoke some time later. Two candles had burnt out, but the remaining one cast a gentle glow over the room. Carefully, so as not to disturb Arian, she extricated herself from the tangle of arms and legs. Arian murmured in her sleep but did not wake. They should move to the proper bed, otherwise they would have cricks in their spines by morning. But first Cassie had to get her head straight.

She walked to the window, although nothing could be seen on the moonless night. Voices echoed on the street outside. Soldiers by the sound of them, returning to barracks after their first night back in Verina. It was not yet midnight, but dawn parade was unforgiving.

Cassie turned and leaned her shoulders against the wall. She stared across the room at Arian, lying curled on the daybed.

"I love you too." She whispered the words softly, so as not to risk waking Arian. "You want to know how things will go? No matter what you might think, you'll find out I'm not the only woman in the world for you. One day you'll meet someone as honest and truthful as yourself. Someone you can trust. Someone who won't be playing games in one political intrigue after the next. Someone who maybe comes close to deserving you."

Cassie crossed the room. She reached for Arian's shoulder, ready to suggest they move, but then paused, mid action.

"And on that day, you'll break my heart."

About the Author

Jane Fletcher is a GCLS award-winning writer and has also been short-listed for the Gaylactic Spectrum and Lambda Literary Awards. She is a recipient of the Alice B Reader Appreciation Awards Medal.

Her work includes two ongoing sets of fantasy/romance novels: the Celaeno Series—*The Walls of Westernfort*, *Rangers at Roadsend*, *The Temple at Landfall*, *Dynasty of Rogues*, and *Shadow of the Knife*; and the Lyremouth Chronicles—*The Exile and The Sorcerer*, *The Traitor and The Chalice*, *The Empress and The Acolyte*, and *The High Priest and the Idol*. She has also written four stand-alone novels, *Wolfsbane Winter*, *The Shewstone*, *Isle of Broken Years*, and *Silver Ravens*.

Her love of fantasy began at the age of seven when she encountered Greek mythology. This was compounded by a childhood spent clambering over every example of ancient masonry she could find (medieval castles, megalithic monuments, Roman villas). Her resolute ambition was to become an archaeologist when she grew up, so it was something of a surprise when she became a software engineer instead.

Born in Greenwich, London, she now lives with her wife in southwest England, where she is surrounded by enough historic sites to keep her happy.

Website: http://www.janefletcher.co.uk/

Books Available from Bold Strokes Books

A Fox in Shadow by Jane Fletcher. Cassie's mission is to add new territory to the Kavillian empire—murder, betrayal, war, and the clash of cultures ensue. (978-1-63679-142-5)

Embracing the Moon by Jeannie Levig. Just as Gwen and Taylor are exploring the new love they've found, the present and past collide, threatening the future they long to share. (978-1-63555-462-5)

Forever Comes in Threes by D. Jackson Leigh. Efficiency expert Perry Chandler's ordered life is upended when she inherits three busy terriers, and the woman she's referred to for help turns out to be her bitter podcast rival, the very sexy Dr. Ming Lee. (978-1-63679-169-2)

Heckin' Lewd: Trans and Nonbinary Erotica by Mx. Nillin Lore. If you want smutty, fearless, gender diverse erotica written by affirming own-voices folks who get it, then this is the book you've been looking for! (978-1-63679-240-8)

Missed Conception by Joy Argento. Maggie Walsh wants a relationship with Cassidy, the daughter she's only just discovered she has due to an in vitro mix-up. Heat kindles between Maggie and Cassidy's mother in a way neither expects. (978-1-63679-146-3)

Private Equity by Elle Spencer. Cassidy Bennett spends an unexpected evening at a lesbian nightclub with her notoriously reserved and demanding boss, Julia. After seeing a different side of Julia, Cassidy can't seem to shake her desire to know more. (978-1-63679-180-7)

Racing the Dawn by Sandra Barrett. After narrowly escaping a house fire, vampire Jade Murphy is unexpectedly intrigued by gorgeous firefighter Beth Jenssen, and her undead existence might just be perking up a bit. (978-1-63679-271-2)

Reclaiming Love by Amanda Radley. Sarah's tiny white lie means somehow convincing Pippa to pretend to be her girlfriend. Only the more time they spend faking it, the more real it feels. (978-1-63679-144-9)

Sol Cycle by Kimberly Cooper Griffin. An encounter in a park brings Ang and Krista together, but when Ang's attempts to help Krista go spectacularly wrong, their passion for each other might not be enough. (978-1-63679-137-1)

Trial and Error by Carsen Taite. Attorney Franco Rossi and Judge Nina Aguilar's reunion is fraught with courtroom conflict, undeniable chemistry, and danger. (978-1-63555-863-0)

A Long Way to Fall by Elle Spencer. A ski lodge, two strong-willed women, and a family feud that brings them together, but will it also tear them apart? (978-1-63679-005-3)

Barnabas Bopwright Saves the City by J. Marshall Freeman. When he uncovers a terror plot to destroy the city he loves, 15-year-old Barnabas Bopwright realizes it's up to him to save his home and bring deadly secrets into the light before it's too late. (978-1-63679-152-4)

Forever by Kris Bryant. When Savannah Edwards is invited to be the next bachelorette on the dating show When Sparks Fly, she'll show the world that finding true love on television can happen. (978-1-63679-029-9)

Ice on Wheels by Aurora Rey. All's fair in love and roller derby. That's Riley Fauchet's motto, until a new job lands her at the same company—and on the same team—as her rival Brooke Landry, the frosty jammer for the Big Easy Bruisers. (978-1-63679-179-1)

Inherit the Lightning by Bud Gundy. Darcy O'Brien and his sisters learn they are about to inherit an immense fortune, but a family mystery about to unravel after seventy years threatens to destroy everything. (978-1-63679-199-9)

Perfect Rivalry by Radclyffe. Two women set out to win the same career-making goal, but it's love that may turn out to be the final prize. (978-1-63679-216-3)

Something to Talk About by Ronica Black. Can quiet ranch owner Corey Durand give up her peaceful life and allow her feisty new neighbor into her heart? Or will past loss, present suitors, and town gossip ruin a long-awaited chance at love? (978-1-63679-114-2)

With a Minor in Murder by Karis Walsh. In the world of academia, police officer Clare Sawyer and professor Libby Hart team up to solve a murder. (978-1-63679-186-9)

Writer's Block by Ali Vali. Wyatt and Hayley might be made for each other if only they can get through nosy neighbors, the historic society, at-odds future plans, and all the secrets hidden in Wyatt's walls. (978-1-63679-021-3)

Cold Blood by Genevieve McCluer. Maybe together, Kalila and Dorenia have a chance of taking down the vampires who have eluded them all these years. And maybe, in each other, they can find a love worth living for. (978-1-63679-195-1)

Greener Pastures by Aurora Rey. When city girl and CPA Audrey Adams finds herself tending her aunt's farm, will Rowan Marshall—the charming cider maker next door—turn out to be her saving grace or the bane of her existence? (978-1-63679-116-6)

Grounded by Amanda Radley. For a second chance, Olivia and Emily will need to accept their mistakes, learn to communicate properly, and with a little help from five-year-old Henry, fall madly in love all over again. Sequel to Flight SQA016. (978-1-63679-241-5)

Journey's End by Amanda Radley. In this heartwarming conclusion to the Flight series, Olivia and Emily must finally decide what they want, what they need, and how to follow the dreams of their hearts. (978-1-63679-233-0)

Pursued: Lillian's Story by Felice Picano. Fleeing a disastrous marriage to the Lord Exchequer of England, Lillian of Ravenglass reveals an incident-filled, often bizarre, tale of great wealth and power, perfidy, and betrayal. (978-1-63679-197-5)

Secret Agent by Michelle Larkin. CIA agent Peyton North embarks on a global chase to apprehend rogue agent Zoey Blackwood, but her commitment to the mission is tested as the sparks between them ignite and their sizzling attraction approaches a point of no return. (978-1-63555-753-4)

Something Between Us by Krystina Rivers. A decade after her heart was broken under Don't Ask, Don't Tell, Kirby runs into her first love and has to decide if what's still between them is enough to heal her broken heart. (978-1-63679-135-7)

Sugar Girl by Emma L McGeown. Having traded in traditional romance for the perks of Sugar Dating, Ciara Reilly not only enjoys the no-strings-attached arrangement, she's also a hit with her clients. That is until she meets the beautiful entrepreneur Charlie Keller who makes her want to go sugar-free. (978-1-63679-156-2)

The Business of Pleasure by Ronica Black. Editor in chief Valerie Raffield is quickly becoming smitten by Lennox, the graphic artist she's hired to work remotely. But when Lennox doesn't show for their first face-to-face meeting, Valerie's heart and her business may be in jeopardy. (978-1-63679-134-0)

The Hummingbird Sanctuary by Erin Zak. The Hummingbird Sanctuary, Colorado's hottest resort destination: Come for the mountains, stay for the charm, and enjoy the drama as Olive, Eleanor, and Harriet figure out the meaning of true friendship. (978-1-63679-163-0)

The Witch Queen's Mate by Jennifer Karter. Barra and Silvi must overcome their ingrained hatred and prejudice to use Barra's magic and save both their peoples, not just from slavery, but destruction. (978-1-63679-202-6)

With a Twist by Georgia Beers. Starting over isn't easy for Amelia Martini. When the irritatingly cheerful Kirby Dupress comes into her life will Amelia be brave enough to go after the love she really wants? (978-1-63555-987-3)

Business of the Heart by Claire Forsythe. When a hopeless romantic meets a tough-as-nails cynic, they'll need to overcome the wounds of the past to discover that their hearts are the most important business of all. (978-1-63679-167-8)

Dying for You by Jenny Frame. Can Victorija Dred keep an age-old vow and fight the need to take blood from Daisy Macdougall? (978-1-63679-073-2)

Exclusive by Melissa Brayden. Skylar Ruiz lands the TV reporting job of a lifetime, but is she willing to sacrifice it all for the love of her longtime crush, anchorwoman Carolyn McNamara? (978-1-63679-112-8)

Her Duchess to Desire by Jane Walsh. An up-and-coming interior designer seeks to create a happily ever after with an intriguing duchess, proving that love never goes out of fashion. (978-1-63679-065-7)

Murder on Monte Vista by David S. Pederson. Private Detective Mason Adler's angst at turning fifty is forgotten when his "birthday present," the handsome, young Henry Bowtrickle, turns up dead, and it's up to Mason to figure out who did it, and why. (978-1-63679-124-1)

Take Her Down by Lauren Emily Whalen. Stakes are cutthroat, scheming is creative, and loyalty is ever-changing in this queer, female-driven YA retelling of Shakespeare's Julius Caesar. (978-1-63679-089-3)

The Game by Jan Gayle. Ryan Gibbs is a talented golfer, but her guilt means she may never leave her small town, even if Katherine Reese tempts her with competition and passion. (978-1-63679-126-5)

Whereabouts Unknown by Meredith Doench. While homicide detective Theodora Madsen recovers from a potentially career-ending injury, she scrambles to solve the cases of two missing sixteen-year-old girls from Ohio. (978-1-63555-647-6)

Boy at the Window by Lauren Melissa Ellzey. Daniel Kim struggles to hold onto reality while haunted by both his very-present past and his never-present parents. Jiwon Yoon may be the only one who can break Daniel free. (978-1-63679-092-3)

Deadly Secrets by VK Powell. Corporate criminals want whistleblower Jana Elliott permanently silenced, but Rafe Silva will risk everything to keep the woman she loves safe. (978-1-63679-087-9)

Enchanted Autumn by Ursula Klein. When Elizabeth comes to Salem, Massachusetts, to study the witch trials, she never expects to find love—or an actual witch…and Hazel might just turn out to be both. (978-1-63679-104-3)

Escorted by Renee Roman. When fantasy meets reality, will escort Ryan Lewis be able to walk away from a chance at forever with her new client Dani? (978-1-63679-039-8)

Her Heart's Desire by Anne Shade. Two women. One choice. Will Eve and Lynette be able to overcome their doubts and fears to embrace their deepest desire? (978-1-63679-102-9)

My Secret Valentine by Julie Cannon, Erin Dutton, & Anne Shade. Winning the heart of your secret Valentine? These award-winning authors agree, there is no better way to fall in love. (978-1-63679-071-8)

Perilous Obsession by Carsen Taite. When reporter Macy Moran becomes consumed with solving a cold case, will her quest for the truth bring her closer to Detective Beck Ramsey or will her obsession with finding a murderer rob her of a chance at true love? (978-1-63679-009-1)

Reading Her by Amanda Radley. Lauren and Allegra learn love and happiness are right where they least expect it. There's just one problem: Lauren has a secret she cannot tell anyone, and Allegra knows she's hiding something. (978-1-63679-075-6)

The Willing by Lyn Hemphill. Kitty Wilson doesn't know how, but she can bring people back from the dead as long as someone is willing to take their place and keep the universe in balance. (978-1-63679-083-1)

Three Left Turns to Nowhere by Nathan Burgoine, J. Marshall Freeman, & Jeffrey Ricker. Three strangers heading to a convention in Toronto are stranded in rural Ontario, where a small town with a subtle kind of magic leads each to discover what he's been searching for. (978-1-63679-050-3)

Watching Over Her by Ronica Black. As they face the snowstorm of the century, and the looming threat of a stalker, Riley and Zoey just might find love in the most unexpected of places. (978-1-63679-100-5)